D0210346

Gilman
Gilman, Laura Anne LAP
Free fall

WITHDRAWN $14.95
ocn181602282
07/09/2008

Praise for the Retrievers novels of

laura

"An entertaining,
and computers exis
highly talented rogu

—*Locus*

"Gilman delivers an exciting, fast-paced, unpredictable story that never lets up until the very end...I highly recommend this book to fans of urban fantasy, especially [the works of] Jim Butcher, Charlaine Harris, Kim Harrison, or Laurell K. Hamilton. This is an extremely strong start, and I hope Gilman keeps it up."
—*SF Site*

"What's a girl to do now that *Buffy's* been canceled?
Read Laura Anne Gilman, of course!...If Nick and Nora Charles were investigating *X-Files,* the result would be *Staying Dead.*
These 'Retrievers' are golden."
—Rosemary Edghill, author of *Met by Moonlight*

Curse the Dark
"Gilman has managed the nearly impossible here: a cleverly written and well-balanced fantasy with a strong romantic element that doesn't overpower the main plot."
—*Romantic Times BOOKreviews* [4 ½ stars]

"Fans of Tanya Huff will cherish *Curse the Dark,* a fabulous romantic fantasy that showcases how talented Laura Anne Gilman is."
—*Affaire de Coeur*

"With an atmosphere reminiscent of Dan Brown's *The Da Vinci Code* and Umberto Eco's *The Name of the Rose* by way of Sam Spade, Gilman's second Wren Valere adventure (after *Staying Dead*) features fast-paced action, wisecracking dialogue, and a pair of strong, appealing heroes."
—*Library Journal*

Bring It On

"Fans of Charlaine Harris, Kelley Armstrong and Kim Harrison will find *Bring It On* a very special treat. The author is an expert worldbuilder and creates characters that are easy to care about."
—*Affaire de Coeur* [5 stars]

"Gilman has outdone herself.... The revelations are moving, the action is fantastic, and the ending is something that makes you wonder what will happen next."
—*In the Library Reviews*

"Ripping good urban fantasy, fast-paced and filled with an exciting blend of mystery and magic...Gilman continues to explore a world where magic runs like electricity...where demons and other non-human breeds walk the streets in plain sight...this is a paranormal romance for those who normally avoid romance, and the entire series is worth checking out."
—*SF Site*

Burning Bridges

"This fourth book in Gilman's engaging series delivers...Wren and Sergei's relationship, as usual, is wonderfully written. As their relationship moves in an unexpected direction, it makes perfect sense—and leaves the reader on the edge of her seat for the next book."
—*Romantic Times BOOKreviews* [4 stars]

"Wren's can-do magic is highly appealing."
—*Publishers Weekly*

"I've been saying it all along, and I'll say it again, this is an excellent series, well worth picking up, and I haven't been let down yet."
—*Green Man Review*

"Valere is a tough, resourceful heroine, a would-be loner who cares too much to truly walk alone. A strong addition to urban fantasy collections."
—*Library Journal*

laura anne gilman
free fall

LUNA™
www.LUNA-Books.com

If you purchased this book without a cover you should be aware
that this book is stolen property. It was reported as "unsold and
destroyed" to the publisher, and neither the author nor the
publisher has received any payment for this "stripped book."

LUNA™

First trade printing May 2008

FREE FALL

ISBN-13: 978-0-373-80267-8
ISBN-10:   0-373-80267-6

Copyright © 2008 by Laura Anne Gilman

Author photo © by Peter R. Liverakos

All rights reserved. Except for use in any review, the reproduction
or utilization of this work in whole or in part in any form by any
electronic, mechanical or other means, now known or hereafter
invented, including xerography, photocopying and recording, or in
any information storage or retrieval system, is forbidden without
the written permission of the editorial office, Worldwide Library,
233 Broadway, New York, NY 10279 U.S.A.

This is a work of fiction. Names, characters, places and incidents are
either the product of the author's imagination or are used fictitiously, and
any resemblance to actual persons, living or dead, business establishments,
events or locales is entirely coincidental.

This edition published by arrangement with Harlequin Books S.A.

® and TM are trademarks of Harlequin Books S.A., used under license.
Trademarks indicated with ® are registered in the United States Patent
and Trademark Office, the Canadian Trade Marks Office and in other
countries.

www.LUNA-Books.com

Printed in U.S.A.

AUTHOR NOTE

When I wrote the first book of the Retrievers series, *Staying Dead,* I was in love with the characters, the world, the magic system and pretty much everything about it. What I didn't know was how everyone else would react. After all, I was coming in as a fantasy/horror writer, and LUNA was all about romantic fantasy. I wasn't writing anything *romantic,* was I?

Wren and Sergei—and yes, P.B.—taught me differently. Because romance isn't just about sexual love. It's about the emotional attachments that form between people—no matter their gender, their background or, in fact, their species. Over the past four books we have seen that attachment grow, be tested and evolve into something quite, well...magical.

And it was in writing *Free Fall* that I realized how very magical love can be. Because when the weight of the past few years finally takes its toll on Wren, it's not spells or weapons or her famed Talent that might save her. It's love.

Oh dear. I'm a romantic after all.

I won't tell anyone if you won't.

Laura Anne Gilman
May 2008

For ChristineH. Because every Calvin needs her Hobbes...

"…And if we ever leave a legacy
It's that we loved each other well."
—"Power of Two"
Indigo Girls

one

Spring, 1910
New York City

The conversation was subdued and civilized, as befitted the surroundings: a large, tastefully decorated library, surrounded on three sides by leather-bound books and a marble fireplace, and on the fourth by a wall of floor to ceiling windows, respectably covered by sheet curtains to allow light in but deflect the gaze of those on the street.

Out of the murmured conversation, a complaint lifted into the air. "We must have a motto."

"Oh, not again," his companion replied. "Who would we tell this motto to, Alan? Where would we place it? Over what mantel would it be carved?" He gestured around the rather plain room they met in, the high ceilings and wainscoting on the walls almost austere in their simplicity. "It seems somewhat counterindicated for a secret society, if it truly wishes to remain unnoticed. If we must formalize our identity, I should think a statement of purpose before a motto."

The argument had been raging on-and-off for three months now, ever since they had gathered to bring in the New Year and officially inaugurate their new organization, and most of the assembled men—eleven in all—were heartily sick of it.

The first man stuck to his guns. "We all know why we are here, Maxwell. A motto will bind us together, remind us of our purpose. Give us light in the darkness."

"A lamp will work as well for that," Maxwell retorted.

There was some muted laughter among the other men gathered, which quickly turned to coughs and covered grins. All eleven were well past the first blush of youth, with graying hair and faces that showed lines of wear. Yet they were all full of energy and vigor; the perfect advertisement for a generation of leaders, the lifeblood of Manhattan society, both business and social. Only under the surface did a difference show, a stern determination inherited less from Society and more from their Puritan forebears.

"Gentlemen, please." Their leader, a relatively young man with a fashionably clean-shaven face and well-cut brown sack suit held up his hand. "Peace. Alan, I am certain that a motto will be chosen when the time is right. It is not a thing to be rushed, after all. Posterity would not thank us for an ill-chosen motto.

"For now, it is more important that we come to order with the day's business. If you would please join me?"

The eleven men gathered around the long, dark mahogany table. It would not have looked out of place in a formal dining room, but instead of china and linen it was set with a three-color map of the United States, a Holy Bible, and a sword of gleaming watered steel placed lengthwise along the center of the table, its tip resting on the

Bible. The hilt was of an Indian style, placing the age of the weapon at anywhere from 300 to 600 AD.

"Lord, we ask your blessing upon this gathering. In silence we have seen the wreck of human nature. In silence we have borne the preditations of the old world, the creeping darkness coming upon us."

In New York, in America, they were safe. But these men looked beyond their walls, considered what might be looking at them with a hungry or jealous eye. And Europe was under more than one shadow, stretching out toward the New World. They knew it, even if the government did not, yet.

"In silence we have watched as the glory of your word was drowned under the work of evil-doings. And so in silence we gather now, to protect those who would be true to their better natures, those who have no defense against the serpent of evil save your flaming sword and fierce justice, and those who, through lack of knowledge, have no salvation. We are the wall between the old world and the new, and we ask your blessing upon our hands, and our weapons, to guide them true."

"Amen," the others chorused. They all sat down, seemingly without thought of placement or precedence.

"All right. I hereby call this meeting to order, on this the 15th day of March, the year of our Lord 1910. Have we any special orders to be brought forward at this time?"

There was a short pause, while the members looked to each other. When no one stood up or indicated they wished to address the group, the Speaker went on.

"Very well then. Have we updates on old business? Yes, Mr. Carson?"

The member so indicated let down his hand and stood up. Now that the meeting had been called to order, their speech was more considered, their address more formal. "The money-lending situation down near Green Street has been resolved. The gentleman in question understands that we will be watching him, and his rates, quite closely for the foreseeable future. I expect that there will be no further unpleasantness."

A few grim nods at that: money-lending was not a crime, nor were the rates the man was charging—no one, after all, was forced to go to him for loans—but it was wrong nonetheless. Business was business, but there were seemly limits.

"Very good." He looked down the table as Mr. Carson sat down. "Mr. Van Stann?"

Van Stann was a short man with sallow skin and a zealot's eye. "The den of opium addicts near the fish market has been closed down. It required some cleansing to accomplish, but the owners will not attempt to reopen."

"Costs?" This had been debated sharply among the members before action was taken, on exactly that question.

Van Stann didn't hesitate. "Two residents were trapped inside, unable to move themselves enough to escape. They would not have lasted long on their own, anyway. I doubt even the kindest of homes would have kept them from the drug longer than a day or two. The building is a total loss."

"We should have it strewn with salt, to be certain," another man at the table suggested. "I know it is but superstition, but at times using their own fears against them is the only way to ensure success."

There was a low rumble of agreement to that. The chairman was within rights to call the meeting back to order, but he allowed the side discussion to go on.

"And yet," Mr. Goddard, a banker who brought a refreshingly practical viewpoint to the table, asked, "If we play into those fears, are we not encouraging them, rather than stamping them out? How can that be true to our charter, to protect them even from themselves?"

Van Stann was back on his feet. "If we can keep another place such as that from being rebuilt? Sometimes, the lesser evil—the much lesser evil in this case—must be embraced, to keep the ignorant from greater crimes!"

"And who are we to determine what the lesser evil is?" Goddard shot back. "I do not claim that level of wisdom for myself!"

"Gentlemen! Please!" The chairman knew his fellow members well enough to intercede at this point. It had never come to violence before in this chamber, and he prayed it never would, but every member of the Silence was full of conviction and fire, else they would not have been allowed entrance to the group.

Once he had them settled down and seated again, he continued, in a more sedate tone. "A suggestion has been raised, and not without merit—and risks. Does anyone second Mr. Van Stann's motion?"

Several hands went up, while other faces turned hard as granite.

"Very well. It has been moved and seconded. All who are agreed?"

Seven hands raised.

"Opposed?"

Three hands.

"Seven to three, one abstaining. The motion passes. Add the cost of the salt to the minutes, if you would, Mr. Donnelly?"

The secretary nodded, his hand flying over his notepad. They had offered to buy him a typewriter, but he preferred the old-fashioned way of doing things.

"Is that all for old business? Very well then, I open the floor to discussion of new business. Mr. Clare?"

Ashton Claire stood, taking his time. He was a slender man, not much over five feet ten inches tall, and not quite so immaculately turned out as his companions, but the empty sleeve in his coat made others give way before him, as befitted a man who served his country in the Indian campaigns with honor, and paid the penultimate price.

"It has been reported that the selkies are back in the harbor. Already, we have lost three sailors to their wiles, two off naval ships at liberty, one a merchantman. The Portmaster begs our aid in the matter."

There was a quiet murmur at that. Many of the men at the table had considerable investments tied up in shipping, and this struck close to home.

"We gave them fair warning, twice before," the Chairman said heavily. "Still they cannot leave our harbor alone."

Mr. Gilbert raised his hand, and was acknowledged. He stood, a tall, angular man, with deep hollows under his eyes. He was an importer, with direct and firsthand knowledge of the problem. "I do not underplay the significance of the damage selkies may do—they have long been a temptation to the sailing man long gone from his home."

Several of the men at the table crossed themselves, or looked horrified, but Gilbert ignored them. "However, we must acknowledge that selkies were once man's allies on the oceans. They may not understand why—to their eyes—we have turned against them."

"That partnership took effect when mankind was still mired in the age of superstition and folly," the Chairman said. "It is a weak relict of what humanity was once, not what it is becoming. Those partnerships are null and void in this modern age."

Gilbert bowed his head to indicate his acceptance of that. "I do not disagree. But they are, as you say, of a different age, and slow to change."

"We have given them warnings. We have told them to leave our men alone. Still, they persist. Is there a man here who would argue that we have not given fair notice?"

Gilbert waited a moment and then, finding himself alone, shook his head and sat down.

"So be it. Have their rocks slicked with oil and set afire. Any of the creatures who do not willingly leave after that, take care of with a single shot to the head or heart."

"We should destroy all of them," one of the men at the table muttered. "Filthy abominations!"

Gilbert would have reacted to that, but the Chairman was more swift.

"They are animals, Mr. Jackson. Of human mien, perhaps, but without the grace of God's touch, and so unable to understand the evil of what they do. Had it been harpies, then I would be the first to agree with you, but selkies… They were, as Mr. Gilbert reminds us, our helpmeets once, and it behooves us to remember that. They are of an older age, and Time and Science has passed them by. Destroy them for that? No. If we must, then let it be only when we ourselves are in dire threat, and only then with a heavy heart. The Lord created them, as he created all on this earth, and it is not our place to judge His works.

"Now. Is there further old business for us to discuss?"

There was none.

two

Present Day

Wren Valere was getting dressed to go outside. It was a lovely spring morning, complete with birds cautiously twitting and an almost pleasant breeze coming off the Hudson River. The sun was bright, the sky was blue, and she was trying to decide if she was going to need the hot-stick or not.

Some genius in the *Cosa* had come up with this over the winter, after the Battle of Burning Bridge. Passed through a security screening, it looked like an insulated tube, maybe part of a thermos, or for bike messengers to carry important papers in. Totally harmless. In the hands of a Talent, someone with the ability to channel current through their bodies, it was the magical equivalent of a howitzer.

It didn't pay, these dangerous days, to go outside unarmed.

She finally decided that she didn't need it, not for a job in broad daylight, and put it back into the drawer with relief. She hated carrying a weapon, even when she had to.

To the ignorant eye, she looked the epitome of harmless and helpless: five feet and scant inches of nonentity. Brown hair, brown eyes, pale skin, and a figure that was neither eye-catchingly curvy nor attractively slim: Wren Valere disappeared the moment you laid eyes on her. It was a skill she had been born with, and honed over the years until she was one of the most successful Retrievers in record.

Now, it made her one of the most dangerous weapons the *Cosa Nostradamus* had. The more their enemies looked for her, the harder she was to find.

Hard didn't mean impossible, though.

It had been three and a half months since the Battle, when an attempt to draw out the leaders of the human opposition had ended in bloodshed and destruction on both sides. Since then, the generations-old understanding between the "normal" world and the *Cosa Nostradamus*—best summed up as "you don't see us and we won't bother you"—had been badly shaken, if not shattered entirely. That shaking was the direct result of a vicious campaign waged, professionally and relentlessly, by anti-magical forces, unknowingly aided by factions within the *Cosa* who had seen only the chance to grow their own power and influence.

The intra-*Cosa* problems had been dealt with—or at least quieted for a while. The other…that force was still a real and present danger. The Humans First vigilantes who had been harassing the magic-using members of the *Cosa* and their non-human cousins the Fatae weren't the real enemy, but merely shock troops employed unknowingly by a far more dangerous and well-funded organization—the Silence.

The same organization her partner—her *ex*-partner—used to

work for. The same organization that had employed her, however briefly, when they were still pretending to be the good guys, the protectors of the innocent, the caretakers of Light and Virtue.

Innate and unwanted honesty forced Wren to occasionally acknowledge that it wasn't that easy, as black-and-white as it sounded. Just as not everyone on the Mage Council was an uptight power-hungry murderer—just most of them—then not everyone in the generations-old Silence was a bigot who hated magic and anything to do with magic.

Only the ones in power. Only the ones calling the shots. The ones who had hired over a hundred of the younger Talent, and brainwashed them into becoming weapons against their own people.

Who had set ordinary human bigots against the Fatae, causing innocent creatures to be harassed, chased, torn apart by dogs and run down by cars.

Who had sworn, at that highest level, to wipe what they saw as the "abomination" of the *Cosa Nostradamus,* the beings of magic, out of existence.

But on this morning, the first Tuesday in May, Wren had nothing to do with the Council, the Silence, or anything else with any sort of organization above and beyond herself. Right at that moment, Wren was lacing up a pair of flat-soled sandals under her carpenter pants and cotton sweater, and getting ready to go out on a job.

Life in wartime didn't mean life without work.

"Hey. You want another cup of coffee?" a voice asked.

She shook her head. "When I get back." She was wired enough; she didn't need the additional push of the caffeine.

The demon nodded, and took a sip out of the mug he held in his white-furred paw. Thick black claws showed darkly against the pale blue ceramic of the mug, which had the sea-wave logo of the Didier

Gallery on it. It was the last one she had: the other had gotten broken during the farewell party they had held for some friends the week before.

Most of the Fatae who couldn't pass for human had left town well before then, through a chain of households and helping hands the ever-irrepressible lonejacks were calling the Underground Furway, ignoring the fact that fully a third of the Fatae had scales, and the other third were plain-skinned. Her fellow lonejacks—human *Cosa* members unaffiliated with the Mage Council—stayed put for the most part, facing the danger with strength, courage, and an unending dose of irreverence.

The strength and courage had surprised her. The irreverence she had expected. You didn't become a lonejack if you were comfortable with the party line, or didn't try to bend it, every chance you got.

Despite being obviously Fatae, and therefore a prime target, P.B. had refused to even think about leaving town. The only concession he had made was to give up his basement apartment—in a crappy part of town the vigilantes patrolled too often—to move in with Wren for the duration. Her brownstone apartment was really too small for two people with personal space issues to live in comfortably, but another Talent, Bonnie, lived downstairs, and between the two of them, they could keep him safe.

They hoped.

These days, "safe" was a relative term.

"I have to go." She picked up her leather jacket off the back of a chair and slid it on. The damned thing showed more wear and tear than she did, but there was comfort in the old familiarity of it.

"So? Go." The demon shrugged. "We still on for the movies tonight?"

"Yeah. Bonnie and Jack will meet us there, they said. We can catch dinner after."

Life in wartime didn't mean you didn't have a social life, either. You just went out in numbers. And armed, at night.

"Did you…" P.B. didn't even finish that thought, much less the sentence.

"No," she said anyway, and, unlocking the four different locks on the metal security door, left the apartment, and the question behind her.

Left alone in the apartment, the demon known as P.B. shook his head. A lifetime spent avoiding conflicts, avoiding ugly complications and useless entanglements, and he finally found his place at the side of a woman who was avoiding the best thing that ever came down the proverbial pike for her. That was karma for you.

Not that he blamed her, entirely. Sergei Didier had been a hero at Burning Bridge, but P.B. was the only one who knew it. On Didier's orders, no less. The human had his reasons, but it didn't make the estrangement between Wren and Didier any easier to deal with.

"She will be able to function better without me."

Sergei loved Wren, and that made him blind, in a lot of ways. In the aftermath of the disaster at the Brooklyn Bridge, the *Cosa* didn't have many leaders left. They were trying to hold together, hanging together, but P.B. had seen it all before, and it didn't look good. They needed Valere, as much as she didn't want to be needed. But he had tried to convince her of that, of her importance in the scheme of things, and failed. The only person who could possibly make her see reason was her partner. *Ex*-partner. In both the business and the personal use of the word.

Something had to be done about that, too. For the *Cosa,* and for P.B.'s own sake. Not only was Wren's mood far sweeter when she was getting some horizontal action on a regular basis, but Didier was the only one besides Bonnie in this building who could actually cook.

* * *

Walking down the street toward the bus stop, Wren had already taken the demon's parting words and implications and put them away where she didn't have to look at them. She and Sergei...it was better this way. Ignoring all the stuff between them personally, which took a major amount of ignoring, the truth was that he had prevaricated to them—to *her*—about the Silence. He had held on to information they needed, information they deserved to have, to protect themselves, in the name of a loyalty he swore no longer existed.

Yeah, he had come clean in the end, or at least she thought he had, but the level of distrust in the *Cosa* toward him was pretty deep, and she...she couldn't afford that. Couldn't afford to be touched by it. Not if she wanted to survive this.

The *Cosa* had dragged her in not once but twice. Made her responsible, when that was the very last thing she wanted. People had died. *Friends* had died. And her city was being torn apart, even as she walked to work, all because the Silence hated anything not—to their eyes—purely human, and the *Cosa* didn't trust anyone not *Cosa*.

Sergei claimed that he had been done with the Silence, had been done with them for years. But at the Battle of Burning Bridge last January, he had been there. Been on the scene, when nobody—not her, certainly not P.B.—had told him anything was going down.

It looked bad, no matter how fast he talked. It looked bad then, and it still looked bad now.

Two cops were standing on the corner of Eighth Avenue. They acted casual—one eye on the early morning traffic, one on the pedestrians passing by—but Wren made a living reacting off unspoken cues, and they were practically screaming unease, to her.

The shorter cop's gaze touched on her, moved on. She hadn't invoked her usual no-see-me cantrip yet, because it was tough enough to get a bus to stop without intentionally making it difficult to see you standing there, but she was naturally forgettable. Unless she suddenly developed wings or green skin or shot at them....

The NYPD was still a little twitchy in the aftermath of Burning Bridge, too. For decades, there had been Fatae in the ranks, until scrutiny got tightened, and most of the older cops had pretty decent memories of a partner who was just a little... weird. But a reminder of that winter morning would not go over well right now. Cops had gotten hurt, too.

For that reason alone, Wren wished that P.B. had made like so many of his cousins and beat feet out of town. Old loyalties and vague memories weren't much to count on when there were so many bloody incidents happening. Because it was quiet right now didn't mean it would be quiet five minutes from now. The tension she could feel constantly in her skin reminded her of that, every moment she was awake and most of her sleeping time as well.

The bus came and Wren got on, sliding between the ranks of her fellow commuters to a place where she could rest against the back of a seat, and not worry about being shoved as people got on or off at each stop.

Other people carried briefcases, computer bags. She had a yellow canvas shoulder bag that had seen better years, and a set of lockpick tools tucked into a leather case strapped against her stomach. Thighs could be ogled, backs-of-back touched, but generally not even the most intrepid of security guards touched a woman's stomach. Not unless you were already in deeper kimchee than a lockpick would warrant.

There was a quiet urge inside her, to reach down and touch her core, just for reassurance. Connecting to her core—the pit of current that lived inside her, and made her a Talent—would settle her nerves, her uncertainties. Not because it was reassuring—it wasn't—but because the level of confidence and control it took to manage it overrode everything else. You went down into the core, you were calm and controlled, or you lost ownership. And once that happened... It was instinctive, by the time a Talent was allowed out on her own. But she couldn't let herself reach for it.

Not unless she wanted to fry every single laptop, PDA, watch, cell phone, and music-playing device on this bus. Her control was, well, in control. But her emotions were totally not.

Damn you, Didier. Damn you for making me shove you away. I need you, you stupid, selfish, arrogant bastard! She had counted on him, and he had failed her.

Her stop came up and she slipped off the bus, weaving her way through the crowds of Times Square. Even at this hour, there were tourists. At every hour, there were tourists. Wren wouldn't mind them quite so much if they'd just learn how to walk. You didn't stop in the middle of a sidewalk to have a conversation with ten of your bestest buddies. You didn't wave your camera around like it was a baton. And you absolutely didn't stand there with your wallet open, counting out your bills after you bought breakfast from a bagel cart.

Wren pocketed the handful of bills almost absently, and decided that the camera wasn't pretty enough for the taking. Anyway, what would she do with it? Her only experience with cameras was ducking whenever her mother's then-boyfriend tried to take a photo of her, as a child.

Her quarry was up ahead: the Taylor Theater. The Taylor was one of the smaller venues, holding on to its dignity with a restored Art Deco facade. Broadway had never been demure, but she always had class, even draped in neon and splattered with six-story-high underwear ads, and the Taylor was every inch a classy dame.

Wren loved living in Manhattan, and she especially loved wandering through Times Square. It was an unspoken law, known to every New York Talent: You don't recharge on Broadway. The neon, the floodlights, the endless uncountable miles of wiring and secondary power sources, they all had an invisible "paws off" sign. Like hospitals and nuclear power plants, you just *didn't*.

That didn't mean you couldn't feel a buzz, walking under the throbbing, pulsing, sweating lights. Wren let it pass through her, not trying to catch any of the current shimmering in the air. It was spring, there had been a thunderstorm over the weekend, and her core was sated and ready to go.

The job had come in two days ago, via a friend of a friend of a former client. A smash-and-grab, without much smash. Not much of a grab, either—an old prop that had some sort of sentimental value to the client, and was being held by another actor as his own good luck charm.

Actors. Jesus wept. They made the *Cosa* seem well-adjusted.

Once, Wren would have grumbled about a job that was, in effect, sleepwalking; she used to thrive on the rev of adrenaline that came from outsmarting a security system, outwitting guards, and getting away with something someone else didn't want you to have.

Now, she was working to pay the rent, and keep herself occupied, and nothing else need apply, thanks. Certainly no more adrenaline.

At least she didn't have to worry about the cost of feeding P.B.—demon couriers were never out of work, especially in times of unease and suspicion, and with him in the apartment on a full-time basis, he was placing regular online grocery orders on his own dime.

Apparently they really *would* give anyone a credit card.

She came upon the theater, and walked past it, giving it a casual once-over with her eyes, and another deeper one with a narrow thread of current. Nothing struck her as being out of place or odd. More odd, anyway, she thought, walking past the Naked Cowboy, trying to strum up some attention. Broadway might have class, but not all of her residents did.

She turned the corner and went into the wine store there, spending a few minutes looking around as though comparing prices on the red wines in the sale bin. The only thing Wren knew about wine was that she usually liked whatever Sergei suggested, but it was a good way to kill a few minutes. People spent hours trying to decide wines—clerks generally left you alone if you looked like you were a serious shopper, until you made eye contact with them.

Four minutes later, Wren shook her head as though disappointed with the selection, and walked back out of the store, back toward the theater.

There were three different ways you could enter a building you weren't supposed to be in. You could sneak in through a nontraditional entrance: window, sewer, skylight, loading dock. Wren had once had herself rolled in via a beer delivery. You could walk right in through the front door, brazen it out and hope nobody thought to challenge you. Or, you could find a commonly used entrance, and slide in with a crowd.

If you were a Retriever, you had a fourth option. You went invisible.

She had tried to explain it to Sergei once as being just the next step up from pretending that you weren't there. Everyone did that; praying the cop would pull over the guy next to you even though you were the one speeding, that the gym teacher would pick on someone else, that the bum on the subway would sit at the other end of the car and leave you alone. The difference was, when you had current and skill to back you up, your chances for success went up.

Way up, if you were Wren Valere. And if there were days that she wished every head would turn when she walked in the door, it was nonetheless a skill that made it possible for her to call the tune of her own life.

"Impose this
upon their eyesight:
blindness falls."

Two young men walked past her, and as the last word of her cantrip hit the air, the one nearest to her stumbled and went down to his knees, crying out in shock and not a little fear.

"Charlie?" His friend went to him, shifting his coffee to his off hand as he tried to help his companion up.

"Jesus! Everything went black!"

Wren winced, but didn't hesitate as she moved past them, opening the heavy metal doors of the theater and slipping inside to the lobby. She hadn't meant it to be quite so literal! Hopefully it was only temporary.

Tone it down. You're too full, *too charged. This isn't a fight. It's a job. Finesse, not fury. Don't let it control you, you control it.*

Right. She took a moment to stand still, settling the current down into her more securely. Too much was as bad as too little. Worse, sometimes. All it took was one instant for the core to escape control… Mirroring the neon outside, the current glowed around her bones, slithering like snakes, always restless at the hint of action.

Control, control. Only the small amount I need, and the rest of you, sleep…

According to the emerging theory her neighbor and fellow Talent Bonnie had told her about, there was a weird mucous lining on their cells that allowed their bodies to channel current. That didn't fit well with her visual of the core as being a dry pit filled with muscled neon snakes, but it made a lot of sense, otherwise. It was also, in a word, disgusting. She preferred to think of it as willpower and self-control.

Control. Yes.

The tension in her skin eased for a second, and she felt almost normal.

Confident now that she would pull only the current she needed, Wren started moving again.

The job literally was a grab. No cursed objects, no semisentient entities, no high-magic or low-tech security systems. Not even any half-awake, geriatric guards to work around. Just the cast and crew of a Broadway play, the normal preperformance nerves shimmering in the air, and a silver hip flask engraved with a Fleur de Lys that if Wren was really lucky, would have something potent inside, and she didn't mean spellwise.

Wren didn't understand why the client felt he needed a Retriever for this, but the truth was that she had become somewhat of a status symbol. Anyone could have something stolen. You had to pay a lot to get The Wren to Retrieve it for you.

Morons. But so long as the check cleared, the client got to be *Mr.* Moron.

The lobby in front of her was everything the façade had promised: red velvet, gilding, soaring ceilings, and the faint but unmistakably tangy scent of an overworked air circulation system. Nice, if you were into old buildings.

Her blueprint of the theater showed a series of tunnels running under the stage itself. She supposed they had been used to move sets and actors around, since there wasn't much actual "backstage" to be found. What she wanted was—allegedly—hidden there.

If Sergei…

Sergei wasn't.

But if he was, you'd know for certain. He would have pulled something from one of his contacts….

Contacts that, more often than not, came from the Silence.

Her voice fell silent, unable to argue the point.

It's not the Silence….

Jesus wept, shut *up.*

The voice shut up again. But that didn't make the truth of what she didn't let it say any less. It wasn't his connection to the Silence that kept her from returning his phone calls, weeks ago when he still left messages for her. Everyone else might think that, but she knew better. So did he.

Sergei was an addict. He was addicted to the feel of her current; mostly when they made love, but any time he could get it. Current took the signature, the feel of the person using it, once it was in the core for a little while. Sergei wanted that, wanted the rush of it—of *her*—in his system.

Only problem was, he wasn't a Talent. He was Null. And current damaged Nulls.

It killed them.

Sergei knew that. And he still craved it. Asked her to give it to him.

And she, damn her, did. Because she couldn't refuse him anything he needed that badly, especially when it was all tied up in how much he felt for her.

So she denied him. Everything. Her. Kept him safe by giving him up.

Because she could forgive him anything—anything—except using her to kill himself.

"Who left the damn door open?" A very tall man clad entirely in black, with a long ponytail of red hair reaching between his shoulder blades breezed into the lobby, and shut the door Wren had entered with a resounding slam. "Idiots think that just because it's springtime we don't heat this place no more? Actors. Only thing worse than actors are musicians, and the only thing worse than musicians're the crew…"

He breezed out again, muttering under his breath about the useless bags of meat he was sent to work with.

"The director, I presume," Wren said, amused. She had never been a theater person, but one of her friends in college was, and between Suzy and Sergei's own dealings with the artists he showed in the gallery, or met on the circuit, she'd heard countless stories about the "temperament" of the artistic types.

Her only real friend in the arts had been Tree-taller, and the sculptor had been as calm and measured as one of his sculptures. But that came from being an artist with Talent—working metal with current made you cautious, or it got you dead.

She winced. He had gotten himself dead anyway, hadn't he? So many dead…

Focus. A different voice this time, sharp and unforgiving. The voice she heard too often in her dreams, now. An unfamiliar, unforgiving voice, refusing to let her rest. A combination of all the dead: the Talented and Fatae dead of this city, trying to drive her forward into things, places, she didn't want.

Bite me, she said to it now, and followed the director down into the theater. The set was dark; if the rest of the cast had arrived for the matinee already, they were elsewhere in the building.

The blueprint said that there was an entrance to the main tunnel to the left of the stage, just behind the pillar. Wren looked around to make sure that nobody was lurking, then vaulted to the stage, careful as she landed not to make so much noise that anything echoed. They might not be able to see her, but they'd still be able to hear her.

"Okay, door. Where's a door? What looks like a door?"

To someone used to the stage, it was no doubt obvious. Wren, in the dark in more than one way, had only her natural sense of sneaky to guide her.

Well, that and a little extra fillip of Talent.

"The way down
is the way to go.
Lead me there."

Thankfully cantrips didn't have to be any kind of great poetry. So long as the words helped you focus, they were effective. A faint blue shimmer of light flickered off her fingertips, tiny cousins to the neon flickering outside, and floated off as though they had all the time in the world.

"A little speed, willya?" she urged it in a whisper. In response, the lights brightened a little, then moved en masse to a spot just to the left of the pillar. Wren followed, noting as she moved that she was now out of sight of anyone in the audience.

The blue lights spread over the wall and thinned into a bare thread, outlining a narrow door.

The tunnel.

She held up her hand and the blue current sped back to her. You didn't leave evidence behind on a job. She might have been careless before, not thinking that it mattered, but having Bonnie living in the building with her had been an eye-opener as to what the PUPIs—

Private Unaffiliated Paranormal Investigators—could do with even a scrap of signed current. And she had been holding this in her core long enough for it to "taste" like her to anyone who bothered to test it.

She eyed the door, trying to get a feel for any alarms or other wiring securing it shut. Nothing. As far as her abilities could tell, it was just a fitted wooden door. Which led to the next choice: fast or slow? You could open it slowly, and risk one of those soul-killing creaking noises. Open it fast, and who knew what might happen. Either way, there was a chance of alerting people to an intruder.

"Screw it," Wren said, and opened the door normally.

It slid open without a sound. A black light went on overhead, lighting the steps down. She frowned at it before realizing that the black light was probably so that nobody onstage or in the audience might see a distracting glow when a performance was running. Nice. She was going to have to experiment, when she got home, and see if she could create the equivalent with current. A handy thing, if she could make it work. Handy, yes, and possibly profitable? If she could bottle it somehow, the way some Talent made prepared Transloca-tion spells—they overcharged so much, she only used them when there was no other choice, and they had to be individually set and had a limited lifespan, but a current-powered blacklight…hell, a prepared current-light, period…

Worry about it later. Just because this is a cakewalk, no reason to get sloppy. Bad things always seem to happen when you get cocky.

The stairs were surprisingly comfortable to walk down, even keeping her back to the far wall. There was some sort of rubber padding tacked to the steps, which had the advantage of both muffling footsteps and keeping her footing secure when the stairs turned sharply.

At the bottom, the tunnel was much larger than she had expected; rather than a narrow walkway, it was a broad and arched hall with a track of modern lighting running along the ceiling. The air was cool and dry, not musty or stale, indicating that they had at least a basic air filtering system in place.

Nice. With a little work, you could probably turn this into the trendy new living space, and make a fortune.

All right, enough with the money-making plans, Valere. Get the job done.

She set her back against the wall, feeling the cool stone even through her leather jacket, and tried to orient herself. She had come down *here,* and she was facing *there,* so...It might be cheating, triangulating via the pulse of Times Square, but you used what you had. Confident now that she knew where she was going, Wren pulled her lockpick tools out of its tummy sheath, and stepped forward confidently.

There was no warning. One moment she was moving forward, the next she was pinned against the wall again, only this time there was a heavy forearm against her throat, and the smell of hot breath on her face. A white cloth mask was pulled over his face, showing only narrowed brown eyes above the fabric.

Wren reacted the way she had been trained: fast and hard, but not lethally. Her mentor, John Ebeneezer, had been a huge fan of not killing people, and even years of Sergei's "survival at all costs" attitude and P.B.'s casual disregard for bloodshed had not been able to quite eradicate that early influence.

She didn't even try to shove back physically—she was in shape, but her strength was not in meat and muscle. A hard pull down on her core, and thick-bodied snakes of sizzling red and gold came to her, coiling up her arm faster than she could visualize them. There was enough power there to jolt any assailant back on his ass and crisp the ends of his short-and-curlies.

The guy jerked and grunted when she hit him, but didn't let go. And he absolutely didn't fly back onto his posterior the way he was supposed to. Instead he slapped her across the face, hard enough that her vision swam and her face burned.

"Bitch sparked me," he told someone else over his shoulder. "Stupid cunt."

He relaxed his grip slightly, but before she could take advantage of it, another set of hands pulled her off the wall, shoving her down to her knees on the floor. From that position, she could see that they were wearing thick-soled work boots, and dark green carpenter's pants.

Two of them. Then another set of boots came into view, and she upped the count to three. At least. Damn, and also, damn. Two she might have been able to take in an unfair fight. And they had expected her to use current. They had warded themselves somehow.... Rubber. The soles of their boots, probably fibers in their clothing, at least enough to absorb a nonlethal blow. They weren't warded, magically; just basic physical forensics and a trip to the Army-Navy store. They knew about Talent. And they didn't seem to be friendly.

A shove in the small of her back, and she went facedown on the stone.

Nope, not friendlies at all. Stay calm, Valere. Stay calm. Damn it, I should have brought the hot-stick.

A thin, thin filament of current stretched out from deep within her core, imbued with as much of her personal signature as possible. She sent it out, searching for anyone on the street above who would be able to hear her. There were people she could specifically tag, reaching out to their mental signature across the city, but by the time they understood what was going on, it might be too late to be of any use.

The filament didn't find anyone other than Nulls on the streets above. No Fatae, no Talent.

Looks like you're on your own. Figures. So much for the Patrol still hanging around.

Who were these assholes, anyway? Random goons who got lucky? The fact that they were prepared shot that idea down. They weren't Council, and she doubted they were here to protect her target, so that left only one answer.

Vigilantes. The Silence's goons. Fuckitall and why did she never get a break?

"Hurry up," one of them urged the other two. "Let's get this done." She lay very still, trying to distinguish their voices in her mind. The one standing up was a tenor, she thought. He had a faint rasp to his words, like he had a cold. Not a local—she didn't recognize the way he worked his vowels.

"Ain't nobody down here," the second one said. He was kneeling beside her now, and she repressed a shudder when his hand landed flat on her back, just above her waist. "They're all upstairs getting made up."

Local boy, definitely. Probably Staten Island. His hand slid up her back, and now Wren did shudder. The touch was more than un-friendly; it was unfriendly with Intent. And she didn't want to think about that intent.

The last man to touch her with intent was Sergei, their last night together. Ham-handed boy got to take no such liberties.

The third guy was silent, just standing there, watching. She could hear him breathing, though. He sounded like another big guy, like he had a thick chest, and probably the weight to match.

"I wonder if what they say about their kind is true? Seems such a waste, dropping this little bird so quick." Kneeling boy laughed at his own wit, and Wren would have rolled her eyes if she hadn't been so nervous. Please. Like she had never heard that joke before? Her nickname came off her given name, Genevieve, and because she was hard to see, like the wren in a bush, but people always made the size assumption.

Her mind came back to the here-and-now with a nasty snap. Two hands now, one on each shoulder, pressing her into the floor, and a weight still on her back. His leg?

Oh shit. She was starting to get pissed off, the snakes in her core sliding against each other, their scales dry and scratchy, letting off static in a low hiss. *I really don't have time for this....*

"George, don't."

George. Wren grabbed onto that. Local boy's name was George. That was dumb, using names.

Then Wren really did shudder. Unless they weren't dumb, just careless. Because she wasn't going to be around to tell anyone. *Oh shit,* she thought again, this time with more emphasis as the pieces came together. "Their kind." Talent. The insulated boots and clothing. "Little bird." They were here for her specifically, not just vigilante yahoos looking for a Talent to bust, or even unwary legs to spread. They were hunting The Wren, and she'd walked right into them.

Or been *sent* right into them. The entire job, a setup? Or...*it doesn't matter, Valere! Just get out of there!*

"Come on, you musta heard the stories." He shifted, and Wren could feel him straddling her, sitting on her upper thighs. Then he leaned forward, covering her entire body, and she felt his erection pushing against her ass, even through her jeans. "Like dipping into an electrical socket, I've heard. Hottest shit ever."

Thou shalt not kill, a memory said, oh so quietly in the back of her brain.

"Yeah, and you hear what else they say? They're not human, man!"

"So?" George clearly wasn't worried about that. He shifted again, one hand leaving her shoulder to reach around and wrestle with the snap of her jeans. "Come on man, help me. I'll let you have a taste, after I wear her out, if you're too scared to get in first."

The other guy didn't sound tempted. "The Man hears, you won't think it worth it. Aw, hell. You remember what happened with the last one we popped? Bitch near tore his head off. You gotta get some, damage her first and you can get in and out before she dies."

George didn't stop his movements. "Whaddreyou, sick or something? I'm not doing a corpse! Anyway, I like 'em when they fight. Spicy." His fingers got under her waistband, and started moving down, shoving aside her underwear.

The last one we popped...echoed in Wren's brain, rattling around like dried beans. Bastards. They got off on this. They thought they had the right to do whatever they wanted, because someone told them they were superior, that they were *better.*

The frustration of the past few months, the anger building up for the past year, rolled like the tide against her shores, and she was so very tired of holding it back, of not being able to vent her emotions on the world that kept trying to slap her down.

Control, she told herself. *Control.* But her core was suspended in black tar, and current raged overhead and underfoot, and blood ran like the river tides. She could not feel anything other than that, oblivious to the outside world, not caring what was being done to her body as she fought for control she wasn't sure she even wanted, any more.

The third man spoke then, finally, breaking her out of her mental prison. "I'll kill both of you, you touch that thing." It didn't sound like he was bluffing.

"What, you're trying to protect it?"

There was a snick of a knife, and George's fingers stopped for an instant.

"Don't be even more of a moron than you have to be. You're human. It's not. Don't sully yourself."

"You'd kill him? *For that?*" The second man, incredulous.

It's not human. Three on one. They're armed. Thou shalt not kill. 'The last one we popped.'

A memory: of bodies facedown and faceup, sprawled in their own blood, pools of black on dirty snow. Entrails, shit, and teargas making her gasp against tears. Ohm's bane, flickering dark red against the dawn sky, up and down the skyward-arching form of the Brooklyn Bridge. A long black car, driving away. Sergei's face, stone and sadness.

Inside, Wren felt something give way; a brick wall under assault, an earthen ditch crumbling. She grabbed for the pieces, held it together. But it was slipping under her fingertips.

"*Aid!*" An involuntary blast of streaky purple current like a signal flare shot into the ether, the agreed-upon signal of the Truce Patrol, whatever was left of it. "*Aid and assistance down here! Vigilantes!*"

And then she was falling, falling into the tar, falling into the darkness where even current did not shine.

She had asked for help. She wasn't going to wait around for it.

It was a simple matter—almost instinctive—to reach for the proper fugue state. Once, she would have had to do deep breathing, ground and center, concentrate. During the past year, Wren Valere had used her current more on a daily basis in order to survive, to protect those around her, than she used to call up in a week's time, even including jobs. She had stretched and grown, almost unknowing; so much so that now she simply *let go* and fell down into her core.

The first awareness was always the sound. Dry slithering, and hissing. Paper-against-spark, the insentient patience of current, coiling and recoiling in an endless loop.

Next were the colors. She opened her not-eyes and colors consumed her. Dark and scarlet reds and royal-blues, dark greens and iridescent purples, streaks of gold and silver, and underneath it all the dark, dark muscled bodies of a color she had never been able to name.

And then the warmth that seeped into her bones. Stone-warmth, like lava rising from the gut of the earth. It called, seduced, tried to make her give in, relax, come down into the pit and lose her way.

The moment she did that, the current would destroy her. Self-control was everything in the core.

Come to me, she told it. Not a single thread, the way she normally did, or even a braiding, but all of it. It surged up in response to her call, her will easily overpowering them. Sparking and sizzling into her veins, bloating her with power. *Not you,* she said to the dark, dark current, sticky like tar.

???!!?

Not you, she repeated. She didn't know why, but something deeper even than her core warned her away from it, denied it access.

Dimly she was aware of her body shoved forward, her pants around her thighs. Hands gripping her wrists, a knee between her shoulder blades. The snap of latex. She almost laughed. They thought it would get that far?

"For God's sake, I'll buy you a whore. I'll buy you two." The third man, again. "Just kill it already. Once it's dead, its familiar will be unprotected, and we can finish the job."

P.B.? Her thoughts fluttered. P.B.!

The demon could protect itself. That wasn't the point. She hadn't been thorough enough vetting this job, hadn't been careful enough, and now they thought, these pitiful, rubber-suited *Nulls* thought they would clear the board, with their flick-knives, their dicks, and their self-righteous bigotry?

They thought they were better than her, because they could not feel the current in everything around them?

The smell of shit and tear gas filled her nostrils again, and she breathed it in, deep. Her attention off of it for that split second, the black thread in her core rounded in on itself, and no longer tar but black lava, struck upward, straight into her spine.

Wren almost laughed as the full impact of her core surged through her, crackling and snarling. No longer snakes, not serpents, but dragons now, full-winged and fire-breathing and deadly to behold.

They erupted from her, soaring free and high. Black opal-bodied, all the colors of the universe contained within, the hot sludge of their blood thrumming like a bass drum. Thunderheads formed around them, great anvils of Thor, and their wings smashed them, drank them in, filled their roars with the sound of thunder and the cold buffeting rain. Tangled and soaked, Wren opened her throat and screamed with them, her arms thrown into the air. The current jumping from them to her and then back again until welts formed on her skin, creating a pattern of diamond scales.

Somewhere, in some small corner that was still Wren, she was screaming for a different reason. But it was a small, thin voice, and impossible to hear. Possible to ignore, in the orgasmic fury of the storm, that one whisper of dissent: of denial, of fear. Of sanity.

Then a sudden downward spiral, shooting back toward earth, not so much picking up speed as becoming speed, a lightning bolt of a thousand dragons of unheavenly ire. The hit was better than speed, was better than sex, was better than anything she had ever felt before, and her body convulsed around the sensation, throwing her heels over head into a blast of colorless current that cut off her breath and dropped her into unconsciousness.

three

Wren?

It was quiet where she was, quiet and comfortable, and she resented the voice for disturbing her. "G'way," she told it, batting a mental hand at the sound, like a pesky moth fluttering in her face.

Wren? The moth was more urgent now, refusing to be batted.

She murmured something rude, feeling lazy and sluggish. Also fried. So fried she was pretty sure her hair would crackle if she touched it. As though the thought forced the movement, her fingers twitched slightly.

They were wet.

No, they were *holding* something wet.

Wren!

That woke her up, the near-frantic shout into her brain. Not a moth any more but a hornet's sting.

She identified the voice, uncertainly, as not being her own. A ping, from not so very far away. Why were they yelling?

Yeah, she responded, just trying to get the voice to stop shouting.

We heard you! Are you okay? I'm on my way! The nonverbal words carried a sense of urgency, of fear, of forces being marshaled and ready to break down the door, wherever the door might be.

Wha? Confusion, then memory, coming back to her, a trickle at a time. She had been on a job. Attacked, taken out by three vigilante goons. Idiots. They were going to rape her, rape and kill her, and then—

She sat up, and looked down at her hand.

Ten minutes later, she was huddled against the stairs, her gut empty and her throat aching from the continuous dry retching. The wide tunnel floor in front of her was strewn with flesh and bones, scorched to black with current. The remains of three humans, obliterated.

Her hand, still clenching the sticky strands of something she didn't want to identify, and couldn't bring herself to wipe off.

Wren! That voice, screaming now inside her, an entire nest of hornets.

There was barely enough control left in her to grab onto that scream, send it back on a quieter note. *It's over. I'm...okay.*

You sure? Whoever this Talent was, he didn't sound convinced.

No. She wasn't okay. She wasn't ever going to be okay. The stickiness itched, and she finally wiped her hand against the wall, trying to scrape it off her skin.

Yeah. I'm good. Thanks.

She cut the connection, and sat there in blessed silence. Until the silence started to talk back.

You did what you had to do. A seductive whisper of justification, of reassurance. She was one of the good guys, relatively speaking. They had tried to hurt her, and she had struck back. Nobody could blame her. Nobody would.

Thou shalt not kill. Wren had never been much for religion, not even the remarkably mild and mellow Protestant God she had been raised with, but certain things hit hard when you were a kid, and stuck. Thou shalt not steal was right out, and she coveted and blasphemed on a regular basis, without any guilt whatsoever. Ancient commandments should not haunt her, not now.

She wasn't to blame. It had been a setup. She didn't know why she was so certain of it, but she was. She had walked into a trap. No matter if the job was real or not, nobody had been here, nobody had come when she—had she made any noise? How long had it taken? No way of knowing. Nobody came. They, whoever they were, had targeted her, maybe seen her as a weak spot in the defense—

Thou shalt not kill.

Wren's fingers closed into fists, her close-cut nails digging into the flesh of her palms. She had killed before. Had used current...

Chrome and blood. Exhaustion, pain: the aftermath of their first, disastrous face-off with the vigilantes. Plastic cups and white plates, and blood and gore and...

She shut the memory down, locking it back in its box. Stephanie. The lonejack turncoat, who had sold them out to KimAnn Howe and the local Council. Wren had been part of the group that stopped her...stopped her with deadly force. But she had been part of a whole, then. A consensus, if hastily and wordlessly achieved. Her hand had been on the current that eradicated the woman, but other hands had been laid upon hers, the decision to use force spread out among many minds...

This time, she had no one else to turn to, no one to share responsibility. Wren shook her head, and again scraped her palm against the wall, focusing on the cool texture underneath her skin.

But the coldness in her gut wouldn't go away, nor would the fact that worse, far worse and far more damning, this time, she hadn't used current. Current had used her. Her fear, her rage, her exhaustion. She had failed, every inch of all of her training, and she had failed. It had escaped the core, escaped *control,* and thrown her up into it.

Thrown her into... She had...oh God.

Her hand fisted against the wall, and her face squeezed together in a pained grimace.

What she had done, what she had almost become, clogged her brain and stopped her heart for a godforsaken moment. Hysteria threatened, the waves becoming a tsunami that threatened to drag her under.

Don't go there. Don't think about it. Don't...

Mental doors slammed, control reasserted itself, walling off even the faintest trace of the awful glory. And a chant from her brain to every single cell of her body: Don't ever think about it, don't ever remember it, don't ever linger on it, or you *will* go insane.

Again.

Her fist opened, her face relaxed, and Wren let her now-clean, if stained, hand fall away from the wall. She reached down and pulled her pants back up, zipping and buttoning the fly. Her leather jacket had vomit stains on it, and she absently made plans to drop it off for dry-cleaning. Current could clean it up but...

No current. Not right now.

She had murdered three people.

Thou shalt not kill.

She could have held them off without killing them. She had done it before. Even three on one. She had held off hellhounds. Talked down revenge-driven ghosts. Captured malicious, evil sentient boogums and ancient bansidhes.

These were just three Nulls. Three humans. She could have stopped them some other way. There had to have been some other way.

Tears soaked her cheeks, but inside, inside she was sere and dry. Inside, without thought, something hardened within her.

It's not human. Kill it.

The memory of bodies strewn over the length of the Brooklyn Bridge.

A small winged Fatae, torn to pieces by a dog while its owner urged it on.

Michaela, her gypsy colors muted, lying still and motionless in a bed, white sheets pulled up around her. "She's gone too deep. She won't ever wake up again. She doesn't want to wake up again."

Death. All around her, death and hurt, and it was too much. She didn't have anywhere to put it any more.

Wren closed her eyes and counted to ten. When she opened them again, nothing had changed. "No more. No more." She wasn't sure if she was asking the universe, or telling it. She was pretty sure, either way, that it wasn't listening.

Fine. Whatever.

She turned and looked at the debris, and flicked the fingers of her left hand at it, almost negligently. The dead man's skin sizzled and dissolved, the bones aged into dust, the blood dried to an antique stain. All gone, bye-bye.

The flask. Now get the flask. Always finish the job. Sergei's mantra. Her mantra.

Something cold and wet, like fog, settled over her, filling in the dry desert places inside her. It was cold, but it kept her warm, replaced what had been taken. "No. Screw that. There's another job I have to finish, first."

* * *

P.B. was exhausted. There was no reason for it; he'd just been puttering around the apartment, playing with color swatches of paint and fabric, wondering what Wren's reaction would be if she came home and found her apartment-white walls painted Victorian Mint, or Honeybear Brown. A terrifying thought, but hardly an exhausting one. And yet, all he wanted to do right now was crawl onto his cot in the office, and take a nap.

He resisted, standing in the hallway and doing stretches, feeling his thick muscles creak and complain while he worked them. His body was not designed for yoga, but it seemed to do the trick: he was still tired, but it wasn't quite so overwhelming.

The delicate, hand-painted fabric on the wall in front of him—a gift from their friend Shig, a Japanese businessbeing—stood out like a sore thumb. Or, more accurately, it stood out like a perfectly formed thumb on a gnarled, battered hand. P.B. had asked Wren once why she never actually bothered to do anything about her apartment, and she had simply shrugged. How a woman partnered to an art dealer could be so blasé about home decoration P.B. did not understand, and had threatened more than once to call an intervention on her design sense.

Their most recent discussion—too much to call it an argument—had been two nights before, and she had finally told him to do what he wanted, so long as he left her alone on the subject already. He had barely waited until she was out of the apartment this morning before pulling out the paint and fabric swatches. But he hadn't gotten beyond her office when the exhaustion hit.

Once he felt confident that he wasn't going to collapse in a pile, P.B. went back into the kitchen and pulled a soda out of the fridge.

Diet, of course—didn't Valere know those things were going to kill her?—and downed it in one long gulp. Only after he had crushed the now-empty can in his paw did he realize that it was caffeine-free.

"Christ, woman, what's the *point?*"

He paused, feeling something shift, even as he spoke her name.

"Valere? Wren?"

Silence, not unexpected, answered him.

If he really needed to, he could reach her; they had shared enough of a connection the times she had grounded in him that he could find her, anywhere, if need be. He considered it, then shook his head. Probably his imagination, that shift. She should be well into the job by now, whatever it was. She'd only spent a day preparing for it, so it wasn't a big deal. There was no need to be concerned. And if she ran into any real trouble outside that, she could handle herself. There was no need for him to worry.

That decided and put to rest, there was no reason at all for the sound of a high-pitched buzzer blasting through the apartment to send him a foot straight into the air.

"What the *hell?*"

The intercom. That's all it was. Sergei had gotten it fixed, but they never used it: if anyone wanted in, they could ping, or climb up the fire escape, the way he did.

Except Wren wasn't here, and Bonnie'd gone to work, so nobody was around to hear a ping, you idiot, he told himself, going to the door. Which meant that whoever was out there knew it was just him in the apartment, and didn't feel like climbing the fire escape to gain access.

"All right, all right, hold your horses, I'm coming," he grumbled, trying to remember where the intercom controls were.

"Right. There you are." Right by the front door, which made sense.

Two buttons to talk and listen, and one to unlock the building's front door.

Not thinking, he hit the buzzer to let them in.

It took Wren another ten minutes to work up the energy to get back up the stairs from the tunnel. The stage was still empty when she emerged through the door, but a spotlight was fixed on the sofa that made up the main of the set, and there were sounds to indicate that the crew was hard at work behind the scenes. Wren hunched her shoulders and slid into the shadows.

The lobby was now humming with soft instrumental music, and there were several someones now moving around in the box office. Wren left by the same door she had come in, without notice. She didn't even have to think about not being seen: she wasn't. It was all automatic. From her breathing to her thoughts, the entire system was running without conscious direction.

Out on the street, in the daylight, the wreck of her leather jacket was more apparent. Wren considered, briefly, braving mass transit and the chances of something jostling her, or making a comment, and decided not to risk it. Her nerve endings were twitching, and she wasn't sure what might happen if someone got in her face.

Walking though the crowds back to Eighth Avenue, she was just another New Yorker not making eye contact. A cab came along when she stepped into the street and raised her hand, with a driver who didn't even notice the smell and didn't want to talk. You took the miracles where and when you got them.

She had just enough cash on her to pay the driver off, and staggered up the steps to her apartment. She made it to the third landing, and had to stop out of sheer exhaustion.

"Wren?"

"Bonnie." Wren rested her head against the wall. The sense of being an automaton was starting to wear off, and she waited for the pain to come back, but it didn't. She still felt numb, blank.

Shocky, part of her mind diagnosed. *Get upstairs, eat something. Take a hot shower. You'll feel better.*

The other lonejack in the building had come out of her apartment—based on the white plastic bag in her hand, to make a garbage drop—and was regarding her with concern. She was wearing a black short-sleeved T-shirt with a pink kitten on it, and black cargo pants with heavy black boots underneath, and had a new haircut, something cutely pixielike that made the newly white-blond strands curl around her chin and ears. She looked like a goth pixie, but her expression was less mischievous and more oddly maternal. Considering Bonnie barely qualified as twenty-something, the motherly face didn't quite fit.

"You look like…Actually I don't want to think about what you look like. Go take a shower. I just made brownies. I'll be up in fifteen."

Sugar. Yes. "Make it thirty."

Wren made it the rest of the steps, unlocked the door, and fell inside. Only then did her back stop with the prickling as though someone were targeting her, and the muscles in her jaw relaxed enough so that she was no longer grinding her teeth together.

"Hello?"

Silence. A moment of panic shivered through her, cutting the fog, then she saw the piece of paper tacked to the wall, just at eye-level.

Danny came by, the note read. *Out for coffee. Will pick up milk and etc.*

She let out a breath, feeling her lungs empty and then fill again in relief, even as she took the note off the wall and crumpled it in her hand. Danny was another Fatae, one who Passed well enough to have spent a number of years on the NYPD before going private. The two of them might get into trouble together, but they could get out of it, too. P.B. would be back. He wasn't out there alone. Danny was a damn good scuffler, and probably armed. He would be fine, P.B. would be fine.

Stripping off the jacket, she went into the kitchen and got a plastic garbage bag to put it in. If Danny managed to survive shopping with P.B., it would be good to see him again. And she had a use for him.

For everyone she could bring in, for that matter. P.B., Danny, and Bonnie, Bart, if she could find him. There were things to be done, and she wasn't fool enough to think she could do them alone.

She dumped the jacket in the bag, and put it on the chair. She should toss it. There was blood on it, hers, and...other people's. A dry cleaner might clean it...or they might report it. No way to know. She might be able to get the stains out with current but...

The crumpled bit of paper in her hand crinkled unpleasantly. For an instant, she had the overwhelming urge to brew a pot of tea. She scrunched her eyes shut, conjured the wet fog, and slowly, reluctantly, the urge passed.

Tea meant Sergei. She couldn't allow herself Sergei, his common-sensical, rational, nonmagical comfort. Not now. Not with everything still messy between them. And this... She looked at the bag on the chair. This was a matter for the *Cosa Nostradamus*. Nulls need not apply.

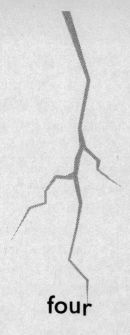

four

The atmosphere at Eddy's was calm, even at the height of the lunch rush. The tables were set with linen so pale blue as to look white, and the floral displays at the front door were placed so perfectly that every table got only an occasional hint of their perfume, so as not to overwhelm the taste or aroma of their excellent, if overpriced food. Conversations were quiet, occasionally intense, and always, as befitted the surroundings, civilized.

Sergei Didier, art connoisseur, boutique gallery owner and trend-setter, former man about the art scene, had spent the past ten years looking for an excuse to eat here. He wasn't about to waste the experience. But he couldn't avoid the reason he had finally gotten here, either.

His companion waited until the waiter had finished refilling their glasses and moved away before speaking again. "You're asking me if I believe in things that go bump in the night."

Sergei lifted his glass and admired the way the red liquid looked almost brown in the light. It was an excellent vintage, and the aged tannins suited the wild boar on his plate to perfection.

He took a sip, letting the wine slide down his throat with the quiet appreciation it deserved, and then placed the glass on the tablecloth next to his plate. "I am asking if you are willing to admit what you already know."

The other man at the table raised a white eyebrow at that. "I never admit to anything that will not profit me."

Sergei knew that. More, he was counting on it. Finding the chinks, the weak spots, within the ranks of his former employer took resources. Some of those resources he already had. Some of them he had to acquire.

Acquiring took delicacy, discretion, and knowing when to bull forward and damn the usual rules. But bull forward *carefully*. "It is said, in legend and story, that the gratitude of the wee folk was to be valued."

There was another period of silence as they ate. The business that had, superficially, brought them here was long-finished, the arrangements for a private showing at Sergei's gallery of this man's collection all but nailed down in discreet, gentlemanly fashion, waiting only for the lawyers and the insurance companies to agree.

"You're claiming that there are fairies running around Manhattan?" His dining companion was one of the most famous unknown men in the City. He paid a lot of people a lot of money to make sure that was so. Or rather, his company paid people a lot of money to make it so—and to make sure that nobody disturbed him from his work, which was to determine what the stock market was going to do before the market itself knew.

He was not a man who believed in fairies.

"I am not claiming anything," Sergei said peaceably, not retreating.

"No. You're asking me to do so."

It was an odd conversation held by an odd couple: a seventy-something bald-headed, pug-faced man in a thousand-dollar blue suit and an old-fashioned bow tie, and a forty-something man with a full head of silvering-brown hair and a face perhaps a shade too sharp-lined to be considered handsome. He wore a less expensive but better-fitting suit, and his monochrome tie was perfectly tied, the picture of the confident underling: exactly the picture he wanted his companion to relax into.

The old man wasn't buying it.

The waiter came by and refilled their wineglasses with silent precision. Sergei let the conversation lapse again: there was nothing to be gained by pushing further, and the meal was worth his full attention.

"I knew a girl once…"

His companion let the sentence trail off, waiting for Sergei to show interest.

"Indeed?" A polite cock of the head, but his attention still on the meal. It was like coaxing a feral cat, like the one that lived out behind his gallery. If you gave them any attention whatsoever, they suspected the worst. Ignore them, and they were intrigued.

"She had claws."

"Indeed." Sergei had no idea what breed of Fatae had claws, but he was sure there were at least three different types. Maybe more. Wren might know, if she would ever pick up the damn phone when he called. He shut that thought away. That was personal. This was the job. All his attention had to be on the situation, nowhere else. He could not allow himself to think of anything other than his goal.

The Silence had taught him that, when he was a wet-behind-the-ears college graduate, ready and eager to believe he could help save the world from itself. They had taught him how to concentrate, how to shut out distractions. They had also taught him how to lie, to cheat, and to kill.

And how to betray.

Wren would answer the phone, eventually. Or she wouldn't. He was the one who had screwed up: he had to wait for her to decide.

"Claws, yes. And eyes that were almost…they were like opals. Dark but filled with color. She wore sunglasses, all the time."

"And you thought she was human." He had once thought the entire bipedal world was human; working with Wren Valere had taught him differently. Not even the humans were human, sometimes.

"No. I thought she was a dream. And, like all dreams, eventually I woke up. And she was gone."

The man was seventy-four, and for a moment his voice was that of a man in his twenties.

Sergei could relate. Magic did that to you. But what he was doing here had nothing to do with Wren for the duration. Not in that way, anyway. The *Cosa Nostradamus* might not want him, either, but they *needed* him. Needed his contacts, his skills. His ability to get past the front guard of the Silence, even now. Especially now.

Andre Felhim, his former boss, was still inside, fighting to reclaim the organization from the corruption eating it from the top down, the force that had turned it from benefactor of the innocent to persecutor of the different. Sergei didn't think that the old man had a chance in hell, but hell had been known to throw some wild dice.

In the meanwhile, Sergei stood just inside the door and tested the foundation for weaknesses. A way for the *Cosa* to defend themselves, come the next attack. Because it would come, there was no doubt of that.

"You never tried to find her again?" he asked his companion.

"Of course I did. But after a while… You let dreams go. Or you go insane trying to convince others that it was real."

They ate in silence. When the waiter came to take their plates, Sergei's host raised weary eyes to him. "They are real."

Sergei nodded. The knowledge did not seem to bring the older man any peace.

"What do you want me to do?"

Sergei's next meeting didn't go quite as well.

"No." Flat, unbending, and final.

"Joanie…" He tried for a reasonable tone.

"No." She kept walking, looking straight ahead; no sideways-slanting glance that might give him hope. She had a black leather pocketbook slung over one arm, and black leather sneakers on her feet. He had caught her on her lunch break, taking a power walk.

"Joanie." He kept pace with her, letting a hint of calculated wheedling slide into his voice, just enough to make her laugh and give in, once upon a time.

"I hate you."

"You always did."

Her mouth twisted, and she glared at him. Joanie was tall, and blond, and had a chest that just asked for a deep breath and a low-cut neckline. But the way she glared made her cousin to Wren in attitude, if not looks.

Don't think about her. Don't go there now. Damn it, focus!

They were walking along a glass-enclosed arcade, under artificial lights replicating sunlight. The stores lining the walkway were trying very hard to look expensive and exclusive, and the women walking in and out of them, bags in hand, were doing likewise. He had just come from his lunch, with the results of it tucked securely away by means of one phone call to a very discreet private bank, and an electronic transfer to another account set up within the same bank. Sergei felt a little dirty about it all, but that wouldn't stop him from using every penny, and going back to ask for more, if needed.

"I can pay for information."

"You think I'm holding out for *money?*" Her voice went from reluctant to honestly annoyed.

Nobody who worked for the Silence ever needed to take a second job, even if they had the time or energy for it. "No." He didn't think that. "But it will make…whatever happens, easier."

He had no idea what was going to happen, but playing on someone's fears of the future was usually effective. He'd learned that from his tax guy.

Joanie shook her head, blond ponytail wagging. "Nothing's going to happen. You're wrong."

"I'm not wrong." He paused. "Joanie. I was there. I saw what I saw."

She didn't bother arguing that point. "You never killed for the cause?"

He had. He had, more than once. "I never killed an innocent. I never killed one of our own."

Poul Jorgunmunder had. Poul, Andre's protégé, his replacement once Sergei left the Silence.

And the innocent he had killed was Bren, Andre's left-hand woman. A good woman, as far as Sergei knew. Poul had killed her in cold blood, in order to implicate the Fatae in the murder of a Silence employee, setting a trail of clues that would have fired up anti-Fatae sentiment even higher, caused even more deaths.

Sergei had seen it happen. So had Andre. Only one of them had been horrified.

"I was an Operative for ten years," Joanne said. "I worked with Poul, when he first came on-board. Smart kid. Sharp. Everyone knew he was going places."

"Yeah," Sergei agreed, tasting something sour in his mouth that wasn't from lunch. He had never liked Poul, but he had trusted Andre's judgment on the man. They had both been wrong. "He went places...right to Duncan's side."

She looked puzzled. It seemed honest. She didn't know. She wasn't part of it.

He had picked right. Sergei allowed himself a faint breath of relief.

"The Silence, they're using the FocAs, Joanne. Our kids. They're using them as *weapons*. Against their own kind. Against *innocents*."

FocAs. That was Silence shorthand for Focused Active Agents. Talented Operatives, brought in by the Silence—by specific Handlers like Joanne and, once upon a time, Sergei, to work on very specialized situations—using magic to fight magical threats. Most of them were low-res, to use Wren's term. Not Pures, not extremely strong, but still Talent. Young. Hell, most of them were *children,* in all the ways that mattered. Most of them had been under twenty when they signed on.

The Silence was twisting them. Brainwashing them somehow. Using them against the *Cosa,* and then throwing them away.

They had been the greatest victims of the Bridge, killed by their own kith and kin in self-defense.

The more of this he told Joanie, in just a step more detail than he estimated she could stand, the greener her pale skin became, until she tuned away and was sick in a potted plant outside one of the stores. He watched, feeling only a little guilt. He did what he needed to do, to get the results he needed.

A salesgirl glared at them, but made no effort to come out and either help, or chase them away.

When Joanie finished, he took her by the arm, and walked her to the nearest public rest room. He waited outside while she washed her face and flushed out her mouth. His point had been made; there was no need to punish her further.

When she came out, her skin was still pale and green-tinged, but the control that marked a good Operative was back in place. She opened her mouth, and the party line fell out. "We do good work. The means aren't always just, but…"

He wished he was more surprised at her words. "Is that justification for murder, fraud, and setting up more innocents to die?"

"Are they innocent?" she asked. "Are any of us really innocent? Bren…I never met her. But she was a member of the Silence. To protect the innocent is our reason for existing. That means we take on the onus of not being innocent. We see too much. We know too much. Sometimes, we do too much. That's the cost."

It wasn't, Sergei reflected sadly, only the FocAs who were brainwashed. He had been there once, too. It had taken a case going horribly wrong before he had found the strength to walk away, and only Wren had kept him from going back.

What would it take to get Joanie to walk away?

"Are you willing to wake up at three in the morning, knowing what cost you've paid out of your soul, if you sit and do nothing, now?"

She looked away, watching the progress of a pair of young women down the escalator below them. "I'm awake at three in the morning anyway, Sergei. Aren't you?"

Once, he would have been silent. Now, he had an answer for her.

"No. I'm not." It sounded priggish, but it was also the truth. "I don't wake up and stare at the ceiling, or listen to the clock tick. I go to bed, and I sleep through the night, now."

And with that small white lie, he walked away, hoping that what he had said had been enough to seed doubt, that even if she would not question her loyalties, she would not turn around and betray him.

He didn't look back, but he felt her staring at him.

Three hours later, sitting in an office in another part of town, surrounded by exotic woods carved into seductive and somewhat disturbing forms, his cell phone rang.

"I'm sorry, if you'll excuse me for a moment?" he asked the man he was speaking with. Taking the nod as permission, Sergei walked a few steps away and flipped open the phone. "Didier."

"Maxwell's Tea House. 4:00 p.m."

The connection broke off, and Sergei pocketed his phone with a thoughtful frown. He hadn't recognized the voice, or the number on the display. Not that those facts alone meant anything, good or ill. His phone number got around, and he had been sowing the ground pretty intensely over the past few months since the fiasco downtown. But he would have been slightly more comfortable if he knew which tug on what rope had produced that invitation.

Maxwell's was, if he remembered correctly, not particularly in one group's territory or another, and he had never met anyone there before. In fact, the only reason he knew about it at all was that Shig, the Japanese Fatae friend of P.B.'s, had mentioned it as having a particularly authentic tea ceremony. And that it was a good place to hold delicate discussions.

So it could be an honest meet. Or a setup. Or both.

It could be anything. So why did he feel a nervous chill in his bones?

Because he knew too well what all the players were capable of. And he had no backup.

"I'm sorry." He went back to the man he had been speaking with, who was waiting patiently. "I'm afraid I am a man in demand, today." The other man, an art dealer from New Zealand, accepted the comment as it was offered, with a smile, and they continued their negotiations.

Even in wartime, business continued.

five

The building that housed the Silence elite was a discreet brick structure on a street of similarly discreet structures, all dating back to
when the island was known as New Amsterdam, not Manhattan.
The original Board had met here, at the turn of the previous century,
laying the groundwork for what would become the multinational,
multimillion-dollar foundation known as the Silence, and some said
that their ghosts still lingered in the hallways and boardrooms,
watching and judging what their heirs did with their inheritance.

For all that history, the building was completely nondescript the
way only the very wealthy and the very confident can afford to be.
To walk down this street, under trees almost as old as the buildings,
it would be difficult to guess who lived and worked here. The only
identifying marks on the rows of buildings appeared on small plaques
with the years of their founding engraved on it, and a well-placed
buzzer to call for admittance.

The Silence's building, number 27, did not have even that. You either knew, or you walked on by without a second thought. It wasn't magic that kept them unnoticed, but practical camouflage. This building is exactly like all the others. *This is not the building you thought that you were looking for.*

And if it was the building you thought you were looking for? The Silence had security for that, some nonlethal, some very lethal, and all perfectly legal.

But some unwanted visitors were more persistent than others. And they didn't need to ring the buzzer to gain entry.

"Seven," Christina was saying. When she had first joined the Silence as an Operative they had called her Tina. By the time she made Handler two years later, she was Christina. To most of the rank and file, she was now ma'am. "Seven times our security has been compromised." She didn't mention how many attempts had been made that failed, and nobody asked. A failed attempt was part and parcel of the job, and not worthy of comment.

The man at the head of the table nodded thoughtfully. "Seven attributed to the same source?"

"At least four of the seven, likely closer to six." It was probably all seven, but she could not confirm that.

"Has there been any actual penetration?"

"No, sir. Each time we were able to reroute our protections and deny entrance." If it had been otherwise, heads would already have rolled. "But they are learning our patterns, and there is only so far we are able to alter them without compromising ourselves in the effort."

Andre Felhim listened, not to what Christina was saying—he already knew, having used his still not inconsiderable resources within the organization to get his hands on and read the report before it went to Duncan. He listened now to what was being said by the rest of the people in the room: not voices, but bodies. Too many people were surprised by the fact that there had been any incursions on their security system; that news should have spread within three hours of the first attack. The Silence's main currency had always been information, both within and without, and the more you held the more power you had.

At this level, in this room, new information should have been blood in the water, and yet there had been no frenzy, no desire to know, to acquire the details, and dig—or, if you had enough status, have someone else dig—for more.

Some might say that was the sign of a well-trained team, focused on their task.

Duncan did not have a team. He had a cadre. Zealots. True Believers, who saw no need to know anything beyond what the Man Himself needed them to know to accomplish their goals.

Andre had seen terrible things in his thirty-plus years with the Silence. He had done terrible things, and allowed terrible things be done to others, all the while believing in their call to arms: to defend the innocent and the unknowing against the things in the world that would prey upon them. He believed, wholeheartedly, in the mission.

The people in this room terrified him.

"How long will it take to implement and install a new system to underlay the original?" Duncan asked as though he expected the answer to be "it was done yesterday."

Christina hesitated, and looked to her left, where her group members sat. "We should have the underlay in place within four days. It has yet to be tested, however."

The room went still.

Duncan considered the words, and Andre considered Duncan, carefully, observing their leader no more and no less obviously than anyone else in the room. His lean and angular form, draped in a suit of very expensive, quietly classic cut and fabric, gave nothing away. Duncan was a natural mute when it came to body language. It was part of what made him so dangerous.

"You can test it without disrupting the original security?" he asked Christina after due consideration, just long enough to make her sweat.

"Yes, sir."

"Then get it in place and run the tests." He dismissed her almost casually, to imply his greatest faith in her ability to perform perfectly, and she fell back into her seat with the expression of a woman who had been kissed by the gods. That was the other part of what made Duncan a real and present danger: charisma. "What's next?"

"Sir." A solidly built Asian man stood, formally waiting to be recognized. "If I may?"

"Please." Their leader oozed both charisma, and a disarming grace of manners. Duncan had not gained any of his power by being rude, even the politely confrontational manner of the new speaker's posture did not trigger anything but graciousness in him.

"This intrusion, it is the work of these so-called Talent?"

There was a burst of nervous laughter, quickly stifled, from someone sitting in the row of straight-backed chairs lining the far wall of the conference room. A junior, someone's assistant, who would catch hell later for that.

Duncan almost reacted, leaning forward to deliver a rebuke. "There is no so-called about it, Reese. They are quite definitely talented, and should not be underestimated. I believe that the events of last January should have brought that home to everyone in this room?"

There were nods around the room. Not that any of them had been there; shock troops had died on the Bridge, not these privileged officers. None of them had been on the front lines...none of them save Andre, and Duncan himself.

And Duncan's hand-picked lieutenants, including Poul Jorgunmunder, who had once been Andre's own protégé/right-hand man.

Poul was no longer with them, dead at Andre's own hand. Dead, after he had first killed one of their own, his former teammate Bren, Andre's left-hand woman and trusted aide d'office.

It had been a bad day at the bridge, that cold winter morning. Bad all around.

Andre wondered briefly what cold hell Poul was populating now, and then gave his attention back to Reese, who was still speaking.

"Sir, why have we not struck back at them? We know where they are, we know *who* they are. What is to stop us from simply making them..."

"Disappear?" Duncan asked, his voice dangerously soft and inviting.

"Sir. Yes, sir." Reese was cautious, but he did not back down.

Duncan looked at him, and then looked across the room at the rest, some thirty bodies all eager to prove themselves, to please their master. "Andre."

"Sir?" Oh, it grated on him to say that, and Duncan knew it grated, damn him.

"Would you be willing to make a Talent...disappear?"

"Not alone, sir. I know firsthand what they are capable of." Maybe half of the people sitting in this room had started out in Ops, the active field unit Andre had worked with for twenty of his thirty years with the organization. Maybe ten people in this room had ever been Handlers, had ever directed an Operative. None of them had ever worked with a FocAs, a Talented Operative. The Handlers who were assigned FocAs did not go to Duncan.

Andre knew for a fact, thanks to his researcher, Darcy, that most of the Handlers who worked with Talented Operatives were either dead or in "rehab" now, recovering from reported emotional break-downs. A comfortable, secluded rehab, on the Silence's tab, of course.

Andre had worked briefly with The Wren, Genevieve Valere. He had been the one to coax her to the Silence's side, if only for a short time. Everyone in the room knew that. They assumed that was why he was here, to give Duncan the inside scoop on the lonejacks' unwilling figurehead.

For all Andre knew, that was what Duncan himself believed. But he doubted it. Duncan understood Andre well enough to know that whatever information Andre were to give up on the young Re-triever, it was limited and out-of-date. Ms. Valere had never trusted him, and Sergei—now dead-set against him—would be sending them no further details of the *Cosa*.

Sergei had been there that day as well, when Poul killed an innocent on Duncan's orders. Duncan had given the order, and then left before it was carried out. He had not been there when Andre turned his coat back to its original color and killed Poul, striking while the man's back was turned and his attention was elsewhere. Andre and a touchingly shocked Sergei had arranged the scene afterward, making it look as though, rather than the Fatae killing Bren as originally plotted, that Poul had done the deed, and a Fatae had killed him in retribution. No one could argue with a little street justice, on a day already so bloody.

"*Lies built on lies, to protect the truth. This world turns on chaos, and we all fall into the fire.*" He had said that to Sergei, before they parted. He had known, as he said it, that they would not meet again.

He missed the boy.

Shutting off those thoughts, Andre returned his attention to the meeting, turning his hands palm-up and considering the mahogany skin of his fingertips as though his script were printed there. "The *Cosa* knows where we are, physically." They had left two bodies on the front steps earlier that year, as a message, although Sergei insisted that the *Cosa* had not done it. "They know where we are cybernetically, that much is clear, and they are showing us that we are vulnerable to them even through our electronics, where they should not dare to go. And yet, the attacks they have made? Are not even half of what they are capable of, if driven to it.

"To this point we have been protected by their own disorganization, and the fact that even the most arrogant of Talents is hesitant to take a life. If we were to push them over that line..."

Duncan definitely leaned forward now, waiting to hear Andre's concluding thoughts, as though anticipating they would match his own. "Yes? If that hesitation were to be pushed, by action on our part? If these Talent were to lose that inhibition, that veneer of civilization?" Duncan sounded honestly curious. That worried Andre, but he couldn't hesitate. His answer would not change, anyway.

"Then we would be in trouble. Sir."

"We" was such a curious word. The others in the room took it to mean all of them, as the alpha lions of the Silence pride. Where "we" went, the Silence followed. Andre meant the Silence itself, the Silence he joined, the one he wished to preserve. And it had no room for Duncan or his cadre of faithful fanatic in it.

Duncan? Who knew what Duncan thought, or believed, or planned? He spoke often and convincingly of a humans-only city, a humans-only civilization, where the reliance on superstition and magic was a thing of embarrassed memory, but for what reason? What end?

Andre didn't give a damn. Andre was just there to limit the damage

Duncan could do to the Silence as a whole, and remove him from his seat of power as soon as possible, however and whatever means it took to do that. Wren and her people—including Sergei, now—would have to fend for themselves. He wished them well, but unless their interests overlapped with his right now, they were no longer his concern.

"Ah. Yes. So you see, Reese, there is a logic behind my plan. Unless you have information we have somehow missed?"

Reese blinked, seeing the sword metaphorically being offered him, and declined to fall upon it. He sat with a little more haste than grace, and if anyone in the room blamed him, or thought it was amusing, you could not tell it from their expressions.

"All right then. We all have other things to do this day, so I ask again, what's next?"

The next item up for discussion was one of great interest to Andre: the matter of a Silence director who had gone on record as being opposed to the money spent on one of Duncan's projects. The code name for it—"Brunswick"—was one that Andre did not recognize. Before, Andre would have gone to Darcy—still faithful despite her boss' sudden and unexplained change of alliances—and she would find it for him. Now, however, it was more important that Darcy remain his ace in the hole, protected from any overt association with him.

What was more important than the project was the attitude taken toward the dissenting director, a man who was not part of the invited cadre, was not in this room to protect himself, or negotiate allies among those who might do it for him. If he were able to warn this man of the danger he faced, would he win an ally? Or open himself to the same fate, should Duncan learn of it?

That was a question to ponder, and carefully. There was too much at stake to act impulsively.

six

Wren stood in the kitchen, and stared at the crumpled bit of yellow paper in her hand as though it would suddenly give her a clue about what was going on.

"I came in here to…" To do what? The thoughts came slowly, not her usual quicksilver stream, and she was having trouble focusing on things, remembering things. Why was she worried about the demon? Her head hurt, like an old hangover. Why had she come back here? She hadn't finished the job, why was she home? She had been standing there, this scrawled note in her hand, for too long. She knew that much, at least.

Shower. She needed to take a shower. Hot water always made everything better.

Shedding the rest of her clothing in the hallway as she went, Wren headed for the bathroom. By the time she reached for the shower taps, turning the hot water on as high as possible, she was naked and shivering, despite the apartment being seasonably warm; for once, P.B. hadn't left the windows open.

She stepped under the spray and bent her head under the water until the pounding outside matched the pounding inside. Slowly she remembered. Not everything; she was aware that her brain was withholding information, but she wasn't too worried about it. She had been set up, and attacked. She had dealt with the attackers; now she was going to deal with the ones who had sent them, who had set them on her for the sole fault of being a Talent.

The Silence. No matter what Sergei once thought of them, no matter what her ex-partner still thought of them, they were the enemy. Elegant Andre, his errand-boy Poul, even the blond woman who had tried to warn Sergei to back off…all of them ranged on the wrong side of this war.

And Sergei? Where was her former partner, her lover, her love, in all this?

Wren let the water hit her face, washing that question away. She couldn't answer it. She wouldn't deal with it. Not right now. Let him just stay out of the line of fire, and she wouldn't have to deal with it.

After the initial tears, after the attack, Wren's tear ducts had dried up. She had thought she was holding back, but now that she was safe, in the safest place she could think of, the tears didn't return.

The water might be washing her skin and soaking her hair, but inside, she was dry and still as a summer desert at noon.

Turning off the water without even bothering to soap up or wash her hair, she got out and wrapped herself in the first towel that came to hand. Her hair in wet chunks against her bare shoulders, she started for the bedroom when a knock at her front door stopped her.

"Who is it?" she yelled.

"Bonnie!" the voice yelled back, in a "who the hell do you think it would be" tone. Wren had forgotten she'd invited the other lonejack up. *Brownies. Right.* Wren didn't even need to reach for current to unlock the door; it was already in her veins, doing her bidding before she thought the command. "Make yourself at home," she said, and continued down the short corridor, into the bedroom.

Twenty minutes later, she came back out, dressed in sweatpants and an old cotton sweater, thick wool socks on her feet. Her hair was still wet and slicked back, and her face was pale and pinched around the mouth and eyes.

"Jesus, Wren." Bonnie practically shoved a still-warm brownie into the Retriever's mouth. "You still look like hell. What happened?"

Choking on the chewy goodness of Bonnie's baking, Wren could only laugh, helpless. She chewed, swallowed, and said, "There's a damn story, all right…"

"Come on." Bonnie tugged at her hand, leading her like one would a child. "Sit. Eat. Get something into you. We'll worry about protein later."

Bonnie was such a little mother, Wren thought, letting herself be led into the main room and settled in the oversized chair that was still her favorite piece in the space.

"I thought you said you were going to make this place look a little more, ya know, lived in?"

"I did." She had. The room now boasted a sofa, and a coffee table, bought under repeated prodding from P.B. to "start living like a grown-up already." And she had even bought a café table and chairs to eat dinner on. All right, so they were stored in her office most of the time. She really didn't need a dedicated dining space, considering most of her meals were eaten standing up at the counter, or sitting on the floor in her office, working.

"Wren... A rug, maybe? Something on the walls? A cabinet for the stereo?"

Wren felt unutterably weary, and more than a little snappish. "Don't rush me."

She still wasn't sure how to decorate, anyway. She had Talent, but no talent for that kind of thing.

The first time she had walked into this apartment, trailing behind the Realtor who had better things to do than show twenty-somethings apartments they couldn't possibly afford, she had fallen in love with it. The kitchen defined "small," the plaster was cracked in places, and the traffic outside was pretty much 24/7. But the fifth-story walkup had large windows, hardwood floors, high ceilings, and a sense of comfort and energy that could only come from being situated directly on some source of current, be it traditional magical ley lines or an underground thermal generator or sheer good vibes.

She had dug deep into her savings, and rented it on the spot.

Almost a decade later, sitting in the main room, she didn't feel quite the same sense of comfort within those walls. Too much had happened there, both good and horrible, for it to be a refuge without flaw. So she resisted making it feel too homey.

And yet, the sense of current running through the walls and floors remained, and the thought of moving elsewhere gave her physical pain. So she stayed, barren walls and all, and only occasion-ally—like now—wondered why.

This time, she asked it out loud.

"It's like a fortress," Bonnie said in response. Her legs were curled up under her as she sat on the sofa chewing on a brownie, the half-empty pan on the coffee table between them. How had they eaten so much, so fast? "Even as empty as your place is. The building's soaked up so much current over the years, it's *in* the building now. That's why we both just had to live here. Probably why P.B. spends so much time here, too. I can barely get the guys to go home, some mornings."

Wren didn't want the details. Bonnie was cheerfully if discriminatingly polyamorous, and while Wren had no problems with that, she was going through a self-imposed dry spell, and didn't need the reminder of what she was missing.

"I bet that's why that psi-bomb didn't do any damage," Bonnie went on, thinking the problem out logically the way the PUPIs—the forensic scientists of the *Cosa*, for lack of a better term—were trained to do. "The building practically deflected it, the way treated glass does UV rays…"

The bomb had been planted by the Council—suspected, not proven—back when they were trying to scare the lonejacks into signing on to the Council's agenda. A classic tactic that had backfired because the Council forgot one basic lesson when dealing with lonejacks: when pushed, they get ornery. And even more stubborn.

Wren had heard, and seen, stranger things. "Or maybe it's just a really well-built building."

"Yah, maybe. Got no complaints about the soundproofing, that's for sure."

"Oversharing…" Wren murmured.

"Speaking of which." Bonnie could switch topics without warning, giving you mental whiplash. "What the hell bit your tail? And don't tell me nothing. You never eat four brownies in one sitting like that, so I know you're seriously wiped out. You were on a job this morning, weren't you?"

Wren didn't talk to Bonnie—or anyone—about her jobs. Part of the service she provided was privacy and confidentiality about the details of what she did. But the actual nature of her work wasn't exactly a secret any more, not among the *Cosa.* And certainly not to the PUPIs, damn them.

"Yeah. It was a setup. Someone played me, lured me out there, and jumped me."

"What?" Bonnie's normally half-asleep expression woke up suddenly, and she leaned forward, peering again at Wren. "You're okay. They're not, I take it."

"They're not," Wren agreed.

"You need to…" Her voice trailed off. The PUPI were formed with the single goal of bringing justice to the *Cosa,* finding the truth behind things the Null justice system couldn't or wouldn't handle. But Bonnie was clearly having difficulty determining how they would be able to help Wren, in this instance.

"I know who they were." Underneath the fog, a cold clarity had settled over her on the trip home, and the warmth of the shower, and the gooey sugar of the brownie hadn't broken it even slightly. Now, when she needed it, it rose to the fore. "I know who sent them. And I know what to do about them."

"Who, and what?" Bonnie sounded like she wasn't sure she wanted to know, but couldn't stop herself from asking.

Wren stared at the ceiling, then got up to go into the kitchen. "Valere!"

Wren poured herself a mug of coffee and came back into the main room where Bonnie was sitting.

"I'm going to take them down," she said, simply.

"The Silence." It was a logical conclusion, and for all her perky-goth casualness, Bonnie was bone-deep logical.

"Yeah." Wren drank her coffee, and watched Bonnie mull over what little she knew, fitting the pieces together with recent history.

"You're serious about this?"

"I'm serious."

"Why now? I mean, no offense, Valere, but you were offered leadership shit back when this all started, back when it was just a bunch of random vigilantes and their pit bulls." It had been mastiffs, actually, the ones Wren had seen, but she didn't correct her. "And it's not like you didn't know how serious it was, that they wanted us all dead and gone and never-existed."

"I couldn't do it then," was all Wren said, but after a minute, Bonnie seemed to get it. You could know something in your head, and in your heart, but that wasn't the same as knowing it in your gut. Down where you can actually do something about it.

"So...how? You alone? Or you knock on my door and say 'It's time to do this' and I'm supposed to fall in lockstep behind you? All of us are? On your say-so, you whose partner is part of the problem?"

"No." Wren knew that Bonnie was just being devil's advocate, and didn't take offense. "Exactly the opposite." She was still trying to work it out herself, so she was choosing her words carefully, trying not to get tangled up in her own thoughts. What had been so white-hot and clear walking out of the theater cooled slightly under rational considerations, but Wren knew she had been right, in that heat.

"We went about it the wrong way, before. We tried to organize, to become an army. A solid force of opposition."

"And that's not going to work?" Bonnie asked. "Then what the hell is?"

"You study any history when you were in school?" Wren asked. "American history, I mean."

"A little, I guess," Bonnie said dismissively. "I wasn't much for classes back then."

"Me, neither. But I liked the textbooks. And some stuff stuck, even when I didn't know it was sticking." Never any of Neezer's classes—she'd had no head for biology, and Neezer kept her away from any of the expensive microscopes, since her control back then had been for shit. But history had intrigued her.

"Back in the American Revolution, the British sent their troops in. They marched like they'd marched in Europe—straight lines and squared off formations, and bright red uniforms. Soldiers."

"Yeah, so?" Bonnie wasn't following, for once.

"The rebels were frontiersmen," another, deeper voice said.

Both women jumped: they hadn't heard P.B. come in. Wren had been expecting the usual tap on the window, forgetting that he now had his own key, now that he was staying with her on an official basis.

"They wore brown, to blend in with the forest and the crops. They shot from behind trees, lying behind rocks. They were snipers, not soldiers." The demon paused, sounding as though he were lacking only elbow patches and a classroom to go into academia. "A lot of that's historical legend, actually. But there's truth in it, too. You thinking of turning us into snipers from behind mailboxes and fire hydrants, Valere?" Then he saw the bruises on her face and his oddly flattened, bearlike face went from amused to furious. "What happened?"

She had almost forgotten how bad she looked, even with the blood washed off. "Welcome home. I got jumped. Down in the theater district. Someone used the job as a chance to get me alone."

"He dead?"

"All three of them are."

"Good." The thing about demon: they didn't much give a damn about violence. Wren didn't know much about the breed, and she knew more than almost anyone, from what P.B. had told her over the years. But the one thing everyone knew: the reason they made such good couriers for top-priority or dangerous packages was that a demon would kill you if he felt threatened, and feel no guilt about it. They didn't *have* guilt.

"Silence?" Danny had come in behind P.B., taking the time to remove his coat and hang it up in the closet. He was dressed in his usual jeans and cowboy boots, with a baseball cap over his curly brown hair to cover the small, curved horns peeking out.

"From what they said, I suspect so. The plan was to take me out, and then come get P.B."

Bonnie hadn't known about that. Wren had almost forgotten, herself.

"And you killed them first. I never get to have any fun." P.B. was being jovial, but his jawline gave it away, if you knew what to look for. Black gum showed against his white fur, like a dog preparing to snarl, emphasizing the polar bear–like appearance that gave him his nickname. He might be causal about killing, but he knew—they all knew—that Wren wasn't. So there was more to the story that she wasn't telling.

She twisted her mouth into an almost-smile, wincing when it hurt her face. "You're still pissed off because I stopped you from interfering in an attack, last winter."

"I remember." He was looking at her, and she held his red gaze steady, until he was the one who looked away. But he didn't seem displeased by what he saw, despite that. In fact, she almost thought that he looked…smug? "You said to hold off, because the Patrol was coming. You were right. Bart agreed, and it all came out right. Patrol power. Yay." They had argued about that, at the time, and afterward. Clearly he still thought he had been right.

"The Patrols are still going on," Bonnie said, starting to recover and regroup. "Not organized as such, but if there's a problem——" a nice way of saying "if someone was attacked" "——they have help nearby, ready to come. Did you call?"

Wren nodded, remembering the voice that had pinged her when she called out. They hadn't asked "what" but only "where." A willingness to help. But it was after the fact. Too late. They were moving too slow, too late. They needed to move fast, like lightning. Like current.

"Fatae and lonejacks, yeah. Council has totally skedaddled." Danny was dismissive the way only a Fatae could be about the Council. Neither group had much use for the other, even at the height of the Truce.

"It's something," Bonnie said, defensive. She was a member of the Patrol: all of the PUPI were, by order of their bosses. On-the-job training, if they were at the scene of a crime before anyone else. Before the evidence could be trampled by clueless *Cosa* who weren't used to thinking beyond "fight or flight."

"No more Council. No more lonejack." Wren wasn't looking at anyone when she said it, staring at something only she could see, off somewhere else. "No more Fatae."

"Excuse me?" Danny looked at her, then looked at Bonnie, as though asking if the bruises on her face and arms were matched by a crack in the Retrievers' skull. Bonnie shrugged, as at a loss as the faun.

"No more *Cosa?*" P.B. asked softly. She looked at him, and saw by his face that he understood. He knew the coldness in her core, the sludge in her veins. And he approved.

"More *Cosa,*" she corrected him. "*Real Cosa.* One family. Get us thinking like one beast, not three. Or we might as well just roll over and die now." She finished her coffee, and stared down into the mug. It was easier to say than she thought it might be. "You were right,

P.B., and I was wrong. We've been treating this—all of this, from the very beginning—like a personal attack, at worst like a hate crime. A private dispute that could be mediated, discussed. Like something that we could deal with like reasonable beings, patrol and protect and wait it out, and get away without getting our hands too dirty."

"We can't?" Bonnie was listening intently now, as was Danny. Wren turned to P.B., her eyes asking him a wordless question.

"You can't deal with someone who doesn't believe you have the right to exist," P.B. said, answering her question from the depths of his own experience, a voice filled with conviction. "You have to eradicate them. Before they eradicate you."

"We tried that," Danny said. "The patrols, the Battle..."

The Battle had been intended to be a demonstration, bait to lure out the leaders, the shadow-figures behind the hatred. As such, it had failed.

"No, we didn't," P.B. disagreed. "We fought the foot soldiers. And then we tried to draw out the leaders, yeah. Each time, we dealt them an injury. But it was half-measures and preventatives, aimed at figuring out what was wrong and how to fix it. All that did was buy us time.

"Only it bought them time, too. It showed them what we are, where we are, and what we can—and can't do. We showed them our entire hand."

"No. They only think we did." Wren put her mug on the floor and stood up, pacing. She had learned over the years that it was easier to keep people focused on her if she was moving. It also helped her concentrate. "But the truth is that they don't know half of what we are. Because we don't know half of what we are."

"Okay, huh?" Bonnie cocked her head and scrunched her face up in exaggerated puzzlement. Sometimes Wren forgot how much younger the other woman was. Ten years wasn't much between her and Sergei—they both had the mileage to make up for it. But Bonnie's life had been a gentler one, and even now she worked in the scale of evidence and evaluation, not experience.

"We've gotten civilized. We're *modern*. We use current, and distance ourselves from the old ways, as much as the Silence is trying to."

"Old magic was inconsistent and less effective," Bonnie said, parroting the accepted line.

"True. And it had a higher cost," Wren said. "A cost we don't have to pay any more, thanks to Old Ben and his magic kite. We've come a long way. It's been a good thing. But that doesn't mean the past isn't as much in us as the present." She couldn't believe she was saying that. She had always considered herself totally modern, knowing only as much about the old magic and the past ways as Neezer had insisted she learn.

She still was. She still preferred to take her strength from current—it was cleaner, more secure, and less prone to backfiring on a user. Old magics had to be coaxed, bribed to hand, and if anyone could use them, nobody could guarantee results. And you paid for it, oh how you paid.

But it was the same stuff. She knew that now, with what she had done, that dark current that Neezer had always warned her away from, still heavy like sludge in her core. Old magic. Emotionally charged. Unpredictable. She might have refused to see it, refused to use it in the past…but it slithered in there with the neon brights, just the same.

You were what was inside you. You were what formed you. Love, hope…anger, hatred. Fear.

The sludge, the tar, it wasn't something that came from outside. It was in you, all the time. Waiting for something to trigger it. The fear. The anger. The *hatred*. The cold stillness she could feel inside, now.

It wasn't more powerful than external current. It wasn't easier. It fed off of her in a way that current never did, and made her weak, in the end. But when it heated, it heated faster and hotter than any modern current ever could.

That was the danger, the risk. Old magic consumed the user. Old magic ate you whole.

But oh, the things it could let you do, in that heat. No control needed at all. That was the lure. That was the danger. D'anger. The anger. The wordplay almost made her laugh. Almost.

"I never wanted to kill anyone," she said quietly. "I never wanted to fight when I could run, and I never wanted to run when I could just stay out of sight. I'm not a troublemaker or a troubleshooter. But we need to survive. We need to do more than survive. And we can't do that if there are people out there who aren't even willing to give us the respect of being people, in their eyes. And we can't change their minds, that's been proven already."

P.B. shifted uncomfortably, causing the other three in the room to look at him. He glared back at them, then looked at the Retriever.

"That's the one thing you never wanted to hear, Valere. You know it now. There *is* such a thing as justifiable violence. There is such a thing as a just war——or at least a necessary one. Necessary death. Necessary killing. There comes a time when you can't run any more, because you've been running so long you've run out of anywhere to run to."

Wren wanted to deny it. But the sludge stirred in her, and she felt the tarry sweetness on her tongue, and was stilled.

"And you know this because…?" Bonnie challenged him.

"Because I've been there, puppy. I've been there over and over again."

Wren had asked P.B. how old he was, once. He had slid around answering her directly, but the implication had been that he was older than the normal human lifespan. She wondered, suddenly, how *many* times older.

"You?" Danny scoffed; the Fatae as a rule were less accepting of demon than Talent were, because the demon were a created species, their origins never spoken of except in speculative whispers. They didn't have a clan or tribe or herd, they didn't gather together—in fact, they seemed to dislike being in each others' company—and not one of them looked like the other, except for the eyes all being that exact same shade of dark dried-blood-red. Danny didn't mean to be insulting, Wren thought. It was just that the Fatae were used to thinking of demon as second-class members, without a history or tradition of their own.

"Me, faun. When you were still wobbling around on your hooves, trying to figure out what your tail was for."

A faun's tail was a sensitive subject, and Danny flushed under the baseball cap, but held his tongue.

"I'm not trying to be rude here," Bonnie said, "but I'm going to be anyway, so what the hell. You've been in the thick of things since all this started. You're the one who got Wren involved, stirred up the Fatae, got the word out. Got everyone sharing information. And you're a demon—you've never avoided violence in your entire life. So what the hell do you know from running?"

Wren closed her eyes and counted to five. When she opened them again, nobody had moved, and P.B. was watching her.

"I am demon," he said, finally. "What that means…The Fatae

never wanted to know. The mages have forgotten." Mages——the old term, the one only the Council used any more, and then only formally. The word sounded strangely right on the demon's tongue. "For generations, we were content that way. It was better to be forgotten. Safer. No one could use us, then."

You can ground in me. P.B.'s voice, offering her sanctuary, protection from overrush. *It's what I was created for.*

Never without your permission, she had replied.

Her eyes were too dry to tear up in realization. Once, clearly, permission had not been sought. Or granted.

"But I am older than all of you put together. And I didn't get that way by throwing myself under every passing trauma-train. When I hear marching boots, the sound of rifles, the screams of a mob...I run. I ran. From old Amsterdam. South Africa. From Germany. Over and over again. I ran." His eyes couldn't really have darkened; it had to be a trick of the light. "And people died, who might have lived, if I had taken a stand.

"But I lived. Lived, and came here. And if I had any brains left I would have run again." He sounded so disgusted with himself, so totally *P.B.,* that the spell he had been weaving with his words was broken, slightly, and Wren found that she could breathe again.

"But you didn't," she said softly. She had never asked why.

"I didn't. I thought about it, once. Maybe twice. But after a while...you want to be needed. To feel like you can change something, that it doesn't have to be bad, all over again."

He laughed, not even slightly bitter. "And now it's too late, even if I changed my mind. They jumped you, were coming for me. Again." He had been attacked once before, in this apartment, as a message to Wren.

"Walking away——running away——isn't an option any more. The

world's gotten too small. And doing things halfway and bass-ackward isn't going to get the job done.

"You were talking when we came in, Wren, about sharpshooters versus an army. It's a good idea but it's not going to work, because they've already scoped out the best places to shoot from. We'd still be playing catch-up."

"I wasn't thinking about shooting at them," Wren said, a glint in her eye that none of them had ever seen before, somewhere between mischief and malice, with a dose of vengeance. "You guys get to do that, once I level the playing field. Better than level it. I'm planning on taking away their ammo."

Danny and Bonnie stared at her, but P.B.'s face was slowly transformed by a distinctly evil grin that suited his ursine features perfectly. He knew. He knew *her*.

"They're using our own kind against us," Wren said, explaining it for the other two. "The Lost. The FocAs, they call them." The Talent who had been twisted into weapons by the Silence. The disaffected, unaffiliated young adults Sergei had told them about, the ones they had lost track of, somehow, failed to bring into the fold. "That has to stop."

"How?" Danny asked.

"We have to do what we should have done a long time ago, if we had been paying attention the way we should have been. If we had been a real family. We're going to get them out." She paused. "I'm going to Retrieve them."

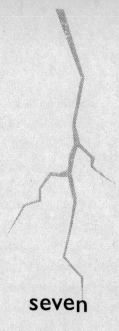

seven

The morning sun was bright and the air outside was surprisingly clean and fresh. Wren wanted another cup of coffee, and she wished that she smoked. Not that the law allowed cigarettes within twenty feet of another living human being any more, but at least nicotine addiction denied would be a valid excuse for being so damned cranky.

The last time Wren had gotten involved in anything other than her own life, she had been dragged in bass-ackward, and gone about it in a scatter-shot, fact-finding way. This time, she was treating it like—well, like what it was: a Retrieval. She had a goal, a plan, and a specific and narrowly focused zone of attack.

It wasn't making her feel any better about the whole thing. Organized and efficient, yes. But not better.

Three days after that meeting in her apartment, three days of brainstorming, of tossing in and tossing out ideas, they were making their first—and probably most important—recruit. He seemed less than thrilled to be so honored.

"Let me see if I've got this straight. You want to walk into the secret stronghold of an organization that has sworn to destroy us, limb by limb if need be, a stronghold that nobody even knows where it is, exactly. You're going to go in—alone—and Retrieve an unknown number of brainwashed Talents who will also try to kill you. And bring them out, and unbrainwash them, or otherwise render them useless to the Silence."

"Nah," Wren said, casually leaning against the wall and watching Joe Doherty sit on his battered wooden desk and reiterate her plan like he was dressing down one of his smarter but still clueless students. "The unbrainwashing I'm going to leave to you."

"Lovely." His tone indicated he thought that it was anything but.

P.B. chuckled. He had been doing that a lot over the past few days as they moved through the remaining *Cosa* structure like a hot chainsaw, narrowing down the list of the few people Wren thought that she could trust with this plan. His human's new bloody mindedness seemed to please him immensely.

Wren wasn't so sure it made her anywhere near as happy. What she was going to do—that was good. That was better than good. What she was asking other people to do, on her say-so, on her belief...

The *Cosa* had survived for generations by staying low, by blending in times of trouble, and making themselves useful enough to people in power, when needed, that they always had some bargaining power, some wiggle room.

The Silence did not want them. Would give them no room, no power. Nothing but the echoes of a deleted history.

Her clarity didn't waver; there was no hazy morning-after of regret or doubts. But every time she tried to sleep, the dead came to visit her. Not as ghosts—she believed in ghosts now, having encountered the sadly vengeful ghost of the Council architect, Jamie Koogler, several years back. Ghosts would have been easier to handle; you could reason with them, to a certain extent. You could find out what they needed, and soothe their restlessness. Guilt manifestations of things yet-to-come, not so much.

Not that she felt any guilt herself, personally. She didn't. She didn't feel much of anything. Those tears never came back, even when she lay awake at night, staring at the ceiling. She didn't have regret, or flashbacks, or much of anything, in fact. The details were fading from her forebrain. Just the sound of all the boxes in her brain, clicking down their lids, keeping things she didn't want, but couldn't seem to throw away.

And there was something else tickling at the back of her brain, keeping her from sleeping. Something she needed to deal with, to acknowledge and process, some bit of information that might make the difference in...something. She could feel it there, but every time she tried to touch it, to identify it, it shied away, danced behind something else and hid until she was distracted by the day's chores.

And there had been a lot of distractions lately, from the moment she came to in the Taylor Theater's tunnel. It was almost as though something had taken possession of her brain: she was as tightly focused as she ever had been on any job, on any task, and yet there were parts of her that seemed butterfly-erratic, always catching one breeze or another. Even in the middle of a thought, Wren felt as though there was something else going on, something she didn't have a handle on. It unnerved her, when she thought about it. So she didn't.

Despite all that, her plan was moving along to something resembling action. P.B. had been onboard immediately, as expected. Danny had, surprisingly enough, followed. Although maybe not so surprising after all: the Fatae had been a cop, not so long ago, before becoming a private snoop, and if there was one thing that cops and snoops both hated, it was being left out of the action.

Between the two of them, and her own contacts, Wren had a pretty good pipeline into the Fatae communities. But they weren't the ones that she needed. They weren't the ones who had to be onboard, for this to work. She needed Talent. Strong ones.

Bonnie had left Wren's apartment that first night, clearly distraught, and the Retriever hadn't seen or heard from her friend since then; no small trick considering there was only one stairwell and one entrance to the building. But she hadn't pushed it. Anyone who came along for the ride had to be totally committed.

The advantage she had over the Quad and their Truce Board was that she wasn't trying to build a consensus. She didn't need allies. She didn't need backup.

She needed people willing to act, not react. People who were willing to do what needed to be done, without hesitation or moral second-guessing.

Professor Doherty had recovered from his shock, and was talking again.

"Well, that explains why you've come to me." There weren't many Talented doctors— medical school tended to be a problem, not to mention residency, with the combination of stress, sleep deprivation, and all that finely tuned and very expensive electronic machinery. There was a reason Dr. Doherty went into teaching rather than a more lucrative regular practice, and it wasn't idealism: a career in a hospital might end up killing more than he would cure, simply by having a bad day near the emergency room. He wasn't a mover or a shaker in the *Cosa* community, but he had a real and fervent following among his students, both Talented and Null, and the patients who hailed him as a brilliant, if unconventional thera-pist for borderline personalities.

"Do you have any idea how you're going to manage this rather impressive stunt?"

His voice was dismissive, and more than a little patronizing, and Wren—having neither time nor patience for Attitude that got in her way—abandoned any pretense at being casual.

"Who am I?" she asked him.

"What?" His round face showed confusion, and the faintest wonder if maybe the woman in front of him wasn't entirely there.

Wren had wondered that herself, a few times. It would explain a lot, if she were actually in a hospital bed somewhere, hallucinat-ing all of this. Maybe she would schedule an appointment with Doherty when all this was over.

Black threads. Black ooze. Old magic only goes so dark before you can't see and it's very very dark inside. What is in your brain, little wren?

She shook the quiet mental voice off. "Who. Am. I?" she repeated.

From the nervous look he gave Danny, leaning against the wall opposite her, Doherty was pretty sure now that she had snapped her mental leash. Danny just grinned at him, no help at all.

"You're Wren," Doherty said in a tone designed to soothe the crazy woman. "Genevieve Valere."

"Who am I?" she pushed, her voice getting even colder.

He finally twigged. "You're The Wren."

Good boy. Slow, but good. "I'm The Wren. I am, by most accounts, the best Retriever on the continent. Possibly of my entire generation."

"And humble, too," Danny muttered. He was leaning in a pose similar to Wren's earlier position, his gimmie cap pulled down over his forehead like something he had seen in a trucker movie from the

1970s. He was still grinning, and it wasn't a pretty grin at all. Wren had a suspicion that he had started filing his front teeth into points, like his feral faun ancestors.

The two Fatae had become her bookends since the attack; she wasn't sure she had seen either one of them sleep since then. She wasn't sure P.B. even had to sleep, actually. Had she ever seen him, ever heard him snore? She hadn't.

They were playing bodyguard, she realized, taking the attack on her more seriously than she had. Or they thought she was crazy, too, and were there to keep her in line and harmless.

Maybe she was. Crazy, that was. Maybe she had to be. "I don't have to be humble," she told the room. "If I say the job will get done, it will get done." *The Wren always finishes a job.* She could say that now; she had found the bansidhe she had been chasing for years, finally. It was still under wraps in the storage room in Sergei's studio, waiting for its nominal owners to arrange shipping back to the U.K., but she had found it, bagged and tagged and boxed it up. The Wren always finished the job. Once she was idiot enough to take it on. "All I need is some information…and a distraction."

"And for that, you need us." Doherty was starting to catch on.

"That, and a holding space." She couldn't shove them in with the bansidhe, after all. And her apartment was too small. How many children did the Silence still hold? How many survived the Bridge? If they'd survived, what condition were they in? Details. She would work the details out later.

"And the unbrainwashing," he said, clearly already running names and talents through his head.

"Or to kill them," she said.

The words fell into a sudden silence, colder than the outside temperature could warrant.

Thou shalt not kill.

Danny made a noise that might have been either protest or agreement. Doherty was clearer in his shock. "The *hell* are you saying, woman?"

Cold. Damp cold tar, cushioning the blow, letting her say what needed to be said. "I faced them, on the Bridge." Wren's voice was even, calm. "These...what does the Silence call them? Focused Active Operatives. Only four of them, me fighting with Michaela and Bart, and I was the only one who walked away on my own power. What the Silence did to them, the way they twisted them...you can't imagine." She could barely comprehend it, and she had seen it, had heard the details of Sergei's final report to the Quad. "They exist on the edge of wizzing. They have no way of shutting off, the way they are now. They're not sane."

"Then we should kill them now." Doherty wasn't as wussy as he sounded, at first. Good.

"We should, yeah." Wren stared at a stream of memories the others couldn't see: the sight of blood splattered across a New Jersey diner's chrome table; body parts strewn down a stone-walled tunnel; her hand, holding the stringy bits of entails of a man she had killed with a blast of thick, angry current.

Black current. Her mind touched on the memory, and skittered away again.

Never touch the black. Neezer's voice, faint with years. One of her earliest lessons, when the core inside her was small and populated with slender snakes that were more potential than power. *Never touch the black. It's old. More than old. Wild. You can't control it. Nobody can.* Nobody did. Not and live to talk about it, anyway.

The memory faded, was gone.

"We don't kill the wizzed. We take care of them." It was a lesson

Neezer had hammered into her head, even before he knew that he, too, was teetering on the edge. "But if the only way we can stop their suffering is to end it…" She came back to the room with an almost audible snap. "I'll do it. Nobody else will have to."

Not alone. together P.B.'s mental voice in the back of her head: cool, alien, and comforting. *You'll never be alone again.*

Wren knew that the demon meant…not well, maybe, but he meant it honestly. He was *her* demon, by his own choice, and that meant everything to her.

But she was still alone. She would always be alone.

Sergei wasn't there.

Sergei didn't want to be there. He didn't need to be there. The gallery was practically running itself. Or, more accurately, Lowell was running it. Day-to-day, customer by customer.

Sergei stood on the catwalk where he had been double-checking the lighting over a new installation—tiny blown-glass objets d'art that made him think of tetanus shots, for some reason—and looked over the railing at the main floor.

"Why yes, you can pick it up as soon as the exhibit ends." Lowell had his hand in the air just outside the customer's personal space, encouraging without intruding. His immaculately groomed blond hair, fine-boned face, and clearly upper-class manners gave the impression that he wasn't doing this for the money but the love, and his voice brimmed with confidence and congeniality.

The boy was good. Not great, but good. Unfortunately being good with the customers didn't mean that you could handle the back room stuff; the invoices and the bills of lading, the insurance issues and the bank loans…

He could learn.

True.

You just hired a new receptionist for the busy days. If he took over some of the back office work, you'd have time to—

To do what?

Good question.

Even if the Silence survived the internal battle for power *and* the inevitable showdown with the *Cosa,* that door was closed to him, forever.

You could work more with Wren, then.

That was a painful thought, since it depended on her wanting him as her partner, business or...otherwise. He wasn't a total idiot—whatever reason she gave, he knew what she was really afraid might happen.

The first step is admitting that you have a problem.

Right. He took a deep breath, unaware that his hands were gripping the wooden railing tightly enough to whiten his knuckles.

"Hi. My name is Sergei Didier, and I'm a current addict."

He almost expected to hear a chorus of voices echoing back to him "Hi, Sergei," and was ridiculously disappointed not to get it. Of course, the way his luck was going, a customer would have come up the stairs behind him at just that moment, and some garbling of his words would be gossip among the arty set by the weekend.

It was a small world, and nasty at times.

Was there any part of any of his worlds that wasn't nasty? Beautiful, but nasty.

Like fairies. The old-world ones, the ones with pointy teeth and moss in their hair, the stories his Russian grandmother used to tell him, to scare the bejasus out of him when he was still a toddler, until his father came home and made her stop.

He missed those stories, when she died. He wondered if, maybe, without them, he would never have taken so easily to the fact of real magic in the world: real, dangerous, deadly magic.

Deadly...

Wren could die. He had always known that, but the past year had made it real. Too real. She had enemies now. Not just former targets who might or might not know who had Retrieved from them: people who held actual, ugly grudges.

Wren could die. One wrong move, one slow reaction, one day of not being at the top of her game, and...

And what's the point of all this, then? What's the point?

He didn't know. And, for the first time in his entire life, he didn't know what to do about it. Couldn't do anything about it. Not until— if—Wren let him back in.

"Good Lord, Didier. Enough," he said, disgusted with himself. "Just...enough." He went down the staircase and into his office, grabbing his coat and leather document case off the rack, and went out into the gallery. Lowell had finished with the client, and was going over something at the front desk.

"Hey."

The boy looked up at him, expectantly, and he felt old and bosslike.

"I've got a meeting, won't be back today. Shut down and lock up, and I'll see you tomorrow."

Lowell was too well trained to show any reaction to being left in charge so suddenly, or to express any surprise that Sergei suddenly had a meeting that wasn't on the computer's agenda, but there was a definite smug satisfaction at the unquestioned responsibility.

Let him have his rope. See if he hangs, or swings like Tarzan.

Without giving any more information, Sergei shrugged into his trench coat and went into the late afternoon sunshine.

He didn't have a meeting, of course. But if he was going to be morose and cranky over things he couldn't change, he might as well do it over an early dinner and a glass of wine.

He wasn't in the mood to cook, but this was Manhattan: finding a meal at any hour of the day was never a problem, eat in or take-out. The only dilemma was deciding what you wanted.

When it came to food, Sergei had a secret. It wasn't a Dark Secret; more along the lines of a white lie that had taken on a life of its own.

He didn't like Chinese food.

He didn't hate it, exactly. There were dishes and flavors that he could appreciate, and the value for the money was undeniable. But given a choice, he would always have chosen Thai, or Japanese, or…well, pretty much anything except take-out Chinese. Even Jimmy's noodles didn't sway him from that preference.

But Wren loved her Chinese food. It made her happy, even when she was ducking the fortune cookies. And for the way she tucked into those white cartons, the way the spices seemed to make her mind work faster, her words tumble out of her with more energy—it was worth subduing his own preferences.

But on his own, he usually chose to visit his local Thai place, not Chinese. And that was what he did, on the way home from the gallery. For today's mood, a container of khao khluk kapi and a glass of Riesling would do the trick.

So when he got home and opened the bag from the restaurant, he was very surprised to discover a cookie twisted in a very familiar shape sitting on top of the container.

"Damn it," he said, then he laughed. "They always get you. Always."

He put the plastic take-out dish on the counter, the fortune cookie untouched on top of it and went about getting down a plate, and a glass, and opening the bottle of wine.

He poured a glass of wine and wandered out of the kitchen and into the great room. He looked out the huge windows, sipping the Riesling and trying to pretend that he wasn't hungry.

Wren had tried to avoid getting a fortune cookie for months, down to swearing off Chinese food entirely. For her, that had been a real hardship. Hadn't mattered, though. The Seer who worked at Jimmy's Noodle Shop had chased her down on the street. The Seer was an ancient figure—cricket-old, Wren had described her, tiny and frail—who shouldn't have been able to get out of her chair, much less track down a healthy young woman in a relatively large city. But she had, and given Wren the fortune directly, hand-to-hand and no way to dodge it.

That was the damnable thing. You could run. You could even hide. You could pretend it wasn't a real Seeing. It didn't matter.

They always got you.

Even if you didn't know you were a target.

Finishing the wine, he left the glittering view, and went back into the kitchen.

"All right. What?" he asked the cookie, picking it up, and weighing it in his hand. Unlike commercial types, this wasn't wrapped in plastic, but rather a familiar parchment paper twist. That damned Seer got around.

He opened it, broke the cookie open, and withdrew the small slip of paper.

Falling is not failure but a failure to resist.

"Wren was right," he told the slip of paper. "All Seers should be shot at birth."

eight

"You're slow. And clumsy."

Wren rubbed her hip, and glared. She hadn't been called clumsy since she was a four-year-old in a pink tutu trying to figure out how to do a plié. And she resented it, both the name-calling and the bruises that accompanied it. She had things to do, damn it. People to harass. A Retrieval to plan…

The tall human stared back down at her, completely unmoved by the force of her glare. He reached out a hand to help her up, which she took. They were in the middle of the main room—also known as the living/dining room/emergency meeting space—of her apartment. All the furniture and the stereo system had been shoved up against the walls, or into the hallway, to avoid being damaged. She might not be certain about her recent purchases, but she had spent money on them, and was therefore protective of their well-being.

They were certainly faring better than she was.

Morgan had appeared at her door that morning with a canvas bag over his shoulder and a hard case in his hand. The bag contained a fall-mat, and the case....

The case was filled with sharp-edged toys packed in hard foam.

"You're going to teach me to throw those?" She had been incredulous and just a tinge excited. The Null shook his head.

"I'm going to teach you to *duck* them."

Which was exactly what he was doing, to variable success.

"Nice tumble, Valere. You go through windows that way?"

P.B. had come in about halfway through the lesson, and been critiquing—catcalling—ever since. He denied siccing Morgan on her—denied even telling the human about what Wren was up to—but clearly thought it was a wonderful idea.

"Best there is," he reminded Wren when she complained. The human Morgan was a martial artist of—apparently—considerable reputation. He also worked part-time for a moving company, which was how Wren and P.B. had first encountered him—when she had executed a job on a member of the Council while the target was distracted by moving.

She later learned that he had been hired by some of the more pacifistic Fatae breeds to teach them how to protect themselves, and the next time they ran into each other, he had been elected a street captain of the Truce Patrol, despite being a Null.

Null or not, he had to have some current in him, Wren thought now, to be able to move so damn fast. She could barely tell when he threw the knife, and the fact that it hit her with the hilt rather than the blade was not because he misthrew it.

"You really think the Silence is going to go after me with tableware?" She was tired, sweaty, bruised, and cranky. Her plan for the day had been to track down the blueprints for several buildings they suspected the Silence owned, to see if any of them might be housing what was left of the Talent Operatives. Nowhere on her calendar had "be beaten up by an unexpected ally" been penciled in. She was pretty damn sure of that.

"They're smart. And they'll know you're coming. They won't try to use guns."

"How the hell are they going to know she's coming?" P.B. demanded from his perch on the back of the chair residing in the hallway. She hoped he wasn't using his claws to hold his position: the chair might be old but it was still in good shape.

"Because they're smart," Morgan said calmly, shoving Wren back into position on the fall-mat and picking up a nasty-looking cudgel with teeth. "And because it's what they would do."

"You disapprove?" Wren asked. Her T-shirt was soaked in sweat, and there was a tear in the lower leg of her sweatpants where a blade had almost gotten her. She really wanted him to try for the moral high ground, so she could go to town on her tormenter vocally, if not physically.

"It's not my place to approve or disapprove," he said, and the cudgel whirled at her kneecap. She twisted and dipped without thinking, and the teeth sank into the mat an inch behind her.

"Better," he said. "But not better enough."

The Fatae on the patrol adored Morgan, enough to make him their captain. She didn't understand why.

"Why not?" she asked. She wasn't talking about his evaluation, and he knew it.

"I'm not *Cosa*," he said. "I'm just hired help. Hired help doesn't get to make moral judgments."

"You came here. That implies some sort of judgment. Unless you were hired to come here." She really wanted to know who had hired him. Someone who didn't think she was capable of handling herself, but didn't want to say anything for fear of a smackdown...she could come up with half a dozen suggestions, and the probable one lived two floors down.

She picked up the cudgel, surprised at how heavy it was, and handed it back to him. "So, as my instructor in self-defense and non-stupid behavior, what would you suggest that I do?"

He took the cudgel as though it weighed as much as a loaf of bread, and she revised her opinion of his body mass upward.

"Play everyone's game," he said.

Wren scowled at him. She did that when she Retrieved, used current and physical skills, each as seemed appropriate. But the way that he said it, there seemed to be more to his words than his words, if that made any sense.

Before she could process that further, he threw the cudgel again, this time with a curve.

Wren cocked her hip and half-turned her upper body, letting the cudgel swing past. But this time she *felt* it coming, and in that blur of being totally in the moment, totally aware, his words clicked in her brain. *Play everyone's game.* Not just hers, not just theirs: Use *everything.*

Before the weapon could land, she reached down and sent just a hint of current under it, calculating the vectors and hitting it so that the combination of momentum and impact swung it like a boomerang, and headed back around to Morgan's hand. *Use everything. Not just as needed—all at once. All the time. No black and no white, only shades of almost-identical gray.*

He caught the cudgel easily, and set it down.

"Bastard," she spat, reaching for anger to keep her going in place of stamina, because her knees were about to give out on her in reaction to both the assault and the understanding. "You were trying to really hit me that time!"

"You should have aimed it at my head," was the response she got, the only praise he gave. But he—almost, maybe—smiled. "Enough for today." He started to pack up his toys. "Hot shower, aspirin, and a good meal tonight. Carbs, if you can do it."

"Right. P.B., make yourself useful and help Master Pain over here move the furniture back. I need coffee, and yeah, a shower."

"Please," P.B. said, sniffing the air ostentatiously.

She clouted him on the shoulder, hard, as she passed, and they both winced.

The entire bathroom had filled up with steam and her coffee had gone lukewarm by the time she finally dragged her aching body from under the scalding hot spray, and she moved like a woman twice her age as she wrapped herself in a towel and inspected the damage.

"I feel like I went ten rounds with a wood chipper." She rotated her left shoulder carefully, and moaned a little as another knotted muscle gave in and relaxed.

There were a few nicks and a lot of bruises reflecting in the mirror, including a doozy on her hip that was going to take a few days to heal properly unless she had someone zap some current into it. She could do it herself, but she was so damn tired, it seemed a better idea to sit back and let someone else do the doctoring: self-healing was the trickiest of current-use, even on surface wounds, because it felt so good—it was easy to get overenthusiastic and "fix" something that wasn't actually broken; never a good idea.

The brown strands of her hair clung to her neck and shoulders and she thought about getting her hair cut again, maybe finally giving in and getting a buzz cut for simplicity's sake. But it seemed like one thing too many to deal with, so she mentally tabled it for later. Much later. Like a year from now, maybe. If she even had hair to worry about, then.

She drank the last of the coffee, wincing at the taste, and pulled on a clean sweatshirt, underwear, and a pair of jeans.

"Anyone else want to order in a pizza?" she asked as she walked down the short hallway from bathroom to the main room, only to be greeted by the smell of grease and pepperoni.

"I took the liberty," Bonnie said from her spot on the sofa. She was wearing her jacket with the PUPI patch on it, so she must have come directly from work, but her shoes were off and she was in what seemed to be her default position, feet curled under her on the sofa, and one of Wren's plain white plates on her lap. There was a two-foot-square pizza on the coffee table that—from the smell—had never come from any delivery place.

Bonnie lifted a slice off her plate and stopped with it halfway to her mouth at Wren's inquiring look.

"My mentor gave me a pizza brick for my birthday," the Talent said.

Bonnie's cooking was legendary, in exactly the opposite way that Wren's attempts at cooking were—it wasn't the only reason Wren had told Bonnie about the apartment on the floor below becoming available, but it was a kickback the Retriever didn't mind at all.

P.B. hadn't waited for anyone—from the smears of sauce in the fur around his muzzle, that wasn't his first slice currently disappearing down his gullet. Morgan was nowhere to be seen.

"You just stopped by for a lunch call?" Wren didn't mean to sound accusing, especially not to a woman who had just brought a massive homemade Sicilian pizza with her, but she hadn't forgotten the way Bonnie had flaked on them after that first meeting.

"I thought you would need sustenance," the younger woman said, not at all defensive. Wren got the message. Bonnie might not be able to embrace what Wren and the others were intending to do, but she wasn't abandoning them, either.

"They also hang those who bake and serve," she warned Bonnie, who folded her slice in two and popped it into her mouth, chewing vigorously. The Pup shrugged, and, when she could speak again, said, "They'll hang me anyway. Or burn me, or stone me, or drown me, or whatever their preference of the week might be." She moved the plate to the coffee tale, wiped her mouth with a paper towel, and met Wren's gaze evenly. "I'm not a fighter. I hit like a girl and I faint at the sight of my own blood, and I really believe in pacifism and discussion as the solution to most of the world's problems. But I also know when to get out of the way and let other people do their job."

She let her rosebud mouth quirk up in a grim smile. "And I can at least feed the troops."

"And send them guardian fight-angels?"

Bonnie looked at her blankly.

"You didn't hire Master Morgan to beat the crap out of me?"

Bonnie shook her head. "No, but I would have if I'd thought of it. You think he'd be willing to teach me?"

"To fight?"

Bonnie's face lit up as she smiled, a crooked, mischievous smile that never failed to captivate anyone who saw it. "Nah, just to toss me down on the floor and tell me I've been a bad, bad girl."

P.B. choked on his pizza, and Wren closed her eyes and shook her head. Bonnie was *hopeless*.

"Danny called while you were in the shower," P.B. said, changing the subject. "He wants us to meet him downtown."

Wren finger-combed her hair, thinking hard. So much for getting someone to patch her up any time soon; it took more time than they had to spare, apparently. "Any reason?"

"Someone we need to meet with," the demon said, shrugging. "I didn't ask specifics, figured we'd find out soon enough."

"Fine, whatever." Wren really needed to get her hands on some blueprints, and start narrowing down whatever buildings the Silence might be using, but that could wait another few hours in addition to the hours already lost.

They ended up meeting Danny and his mystery guest in one of the every-other-corner Starbucks that still littered the financial district. Above the Fifties, they were starting to get priced out by the real estate market, but traders and brokers needed their stimulants, and were willing and able to pay for them.

Wren had grown up in New Jersey, where you could hold down a table in a diner for twenty-four hours straight, so long as you kept buying coffee and, if it was a slow day, not even that. Starbucks was the modern Manhattan equivalent, but their coffee was a lot more expensive. And the tables were smaller.

On the plus side, the coffee was light years better.

P.B. and Wren walked in and saw Danny with another male holding up a wall. Danny made a series of gestures by which Wren determined that the two men were scouting for a table to come free, and that Wren should go stand on line for coffee.

Danny understood the priorities in life.

The line wasn't long, but it was moving slowly. Wren let out an impatient breath, and the woman in front of her looked over her shoulder, then did a double-take.

"Oh. Hi."

The voice was familiar, but it took Wren a moment to place the face in front of her. "Um. Hi."

"Well." The woman smiled, a polite little grimace. "Isn't this awkward."

Colleen. The former unaffectionately-nicknamed "Mouthpiece," for the Mage Council, one of the representatives to the Truce Board, back when there was a Truce Board.

She had been tough and tough-minded, and Wren respected her as a worthy if annoying opponent-turned-ally-for-now. She hadn't disappeared when the rest of the Council slammed doors and turned tails. Points to her. But when the Battle went down, she hadn't shown, and nobody had seen her since.

And now she was here, on line in Starbucks. Small city.

"You look like shit," the Retriever said bluntly.

"I know." Colleen had never been a beauty, but she was striking, with a sort of 1940s femme fatale style. She had been a snazzy dresser, the same way her mentor had been.

Her mentor had been KimAnn Howe, leader of the local Council. KimAnn had also not been seen since the Battle. Rumor had it that other Council leaders had come to town for a powwow, just before, but that was where rumor ended and wild speculation took over. Someone might know where the old battleax was, but if so, they weren't talking.

Wren honestly hadn't cared, one way or the other. Madame Howe had been behind some of the worst Council-directed offenses against lonejacks ever, and the failure of the Council to join with the rest of the *Cosa* during the Battle was directly due to her orders.

But Council membership alone did not a bad person make. Her own mentor's mentor, Ayexi, had gone across the river to join the Council, and Ayexi was a good man to the marrow.

The barista pushed Colleen's latte across the counter, and she picked it up. "You....you're doing okay?" she asked Wren.

"You care?"

Colleen flushed, but didn't look away. "Actually, yes, I do. I heard... I heard what happened."

"I bet you did." Wren hadn't known she could put that much snark into four little words. She also wondered exactly what Colleen had heard. Was she referring to the Battle, and the fallout from that? Or... Wren couldn't remember what else Colleen might have been referring to.

"You know what? Fine. Whatever." Colleen's icy reserve returned, and she was once again the überbitch Council Member trainee, mentoree of Madame Howe, no matter how shabby her sweatshirt or bare of makeup her face. "Stay alive, Valere. But stay out of my way."

She took her coffee, and walked out of the store.

"Not smart, pissing her ladyship off like that. We could have used her," Danny said as he came to help her collect their coffees. Wren couldn't argue with him. But they also needed people they could trust, and Wren would never trust anyone who had worked that closely with Howe.

"Manhattan's a small island," he went on. "Eventually we're going to run into other Council members. You plan on dissing them all?"

"You really want to run out and embrace them?" she asked in return.

Danny was *definitely* sharpening his teeth. "Only if I can do it with horns and hooves showing."

Council didn't hate the Fatae. A lot of them were better than lonejacks in terms of accepting the nonhumans as cousins, in fact. But getting hugged in public by a bare-assed faun... It would probably not be one of their favored moments, no.

"You are a bad, bad man," she told the investigator, laughing despite herself. "Now let's go put that bad brain to better use."

Danny had scored them a coveted checkerboard table, tucked in a corner as far away from the door and windows as they could find, and large enough to seat all four of them comfortably: Wren, Danny, P.B., and a skinny, slow-spoken guy named Ron. Danny said he had been recommended by Doherty as a solid planner without, according to the psychologist "too many issues that might impede him being able to take action." In other words, he was not squeamish about bloodshed. It made Wren wonder how Doherty knew that, but you didn't look gift conspirators in the mouth.

"Right. Ron's been briefed on the basics, which means that he knows that you're both insane and is willing to overlook that."

Ron no-last-name didn't crack a smile. "My specialization is procurement," he said, a slight Southwesternish tang in his voice.

"Yeah, and what can you procure for us that we don't already have?" P.B. sounded belligerent but Wren knew him well enough to practically hear the "bad cop" costume click into place. Anyone else, it probably would have worked—a middle-aged Southerner, faced with a slightly-built young female and a fierce-looking demon? But Ron was *Cosa,* and he came in with Danny. He knew the score already.

"People. Troops, already trained. If you're going to plan this right, you're going to need a distraction, something to draw off the watchdogs, or at least divide their attention, not to mention their firepower. Plus, you don't know what shape these kids are going to be in, once you get them out. I can handle the extraction." He paused. "And whatever medical aid is required."

"How about beforehand?" Danny was a straight coffee, two sugars guy, and he had them lined up in front of him like soldiers, dying one after another. He ripped open two packets of sugar, dumped them in, and took a pull off the fresh cup. "What it all comes down to is knowing what you're going to face. It won't matter what we can or can't do with them after, if you can't even get in. And don't give me that I am The Wren bullshit you pulled on Doherty—I know how much work you and...you used to put in before each and every job. Blueprints and schematics and piles of insider information."

Wren appreciated the fact that Danny had tried to skip over Sergei's name, but it wasn't as though not mentioning him was going to make his shadow go away. It hovered over everything she did. Even here, out of the apartment, in a place Sergei would never willingly enter. Sergei thought that Starbucks was an abomination unto the landscape. And even that wasn't helping, much, if she kept thinking about what Sergei thought.

Breakups sucked. Especially when they weren't really breakups. Breakups were about not loving each other any more, right? This was just a...a dissolution of partnership for reasons of...

No. Wasn't helping, either. Enough, Valere. Cut that part of the brain out, put it away. Little boxes. She was good at that, did it all the time with the things she Retrieved, the dangerous things. Construct, fill, close the lid, and click the lock shut. A brain filled with little boxes, and nobody gets hurt.

"We can get that," P.B. was saying. Wren frowned, trying to backtrack to what they had been talking about before her brain butterflied. Get what? Oh, right. Information.

"How? No offense, but we're not going after a museum, or a store, or even someone's home, or anything with normal access to information. This is the Silence, who managed to operate how many decades, right under our noses, without us ever knowing. Who managed to *hire our people,* without us ever knowing about them." Ron drank espresso, three shots at a time. Wren liked him, just for that.

"To be fair, we operated for even longer under *their* noses, and they hired *our* people, without knowing about *us.*"

"Great, so we're both really good at being quiet and sneaky and totally oblivious. That was then. This is now. We know where their headquarters are…"

"And when we went there, they'd already shut down any possible access to the building." A nondescript office building on a nondescript street, the Silence had been there long enough to ensure that the normal underground accesses were controlled from within the building, and that they could work, for at least a short time, off their own, warded, generator. To outsiders, it looked as though they were prepared for another great blackout. To a Talent, it spoke of preparation for a siege. Specifically, against current, and current-backed attacks. Like Wren's assailants with their rubber-soled boots and gloves, they knew their enemy.

"Anyway, what makes us think that that's where they're holding the kids? It was an office building, not a long-term dormitory. Or a laboratory." P.B. was sulking, because Wren had cut off his caffeine after his second coffee that morning, and refused to let him order a cappuccino, so he was stuck with herbal tea now.

"That we know of. Anything could be inside that facade."

"No, if they were trying to run anything on that scale—there were how many missing? Thirty?" Ron asked.

"About that, yeah. As far as we've been able to estimate." There might be more, there might be less. There might have been a *lot* more, once upon a time. Part of what she needed was names— names and ages and descriptions and when they went missing. She needed someone who could coax that information from the families, and run it against the known bodies recovered after the… After. Wren made another notation on her notebook and poked her nose back into the conversation.

"If there were thirty, even just at the start, they would have needed more power than an ordinary office building. Not just electricity but water use, and the demands on their air system, and...trust me, it would have showed up on the grid when we did our preliminary run-through."

"Would it? Things weren't all that careful or coherent, right then."

They had discovered the Silence headquarters not through their own searching, but because they had been suspected of killing two of the Silence field operatives and leaving them on the doorstep of that building with a warning burned into their skins.

The *Cosa* had not done it, or if members had, it was neither authorized nor known to the Quad. Wren would have heard a whisper of it, if that had been so. And none of the Fatae were owning up to it—and they were, as a group, totally incapable of not bragging about something like that. Fatae might be nasty, but they were also self-admitted egomaniacs who liked nothing better than to gloat about a nasty prank done well.

Not all the fairy tales were lies, and most of them weren't even much of an exaggeration.

"All right." Ron pulled out a small stenographer's notebook and a stub of a pencil. "Let's get down to the hard details, let's."

Wren had kicked back in her chair, staring at the debris on the table even as she judged the distance of everyone around them to their table. When someone came by just a smidge too close, P.B. noted that she tensed up, but so far it hadn't been anything more than the usual crowding. P.B. started scanning a little more closely, reacting to her tension. They got a few dirty looks, but that was only because they were hogging one of the best-placed tables, and showed no signs of giving it up.

"So we've got a handful or two of people we can probably count on for supplies and support. Probably. Ron, you sure about the people Doherty's bringing in?"

The human nodded. "Two of them lost family members in the past year—one of them dead, the other they think was swallowed by this Silence. They'll give you blood and bone. The others aren't Talented, but they are damn good therapists, and won't walk away from kids who need help." He paused to think about that, and added another name to his notebook. "And a guy I know: Mack's not a professional, but he worked in homeless shelters. He specialized in dealing with the wizzed community. If the non-Talents need help—" in other words, if they needed protection from the possibly traumatized Talent lashing out "—he's the guy we'll need."

A good thought. P.B.'s opinion of this guy went up a notch.

"So the next and most important thing we need to do is figure out where they had our kids. And then figure out if they're still there."

"And then you can get them out?"

"I haven't been stopped by anything yet," Wren said. "That's not to say that there isn't a security system that could stop me, but..." She shrugged. "I haven't run into a system yet that doesn't have a weakness. The trick is being patient enough—and sneaky enough—to find it."

"Which comes back to the original question," Ron said. "How do we figure out where this ready-to-be-cracked-open location is?"

Danny looked at P.B. P.B. looked at Wren. Wren looked *down* into her coffee.

"Wren." He knew her M.O. He also knew what was currently missing from her M.O.

"I can't." Her voice was flat, which meant that she was panicky inside. He hated doing this to her. He really hated it. But it had to be done.

"Of course you can. You won't. You're not done sulking."

"P.B...."

"I know." And he did. He was the only one who did. "But he's the one who's got the information. And you're the one he'll give it to."

The entire Starbucks didn't quite come to a halt. P.B. knew that. But it sure as hell felt like it, as Ron slammed his coffee cup down on the table and demanded, "You're thinking of going to that turncoat?"

"He's not a turncoat!" Wren retorted, stung into defending her former partner.

"No, because he's one of them! He betrayed us!"

That was the rumor, spread in the aftermath of the Battle of Burning Bridge. That the reason they hadn't been able to draw out the leaders was that Sergei had warned them.

P.B. knew it wasn't true. He had seen Sergei face down those leaders, and been forced to an uncomfortable, impossible stalemate. What had happened after that he didn't know—the human had sent him off to help Wren. Not that he had needed much sending.

"Sergei Didier was one of the few reasons that we survived even half as well as we did," the demon said now, his voice low, quiet, and dangerous. "You will not speak ill of him in my presence." Only Wren got to do that. Only she had the right.

"Then where is he now?" Danny asked. "Because we sure as hell could use him."

A good question. Unfortunately the only way to answer it that didn't make people think that the rumors were true would be to lay open the relationship between Wren and Sergei. While P.B. had absolutely no hesitation about discussing anything—the Fatae didn't have many taboo topics, and sex certainly wasn't one of them—he knew intimately how badly Wren *didn't* want it known.

She was private even for a human, and Didier was even more so.

"I sent him away."

"You what?" Danny looked like someone had slapped him. P.B. felt much the same, even though he'd known the truth. Or, most of the truth, anyway.

"I sent him away. Not because... He's a Null, Danny. Ron, do you understand what that means? Do you really understand?" Talent wasn't always a genetic inheritance, but it did tend to run in families, and even an unTalented parent of a child with skill usually had some ability, even if it wasn't always trainable or useful. To be Null, however...

"My mother is a Null. My partner is a Null. That means that they have absolutely no way to protect themselves against attack. They can't even use Old Magic—it wouldn't even backfire, it just simply wouldn't work. My mother can't even see most Fatae—they slip her mind the moment she looks away, like... Like I do to everyone else! So in a war like this? They're not just in danger, they're liabilities. They're targets."

Oh, she was slandering Didier. The man was lethal with more than his voice. But she wasn't wrong, either.

"So you sent him away." Danny was blinking at her, his wide-eyed look and curly hair making him look like a particularly befuddled owl.

"I sent them both away. As far from me as I could get them to go."

"Oh, come on." Ron clearly didn't believe her. He didn't know her the way the two Fatae did. "Nobody's going to attack a Null, anyway. I mean, the Silence are Nulls, right? And they're all about protecting them from us, the big scary bump-in-the-night things. You're overreacting. I'm all for getting our kids back, but let's keep everything in perspective, okay?"

"He hasn't left the city." P.B. wasn't going to admit that he had been keeping tabs on the man; if Wren hadn't known, that just meant she'd been really good at not thinking about it. But it made for a good distraction point, before Wren showed Ron what "over-reacting" *really* looked like. "Looks like he's keeping to business—he's an art dealer," he explained to Ron. "When he isn't plotting Wren's life of larceny."

"All you have to do is call him. Or write him a letter. A letter might be better." Under stress, Wren could wreck every cell phone in a two-block radius, and this was going to stress her significantly. "Write him a note, and I'll deliver it." He was a courier by profession; he'd even give her a professional courtesy discount. If she asked.

"I'm not going to write—"

Whatever Wren was going to say was lost when someone's shopping bag swung a little too close to her shoulder, and then hit.

P.B. noted how particularly hard it hit her at the same time she rolled off the chair and down under the too-tiny table, even as he was doing the same. His paw reached up and grabbed Ron out of the way, not caring that his claws cut through his nicely trendy and probably very expensive sweater to do so.

Danny stayed topside, exactly the way he and the demon had planned it, just in case, back when Wren decided on her course of action. P.B. protected the Retriever, while Danny, able to pass in a crowd, took out the attacker.

The shopper, seeing that her intended victim had gone low, reached into the pocket of her jacket and pulled out a small, plastic tube. It looked a little like the hot-stick some of the Talent had started carrying around, but he was going to bet against it working the same way.

Before P.B. could see what the woman intended to do with whatever it was, a metal-shod toe met his ribs, and he let out an embarrassing yelp, even as he was turning to face this new assailant. And the next thing he knew, they were in the middle of a very nasty little fight, probably the first brawl to ever break out in the civilized environs of a Starbucks café.

The table went over, and someone had him in meaty fists, dragging him up by the ruff of fur under his neck until his feet dangled off the floor. Without thinking, he twisted his neck at an angle that shouldn't have been possible, given his apparent build, and chomped down hard on one of the hands, the row of small sharp teeth ripping a chunk of flesh off the human with one savage jerk of his muzzle.

The human screamed and dropped him. By the time his feet hit the floor again he was already turning to find Wren in the scrum. Everyone else could go to hell; he had to make sure she was safe.

It looked like there were maybe seven people involved. Staying low, P.B. did a quick head count. Wren had the original woman and another guy trying to rough her up, using that tube he had seen— from the expression on Wren's face, whatever it was doing didn't involve tickling. Danny had someone holding his arms at a painful angle behind his back, keeping him from getting involved. Ron was nowhere to be seen; if these idiots were targeting Talent, P.B. couldn't exactly blame him. One less human to worry about, anyway.

Two other people had waded in, one of them wearing an employee's apron, and were trying to break things up. They weren't getting far. Everyone else seemed to be either treating the fight like their own personal entertainment, or trying to ignore it, moving their coffees and laptops as far out of range as possible.

P.B. tried to crawl toward Wren, and someone in the process of picking up their coffee stumbled and fell over him. Their coffee went flying, hitting someone at a nearby table, prompting that person to get up and start yelling at the coffee's owner.

The woman with the tube hit Wren across the face with it, and current-spark flashed, strong enough for anyone to see it. Oh, that wasn't good. That wasn't good at all. Wren had a look on her face that did not bode well. Before all this, she would have just used her no-see-em thingy and gotten away. Now? Now P.B. wasn't sure what Wren would do. But as much as he was in favor of finishing a fight by winning it, this was way too public a place. Especially if current was going to be used.

Another employee jumped over the counter and waded in, distracting Danny's attacker long enough for him to get a backward kick in with his cowboy boots. P.B. winced in sympathy—anyone who went into a fight without a cup deserved what he got, but ow!—and reached up to tug at Wren's leg.

Out. Now.

Wren's grin was fierce, and he worried for a moment that she was going to ignore him, and keep fighting. Then she seemed to flicker in his sight, and used current to disappear. The guy holding her just tightened what he had been holding, no matter that he couldn't see her any longer: damn it, they knew what she was and what she could do. Not good. Not good at all.

P.B. lunged forward and hit the guy in the back of the knees with every pound of his body. He was short, but heavy: he was almost entirely bone and muscle, and none of it gave under pressure. The guy's knees, on the other hand, did.

It was a small break, but it was enough. The man lost his hold on her, and the woman swore, trying to track something with the tube, like it was a—

"A current detector?" he whispered incredulously. Oh bad, bad, very, very, very bad. Someone official-sounding shouted, and P.B. decided to get before the getting got worse. Danny was a former cop; he could take care of himself.

He was two blocks away before he stopped to catch his breath. There was a noise, like someone dropping a heavy bag, and Wren appeared, sitting on the pavement beside him with an exhausted sigh.

"Jesus wept!" She had a nasty purpling bruise forming on her left cheekbone to match the one already on her chin, and her thick brown hair was tangled and spiky, like someone had tried to pull it out by the roots. "That was like something out of a Marx Brothers movie!"

P.B. snorted. She was right. It had been. Only except not with the funny. "You're bleeding."

"So're you."

P.B. touched the corner of his mouth where his fur was wet, looked at the red that came away on his fingers. "Not my blood."

Wren shuddered, and looked away. "Don't tell me."

"They were hunting. Talent-hunting."

"I know."

"You think they were gunning for you?"

"No." Wren shook her head. "They didn't know who I was. I think they overheard our conversation. Stupid. Who the hell thought they'd be trolling coffee shops for trouble?"

"I don't think they were."

"What, someone told them we were there?"

"Or something. That thing they were using on you, what was it?"

Wren shook her head again, her hands busy braiding her hair back away from her face, wincing when her fingers touched a sore spot on her scalp. "I have no idea. Like a stun gun, only not." Stun guns were like tickling Talent; teens used them at parties, as a gag. "It *hurt*. Like...like suckers, pulling at my skin wherever it touched me. Only hard. Like being French-kissed by a squid."

"Oh, that's just lovely, Valere." He paused to mentally Brillo the image away, then went on. "They were using it to find you, when you went invisible."

"What?" Wren was sharp; it only took her a thought to see where he was going with that. "No." She shook her head once, carefully. "No. It's not possible."

"Yeah well. Lots of things people say not possible to, turns out they're possible after all. Like me and thee, for two."

"Yah. Point. And Ron. What happened to Ron?"

The demon raised one shoulder in a shrug. "Like another Talent I used to know, he got himself out of the way of the fight the second before it happened."

"You think he tipped them off?"

P.B. had wondered it, then decided not. "It doesn't scan," was all he said. "Not unless he's been brainwashed, too...." He paused, then turned his head to look at the human. "Wren? How could we tell?"

"What?"

"If someone was...twisted, by the Silence. How could we tell? I know the ones we fought, they were obvious but...there had to be others in around us, all the time. To report back. And people...their families didn't know anything was wrong, until they started disappearing. So..."

Wren leaned her head against the building's brick wall and closed her eyes. In the afternoon light, there were lines around her mouth and eyes that P.B. knew hadn't been there even two years ago.

"I hate it when you're smart," was all she said. Then, "I'll go see him. Tomorrow."

nine

"Ms. Valere? A pleasure to see you. How have you been?"

Wren grinned despite herself. She could go anywhere, do anything, and not be seen by anybody—except a Manhattan doorman. She had managed to slip into Sergei's building a few times, but always with the sneaking feeling that Max, Shawn, and Ellie, the high-rise gatekeepers, were merely humoring her by pretending not to notice.

"I've been fine, Shawn, thank you. And yourself?" She lingered by the front desk, by habit angling her body to avoid the overhead camera scanning across the lobby. There was another by the elevators, but it would only see her backside right now. Not that she had anything to hide: it was purely professional habit.

"Not too bad, although I could use more sleep."

Wren had to think about that, then she remembered. The last time she had seen Shawn, his wife had been about eight months along in her pregnancy.

"It *has* been a while. Boy or girl?"

Shawn's expression turned wry. "Girl. My life as I knew it is over. Is Mr. Didier expecting you?"

"No." Once, he would have been. Now…

"You want me to call up, or…?"

"I'll just go on up and surprise him," she said cheekily, relieved when Shawn smiled back. Thank God it had been one of the old-timers on duty this morning, and not a new kid who didn't know her. Technically—legally—they weren't supposed to let anyone up unaccompanied without getting the okay from the tenant. But Shawn had seen her enough times with Sergei to let her slide by.

The moment she walked into the elevator, Wren leaned against the back wall and let herself be soothed by the hum of the building's electrical system. It was a fine-tuned, smooth-running beast that almost begged her to take a sip.

She hadn't slept at all last night, listening to the soft snorts of P.B.'s breathing coming down the short hallway. The aftermath of the brawl had been nothing compared to how the desire to see her former partner again, the first time in months, had warred with the fear of actually coming face-to-face with him.

They had not parted well, her and Sergei. She had been exhausted, injured, and emotionally beaten down from dealing with the Silence's brainwashed Talent, from seeing her friends lying bloodied and dying on the ground, from the weight of responsibility she felt for their failure to accomplish the main goal of the day: to find and take down the ones who had been funding the anti-Fatae, anti-Talent vigilantes.

To see Sergei standing there, uninvited, his hair and clothing unmussed, his hands unbloodied and clean…

"Come to watch the show? If I'd known, I could have gotten you better seats."

P.B., holding her up by the arm, started to speak, but Wren overrode him. She wanted to be the one to cut her partner down.

"You proud of where you come from, Didier? You proud of what your people have driven mine to?"

The Cosa *were not killers. They were pranksters and players, but they had never gone to war. Had never honed their skills into violence. And now they had—and she, however unknowingly, innocently, had helped to lead the way.*

Two days later, when she had finally staggered out of bed, and begun the long haul back to some kind of normal mental state, the one thing she could not escape was the look on Sergei's face as he hailed them a cab, then stood back and watched as she crawled into it, P.B. after her.

P.B. had looked out the window as they drove away. She hadn't.

She only learned days after that Sergei had gone directly to what was left of the Double-Quad, had shared with them the information of who they were looking for—and why it would be almost impossible for the *Cosa* to reach them. They were too well-funded, too well-connected for anyone to take down, without equal resources.

The *Cosa* muttered that Sergei had betrayed them, had refused to tell them what they needed to know until after the blood had been spilled, and even then told only enough to play into their sense of devastation, of pointless destruction.

Wren knew differently. Or she hoped that she did, anyway. There was still a kernel of doubt in her. How much had he known? How early had he known it? Could he have done anything to prevent what the Silence did to those children? She didn't want to believe he might have, and had chosen not to. But…she didn't know. Not for certain.

He had refused to tell them anything that would betray the Silence, before. That was true. He could bend his loyalties only so far, without his own honor breaking. But he would have stood with them, if he had been allowed to. He had gone away, stayed away, because she told him to. Before the Battle, and after. Because he wasn't safe around her, and the current-touch he craved. And now she was going directly to him.

"I should have let P.B. ask him," she muttered. But she couldn't. That wasn't fair. Not to anyone. None of this was even remotely fair. And...

She wanted to see him again. She *needed* to see him, like an ache somewhere in her gut, deep and hard.

She had read or heard somewhere that in Chinese theology that was where the soul rested: somewhere below the navel.

The elevator stopped at Sergei's floor. She took a deep breath, tapped the building's generator once for luck, and walked down the hallway.

He answered on the second knock, almost as though he had been waiting for someone to come by.

She had wondered how she would react on seeing him again. What would she feel? What would she do if she felt different? Or felt nothing at all?

The door opened, and Wren wanted to cry. God, oh God how she had missed him.

"Wren." His voice was still low and soft, but those pale brown eyes were wary. "What brings you here?"

"You." She cleared her throat, wanting nothing more to do than to reach out and touch him. Knowing that was exactly the last thing she could do. *Business. This had to be purely business.* "May I come in?"

He stood back, and let her enter.

The apartment looked the same: an open floor plan focused around a pair of comfortable leather sofas and a low table, with artwork and books against every wall except the one filled with tall, narrow windows that looked out across the avenue. It was a mixed-use area: some of the neighboring buildings were condo apartments, some were office buildings. All of them were exclusive. A metal spiral staircase climbed up to the loft bedroom. He had a king bed that was almost too soft; once you fell into it you never wanted to get out.

Wren shoved those thoughts aside, and turned to face her former partner. He looked good. But tired.

"You look tired," he said.

She laughed. "Yeah. I guess all of us do."

They stood there and watched each other.

"You need something." He didn't bother with the smooth chatter he used on would-be clients and customers.

"Yeah. We do. Information."

She expected him to shut down, close himself off. Withdraw, the way he had months ago when the Truce Board had asked him for the same thing: to give them details about the Silence, the organization that had recruited him, taught him, made him into the man he was—for good and for ill—when Wren came into his life. They had asked him then, with that request, to choose his loyalties. He hadn't chosen them.

She only prayed that he hadn't returned to the Silence, either. The Sergei Didier she knew did not like to be beholden to anyone, especially if he couldn't trust them, and she and he both knew first-hand that you could not trust the Silence.

He ran a hand through his gray-brown hair, and shook his head. "You want some coffee?"

"Do I ever not?" she asked, and he smiled, a real, if small, smile. "Come on. I need something, too."

His kitchen was like a chrome and ebony temple to the culinary gods, and Wren had always felt uncomfortable in it, afraid that one wrong spark of current would destroy tens of thousands of dollars of equipment. But it was worth it all to sit at the island and listen to the sound of the high-end coffeemaker hiss and hum while he moved with aesthetic grace to brew his preferred tea.

He had bought that coffeemaker for her. He didn't drink the stuff, except under duress.

He served the coffee just the way she liked it, in one of his black china cups. She had looked them up, once, out of curiosity. Wedgwood. One of the rare types. She refused to treat it any differently than she did her own collection of durable, if stolen, cafeteria-style mugs. If he was willing to use them, he had to be willing to have them broken or chipped, too. Not that she planned on doing it, but if it happened, she wasn't going to apologize more than once.

"You're dodging," he said finally, watching her stir the liquid carefully. "I can hear you slamming thoughts around in your head, even without a bit of Talent."

"Telepathy's a myth," she said automatically, even though that wasn't quite true. Most Talent could at very least ping each other, the way she had when she called for help. But it wasn't good for much more than that, unless you had a really tight connection to the other person, and not always even then.

And she was dodging again, he was right. Damn him.

All she really wanted to do was take him upstairs and give that oversize bed of his a workout. Talk and trauma later.

But that wasn't going to happen. That *couldn't* happen.

And she had to be very, very careful about what she told him. He had already noticed the bruise on her cheek; she had seen the way his gaze flicked to it, then away sharply. He wanted to know, but he wasn't going to ask. He knew that there were things that he had given up the right to ask, to know about. But he could be manipulated by that. By his concern, and his need to know, and the knowledge that he no longer had the "in" to have been there when it happened.

She didn't like thinking about Sergei like a job. But he was.

She was here to Retrieve information. That was all.

"We had a little scuffle yesterday," she said, drinking her coffee. It wasn't perfect—he was still too much of a tea drinker to understand the delicacies of making a perfect cup of coffee—but when you started with the high quality beans the way he did, there was no way it could ever be less than pretty damn good. "Couple of would-be humans-first heroes jumped us. In a Starbucks." She still had to laugh when she thought of it.

"Anyone hurt?"

"Other than a few paper cups and a table? Not on our side. P.B. says he bit someone but I don't think they'll need rabies shots. I picked up a few bruises and a headache."

"Vigilantes."

"Can't imagine who else. You know the *Cosa,* if they have a score to settle they do it somewhere a lot quieter. These boys have stopped caring who notices…or who gets caught in the crossfire."

That got him, the way she knew it would. It was ironic, really. The Silence, he told her, had been set up to protect the innocent and the ignorant from the various "forces of darkness"—and she mentally made quotation marks around the phrase—and now he really and truly bought into it. So much so that he couldn't let go even when he knew—he had to know—that he was being played.

"What do you want from me, then?"

"They knew who we were. Or, they knew *what* we were. Just

sitting there, minding our own business. They had a..." She didn't know if she should call it a tool or a weapon, so she defaulted. "They had a thing with them. A tube, about palm-sized, with a flat end like a spade." She didn't remember much about it, specifically, but the spade end had been what left the mark on her face. That, she remembered. "It gives off a nasty shock when it hits the skin," and her hand went involuntarily to her cheekbone. She was gratified, in a petty sort of way, when his face tightened at the thought. "But that's not what worries us. A weapon against Talent, that's to be expected. In fact, I'm sort of surprised the Silence didn't have a toyshop work something like that up a long time ago."

He neither confirmed nor denied the existence of a toyshop within the Silence. To be fair, he might not know. He'd been a Handler, an Operative out in the field, not one of the office players.

"What does concern you, then?"

"The fact that P.B. saw them using it like a fish-finder. When I went no-see-'um, they waved it around like they fully expected it to light up and whoop when it found me."

The look on his face told Wren everything she needed to know. If this was Silence tech—or Silence magic, as weird a concept as that seemed—then Sergei not only didn't know anything about it, but he immediately grasped what it could mean, and didn't like that one bit at all.

Good. Neither did she.

"If they can find us, somehow pick us out of a crowd...Sergei, the witch trials, the Inquisition? Nothing on what will happen. If they are able to find us and pick us off... Imagine the Nazis without having to worry about camps. Just a flick of that tool, and a sniper bullet to the heart, and they're gone. And soon enough, so are we."

That had been P.B.'s suggestion, using the Holocaust, and his eyes had darkened almost to black when he said it. Someday she was going to have to ask the demon about where he was during the 1930s and 1940s. Or maybe not.

Sometimes, "you don't want to know" really does mean "you don't want to know."

"And once the Talent are gone," she continued, "who is going to protect the Fatae? More, who is going to *stop* the Fatae? Because they're scared. And if the *Cosa* is gone, they're going to get even more scared. And trust me, the Silence does not want to deal with Fairyland in panic mode. Because the Grimm Brothers were down-playing what can happen."

Even the cutest Fatae breed had claws and teeth. And a lot of them were attached to nasty little minds with little historical love for humanity.

"Are you trying to scare me?"

"No. Is it working?"

"I'll put my ear to various walls, see what I can pick up." He suddenly realized that his tea had been steeping all this time, and removed the silver tea ball from his cup, wincing as he moved it over to the garbage and emptied it. The soggy black flakes fell like soot.

"There's more." Only this was the tricky part.

Sergei came back and stood across from the island, looking at her. He was wearing wool slacks and a button-down shirt, like he was about to go to work, but she had noticed when she came in that he was barefoot, which meant that he planned to stay in. She had a thing about feet—his in particular—and it was distracting to think about the texture of the skin of his arch, when she had to stay focused on what she had needed from him.

An hour in the sack—the thought, probably inevitably, came. *One hour, and you'll be all sharp and focused.*

She didn't even know she had moved, before she was next to him, and then his arms were around her and everything was okay, she was safe, the weight of his arms holding her impossibly tight against him was enough to keep the black sludge down and the bad things away.

"Wrenlet," he whispered into her hair. "Wrenlet, I've missed you."

And the black sludge stirred, reaching up to him. Her current sparked, warming her, sliding tendrils through her system and sparking her skin until he was the one shivering in anticipation.

And like that, the comfort was gone, and she was across the room, this time very aware of what it took to move.

Because he was an addict, addicted to the feel of her current when they made love, and she had trusted herself once to say no—and failed. And failure was not something she accepted. Not when the result involved her partner's insides crisping and failing from overrush.

Nulls couldn't handle current. That was what made them Nulls. And what made them dangerous. Fear of what they didn't understand…and desire for what they couldn't have.

Sergei felt his body shaking, cold sweat rising on his skin where her warmth had just been, and forced himself into compliance, slowing his heart rate down and willing his body to behave. It wasn't as effective as a cold shower, but it did the job.

"I've missed you," he said again.

"Yeah." She was shutting down, he could see it. And he could see it because he had taught her how to do it.

Of all his sins, that might have been the worst. But it might also be what was allowing her to survive all of this. Nothing was ever black or white, good or bad, entirely.

Not even the Silence.

"To Protect Against the Darkness."

"What?" She had heard him, she just wasn't sure what it was that she had heard.

"That's their motto. The Silence. 'To Protect Against the Darkness.' The idea was to create a society that had the money and the manpower and the willingness to protect the innocent and the ignorant from the people—and the things—that did not have humanity's best interests at heart. I think they ran into some of your old ones, at some point."

"The Old Ones haven't been seen in hundreds of years," she reminded him. The near-godlike Fatae had either died out or disappeared generations ago, and from what little he had heard, that was a good thing.

"By you, maybe. By them, I'm not so sure. The founders were convinced that there was something—" and he waved his hand in irritation "—Out There that was out to get them, to destroy us all. And I don't think piskies alone could have set them off."

Wren was looking at him as though she expected him to get to the point at some point. He wasn't sure he had one, just a lot of ends and beginnings that weren't connecting. Yet. He kept talking, trying to feel his way to something he knew was there.

"The Darkness, to the Silence, is anything that doesn't have the best interest of humanity at heart. Most of the Fatae don't give a damn about humanity one way or another, far as I can tell."

She nodded, grudgingly allowing the truth of that. Live and let live was the motto for most of the breed, and the ones that were actively anti-human, like the deep-water dragons and the jötnar, tended to stay out of humanity's way in the modern age.

Sergei shook his head. "It's not as though they didn't have enough human problems to worry about. They could have had a full slate, just tracking down and fixing the things human agents screwed up."

"To screw up is human. To really screw it up you generally need magic."

"That a quote?"

She nodded. "One of Ayexi's that Neezer used to use. First time I've ever been able to hand it down."

"Why didn't you ever take a mentoree?" he asked, suddenly wondering. Not every Talent did, but like having kids, it was a topic that should at least come up in discussion, and that never had. Not between the two of them, anyway.

You're a Null. Why should you be involved in that conversation? She probably talked to Lee. Or P.B. Anyone but you.

"There's still time."

It was a clear evasion, and one he had no choice but to respect.

"Meanwhile, whatever reason your old employers have for deciding that we're the cause of all the world's ills, it's become a...what's the term? A self-fulfilling prophesy. Because we *are* out to get them."

Her face was drawn, the gentle face only he ever seemed to be able to recall from memory suddenly crafted less of flesh than wood—petrified wood, full of fine grains and textures.

He knew, almost to the week, when she had stopped being a teenager and become a woman. But when had his Retriever become a warrior?

What the *hell* had been going on downtown?

"You said you needed something else from me." Get this back on track. Get her out of here. His body still ached for her touch, like a junkie jonesing for another hit, and he didn't trust himself not to try to talk her into giving him what he wanted...and no matter what her reaction to that, he would lose. The way he had already lost her trust.

And he had lost that; it was clear the way she hesitated. Once, she would have poured out everything to him, trusting him to sort through her words and discover the important ones, sifting through her thoughts to get to the pertinent facts.

Now, she was doing the sifting on her own, censoring things she didn't want him to know. Didn't trust him to know.

It hurt. And yet, he was almost unbearably proud. Once he had feared that she wouldn't need him any more. Now he knew that she didn't—but he could still help her.

"We're going in." She qualified that: "I'm going in. To get back whatever's left of our kids."

"The FocAs." The Focused Actives, the Operatives he had helped run, once upon a time. The ones he had left behind, when he left the Silence.

"Yeah." She nodded, thankfully not commenting on his ease with the term, although she clearly disliked it. "But we need to know where to look. And how to draw their attention *away* from that location, when the time comes."

She stared at him then, waiting for his reaction. Would he help, or would he walk away again, unable to make that final betrayal?

She didn't know what he would do. She had been wise enough to know that cords still bound him, even when he denied it, and hadn't hated him for it.

"I knew a girl once..."

"And you thought she was human."

"No. I thought she was a dream. And, like all dreams, eventually I woke up. And she was gone."

"I think I have what you need. The information...and the distraction."

She leaned forward against the counter, and waited. He started to pace back and forth, cup of tea in his hand, and for an instant it was just like before: an easy teamwork falling into place, like the tumblers on a high-end lock.

"Andre... Poul was the one who killed Bren, and Andre killed Poul."

Wren had never liked the smarmy, sour-mouthed Jorgunmunder, and she had no sorrow at all in knowing that he was dead. She had only met Bren once, but the woman had risked a great deal that one time to warn him, and she knew that Sergei had respected her.

"Games within games?"

"Silence politics. They tend to be nasty, and they have become regrettably fatal. Andre's playing it deep and dangerous. He thinks there's a way to wrest control of the reins away from Duncan, without bringing down the entire organization."

"You think he can do it?" She didn't; not that Andre wasn't damned impressive, but he had been outplayed by this Duncan more than once before.

"I don't know. But I do know that they're not a unified block. And I may have found a way to widen some of those cracks. Wide enough for some things to fall out."

Without even trying, Wren raised one eyebrow at him—a move she had been trying to imitate without success for years. Sergei raised his own eyebrow back at her, and started to tell her what he had been up to for the past ten weeks.

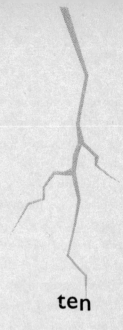

ten

Wren got out of Sergei's apartment an hour later with the information she needed. That had to be enough. Seeing him, talking to him, touching him...and not touching him? Had shredded her in a way she wasn't sure she was going to recover from anytime soon. If ever.

She refused to let the tears fall. She didn't cry. All crying ever did was make her eyes red and her nose run. She didn't look good when she cried.

Maybe she should leave Manhattan, when all this was done. Maybe that would be best: to get away from the reminders. The temptation. The need that hit her every time she thought of him. It couldn't be healthy. This wasn't love, this couldn't be love. It was as much an addiction as Sergei's need for her current-touch.

Love was...

Wren snorted, sounding depressingly like P.B. She had no idea what love was. Her mom had gotten her out of a one-night stand with a guy she couldn't even remember—probably where Wren got her no-see-me from—and all the guys her mom brought home had been better Dad material than lover/husband types. And Wren's own dating history was less a history and more an executive memo: short, and boring.

Love was Sergei. And love sucked.

She started for the subway, then changed her mind midstep. She was out, alone and unarmed. Even in daylight, that wasn't smart. Not after the incident in the Starbucks. Walking to the end of the street, she stepped off the curb and raised her hand for a cab.

"Where to, miss?"

"West Fourth Street, off 6th."

She had to go see a man about a horse. Or, in this case, the entire damned cavalry.

The receptionist at Doherty's office was a tweet—blond and bird-brained, like a canary. She fluttered around so helplessly about office hours and appointments when she asked to see Dr. Doherty that Wren just rolled her eyes and went on inside.

He didn't even look up, at first. "Kara, what—oh. You."

He could have sounded happier to see the IRS appear in his doorway.

"Jesus wept, show some manners. You told me to come see you when I had more details."

Doherty leaned back in his chair and waved Wren to a seat. She eyed the two choices, neither of which were the expected cliché of a sofa, and sat down in a curved wooden armchair that didn't look as though it were used by anyone with significant neuroses. They might not be contagious, but she wasn't in the mood to take chances.

"I know where, and how to get in. Or I will, anyway." Sergei would come through. He always did. Now would be a bad time to change that.

"Into—" he waved his hand, seemingly unwilling to commit to saying anything, even in his own office. She knew that the academic world was tough, but she didn't know it was *that* scary.

"Yeah, to…" And she waved her hand, mimicking him. "I need you and whoever you call in, to be ready. I think you're right. I think they're going to need a lot of help." Based on what Sergei had just told her, she *knew* he was right. If that was how they treated coworkers, what would they be doing to pawns they considered disposable, subhuman?

"We'll need a place," he said. "Somewhere they will feel safe, but not locked up."

"Taken care of." Well it wasn't, yet. But it would be. Mash—an irascible old fart even by lonejack standards—had made his place into a hangout for teenaged Talent, a safe place for them to go when they didn't have school or lessons, when they didn't want to be home, for whatever reason. The Council had taken old Mash out, back before their problems got bigger than family squabbles, but his heirs had kept the brownstone open in his name. A few words in the right ears, and they could have the place for as long as they needed.

All they had to do was get the kids there.

Hey, it was a Retrieval. Okay, so normally she lifted paintings, or jewelry, or things she could fit in her pocket, not things with legs and arms in multiples, but she had done live Retrievals before. The theory was still the same.

Right?

"So. Anything else you want to talk about, so long as you're in the chair anyway?" He had a gleam in his eye that she didn't think was sadistic, but leaned that way. In a purely clinical and caring way.

"Not really." But she didn't get up and leave.

The earlier tone was gone, his voice softer now. "Anything you say in here—it's not *Cosa* business. It's not lonejack gossip or mage-fodder. Just you and me."

"I know how it works. I took Psych 101 in college. Got a solid B."

He sat there, not waiting or not-waiting, and Wren hesitated. Inside her, the boxes trembled, like a subway ran underneath.

"I have a meeting to go to," she said. "Maybe some other time."

She got out of the chair—surprisingly and suspiciously comfortable—and slipped out into the waiting room, past the tweet and a guy sitting there reading a magazine.

She hit the street, taking a lungful of fresh air like she'd forgotten what it tasted like, and turned, ready to book it—she really *did* have a meeting, despite what Doherty probably thought—when someone's hand touched her elbow.

Sua was a griffin, young as that breed went but with a full wingspan and a hard, curved beak that looked completely grown-up. She was also her herd's choice to replace Beyl, the matriarch who had died during the Battle of Burning Bridge. That gave her a gravitas it might have taken another griffin decades to earn.

"Peoples!" Her speech was marred by a slight beak-whistle, but the words were clear. "Peoples, sit down and shut up!"

She was used to shouting down her peers and elders. A room filled with humans and Fatae was nothing. She didn't even have to open her wings. They sat down and shut up.

"Thank you." Danny didn't want to be up there, but P.B. was demon and therefore most Fatae and not a few humans wouldn't listen. Danny looked human, had lived as part of the human world, but was Fatae. Lacking Valere, he was the best one to lead this meeting.

And where the hell *was* Valere, anyway? She had told them where to meet, and when: Had she overslept?

"Thank you for getting your asses down here at this ungodly hour. I see everyone's armed and caffeinated." He got a laugh at that. Not much of a laugh, but they were listening. That made him feel better.

"I suppose you're wondering why you got the call." Literally, in some cases; the Talent and the Fatae with phones had gotten rung up the night before. The low-tech Fatae had been routed by piskie messenger, which was cruel but efficient. Piskies loved delivering unwelcome news. "We have a job for you."

They looked at him, waiting. Twenty-seven had answered the call, out of the forty names Wren and Ron had decided were both useful and likely. Better than expected, not as good as hoped. But in the end, numbers wouldn't determine if this succeeded or not. He wasn't sure what would determine it, but if sheer force were enough, they would have won already.

Where the *hell* was Valere?

The door to the church basement slammed open, and a flurry of movement in the back of the room indicated that someone was coming through. Speak and the devil appears. He squinted, something taking him by surprise. Usually Wren slipped through the crowd like she was a greased fish, but the crowd was moving aside for her—physically turning, noting, and retreating to give her room.

"You warming up the troops, Danno?" she asked as she reached him, the tall, lurking presence of Didier back on her heels like the old days. Except for the fact that Wren wasn't even acknowledging the Null's presence. Not good.

"Like Phyllis Diller for Bob Hope," he cracked, hoping to break the tension, and rolled his eyes when she looked blank. "They're all yours, chief."

She didn't stop where he was, but hopped onto the desk he was standing beside, her thick-soled boots adding to the years of scuffing on the wood surface

Danny shook his head and went to join P.B. at the back of the room. Sergei stayed where he was for a moment, then followed the two males.

Wren didn't even notice them leave, stomping her foot on the desk to regain everyone's attention.

"All right. You know who I am, I know who you are, so down to business. I don't know what Danny's told you. You already know the situation—we got our asses kicked, and now we're walking like wounded cats, spitting but scared."

They didn't like that—not one bit. Wren waved a hand at them, and just like that it was as though she were lit with blue flame: nobody could take their eyes off of her.

Retrievers didn't glow like that. The Wren especially never glowed like that. And yet, tonight, she did.

"You were invited here, not because you're brave, or smart, or beautiful—sorry, Lex—but because we believe that you understand the situation we face, out there on the street. Because you're tough enough to see that, and see what needs to be done next."

She glared at them all. Barely over five feet tall, looking like you could break her in two without much effort, and the current coming off her was like a contained wildfire, snapping and crackling. It was inspiring and motivating, feeling the power she brought into the room. It made you believe that you were unstoppable, that you could do anything, cause anything, solve anything, with that on your side.

It scared the hell out of Danny, and—even though the demon's besnouted face was damned difficult to read—he suspected that P.B. felt exactly the same.

Didier, as usual, was impossible to read.

Wren was on a roll, and not just because she was still pissed at Sergei and his damned presumption, that he could just up and follow her, come in like nothing had changed, just because…because *nothing*. No, she was on a roll because she was *right*. She knew exactly what to say, and how, and where to look…it was a total high, and she'd pay for it eventually, but if it got the job done then that was all right.

"There are still patrols out on the street. And that's good. The *Cosa* is still hanging together, and that's better. But it's not enough. Do you know why it's not enough?" She didn't give them a chance to respond. "Because the enemy we face—the organization that has decided that we—*WE*—are the cause of ill in this modern world— is determined to wipe us out. Not contain us, not 'tame' us. Eradicate us. Exterminate us. Not even with the respect that you would give a wolf pack, but the way you would a germ, a disease."

She could feel the heat coming off the crowd in front of her, the two-dozen-plus who had responded catching her current and letting it feed their own. Part of her, a small deep-down part locked inside was horrified. She was instigating a mob, for God's sake!

The rest of her, the one who could see and was seen—was grimly satisfied. Sergei's story, of the showdown between his former mentor Andre Felhim, her former liaison with the Silence and the de facto leader of the Silence—this Duncan bastard—should not have been a surprise: Sergei's belief in the Silence's mission had never seemed to square with what she knew about them. A messianic hell-razer with delusions of "Null-Humanity First" subverting the core of the organization made all the pieces that hadn't fit before fall nicely and neatly into place.

"We are not going to be treated like an infestation, like a mistake of nature!" she told them, again not waiting for a response. Better to fill them with her certainty than allow any smidge of doubt to get in. That she knew instinctively, the same way she knew they would see her now, that her natural ability to fade into the shadows had been burned out by her fury.

Hands on her back, shoving her down. The casual disregard of her, not only her life but her very existence, as though she were nothing to be concerned over, nothing more than a mud splatter that might stain their clothing...

Somewhere inside her, one of the many small boxes cracked open, just a hairline fracture, and a darkness slid out. She felt it, but was too busy to track it down and slam the box back shut on it.

"We are not going to be exterminated. We are not sheep to the slaughter—we are the *Cosa Nostradamus* and they will learn what it means to be the hunted!"

She had them: she could feel it, a wave of current, hot as lava. It filled the room until there was no more room for oxygen, until it was all you could breathe.

"And we know how to hurt them. We know how to bring them down. And you, my cousins, my sisters and brothers, will be the ones to do it."

And she would show them how. It wasn't pretty, and it wasn't fair, but it would work. They would be the sharpshooters, the infiltrators, the sudden poison in the veins, while the rest of the *Cosa*, however valiantly and futilely, fought what they thought was the front line.

And she——she would be the dagger winging its way from the back, to strike the Silence from behind, and deliver the coup de grace.

The room had emptied, most of the attendees going off in pairs or small groups. It was dark now, and dangerous. Sergei had seen a number of Talent carrying small tubes, some of them obviously custom-decorated, but most a matte black, and wondered what they were for. He didn't think anyone would tell him, if he asked.

Wren was off in a corner, listening intently to a very tall, very lean, very dark-skinned Talent wearing a black jellaba and white sneakers, who was waving his hands in an elegant pattern that might have been spell-casting or simply emphatic gesturing. She didn't seem at all disturbed, whichever it was.

In fact, she seemed almost tranquil, if you could call anything that flickered so intensely with current, tranquil. A narrow band of red strobed her spine from neck to tailbone, mingling with dark blue and darker green bands that wrapped around her rib cage. It was lovely. And very, very disturbing.

"You okay?" P.B. asked, out of the until-then shared silence.

"No."

"Yah." It was an agreement, an understanding, an indictment, all in one word.

The two of them sat next to each other in folding chairs, their legs stretched out, arms crossed over their chests. It looked a little more natural on Sergei, but P.B. pulled it off pretty well, his battered slouch hat pulled over his eyes.

"She did a good job," Sergei observed.

"Yah."

"You see the current around her?" He wanted to make sure he wasn't hallucinating it. Or maybe he wanted to be told that he *was.*

"Like Northern Light, only with more attitude?"

"Yah."

"Yah."

Damn. "If we can see it…"

"Then she's all over the place with it. Full up and going out."

"Yah."

Current was normally an invisible presence in the world. At a certain level it became visible to those who were naturally attuned to it. Taken up a notch, and sensitive Nulls—people like Sergei, who could sense current, but not use it—could see the neon flashes of magic when they were directed by a Talent or Talents. Sergei had seen more than his share of current, most recently shimmering like St. Vitus's dance over the wire rigging of the Brooklyn Bridge. Burning Bridge, the Fatae called it now.

"Everyone saw her. In the meeting," Sergei said after a pause.

"Nobody could take their eyes off her," the demon agreed.

"Yah." Such a useful word, that was. "That's not good."

"No."

Wren had always been proud of her ability to, as she once told Sergei, paint herself blue and waltz naked through Grand Central Station at rush hour without anyone noticing her. It was part of her skillset, how her Talent manifested, and what made her so damn good at what she did.

"She's pushing current," the demon said.

"Pushing?"

"Shoving it too high. Like turning the sound up to eleven on your speakers."

"Yah." A long pause, then Sergei said, "Good way to blow your speakers."

"Yah."

Horrible word, "yah."

Sergei shifted in his chair, studying the tips of his shoes so that he didn't have to look at Wren any more. "You think she's going to…"

"Nah." Now it was the demon's turn to pause. "She knows what she's doing."

"Yah?"

"Yah."

"Good."

There was an uneasy silence, where both of them were aware that the other didn't believe that it was good, at all. Or that she really, completely, knew what she was doing.

"She needs to ground," Sergei said. "If even I can see the current flaring around her…and its dark colors. She's usually brighter, jewel tones. Today…when she was talking, it was all darker." Still bright, still lovely, but the undertones were night, not noon.

"Don't even think about it," P.B. said, pushing his hat up and turning his head slightly to look at the human.

"I'm not." He was, of course. He couldn't not think about it; the hairs on his arms and neck lifted whenever even a hint of her current touched him. But if he denied it strongly enough, it would go away.

"Humans aren't meant to be grounded in, not that way." The demon had slid his hat back down even farther; it covered his eyes entirely now, his muzzle all that was keeping it from sliding onto his chin. "You know that."

Sergei didn't turn to look at the demon, afraid that he might react somehow, give something away.

"Relax, man. I'm the one she went to, after your little dustup. I don't know the specifics but I've seen enough over the years to guess. You got yourself a hunger, and she's smart enough not to feed it."

"She wasn't quite smart enough."

"Huh." P.B. looked thoughtful. "That explains a lot."

"She's going to…burn out." He didn't say what he almost said. He didn't even think it. But the demon heard him anyway.

"No, she won't."

"The way she's—"

"She won't. I'm here. That's why my creator made me. Us. Demon."

The words had the feel of bloody meat, something dragged out unwilling, and Sergei sat, forcibly, on the urge to demand more, to interrogate the demon until he stopped speaking elliptically and started telling the human what he needed to know.

You didn't do that to demon. And you didn't do that to friends.

"Humans aren't meant to be grounded in," the demon repeated. "Not even Talent, so absolutely not Nulls. Not unless you want to kill them."

It was a pointed comment, in more ways than one.

A few years back, he and Wren had run across a number of Talent—wizzed, the crazies of the *Cosa*—who appeared to be bursting into interior flame, like an inverse human combustion. Overrush, Wren had called it. When current became too much, and imploded their systems.

Wren said that they had always thought it was an end result of wizzing, of letting too much current override your system until you effectively committed suicide. Until that job, when they discovered you could cause someone to overrush, by directing—by forcing current into another, unprepared body. Current as weapon.

Sergei had always thought it was the Council's fault, even though Wren, younger and more innocent then, had denied the possibility that one Talent would do that to another. Now, he was all too certain it had been the Silence, testing modes of attack on victims nobody would miss.

Every time he craved her touch, he was asking her to, in effect, do that to him. Assisted suicide, not murder, but all the more cruel for it. All the times she had grounded in him during jobs, had used him, willingly, as a safe harbor…it had fed his addiction, created and enhanced it, all in the name of keeping her safe from her own power.

"She can ground in you?" He knew she could: had seen it, had heard the demon say so, before. But he needed the reassurance, no matter how painful it was for him, personally, to be replaced.

"Trust me, human," the demon said. Then, "I'll be there for her. All her life, whenever she turns around. To my dying breath. That was what you told me to do, isn't it?"

It had been, at the Bridge. He had turned away the demon's offer of help with his own battle, and sent him to Wren. Sent him to where he was supposed to be. Where they both knew he was supposed to be.

"She trusts you."

"I've given her cause for trust." P.B. met his gaze squarely, not blinking.

Ow. That stung, no less for being justified. But hadn't he given her cause for trust? He had told her, over and over again, that he had chosen his side, and she had not believed him. She had claimed to know him, and his motivations, better than he did himself. How much was he to blame, then, for refusing to prove once again where his loyalties rested? Especially when giving that information might have caused the death of people he had once worked with, had liked, respected?

He did things his own way. He always had. And he did not like being backed into a corner. Wren had known that, too, and allowed them to do it anyway.

To drive him away. To keep him safe.

There was a double loop of irony there, but he was too tired to appreciate it.

"Humans are complicated."

"Damn straight," the demon agreed.

Wren had a headache. And a backache. And someone shouting at her.

"Everywhere! I swear, the news is everywhere!"

"What news? What everywhere?" Bamidele was a great guy—class act and class Talent—but he tended to be surprisingly excitable. Wren resisted the urge to duck away from those gesturing arms and instead caught his wrists in a gentle hold. Her hands weren't tiny, but they barely fit around the thick bones, surprising in a guy so tall and skinny.

"'Dele. Details. Slow, and clear. Please."

He opened his mouth, then closed it, as though surprised that no sound came out. He looked down at his now-motionless arms, and opened his mouth again.

She took pity on him, and released her grip.

"The news. About our battle with the…with Them. It's everywhere. I mean, it's gotten out of the city."

"We did sort of make a mess," Wren said wryly. "I'm not surprised gossip has spread." The *Cosa* could gossip like a clutch of hens, when they didn't have anything better to do, and often even when they did.

"Not gossip. We're news!" 'Dele was way too excited; he was exhausting her. She reached down and stroked up some current, using it like a shot of espresso directly into her veins. She was so very, very tired; she couldn't remember feeling this worn down even after the

Frants case, when she'd thought she was going to die. A strand of dark blue slid up her spine, reaching into her brain and sparking her back into life.

"News?"

"News. As in, people calling to offer support."

That was more effective even than current. "Who, and how much support?"

Bamidele subsided slightly. "Verbal support."

"Of course."

He shuffled his feet, and only then did Wren notice that he was wearing snow-white sneakers under his black jellaba. The sight made her blink several times, and lose track of what he was saying.

"Seven e-mails from Australia. Seven! How they heard there, I don't know."

Wren did. Her instant messenger buddy ohsobloodytalented had been busy, as promised

"Two telegrams from Asia. A demon courier from Montreal. And a postcard from Wales. I think it's from Wales. It's in what looks like Welsh. How can we have an entire city of Fatae and nobody who can read Welsh?"

"Welcome to Manhattan. But all we're getting is 'good luck, catch you when it's over?'" She sighed. "I supposed I didn't really expect anything else."

"There are borders and boundaries," another voice said, damnedly pragmatic. 'Dele and Wren both turned to meet the newcomer, who was holding what Wren assumed was the postcard in question. The older man was slight, gray, and dignified. "And they all exist for good reason. They hold, even under stress, especially under stress, for good reason."

"I don't need to be lectured by you, Ayexi."

"I'm not lecturing. And you're leaking current all over the place. Shut it down, Genevieve."

Ayexi had gone over to the Council in his retirement, but he had been the Talent who taught Wren's own mentor, John Ebeneezer, and the lines of mentorship were sacrosanct in the *Cosa*. Wren pulled the current out of her spine and sent it coiling back into her core. "Shut down, sir."

He gave her a dirty look, which turned into a more searching one. She stared back, and they locked gazes.

"Don't you sir me, granddaughter."

Wren let her gaze drop.

"The *Cosa* will hold their lines. The Fatae will stay on their side of the lines. The Council may not be good for much, by your standards—by our standards—but they knew what they were doing when they set themselves up in regional forms."

"KimAnn didn't think so." She couldn't resist the jab.

"And have you heard from Madame Howe recently?"

Ow. He knew she hadn't. Nobody had. She was starting to suspect nobody was going to, either. When the Council mages decided to sit on one of their own, the sittee stayed sat on. They had managed to hide themselves from the Silence for decades, too, before she told Sergei, and Sergei spilled the beans.

"Genevieve." His voice was conciliatory now. "The others cannot interfere."

"But they can offer support." 'Dele was practically bouncing up and down in his excitement, and it wasn't a pretty sight. "That is not interference, is it?"

She returned her attention to him, laser-sharp. "Talk to me, 'Dele. What kind of support are we talking about? And from who?"

He handed over the telegram. Wren scanned it, feeling her

eyebrows rise all the way into her hairline. She finished reading, and handed it to Ayexi.

Even the old man was impressed.

"A nice trick, if they can do it."

"They'll do it," Wren said. Australia was coming through, bless their upside-down stubborn selves. She could almost feel the rush of current come into her system, stirring the coils already in residence. More would follow; she was sure of it. The *Cosa* was worldwide. Split into geographic factions to prevent turf battles exactly like the one KimAnn Howe was—*had been*—trying to stir up, but *Cosa* was *Cosa*. Family.

And, in need, family shared. Money. Food. *Current*.

eleven

"You want another cup, hon?"

Wren nodded, but the waitress was already pouring. In her mind, the only thing wrong with Manhattan had been the lack of a real, true, nontrendy, inexpensive twenty-four-hour diner: when the Mudniks had opened this place last year, not two blocks from her apartment in the West Village, Wren had almost cried from joy. She had been too busy to give them the business they deserved since then, but she intended to make it up to them now. Especially since, contrary to expectation, not only was their coffee not bad, it was damn good.

Besides, she wasn't sure if she'd be allowed into a Starbucks again anytime soon.

It had been the kind of long damn day that needed a cup—or seven—of damn good coffee, too. She had been up and running since pretty much dawn, and while she didn't much care when she worked—morning or night was much the same, to her—she did resent twelve-hour workdays.

She was going on her sixteenth hour now and, from the look of the man sitting opposite her, he wasn't far behind.

"You think you can do it?"

"I don't think it can be done," Ayexi said. He had refused the offer of a refill, and now sat across from her, moving the empty white mug in his hands restlessly, as though if he rubbed it enough a genie would pop out and grant him his wishes.

She waited, drinking her coffee and wishing the slithering coils of current in her core would settle. All day she had been restless, and she couldn't quite pinpoint why. The level of energy she'd had to use in the meeting, you'd think she'd want to crash, not go out and joust with a thunderstorm.

"Yes." He pursed his lips, looked down into his empty mug, and then nodded once, a sharp movement. "I think—*think,* mind you— that we can do it."

"It" was the chore she had set him and his cohorts at—to create a battery of some kind, a long-distance battery that could receive the current being offered and store it until it was needed—and could be accessed by anyone with the proper password. And it had to be done quietly, without any obvious fuss, because if this worked, a battery of that sort could be used in another time, another place, against other Talent, in exactly the kind of turf wars the boundaries were, as Ayexi pointed out, designed to prevent. Talent were no more immune to internecine posturing than the rest of humanity.

She was asking them—Ayexi and whomever else he pulled into it—to create a unique technological magical device…and then destroy it when it had—hopefully—served its purpose. To pull off a miracle, and never be noted in any history books for it. Wren would have felt sympathy, if she had been able to feel anything except the itch and slide of current inside her.

"So go. Do it."

Ayexi nodded once again, as much a salute as she would ever get from the old man, and slid out from behind the table. She didn't ask him how, or who—she didn't want to know. Just that it got done.

Sometimes, you didn't want to ask questions. Sometimes, it was better not to know what was being done at your request.

That thought caused her to raise her eyes and look across the restaurant. None of the offers, however sideways, of help they got, none of it was going to matter worth a damn if the conversation happening over there didn't pan out.

Sergei was sitting very still, spine upright, shoulders back, and head tilted just every so slightly. He was the very picture of respectful attention being paid to the person he was speaking with, if you went by standard body language.

She knew Sergei, though. She knew his body's slang. He was uncomfortable, unhappy, and distracted. The more he looked attentive, the less he wanted to be there.

She hadn't asked him to do this. Or, she had, but only to discover that he had already gone there and done that. Been doing it for months now, apparently. Damn him.

She drank the rest of her coffee, and waited.

About ten minutes later, Sergei's shoulders relaxed. Just a bit, barely more than a half inch lowering of his spine, but to Wren it was like a bell chiming in the chrome-and-plastic dining room. The two men spoke a minute or three longer, then the other man reached under the table. Wren would have tensed, except Sergei's chin was raised, not lowered. He was expectant in a good way, not bad.

Not that Sergei hadn't been wrong, in the past. There was that incident with the crossbow and the farmer in Idaho, for example. And the busker on the V train. And...

For a moment, the memory of simpler, if not happier times occupied her, enough that she almost missed the man reaching across the table to hand Sergei a long, rounded packet; like a poster tube, only shorter.

That was it—no further chitchat or extended goodbyes. Sergei took the tube, stood up, and walked out the door.

Wren waited, catching the waitress's eye and indicating that she'd like one more cup of coffee, please. Not that it would fool anyone who knew them, but gossip knew that they were on the outs, and who was she to mess with gossip? Especially when it suited her needs, to have people think that Sergei wasn't part of what might or might not be happening.

By the time she got back to the apartment, it was nearly 1:00 a.m. She did the math, quickly. Yeah, she'd been awake since 5:00 a.m. the morning before, and in action since 7:00 a.m. Her body was running on the memory of fumes, and even the nonstop whisper of current was turning into a lullaby. Her legs felt like they were filled with helium, and her head like it was made out of lead.

"You look like crap."

She didn't even bother locking the dead bolt on the door, but rested her forehead against the painted metal and closed her eyes, feeling his hands resting on her shoulders. Long fingers reached inevitably for exactly the right points, and began to massage them.

"Blueprints?" she asked.

"Three buildings, all high probability targets. They can wait until the morning."

"It *is* morning."

"Wren." Sergei's voice was an odd mix of amusement, exasperation, and concern. "Sleep. Come on. You need to sleep."

She needed a lot of things. She didn't think she was going to get many of them.

"Come on, Wren. Bed. To sleep." His fingers kept pushing pressure points in her neck and shoulders and she could feel a groan rise in her throat in response. Everything suddenly felt gooey and damped-down. Even the restless core that hadn't stopped growling in days was quiet.

It was safe to be with him. Right now, this moment, he could ask all he wanted, and even if it was her heart's desire, she couldn't have given him even a flicker of current-touch. She was just too tired.

"Come to bed, Wren."

She went.

There was warmth in her bed. Wren reached for it, blindly. Warm flesh. Soft, smooth, familiar. Curving here, straight lines there. And a slight, very slight snore rising from it, like the purring of a great cat. Hrmmmmm. She slinked her way across the bed, snuggling into that warmth, one arm curving around to better fit the pieces together.

This was such a wonderful idea, two to a bed. Why hadn't anyone thought of it earlier?

When she woke all the way a few hours later, her cheek was resting between Sergei's shoulder blades, her arm was around his waist, and his leg was crooked back over hers, as though to keep her still. And he wasn't snoring any more.

"Hrmmmm," she said from deep in her throat.

"Hrmmm yourself," came the response, a little more vocalized. She had known from the lack of snoring that he was awake, but not if he was aware. He always had woken up better, faster than she did. He could probably remember how they had gotten here…

Oh, right. She remembered now. Coming back, wired and exhausted and totally drained. His hands pushing her into the darkened bedroom, *her* bedroom; getting her clothing off with the ease of practice; sliding her under the covers and his weight following her onto the mattress. A brief, light kiss on the forehead, and a touch of his hand on her hip, and before she could take advantage of the promise in that, she had been lost to dreamland.

Well, she was awake now. Sort of. She still felt weak as a kitten, but in her muzzy state, she was also playful as one. And horny. Which wasn't really a kitten-thing, but maybe her brain should just shut off, now?

It did.

Her hand moved from his waist, down over his hip, caressing the skin there before sliding lower.

"Hrmmmmmmmm," she said again. "Looky what I found."

"Wren…"

His voice wasn't warning her off. Far from it, in fact. His body shifted, allowing her better access. Fingertips touched his cock, which was still soft, but she could feel the blood rushing to it as she stroked.

"Missed you."

She wasn't sure which one of them said it. It didn't matter, anyway. He turned within her embrace, forcing her to shift in order not to lose her hold on him.

"Easier the other way," she muttered. "I can never get a good hold at this angle."

"Angle's just fine," he said, kissing her mouth, then her cheekbone, dipping the tip of his tongue into her ear as he brushed sleep-sweaty hair from her neck and nuzzled there.

"You…taste good." His voice, low to begin with, went even

deeper, and she shivered in response. He moved on from her collar-
bone to her breasts, his lips feather-soft, his tongue warm and moist.
He knew that she hated what she called "hound-mouth," and was
careful not to drool too obviously. But she giggled anyway, squinch-
ing away from him.

"Hound."

"And you are a lovely, toothsome piece of meat," he growled in
some sort of mock-masher voice, making her laugh out loud.

"That's horrible. Stop that."

"What, this?"

She arched under his touch. "Oh, no, keep doing that." She was
drowsy still, her body alert and responsive but her brain cotton-soft,
and...

She did an almost panicky core-check, and was relieved to
discover that the usually restless strands and snakes of current
inside her were also blurred and lazy, sulking under a sooty fog
that would have been disturbing if it wasn't such a relief.
Whatever she had done to herself yesterday, it was taking a while
to recharge.

That was good. That meant it was still safe to do this.

She grabbed him by the back of the head, threading her fingers
through his hair, and brought him back up so that they were nose-
to-nose.

"I'm going to make you scream," he told her seriously.

"Go for it," she said in return, and smiled at him, canary feathers
in the corner of her mouth. She planned to make him vocalize, too.

Several hours later, Sergei looked over his shoulder at Wren
where she sat at the counter. "You have food in the fridge."

She rolled her eyes, looking up from the blueprints in front of her to give him the full benefit of the reaction. "You really shouldn't be so surprised by that. I am an adult, capable of taking care of myself."

The look he gave her in return was equal parts disbelief and amusement. "Right. The only reason there's anything more than milk and bread in here is because P.B.'s been crashing with you."

"What, you've been keeping tabs?" He kept tabs on them, and P.B. apparently had been keeping tabs on Sergei—was she the only person in the world who didn't snoop?

Sergei's tone was perfectly mild and reasonable. "You told me to go away. You didn't tell me to stop giving a damn."

"I told you…"

They were going to get into a fight; she could feel it. He was goading her for some reason. Wren consciously relaxed her shoulders, feeling the tension ease out through the elbows, visualizing it dripping onto the floor. Damn. It worked. Lee had been right: controlling arguments was a lot like controlling current, in a way: all about visualizing before you reacted.

She wondered if, when this was all over, she'd be able to teach classes in anger management and argument negotiation to the rest of the *Cosa.* And how much they'd be willing to pay for it.

And only then did she realize that she had thought of Lee without the usual pang of regret and responsibility.

She supposed that, in the wider view, losing one friend no matter how horribly wasn't such a trauma any more. Not after seeing so many die on the Bridge.

That thought left her depressed, and tired. More tired. Any more tired and they could just bury her.

Sergei went back to the refrigerator, pulling out a carton of eggs, milk, and a slab of some kind of cheese that Wren didn't remember seeing in there. Looked like she was going to be fed whether she was hungry or not.

"Refill my mug?" she asked, handing him the near-empty coffee cup. It was a dark blue with red lettering on it; she didn't remember where she had—literally—picked it up, but it was ugly and she determined to break it as soon as she remembered—when it wasn't in use. Her cabinets were filled with mugs she had seen and walked off with, either because she was using them at the time, or just thought it would be nice to have. Some people walked off with matchbooks, or pens—she took coffee mugs.

I'm not a klepto. Really. I just forget sometimes I'm not working.

He handed her the mug, topped off, and she went back to the blueprints, tuning out the semifamiliar noises of Sergei making himself at home in her kitchen. There had been five plans in the packet the man had given to Sergei: three of them buildings she already knew from the outside, and two entirely new to her—one in Albany and one in Philadelphia.

"Christ, anything but Philadelphia," she muttered. Although it could be worse—they could have bought property in Trenton that matched the parameters.

"How much real estate does the Silence own, anyway?"

Sergei didn't stop whisking the eggs. "They've been around since the turn of the last century, and the Founders were almost all wealthy men."

"In other words, a lot."

"Not all of them are occupied by the organization. Several are revenue generators."

"Oh, please. Tell me that they're slumlords."

He laughed. "Sorry, no."

Of course not. She was sure that every property they controlled was spit-shined and perfect—until you opened up the walls and found the rot. Not that she was prejudiced or anything.

Oh, wait. She was.

"This one in Albany doesn't look plausible. The size is right, and they have the facilities to hide a small village in there, but it's too high-tech a building. All it would take would be one Talent breaking free to bring the entire thing down. Sort of like your apartment building."

"Oh?"

"Oh, yeah. That much power in the walls, between all the high-end tech and the extra generator you guys have in the basement, and that elevator...it's like one of those all-you-can-eat buffets in Vegas; you know it's a bad idea but you can't resist filling your plate that one last time, just 'cause there's so much and it all looks so good."

He looked pained like he'd never thought of that before. "Please don't crash my building. I have a lot of money tied up in it."

She shook her head and went back to the sheets. "The one in Philly... It's got the opposite problem. The building's tall and narrow, and entirely aboveground. They'd need a place to bunk these kids while they were..." She stopped, not sure what word to use. "Torture" was probably right, but saying it made her mouth feel dirty, and "training" was too mild for the results she had seen.

"Indoctrinating them."

"Right." As bad a word as any, she supposed.

"So the three in Manhattan, then?" He put a dish in front of her, and placed a fork in her hand.

"Two in Manhattan. One in Queens. I like that one best, actually." She pushed the plate to one side and stuck the fork into the omelet, watching with approval as cheese oozed out the side, then pulled the specific plan out of the stack.

"It's an older building—nice and solid. Plaster and rock."

"Like this place."

"Yeah. Huh." She hadn't thought of that. "Anyway. Four floors underground, two of which are massive, and have their own security system. Only one of the buildings in Manhattan has that, and it's got another company subleasing the top floors. Good for camouflage, but the Silence always struck me as the type to keep their dirty work quiet and tucked away, right?"

"Ain't nobody's business but their own," he said, in a way that made her think that he was quoting something. She assumed he was agreeing with her.

The aroma of the omelet suddenly hit her nose, and she realized that she was starving. Moving the sheets carefully to one side, she reclaimed the plate and started eating.

"So. I'll check out that building in Manhattan, just to see if there's anything onsite that triggers a reaction, but my money's on the one in Queens. I'll do a full reconnoiter on that one." She started to go on, then hesitated.

Once, she would have talked out her entire plan in front of him, trusting him to see where she was forgetting something, or making an error in judgment or expectation. Once, he would have been with her every step of the way, from acceptance to execution of the job.

Once...wasn't now.

Having him here had been wonderful. Sex had been...exactly what the witch-doctor would have ordered. But she could feel the gentle hum of her core waking up, the gray fog that had shielded it dispersing as her body regained strength.

If it were simply a matter of the *Cosa's* distrust of Sergei, she would damn them all to an old hot hell and be done with it. But she still wasn't sure that she trusted him. Not to betray them—he had proven thrice over that he hadn't, that he wouldn't. Not willingly. She might not trust her instincts any more, but she could trust facts. And she could trust P.B., who never let his personal feelings about anyone get in the way of survival.

But it wasn't about that.

If she could feel her current surging again, that meant she was recovered. Normal again. And normal, for her, for any Talent, was the casual use of current.

And that meant a risk for Sergei. Not that she'd fry him just by breathing: she only did that to his electronics. But last night...

You're going to have to figure something out. Some way to either cure him of that need for current-touch, or...

Or some way to insulate him from the damage it caused to his internal organs. Might as well wish for world peace and cheap rents while she was at it.

"What are you going to do now?"

Sergei picked at his own omelet, watching her eat with renewed enthusiasm. It was a small victory, but a satisfying one, to get food into her when she was working.

"I thought I'd go downtown to the gallery, check on things there. We had a new installation in last week—very avant garde. You'd hate it."

"You get the weirdest stuff in, sometimes." And he sold it, too, which always amazed her. Sergei had one hell of a finger on the pulse of what people wanted to display in their living rooms.

"And then—" he was being deliberately casual, which set her warning bells to ringing "—I thought I'd stop by and see P.B."

"Oh?" She could be deliberately casual, too.

"Well, you're on a job, so I thought that he could...catch me up on things."

"I thought that you were keeping tabs on the situation."

All right, so she wasn't quite as casual as he was. He had more practice.

"There's no way a Null could ever keep tabs on the situation," he said without any obvious bitterness. "I was just…going about business. Business that occasionally intersected with the situation, and allowed me a view in."

"Uh-huh." It sounded plausible, which meant that it was probably true. But no way she thought that was the whole story. Not after he was able to dip into his contacts yesterday and come up with exactly what she needed with two phone calls. Sergei was good, but that required some forethought. Priming the pump, like her mother always said. And knowing the way her mind worked, which he excelled at. Of course, he'd had a lot of practice. But then, so had she. At knowing his mind, that was.

Wren blinked, feeling her thoughts get tangled. She was getting fuzzy again. That was happening a lot, even before she went into the theater's tunnel. Not good. And probably not unobserved, based on the vibes she was getting off demon, Fatae, and human at various points since her speech the night before.

"Catch you up on things…and do a little plotting on how to keep Valere from losing all her marbles entirely?"

He didn't even bother to look surprised, or shocked, or any other faux facial reaction. "Do you think you're about to?"

"It's crossed my mind once or twice over the past few days, yeah." Of course it had. Or rather, the fact that it hadn't occurred to her had crossed her mind. Her entire thirty years of existence had involved reacting, not attacking. She had to be hired in order to put herself at risk, and when she did so, she always worked to minimize the danger not only to herself but to those around her.

Life was sacred. Her mother had taught her that. Her mentor Neezer had confirmed it, to the point that he had left rather than endanger her when he started to lose his mind. Sergei, for all that he could be a cold-blooded bastard at times, thrilled to the ways humans expressed their life in art, and his joy in that was her joy as well.

And here she was, planning to kill as many people—as many Nulls—as she could, once she had every remaining Talent safely out of there. Planning to have Talents all across the tri-state area attack—and kill, unspoken but implied—as many Silence Operatives as they could find, on her command. That wasn't a bad sign?

And then there was the weirdness with her current. The gray fog, and the black sludge. The… Thing that happened in the tunnel. That…that was something she wasn't ready to think about yet, much less talk about. She'd rather talk about killing people.

His face was calm and composed, his body language was relaxed, and almost languid. His eyes gave him away; they focused directly on her, not flicking back and forth the way they normally did, taking in everything going on around him without even being consciously aware of what he was doing. She used to think he was just naturally hyper. Now she could recognize the signs of a trained observer. A Silence Operative.

He clearly saw stuff he didn't like, but he didn't push the issue. "So. You go and scout your buildings. I'll pore over paperwork. Somebody may or may not try to kill either one of us today, and if we survive, we get to do more of the same tomorrow?"

"Sounds about right." She could feel herself almost grinning as she said it. "Just like old times." Except not really. And the grin hurt.

"Great. Finish your breakfast, at least."

* * *

Queens wasn't quite another country, but the moment the subway train left Manhattan, Wren had the semihysterical thought that border guards would come through the cars, asking to see passports and visas.

The address she wanted was a hike from the subway exit, but it was a nice day, and she enjoyed window-shopping as she went. She didn't cook, but the Asian grocery stores were fascinating even when you didn't know what anything in the displays were or what it tasted like.

A few blocks out, and the neighborhood changed: fewer storefronts and more offices, old buildings repurposed and renovated. She checked the street numbers and then paused to lace up her boot, making sure that her bag was safely stashed with the handle under her knee, to dissuade any would-be mugger. "Five, four, three, two…"

It was habit more than need, but habit was comforting, and it soothed her nerves. By the time she hit four, Wren had slipped into fugue state, like stepping into a steam shower, warm and comforting. While she knotted the laces, she let herself look at the third building down the street out of the corner of her eye, using both her physical and magical senses to get a quick take on it.

"Oh, not nice. Not nice at all." Auras and tarot cards and crystal-wavers were either con artists or clueless, in her experience, but the building in front of her had distinct icky vibes sliming the walls. Whatever happened in there was not nice, and had been going on for a while.

Laces tied, she grabbed her bag and stood up. To a casual observer, she was merely stretching after bending over. Her leather jacket rode up, letting a breeze hit the T-shirt underneath.

Yeah, that sucker was not very nice. Pity, since it was a pretty building. Dark red brick, three stories visible. Took up almost half the block, which was unusual around here. According to the blueprints, the building went down another three floors, a lot more detailed than the usual subbasements you'd expect to find in this area.

And they had a lot of power in there—a *lot* of power. She could feel it, like a wink and a come-on. Massive generators running.

This was the place. She didn't need to check the slip of paper in her pocket: she knew it.

Fine. She should move on, keep walking and not draw any attention. There was no reasonable reason to linger on the corner. But something kept her there, looking off into space, her lips slightly open, like someone suddenly caught by an important thought.

Do it.

Stupidity.

But it would tell you, once and for all, no doubt...

Or maybe not. You think you could reach in?

Why not? They'd be worried about what's inside...an obvious warning, even if they knew how to do it, would attract attention. Exactly what they don't want.

The logic was flawed. Wren knew that. But the temptation was irresistible.

Hello?

A general ping, sent in a wide wave, covering the entire block rather than the specific building. She waited.

Hello?

Nothing.

Wren tilted her head. Wait...

Hello? she sent again.

Nothing. But…something. There was an echo there, yes. Something that might indicate someone was listening, but not responding.

Wren strode forward again, mixing with the crowd of lunchtime workers. Someone was in there. A Talent. A Talent who was either hiding, or scared. Or both.

The Retrieval was a go.

"They're agitated."

Agitated was overstating it. The three teenagers in the room were talking to each other, their heads bent forward to create the illusion of privacy. But it was the most animated they had been in weeks. "There was a disturbance outside," the lab tech said.

"A disturbance?" Duncan had the poor timing to be in the research building that day, the same day Andre had stopped by. On a Friday afternoon, of all times—the one day he had thought to not run into even the most workaholic of men. Was it poor timing? Or had the Director of R&A made a point to show up here and now, to send a message to his newest reportee? If so, that meant he was being followed, reported on, not trusted yet. It was not unexpected, but meant he had not made as much progress as he had hoped.

"A passing disturbance," Andre dismissed the report, and his own fears. "I suspect someone pinged another Talent in the neighborhood, and it passed through the building."

"Pinged?" Duncan sounded like a broken record, and he knew it, from the scowl on his face.

"A form of communication. Like instant messengering or texting, without the computer or phone." Sergei had mentioned it in several of his reports, back when his former protégé was still sending in reports. They had thought at first that it was a form of telepathy, but research had proven that it was far more rudimentary than that.

To continue the texting simile, it was to telepathy the way a text message was to an essay.

If Talents had been able to communicate at length via thoughts alone, things would probably have turned out much differently. Andre wasn't sure if he regretted that or not.

Duncan turned and looked at Andre. "Yes. I know what it is, thank you. But why would anyone be 'pinging' here, in this neighborhood? Should we consider this a first attack?"

Even the lab tech blinked in surprise at that, although he was very careful to keep his face schooled to impassive concentration on his work.

"Possibly because Talent live out here and someone was probably checking in with a friend," Andre said, trying very hard to keep any condescension out of his voice and off his face. "You elitist idiot," was what he was thinking.

A glimpse at the lab tech, who probably didn't make enough to afford to live even in this neighborhood, confirmed that he wasn't the only one thinking that.

Good. Duncan's hold on his troops wasn't absolute.

Duncan turned his head slightly, looking up toward the ceiling. Andre knew that look—a message was coming in through the device over Duncan's ear. Andre himself would rather wait for a messenger to come down the levels, rather than rely on delicate tech this close to Talent, no matter how tame, but that was Duncan in a nutshell—arrogant.

And, in this case, perfectly correct. The barriers between the control room and the spaces where the Talent were kept appeared strong enough to protect all the technology—although Andre had noticed that the tech wore gloves, and had thick rubber soles on the bottom of his shoes.

"They spotted the Talent outside," Duncan informed them. "Someone has been placed to follow him, and see what he does."

For the sake of that poor bastard's soul, not to mention his health, Andre prayed he simply went back to work or school, and did nothing further to attract the Silence's attention.

Not that it would matter, in the end. Poor bastards, all of them.

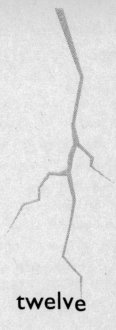

twelve

The speakers dropped the sound of Édith Piaf into Sergei's loft apartment, filling the air with melancholy and grace. Wren always said that it was a bad sign when he went to Paris, but he simply found her voice a boon to concentration. Not that he was doing much concentrating on anything today.

The gallery was closed on Fridays. As per his usual habits, he should have been working anyway, doing something productive on one of the many projects he always had running. He didn't like to sit idle. But he had woken up that morning an hour late, feeling an ache in every inch of his frame. He was getting old, the exhaustion—physical and mental—of the previous months coming home to roost.

Wren had told him last night that she would be busy with a job, and there was nothing urgent on any of his agendas, so he had turned off his cell phone, put a pot of water to boil for tea, and taken a mental health day.

And yet, that hadn't quite worked out as planned. Rather than relaxing, he was restless, unable to settle down with the newspaper or any of the books waiting on the shelf, unwilling to spend any time in the kitchen, but unusually loathe to go outside of the familiar cocoon of his apartment, as though the moment he left something important might happen that he would then miss.

And despite his words to Wren, he had no desire to stop in and chat with P.B. Their brief conversation after the meeting had, he suspected, been at least the partial cause of his restless discomfort.

So he stayed put, and nothing happened. There weren't even any good old movies on the television. A postlunch nap on the sofa was the highlight of the day, and when Sergei woke, he lay there, watching the sunlight play on the matte-textured ceiling, wondering if this was what boredom felt like.

After all that, when the knock came at his door a few minutes after four, Sergei just knew it wasn't going to be anything he wanted to hear, not even to break the ennui.

There was a moment where he considered pretending that he wasn't home. But he was too well-trained for that. He put down the book he had been trying to read, and padded to the door, the hardwood cool under his bare feet.

He had to look down to see who was waiting on the other side of the apartment door.

"We need to talk," the visitor said.

"People who start conversations like that should be shot."

The demon stared at him, and Sergei relented. "All right, come in."

He didn't even bother to ask how P.B. had gotten past the doorman and the security camera. He wasn't sure it was something he wanted to know.

"About Wren."

"I know." What else would the Fatae have come here for, if not Wren? It was their sole point of connection, these days. If something were wrong, he would have said so, right off the bat. Had the demon come to warn him off, again? Because yeah, he'd gotten the message. Nulls plus current, bad. Him specifically, worse.

The demon sat on the edge of the sofa. His short legs made it difficult for him to find a comfortable position, and he looked fleetingly like an unnaturally grave ten-year-old. A red-eyed ten-year-old wearing a white fur suit with clawed gloves.

Sergei reflected, not for the first time, that his life had taken a very strange turn somewhere right after college.

"Wren said that you might stop by," the Fatae said.

"Well, I didn't." God, he sounded petulant. Well, he felt petulant. And not a little cornered.

"Obviously." P.B. picked up Sergei's book, looked at the cover, then put it back down again. "Look, Didier... What, exactly, do you know about what's going on with her?"

"That something's wrong," he said. "Something to do with her core?" He didn't know what that something was, though, and that was concerning him. Wren wanted to just bull on forward and make like it would come all right in the end, because she said so. That was how he handled things; self-medication and stubbornness would make even the worst wounds heal. But it wasn't smart, and it wasn't what he wanted for her. He wanted to bundle her up and put her somewhere safe, the same way she had tried to do to him. Only his damage was old, and hers was new, and there was still time....

"It won't work this time."

"Reading my thoughts now, demon?" It was said lightly, but not meant that way at all.

"Don't need to. Been there, done that. You can't protect her, Didier. And you can't let her hide."

"What's the alternative—shove her out into the middle of the battlefield again with a target between her shoulders and blood leaking out of her veins? All for the good of a group that never gave a damn about her before?" The venom in his voice surprised him: not that it was there, but that he had actually let it show. From the moment the demon had shown up at Wren's apartment years ago, carrying his courier bag and a message from a prospective client, he'd made Sergei uneasy. Was it as simple as—as embarrassing as—jealousy? Or had the events of the past two years— two years P.B. had been front and center and causative for— proved that the demon really was a real threat to Wren's well-being?

"You're projecting, Didier. She's *Cosa*. We have always cared. But we're also selfish and self-absorbed cowards, all of us. Wren included. It's how we're made. Heroics are for your kind."

Sergei pulled back, his voice tight. "So let her be a coward again. Jesus, P.B., I'm a Null and I can feel there's something bad happening around her. If that goes on..."

He didn't know what would happen if it went on. He only knew it wouldn't be good. It wouldn't leave Wren alone, or untouched.

"I love her, too, Sergei." It might have been the first time the demon had ever used his first name. It didn't bode well; the coldness in his gut told him that already. "Different from the way you do, but I love her, much as my kind can. Ways you'll never be able to understand.

"But she's got something to do, here. Something maybe she always had to do, the moment this was all set in motion. You can't run from what you have to do. Trust me, I know."

Sergei had no way to argue that, except one. "And if that means sacrificing her?"

The demon's red eyes stared into the distance, then looked up at him. "We all make sacrifices. If we're lucky, we know about them before the bill comes due."

Sergei's jaw clenched, mimicking the feeling in his chest. "I don't accept that."

The demon almost laughed. "French and Russian pragmatism, trumped by an American veneer. I didn't think you would. But I had to try. You had to hear it." He got up as though to leave, then stopped. "We're not competition, you know."

Sergei didn't bother standing to see the demon out. "Yes, we are. Because I'm not going to let you and your kind consume her for the greater good. I'm done with that, once and for all."

P.B. snorted, a wet, disbelieving sound. "That's why you've spent the past few months gathering support, building an insider column for her to draw on?"

"For her," Sergei said. "Not for you. Not for any of you. To keep her alive." Because he had promised never to abandon her. Even when she sent him away.

Those red eyes were suddenly, unexpectedly sorrowful. "If it can be done, it will be done," P.B. said. "I've given what passes for my soul on that. But it may not be possible, not and do what she needs to do. Can you live with that?"

"Can you sleep at night?" His question to Joanne, come back in a different form to haunt him.

Sergei picked up his book. This conversation was over.

The demon left then, closing the door firmly behind him. And in the silence, Sergei put his book down on his lap, and stared into the abyss.

"No." No, he couldn't live with it.

Where she led, he would follow. And nobody would sacrifice her on his watch, not even for the greater good. Not even Wren herself.

Wren was pretty sure that someone was following her. Considering the neighborhood, which was still quite nice, it probably wasn't a random mugger casing the potentials, although anything was possible. No, considering where she had been, and what she had been doing, Wren thought it might be better to assume the worst: that the Silence had spotted her.

Any other time, any other place, and Wren would have triggered her no-see-me cantrip and just faded from the awareness of whoever was trying to follow her. She could do it; no matter how good the guy was, or even how many they had set on her, she was better than any Null ever trained, and most Talent, too. False modesty had its place, but not on the job.

But not today. Not now. Not these bastards. Her teeth showed in an ugly smile. If they wanted to play, she was more than willing to oblige them.

They'd find that she wasn't quite so easy to take by surprise, this time.

She let a strand of current rise, forming it between mental hands until it was wire-thin, then split it into half a dozen strands, and let them trail behind her, searching for anyone who had their attention focused on her. It was a tricky bit of work, especially since she had to keep moving, and not look as though she were doing anything more complicated than searching for the next Starbucks.

"Mal-intent
be well uncovered
and remarked."

That, she thought smugly, actually wasn't bad, as on-the-fly spell-work went. The words didn't matter so much as the force of will and concentration behind them, but when you clicked the right words, the focus was that much easier. She made mental note of the cantrip for later—a little fine-tuning and she might discover it would do more than the original use.

The strands streamed out in search of anyone who was even indirectly paying her any attention. If found, the current would give them the magical equivalent of a paintball splotch, visible to anyone Talented. If they were Talents themselves—unlikely but possible—they would know that they had been splotched, but not be able to remove it. Only she could do that.

And she wouldn't. Let everyone know. Let them be marked for the rest of their lives.

She paused to look at the most recent Lotto results, and decided on a whim to buy a ticket. Current was crap-all for influencing games of chance—it had probably been much easier when they used chips of bone or wood rather than an automated system, she presumed—and her very limited Precog had worked exactly twice in her entire lifetime, but hey, you never knew, right?

And $40 million, even after taxes, could make life so much easier.

While she waited for her ticket to spit out of the machine, keeping her attention scrupulously focused on the magazines in front of her so as not to current-screw the tech and draw unwanted attention, Wren let her nonmagical awareness of the people around her flow. Talent wasn't everything, and it wasn't the only way to be taken down. Especially with enemies who knew what they were doing—and what she was capable of doing to them.

Nothing triggered any kind of alarm: it was all perfectly normal workweek traffic. A scattering of women in suits and heels and hairstyles that screamed "administrative assistant," more professional-looking women juggling shoulder bags and attaché cases, and a handful of men in suits, most of them wearing receivers in their ears and speaking intently to someone who wasn't there.

"Must be a courthouse nearby" she muttered, reminded of the old joke that you could tell a lawyer, but you couldn't tell him much. Who had told her that joke? One of her mother's boyfriends; not the cop, not the salesman...the accountant, that was it. Steve? No, Shawn.

Wren wondered in passing whatever happened to good old Shawn. He had told some truly god-awful jokes.

"Excuse me?" A young woman came up to the stand next to her, trying to get the attendant's attention. "Excuse me, I was wondering if you could help me?"

The old guy, probably sensing that she wasn't going to be buying anything, just taking time and space that someone might be willing to pay him for, ignored her approach. So she turned to Wren.

"Could you help me? These streets, I'm used to a grid, and I think I'm lost."

Of course. The one day she was running in plain sight, someone decided she was a Good Samaritan tourist guide. Wren looked sideways, and noted a palm-sized orange stain in the shape of a starburst on the woman's forehead.

Huh. Her eyes flicked from the starburst, swept over the woman's boring blue-skirted suit and sensible shoes, and then back again. Bingo. The cantrip must have had an extra fillip to it, to not only mark the target, but bring her forward, forcing her to be noticed.

"Sure. Where are you trying to go?" Wren looked directly into the woman's eyes. They were wide and green and very pretty, exactly the kind of eyes she used to wish that she had.

There was a cesspool behind those eyes. Filth, overflowing, soiling everything it touched, everything it killed.

Rage flared in her brain, fed by and feeding her current, swirling the fog until she was dizzy with it.

There was something she could do, if she dared to...

"The bus into Manhattan?"

"Oh, sister, you are lost," Wren laughed, reaching out to touch the woman's sleeve without taking her gaze off those green eyes.

Follow. Evaluate. Eliminate if threat is determined but otherwise do not approach. Those were the orders the woman had been given. Her spell had overrun that last order.

"Yes, I..." The woman stopped speaking as current sparked from Wren's fingers into her arm, hair-thin and neon black, shooting their way up her spine and into her brain.

"You see nothing. You hear nothing. You say nothing."

Those green eyes turned inward and clouded over as Wren took her ticket from the Lotto machine, thanked the attendant, and turned the woman to walk down the street, one hand on her arm to guide her. There was a bus shelter at the corner, and Wren deposited the woman there, for the benefit of anyone who might be watching.

The woman stood there, deaf, dumb and blind, but calm under the influence of a rough current lobotomy. Someone would notice her, eventually. The Silence would come and pick her up. Or not.

Wren felt no guilt. She had been gentle, and with the right kind of treatment, the woman should be able to recover, mostly.

The woman was alive. That was all the mercy Wren was willing to grant to anyone who worked for the Silence. And even that, not for long.

thirteen

They had been in the middle of an endlessly boring discussion of the next year's budget in the main office Monday morning when word came of a problem. The only indication that something was amiss came from Duncan's sudden and obvious change in concentration from what was being said at the table to what was being whispered electronically in his ear. Whoever had contacted him, it was an exchange which clearly did not please him at all.

His angular face, almost Goya-like in its aesthetic piety, rarely showed any expression, but without his usual dark-lensed glasses, an astute observer could see something move behind his eyes that did not bode well for whomever was speaking.

The rest of the suits gathered around the conference table continued in polite subvocalizations among themselves, not willing to waste time but equally unwilling to do anything that might disrupt their master, or cause his attention to fall unhappily on them. The meeting might resume, and it might not. You had to be ready for any possibility. Andre Felhim sat back in his chair, steepled his fingers in front of him, and waited. To his left, a silver-haired woman with youthful blue eyes pulled out a PDA and entered a hurried series of notes to herself. No data transmission was allowed in or out of the room, except what Duncan controlled, but separating a Silence Operative from their electronics was like asking a cat to give up its tail.

A minute turned into two, and the conversations began to falter; people were unsure how far they might take their sidelines without risking censure.

"My apologies," Duncan finally said, standing with his usual grace and poise. "A situation has arisen that I must oversee personally. In my absence, Karl, if you would please stand in my stead and conduct the meeting?"

A flickering glance swept over the room and a crooked finger indicated that several attendees should leave the room with him. Andre was not sure if it was a good sign or bad that he was among those selected.

The Operative Director knew that he walked a tightrope each moment that he played his game out under Duncan's eye, unsure if the hand on his shoulder would be praise, or the mark of the executioner.

To all appearances he had given no offense. His words were measured, honest, and useful, his body language stubborn but respectful. Anything less, or more, would raise suspicions he could not afford. Meanwhile, underneath, he touched and prodded, testing for softness, for weakness. For allies, even if they did not yet know they would be allies, when the time came.

Duncan had a cadre, yes. But he also had employees, even within the inner circles. And not everyone had—what was Sergei's delightful phrase? Not everyone had drunk the Kool-Aid.

And on the other side of the game, he protected Sergei, as much as he could. Not because the boy had once been one of his—loyalty was only deserved so long as it was given—but because Sergei was a useful stalking horse: let Duncan assume the former Operative was the source of the strikes against them, let Duncan look to the *Cosa Nostradamus* for all his problems, then when Andre made his move, the R&D master's information—the lifeblood and currency of the Silence, and his major source of power—would be shown to be flawed and in error. And that would be the one brick that could tumble Duncan's entire castle.

All this was in Andre's mind, hidden deep, as they left the conference room, the others left behind breaking off into small huddles, plotting whatever plots they thought would rise them to the level of those Duncan had summoned.

Idiots, Andre thought.

One of the other two walking with him was Goran Jay, who had been one of Duncan's faithful from the very beginning. He had never served as an Operative, never done time in the ranks, but he was smart and sharp and not to be underestimated. The other was Gareth Hackins, one of the techs Duncan had brought on board to run his little R&D experiments.

If Andre ever had a chance, he would slip a shiv under Hackins's ribs and leave him to bleed out in an alley. There was much Andre could stomach in the name of necessity. The 3rd Team's Project was not one of them. Plus, Hackins was a slimy toad of a man, with no regard for anything except pleasing his master.

Neither of those men had been subjected to Andre's testing. There was no point: when the time came, they would have to be eliminated along with the man who held their leashes.

They rode down the elevator without speaking. You did not speak to Duncan unless he asked something of you, or you needed to impart something to him. The one crack Andre had ever heard made about the man was that Duncan had been given only so many words to use in his lifetime, and he was jealous not only of them, but of others who had more freedom.

An aide met them on the 2nd sub-level, his eyes worried although his face was calm. Like the others, he wore a sober dark suit and tie, and his shoes were spit-shined.

"Show me," was all Duncan said, but it was a royal command. The four of them moved through the offices to a large, brightly lit room, where seven displays followed twice as many feeds, switching back and forth under the discipline of one technician.

The display in the center showed a young woman seated in a chair. She was well-dressed, blond, pretty, and there was, as far as Andre could tell from her expression, nobody at all at home. Who had she been?

"Genevieve Valere," the aide said.

"What?"

Andre almost seconded that question out loud. He knew Wren Valere; he was the only member of the Silence to knowingly meet and speak with her, and that was not her.

"No, not her. Her." The tech indicated another monitor, as though to say "look for yourself." A photo, unflattering but accurate, the first one Andre had ever seen of the girl, and a scattering of information, displayed on the screen. Government records; sparse and surprisingly uninformative. No driver's license, no voting record, no arrest history. That surprised Andre, since he knew of at least two incidents where the Retriever had ended up in jail, and Talents were not known as effective hackers, to delete such information.

Still, there was nothing to say that they could not hire others to do that work for them.

Duncan stared at it, his eyes narrowing as though trying to make the few details into more.

"That was the intruder we noticed outside the Shelter Friday morning."

Intruder? Oh, the ping-maker? Hardly an intrusion—except anything Valere did she did for a reason. Hackins looked surprised, and then annoyed—clearly, even those associated with 3rd Team's Project were not as privy as they thought.

"A woman, not a man," the technician continued. "Our error."

Duncan made a small hand gesture, as though to indicate that it was a small thing, an error to be forgotten. Except that while Duncan might occasionally forgive, he never forgot. Anything.

The technician continued, avoiding Hackins's eye. Interesting, that, Andre thought. Was Hackins on his way out?

"Our agents followed, to reconnoiter. This agent approached her, against direct orders, and..." His voice trailed off.

And the blond mannequin in the main display was the result, clearly. Andre looked at her face again, forcing himself to study her expression dispassionately. Simply a mannequin, a painting, a thing. There was nobody home in that body.

The Wren Valere he had met was not a woman who would have done such a thing to another human.

He had not seen Valere since the incident on the Brooklyn Bridge, when he had been forced to do things, had justified the means as a way to a desired end.

Who was he to say that Wren Valere had not been forced to the same?

"We found her yesterday. She had been taken to a local hospital, admitted as a Jane Doe."

"Genevieve Valere." Duncan's voice was thoughtful, tinged with annoyance. A dangerous sound. "I know that name."

"Sergei Didier's charge," Andre said, because he had to. Because if he did not, another would, and eyes would turn to him as the obvious source of information that had not been given. "Also known as The Wren. The Retriever." He felt no guilt, no responsibility. Valere had brought this upon herself, by being caught in the act.

"Yes." Duncan nodded, staring at the screen. "Yes." The annoyance was stronger now, but it was not directed at Andre. "So, Didier's pet Talent, snooping around the Shelter. Incapacitating one of my people and abandoning her on the street like so much trash."

For once, Andre Felhim could see directly into Duncan's thoughts, because they were exactly the same thoughts that he would have been thinking, in that position. That he had not paid the proper attention to that particular young woman. That he would remedy that omission, now.

"Clean it up," was all Duncan said, his gaze including Hackins in the order. "Clean all of it up." Then, "Andre. Walk with me."

A cold shiver ran down Andre Felhim's elegantly clothed spine, but he hid it perfectly. Nodding as though he had been granted a great honor, he joined Duncan as they left the control room, and strolled the mahogany-paneled hallway toward Duncan's office.

"Tell me everything that you know of this Genevieve Valere."

"Beyond what was in my reports?" Andre didn't have to fake hesitation: those reports had been remarkably thorough, both the ones he had filed before turning his coat, and the ones taken from him after bowing to Duncan's leadership.

"Is there anything beyond what was in your report?"

"Of course."

Information was the currency of the Silence. You never gave up anything for free. Duncan would not believe him if he pretended otherwise.

"Your reports had indicated that she was not the sort to become involved. That, in fact, her relationship with Didier was a positive, in that it would keep him from becoming involved with anything that might be going on."

"And this was all true."

"Was?"

Andre weighed his words carefully, sorting through his answers as quickly as possible. Information was all. Disinformation was more.

"There have been a significant number of occurrences recently, some of them at our instigation, that have impacted her personality. This has in turn impacted our evaluation of her reactions."

Duncan heard him out without reaction. "In short, she's pissed at us."

Andre might not have put it in that fashion, but... "In short, yes."

"And, in your experienced opinion, what does that...pissed-ness...mean for us?"

It means that she's gunning for you, Andre thought, but he kept that thought down low, almost below his own awareness. "It means that she will be scouting us for weakness," he said out loud. "And if she finds it, she will strike."

"Yes." Duncan sounded almost regretful. "That was what I thought. It is what I would do."

Andre wondered how Wren would have reacted to that compliment. Badly, probably.

They came to Duncan's office, a large, wood-paneled space without windows. An oil landscape that Andre could only identify as being of the Hudson school graced one wall in front of the desk;

the other walls were blank. Once you were in that office, you could focus only on the man who owned it.

That man waved Andre to one of the leather-upholstered seats opposite his desk. They both looked equally innocuous, but so did a rock just before the snake came hissing out from under it. Andre seated himself with the same care he would use in moving one of those rocks. The chair was reassuringly uncomfortable, not something created to put you at ease, and Andre relaxed a little, resting his forearms on the hard-padded armrests even as Duncan settled into his own chair behind the gleaming expanse of desk.

"It is a pity that we were never able to bring her into our plans," Andre said thoughtfully, continuing their conversation. "However, the failure of trust on the Italian situation created a tension that we were not able to overcome."

"Ah, yes." Duncan sounded as though he had forgotten all about that incident, something too minor to be noted. "A regrettable situation, that."

A situation that Duncan had engineered, Andre was sure. The failure of certain important facts to make it into the dossier, and the death of the Operative—one of their own!—who was to have briefed Sergei and Valere on their arrival, were both laid squarely at Duncan's door, although it had been Andre who took the hit.

"However," Duncan said, "and regardless of how useful we have found members of that community, the truth remains that the sooner we are freed of their blighting influence, the stronger our future will be. Wren Valere and her kind are not part of that future."

"So long as she was a leash we could use to control Sergei, she was useful. And Sergei remained a loyal dog so long as that leash was in place." The leash—the contract, the promise of protection and a monthly stipend—had been slipped months before, by mutual agreement, but Andre was betting everything that he had that Duncan was not entirely positive of that fact. It had merely been Andre's word to Sergei: no annulment or amendment had been filed. "The majority of the information we were able to compile on the *Cosa* and their politics came through his reports."

"Yes. And your role in managing that relationship had been noted, and it was greatly appreciated," Duncan said, leaning forward and meeting Andre's gaze with his own, every inch the forthright and appreciative supervisor.

Andre noted the use of the past tense at the exact moment the needles came up through the armrest and entered his forearms.

Idiot, he thought, annoyed at himself, and then the world went dark.

His one consolation was that there were things that he knew that Duncan never would, now.

Like the meaning of the codeword "Distraction."

The bar was crowded and noisy even on a Monday night, and the air smelled like…Wren sniffed, then wrinkled her nose. Yeah, that was hospital-grade antiseptic. Someone must have gotten sick in the bathroom again.

"Nice place." Ron's attitude hadn't improved in the time since they had first met. Then again, hers had gotten worse, so she supposed he was doing better than she was.

"Nulls don't come here," was all she said. Not many *Cosa* would, either, honestly: the Showdown was, not to put too fine a point on it, a hole. Narrow and badly lit in addition to the noise and the smell, it was the kind of place where you'd expect the bartender to hide a baseball bat behind the bar, and the waitresses to carry switchblades under their aprons. He did, and they did.

They also brewed their own ale, and it was spectacular. She raised her glass and toasted him. "Health and wealth."

"And to you." They drank, and she could see his hesitation turn to appreciation. "I take it back," he said. "You were right."

"Of course I was." She didn't drink a lot, but when she did, it was only quality, thank you very much. "Now tell me you have something for me."

"I'm still working on the names of all the possible FocAs," he said, switching into business mode in a way she recognized. Sergei's mind switched back and forth like that. Maybe it was a guy thing. "However, I do have a list of possible distracters from our respondees for you to look at."

Distracters. Cute. The Distraction was what they ended up calling it: P.B.'s idea. It was better than her original "Plan B," she supposed. Volunteers, to sting the bear while she stole the honey back.

He pushed two sheets of lined paper across the rickety, graffiti-carved table, and she picked them up. His handwriting was surprisingly neat and readable, filling the sheets from top to bottom.

"A lot of names." She put her hand out, and he placed a pencil—chewed and worn—in her grasp. "Huh." A scratch through one name, then another. "No, no, yeah, him I don't know…" She looked up at him. "You're kidding, *right?*"

He knew exactly who she was talking about. "Old, yeah, but strong. Lot of juice, and a lot of anger."

"He'll be more trouble than he's worth," she said, but left the name intact. By the time she had reached the bottom of the two-page list, she had crossed off almost a third of the names, and circled a few more. Ron finished his beer while she went over the list again. By the time he came back with refills, she had added another seven names.

"Here. That will give us something to start from. How fast can you get them sorted and ready?"

He took the paper back. "We have a go date?" Everything depended on her: the Distraction only existed to support her movements. Not that she was feeling any pressure at all.

"Soon. Yeah." She hoped. The weekend had gone by in a blur of training with Morgan, broken by fine-tuning a number of her cantrips and spells. Normally she improvised to fit the moment, but normally she didn't go up against fellow, possibly maddened Talent, either. Better to have an arsenal ready; that way she wouldn't need it. Like carrying an umbrella.

Ron folded the marked-up paper and put it in his pocket, and took a large sip off his beer. "This is going to drain people something significant, what you're asking."

"I've got that covered." The battery, once completed, would take the current offered by *Cosa* members elsewhere and store it, allowing Talent here to take a hit off it as needed; recycled current, not as good as fresh, but it should do the job. Again, she hoped. Funny, really. She didn't feel hopeful at all. She felt… Slithery. Dry. Static-y. Full of her own current and none of it making her feel better.

Wren frowned. There it was again, something knocking around in the back of her brain, under the slitheriness. Something that wanted out, but she didn't dare. If she did…

Bad things would happen. She had locked enough bad things away over the past year—including the bansidhe that warned of those bad things coming—that she knew what it felt like. Only this wasn't in a box in Sergei's storeroom. It was in her. A box in her brain—smaller but somehow worse than other memories she'd put aside over the years. And it wanted *out*.

Not yet, she told it. *Hold off a little while longer. Please....*

Let her finish this job, and then she'd have time to deal with it. She'd have time then to deal with everything.

She hoped.

fourteen

"Message for you, sir!"

Sergei ignored the cheery e-mail alert, his fingers flying over the keys as he checked off the lading notices on his desk with the inventory report on his screen. Part of him was still out in the trenches, worrying about what was happening with Wren, how Andre was doing, what was happening that he couldn't see, stuck on the Null side of things. And yet, the minutia of his job—the job that was both cover for his partnership with Wren, and his real passion—claimed much of him the moment he walked in the door of the gallery each day.

It was reassuring, actually, that his daily job could still suck him in like this, even the dreary paperwork side of it. The only thing better than getting a new show in was being able to mark every item on the inventory either Sold or Pending Sale, and not simply for the cash it brought into the gallery.

Sergei loved being the matchmaker between art and owner. Nothing was better than seeing the look on someone's face when they first caught sight of something that spoke to them. It wasn't something he talked about—who would he tell?—but it satisfied something deep inside him that nothing else had ever touched.

So much for retiring anytime soon. Maybe in a couple of years. Or decades.

There was a hum coming over the intercom that connected his office to the gallery proper. Lowell and the new part-time receptionist, Carole, were busy, from the sounds. The exhibit was closing tomorrow, which meant that they had a sudden influx of people who had been meaning to come all week, but...

He glanced at the lower right-hand corner of the screen, where the time clicked away. Another hour, and they could start shoving stragglers out.

The glimpse also reminded him of the e-mail. Stretching his shoulders to release some of the desk-bound tension, he saved the inventory report and closed the file, and then clicked on the icon to bring up his mail program.

To: didier@didiergallery.info
From: ghost@privatemail.com
Be careful, Sergei Kassianovich. Be smart. Be faster.

There was no signature, no indication of who the e-mail had come from. It had been sent to his work e-mail account, not his personal one. The work account was on the Web site, available to anyone who wanted it, if hidden behind spam-blockers. But Sergei knew who the message came from. Beyond the fact that only one person had ever called him by his patronymic, the Russian diminutive of his father's name only his mother ever used, the advice was the same the old man had given him on his first day with the Silence, so many years ago.

"In order to survive, you must be careful. You must be smart. And you must be faster than all the other careful, smart hotshots out there already."

Words to live by.

Words sent via a remailer, suggesting that his first boss—his only real boss—had finally either been less careful, less smart, or slower than someone else.

"Damn. Also, damn." There were other words Sergei wanted to say, but the intercom transmitted both ways.

The old man knew he was playing a dangerous game. The last time they had seen each other, they had been standing over the body of Andre's right-hand man, Sergei's replacement, who had in the span of ten minutes betrayed Andre, killed a coworker to prove his new loyalty, and in turn been killed by the old man himself. It had been an awkward parting.

For the first time, Sergei allowed himself to wonder if anyone had ever come back for Poul's body, or if it had been allowed to rot in the city morgue before being buried in an unnamed grave or, more likely, cremated and dumped with all the other unknowns who wash up on the metal slabs of the city morgue.

He wondered if there was anyone to claim Andre's body wherever it had been dumped, or if that elegant ebony frame had simply disappeared into the darkness.

Something stirred inside him, thick and hot and sour. He recognized it: anger, mixed with frustration. He wanted to strike out, to hit something, take something down hard and vent that anger on it.

He wanted revenge.

Sergei closed the e-mail and deleted it, then cleared out his deleted mail file. There were other steps he could take, to eradicate any evidence of the e-mail arriving on his computer, but he decided to trust the remailer to have muddied the trail enough. If anyone figured out that Andre might have set off a dead man's switch on his e-mail, they would know who the old man had sent it to, and any and all of the tricks he might employ would probably be useless.

Cold reality kicked in, hard and frustrating. Andre Felhim had known the risks. He had chosen to stay within the Silence, play his own game. Revenge was not only a fool's errand; it might jeopardize the things Sergei himself had chosen to follow. The things that were important, now.

Tapping the "off" button on the intercom so that he could hear what happened outside but not transmit his own sounds, Sergei got up and stretched, his arms over his head, fingers almost touching the ceiling. There was a soft crack, then another, as his shoulders were forced back into alignment. He was getting old, and creaky, and he needed to get back to the gym someday.

But not today. Or tomorrow.

Someone had taken the old man out, despite his cleverness and his wariness. Andre had not been without his supporters, his allies, and those who were watching to see which way the game went. The only person who could have shut him down, who would have dared to do it, was Duncan. The man at the helm of the Silence now, no matter that theoretical control still rested with the elected Board of Directors.

If Duncan were making such an obvious, irreversible move, that meant they were nearing endgame, one way or another.

Moving across the office, Sergei pushed the leather sofa out of the way with his hip, shoving it from the wall. Behind it, there was a small touch pad set into the wall. He had moved the safe after the last time his office was tossed, and installed a new security system. No code, no keys: Just a simple prick of the finger and a drop of blood to turn a biogenetic lock that not even Wren had access to.

Inside, there was a packet of official-looking papers, a palm-size black velvet box, and a rough cotton bag closed with a drawstring. There were also two handguns, placed there after Wren's request that he not carry them any longer. Blooded steel made her ill, physically and emotionally, when she came into contact with it, her usually latent psychometry triggered by the memories of violence carried in the metal.

He took both guns, and the box of ammunition.

Wren was staring at a white wall.

Actually it wasn't white. It was a sort of dingy off-cream that probably didn't even have a fancy designer name.

Damn it, P.B. and Bonnie were right. She had never bothered to paint, in all the years she had lived in the apartment. The walls were still the same dingy white. There was still the same brown carpet in the hallway the last tenant had left there, now worn into an even uglier color from her habit of pacing endlessly when she was thinking. All right, she had hung curtains, and a few bits of artwork other people had given her, and her old, bulky, windup wall clock. She had bought some new furniture, and shelved her books and draped her towels.

But she had never painted, in all the years she had been here. Never put her own personal touch on it. Why was that, Valere?

And why the hell was it bothering her now? She had already gone through this with P.B. and told him to leave her alone, already, she didn't care.

Rolling from her side onto her back, she went through the next round of stretching exercises, feeling her body extend and bend, waking up an inch at a time. She had slept most of the day, and woken up with the need to get slapped onto the rack and stretched back into shape.

Lacking that, there was yoga.

The color of her walls kept returning to her brain, even when she was supposed to be focusing on nothing but the feel of sinew becoming less like a rubber band and more like an al dente noodle. Maybe tan. Or blue. Blue would be different

And she would be sick of it within a month. Six months, tops. But maybe a nice cream or mocha…

She finished the routine, and stood up, feeling things in her body move smoothly that had been jammed shut, earlier.

Feeling ready, she collapsed her body into a controlled full split on the hardwood floor. "Thank you, God," she said, resting her forehead on the floor as though genuflecting, then reversing the move in a smooth rise. She wasn't particularly strong, or fast, but she was agile. It made climbing walls and swinging in through windows that much easier.

Rolling up the exercise mat, she shoved it into the hallway closet under the jam of coats and cleaning supplies, then went into her narrow kitchen and ran water into a kettle.

"Rundown. Blues, check." P.B. had dropped off the building plans for the job site, including the wiring and the plumbing plans. She wished, not for the first time, that she could transfer them to digital format and carry them with her the way some of her non-Talented competitors did. There was only so small you could shrink details and have them be readable, in print format.

"Slicks, check." She'd had to dip into her savings account to pay for all of the upgrades she wanted, but the money was there, and she wanted them. Sweat-wicking fabric with a light-absorbing texture, a self-repairing seal up the side for ease of getting in and out under stressful and occasionally cramped conditions, adhesive clips on wrist and ankle that attached the new and outrageously expensive nonslip-grip gloves and foot-covers which folded into a tiny pocket-size packet when not in use... She was salivating, just thinking of the outfit waiting in her office. Little kids at Halloween didn't look forward to their costumes the way she loved her new slicks.

"Valere, thou art geek." Hey, if you couldn't drool over new tech, and didn't own a car, or get worked up over a gourmet kitchen, why not geek out over the latest in spy- and thief-wear? Everyone had their own kink.

The kettle whistled, and she poured the steaming water over the metal tea ball filled from the canister on the counter, making sure that the ball moved around the mug to get the full flavor, the way she had been taught.

"Hi."

"Hey." She handed him the filled mug, still going over the checklist in her mind.

"Hot-stick, where's the hot-stick?" Bonnie had dropped an updated and improved one off that morning, leaving it propped against the apartment door as though by not handing it over directly it meant that she still wasn't involved in what was going on. The fact that it was black with a hot-pink stripe down the center sort of gave it away, though. Only Bonnie would personalize her hot-stick like that.

Smaller than the prototype she had been given originally, this version would fit easily into one of the thigh pockets of her slicks without making an unsightly bulge that might attract attention. It also meant that it wouldn't conduct as large a charge, but the plan was to go in and get out clean, not leave a swath of twitching corpses.

The rest of the team, the Distraction, would be getting to do that.

"Speaking of which, I need to kick Ron for that list." She turned to head to the office, and almost collided with Sergei. "Jesus wept! When did you get here?"

He looked at her over the rim of his mug, his pale brown eyes showing amusement even though his face remained deadpan. "About two minutes ago. I said hello. You said hi back."

She vaguely remembered that. Vaguely.

She also noted that he was drinking tea, and had a vague memory of making that, too. Not that making tea while in a fugue state was unusual for her. Once, she had known when Sergei was coming over to the apartment by the urge to boil water. She had thought that particular twitch had gone away. Apparently not.

"Right. Do you actually want the tea I make, or do you drink it just to be polite?"

She had never wondered that before. From the surprised look on his face, she wasn't sure if Sergei had ever thought about it before, either. He walked in, she handed him tea, he drank it. But did he actually want it?

"It's a ritual of sorts," he said. "Some people get a kiss on the cheek, or a handshake. I get tea."

He looked prepared to delve into it further, but she had already gone back to her checklist.

"I still need rope. Something light, but tough to break. About seven feet of it. And I should work on that blacklight cantrip some more, because if I'm going to need it I'm going to need it fast, and it still takes too long to come forward." She paused over that thought, her brain trying to remember specifics, but it was hazy around the corners, as though she had created the spell years ago, instead of days. Shrugging it off, she went on with her verbal list-making.

"And the list. Damn it, Ron, I need that damned list, so I know who and how many I'm supposed to be Retrieving." Bad form, to go on a job with only a half-assed idea of what you were supposed to bring back.

"They still haven't gotten it to you?" Sergei's expression was a cross between astonishment and concern, the lines around the corners of his eyes and his mouth turning down, even as his eyes widened in surprise at the omission. If she didn't like going in unprepared, he *hated* it.

"No. Ron's having some trouble putting it together. I think some families don't want to admit they might have someone on it." She didn't blame them—not a bit. Better to think that your teenaged son or daughter took a runner, rather than think of them there. "There are twenty, maybe twenty-three still unaccounted for, by last count. You said there were originally forty-seven Talent on their roster?"

"The bed count was for fifty, and three beds were never used, yeah." That mysterious meeting at the teahouse had yielded not a person, but a file, left for him with the server, along with a pot of white tea and some inedible biscuits.

He hated white tea—it was too delicate a taste for him. It was either a bad choice, or a carefully made statement, saying God knew what, courtesy of his unknown benefactor. He hadn't figured out which yet, or which of the many strings he had tugged over the past few months had resulted in the contact. It didn't really matter: the information seemed to be solid. If their source wanted to remain unknown even to him, Sergei couldn't blame their caution. Especially not now.

The shock of loss that slapped him at that thought came as a surprise. He might have processed the detail earlier, but now it was suddenly, impossibly real.

Andre was gone. Andre was dead.

"What?"

Wren was watching him, her hand caught halfway through combing her hair off her face. He shook his head, unable to vocalize. Placing his tea on the counter, he backed her against the counter, his hands resting on her shoulders. She was so tiny, he forgot sometimes how tiny she was. Not fragile, no. But small. Slight. So easily damaged...

Inside and out, a whisper reminded him. *Inside and out.*

"Be careful, Zhenchenka," he said. It was an order, as much as he was ever able to order her around. "Come home to me." He had no right to ask; they had never formalized anything, even before she sent him away, and he had come back without permission, without invitation, but...

She leaned forward, resting her forehead against his chest. "I'll do my best." Her flesh was warm, and smelled of baby powder and Ivory soap. Ivory floated. A bit of trivia he'd forgotten. When he was a kid, he used an old penknife to carve bars of soap into boats, and floated them in the kitchen sink. A thirty-five-year-old memory, and he could smell the bacon and coffee smells of his mother's kitchen in the morning, hear the radio in the background, as his parents dickered over who got what part of the newspaper to read, and exhorted him to get a move on, or he'd be late for school.

She used a scented soap on normal days. Ivory was for jobs.

"You went to scout the scene?"

"Yeah." Her voice made it clear that she didn't want to talk about it. That was all right. He didn't want to talk, either.

His hands rose, resting on the back of her head, sliding down the soft fall of her hair, for once not pulled back in a braid or knot. Not long enough for that any more. A hundred shades of brown, if you knew how to look. If you got close enough to look, and could see.

He liked it better when he was the only one who could see her.

When the rest of the world skipped over this treasure, left him the only one aware...

He wasn't a jealous or possessive man, as a rule. But with Wren, the rules seemed to change a little.

"You should go." He heard the tremor in her voice, echoed in the shiver that ran through her skin, a reminder that as right as this felt, it wasn't. *They* weren't.

"Wren."

"You should go."

Her voice was flat again, and even he could feel the current crawling around underneath it. He shivered, and for once it wasn't in anticipation. Her current was jagged, rough-edged; it felt like the thunderstorms she so adored, the dangerous ones that crashed in out of nowhere and left tree limbs downed and power lines tangled. But he still didn't want to go. "Let me just hold you a little while longer."

She snorted, the sound muffled by his shirt. "That's, like, the oldest line in the book, Didier."

It was. It really was. And what was even worse was that he actually meant it. He just wanted to hold her, like that might keep her safe. Safe from what she had to do—and what was already inside her. If P.B....no. He couldn't think that. He wouldn't think that.

Something was breaking inside her, and he not only couldn't fix it, he was being told *not* to.

He dropped a kiss on the top of her head, and moved back just enough to be able to see her face. "You're ready to go?"

"As soon as the rest of the team gets their shit together. P.B.'s started calling them The Distraction."

He shook his head. It was, he supposed, as good a name as anything the Department of Defense had ever come up with. But it lacked a certain flair.

The *Cosa,* he sometimes thought, had used up their entire sense of whimsy when they named themselves. Then again, anyone with any ties at all to a secret organization called the Silence had no room to nitpick, as she had more than once pointed out.

"When do you think they'll be ready? Tomorrow? Next day?"

She lifted a shoulder as though to say "who knows?" "Any or none of the above? I'm asking them to do something...new." He thought that she was going to say something else, and wondered at the mid-sentence change. He didn't know what this Distraction was supposed to do—nobody did, except the ones involved. It was better that way. Safer.

"Why?" she asked him. "You know any reason we should up the timetable?"

"I don't know." He frowned, chewing over what he knew, and what he suspected, and what he thought might happen. What he thought had already happened. "Probably not." It wouldn't make any difference now; the wheels were in motion, but if she rushed on his say-so, those wheels could so easily crush her....

She pushed him away, not unkindly but so that she could look up into his face easily. "What?"

He didn't have time to come up with a good substitute story, to keep her from worrying. "I got an e-mail today. From Andre. Or, not from Andre."

"Someone pretending to be Andre?" She tilted her head at him, confused.

"No. It was him. It..." He realized he was tripping over the ex-planation, and stopped. "It was rerouted. Sent through an anonymous remailer. Probably more than one, knowing Andre. He probably had a trigger set up to route it to me if he didn't countermand...." He saw her look of confusion, and reminded himself that Wren might use her computer, but it was at a careful distance. Things that were second nature to a child of the tech age weren't, to her.

"It's a way to send e-mail through various blinds, to hide where it came from, and where it's going."

"Ohhh." The light went on. Sneaky, she understood. "And this e-mail said...?"

"It was what it didn't say that said something." Suddenly he needed to pace, to burn off energy. He broke the light embrace, stepping away from her somewhat more violently than the space allowed. He hit up against the other counter, and swore, not as colorfully as usual. "It was a warning. And a goodbye."

He didn't have to say anything more than that. "I'm sorry."

She was; he knew that. She hadn't ever liked Andre, and not only because she and the old man had fought over possession of him like two terriers with a rope toy. As much as Andre had admired her for her grit and style, she had despised him for his...

For his morals, actually. Although neither of them would ever have used that word. Wren lived far more in the gray than Andre could fathom, by her very nature.

"It's not certain. Just...likely."

"What do you think happened?" He had never told her exactly what had gone down between the two of them on that cold winter morning in an alley downtown, just the information he had learned, the details that she—and the *Cosa*—had needed. Nothing of the smells, the sounds, the visuals that had stayed with him, nights afterward.

The old man, two bodies at his feet. Poul's blood on his hands literally and metaphorically. Bren's blood, metaphorically. Andre's decision to go back to the Silence, to fight for the organization he had dedicated his life to—and given his life for.

"I think someone was faster than he was," was all Sergei said now. "Wren, I really don't want to talk any more tonight."

He reached out and gathered her back to him, wrapping his arms around her form until he could feel her heart beating through his own skin.

"I love you," she said, the words breath-soft against his shirt.

He closed his eyes against the rush of tears that threatened. They might not be able to have sex, to show how they felt, how they connected, physically, but those words…those words were what he needed to hear.

Come back to me, Wrenlet, he thought. *Come back whole to me.*

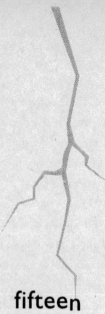

fifteen

Wren dreamed of bees. Room after room of half-filled hives, each bee was larger than she ever remembered seeing in nature, buzzing over the honeycombed sections as they worked. Moving from room to room as though looking for something, she had to turn sideways and slide through, the narrow hall and jagged turns scraping against her arms and chest as she slipped away. Each moment she expected to feel the stingers hit flesh, as the bees realized they had an intruder, but not only did they not seem upset, when one did land on her, she felt a strange sense of comfort, as though she had been set upon by a round, winged, buzzing, St. Bernard puppy.

She woke alone, on her side, the covers tucked around her and a line of sweat down her back. "That," she said thoughtfully, "was weird." Bees. What the hell did bees mean?

Wren shoved the covers off, grabbed her robe, and shuffled down the hallway to the bathroom. The water heater had obviously been primed, because it only took a few seconds before steam started to rise. But what the building's heater could deliver, and what she needed this morning, weren't even close. She rested her hand on the shower spigot, and turned the heat up another notch higher than the heater could really deliver. Only then could she relax under the scalding spray.

Hot water, and indoor plumbing. Right there, you had proof that humankind had a right to exist and expand. Wars and politics be damned; there were *showers*.

She let the shampoo rinse from her hair, then stayed under the torrent a while longer, letting the steam fill the bathroom, until she heard the unmistakable clink of a mug filled with coffee being placed on the sink.

She had tried drinking her coffee in the shower once. It hadn't gone well. So she turned the water off, reached for a towel, and dried herself before stepping out of the shower and reaching for the mug.

Sergei hadn't waited. Probably just as well. They had managed to sleep together, huddled under the quilt like old times...but he had kept his shorts on and she had slept in a T-shirt and that wasn't like old times at all. She wanted him; she wanted to wrap herself around him, have him moving inside her; she craved him the way some people craved comfort food, to devour as an antidote to fear, or depression.

The problem was that was exactly what she might do: devour him. In her need and her love, she might become as much a killer as anything she had ever been part of putting away.

Part of Wren's brain knew that she was overreacting slightly. Maybe even more than slightly. There were ways around this. There had to be. Something other than being totally current-drained before she had sex, anyway. It was just that there was no time or energy or space to think of anything. Not right now.

Old Sally had been right. If Wren had been smarter, she would have realized that the moment she took the job: the damn bansidhe hadn't escaped that glass case on the other side of the ocean just to stretch achy, sawdust-stuffed horse-legs. Old Sally always had a mission; it had come to give notice of doom and death.

That was why the owners had been so dead set on hiring Wren, specifically, to find the damn thing. Not because she was the best— although she was—but because that was the only way Old Sally could find her: to have her find the bansidhe.

Magic worked that way, with its own sort of internal logic that made your head hurt.

Hindsight was not only twenty-twenty; it came with a side-view mirror that let you see things after they hit you.

Wrapped in her robe and clutching her mug, Wren shuffled from the warm bathroom out into the shock of the relatively cooler and dryer air of the hallway, and down to her bedroom. No Sergei there, either. Underwear, a bra, a long-sleeved T-shirt in a shade of pink nobody would ever believe that she owned, and a pair of jeans so worn they were more white thread than blue. A pair of thick pink socks that had been white before she washed them with a red sweat-shirt, and she felt ready to face the day. Or at least, her apartment.

"Hey there, sunshine." A husky voice greeted her from the depths of the single comfortable chair in the main room. It wasn't the voice that she had been expecting to hear.

"I'm taking back my key," she muttered, going into the kitchen for a refill on her coffee.

The demon made a whoop-de-do gesture with one paw, not looking up from the crossword puzzle he was doing.

Crossword puzzles were not the usual brain teaser of choice for most of the Fatae breeds. The longer Wren knew P.B., the more she was reminded that demon were not the usual sort of Fatae.

No Sergei in the kitchen, either. Unless he was working in her office—entirely possible—he had already left the apartment. She looked at the clock: 8:20. Later than she had thought; he probably already had gone off to the gallery. It wasn't a Friday, so they were open.

She went into the main room, and sat on the other end of the sofa, shoving her feet under P.B.'s furry leg and putting the right amount of caffeine into her system. "What are you doing here?"

"Nice, Valere." He shoved her feet away. "Very polite." He could have been referring to her greeting, or her toes, or both. "What's a four-letter word for an inept or stupid person?"

"Dork."

"Huh." He stared at the crossword, then wrote the word in. "*The Times* is slipping in their vocabulary use."

"'Dork' is a perfectly acceptable crossword word."

"If you're a dork, sure."

"You're the one doing the puzzle, not me."

"Yeah well, you need a hobby. How about interior decorating?" He reached underneath him and offered her the Style section of the newspaper.

"Don't start on me again, demon. Yes, I saw the paint samples you left. I don't like either one of them."

"So, fine." He went back to his puzzle.

She waited. Eventually he'd tell her whatever he was here to tell her. Not that P.B. wasn't perfectly capable of lounging around the apartment to no purpose, especially these days, but she had known him long enough to be able to recognize when he was being purposeful about his lounging.

"You're out of milk," he said finally, as though that was an answer. She knew that already; it was on the list tacked to the refrigerator. The demon had been handling the food shopping duties for the past month or so; was this his way of saying that she was on her own? Or was it just a random comment?

Or...oh.

"Surprised to see Sergei here this morning, huh?"

"Not really." P.B. folded the newspaper carefully and put it on the floor beside him. Wren had the fleeting thought that all the demon lacked was a pair of wire-rimmed glasses low down on his snout to look over, and he'd have the disapproving professor thing down pat.

She really needed a vacation. Or something.

Something's wrong. The gray fog was back, hovering at the edges of her awareness, trying to slip its way in. She held it off, but without much hope.

P.B. was talking again. "Sending someone away only works if you hurt them bad enough they'll stay away. You couldn't do that to him."

Wren didn't want to go into this, not after the roundabout she'd just had with her own brain in the bathroom. She hurt everything she touched, the fog whispered to her. She was dangerous. She should wrap herself in it, and be safe. "You think I should have. Sent him away, and made him *stay* away."

"I think anything you did to hurt him that bad would have hurt you just as badly." But he didn't deny her comment.

Both were true. She should have made it final. It would have been like cutting out a part of her soul, and shredding it. "He's been helping us. All along."

"Well, d'uh." He gave her a look that was a few degrees shy of scathing.

All right, she deserved that. She hadn't allowed herself to think about how Sergei was spending his time, but if she had she would have known that he wasn't the sort to simply sit and spin his wheels. Even after she had made it clear that this was a problem for the *Cosa Nostradamus,* not a Null, however well-intentioned. Especially not a Null who had earned the distrust of already spooked Talent.

"I'm not sleeping with him. We're not having sex." P.B. was the only one who knew, other than the two of them, what the real problem was. He was the one she had gone to when things got out of control, when she realized that, as much as Sergei was addicted to her current, she was addicted to him, that she was not capable of saying no, and sticking to it.

"You ever get the feeling that relationships are more trouble than they're worth?"

The look she got in response to that made her realize, for the first time, that irony had an actual weight. And also, that she had never seen—or heard of—a female demon.

"Right. Never mind." She leaned back and let the gray fog slip into her system, softening the ragged edges at the same time it sped up her brain. "Why are you here?"

"I live here?"

"Not if you're not doing the food shopping any more, you don't."

"Stan got jumped last night. Four humans, over on Sixth and Minetta. They had one of those tube things with them. Picked him out of a crowd, herded him into an alley, and bam."

"Stan?" She couldn't place the name.

"Little guy, skinny like a stick, weird eyes, lives in a furnace?"

"Oh. Right." She could picture him now: like a cricket standing upright. Wren didn't think she had ever known his name. She had absolutely no idea what his breed-name was, or if there were more of them in the city. "Is he okay?"

"He's dead."

Another death. Wren knew that, once upon a time, she would have felt something at that calm, factual bit of information. She would have been outraged, or scared, or angry, or all of the above.

Now the fog swallowed her emotions, and she merely nodded, as though it were not only expected, but according to plan. Another death for the Silence to pay for. Add his name, and Andre's too, yes. Another reason to go ahead with her plan.

"How goes the Distraction?" It was supposed to be his job to keep track of everything, to make sure all the smaller details went smoothly. He was also supposed to be checking in on Ayexi and the battery, but either that was going to work, or it wasn't, and if it did they would tell her. No need to fill her in on the failures.

P.B. flicked his dark red gaze over her, then looked away. "Everyone's ready. The moment you give the word, I get to push the start button."

"Good. And the rest of the *Cosa?*" The thousands of Talent and Fatae who were not part of this, either by choice or lack of usable skills. Even if every one of them wanted to take part she would have said no—too large an army become a target, and she needed snipers.

"The ones we could reach, they know to hunker down and lay low. The ones we couldn't…hopefully word reached them. Or they're already out of town."

"Good." She didn't know what else to say. It wasn't good. It wasn't good at all. But it was what it was. What it had to be.

Wren mentally reached to touch her core, brushing over the stored current there the way you might stroke a cat, or finger a lucky charm. The coils were thick and sluggish, like snakes in cold weather, but she could feel the power stored in them, like a thundercloud waiting to break. And over it all, a wet coating, like condensation on a window. The fog.

"There's something wrong," she said, not meaning to open her mouth at all. "With me."

P.B.'s eyes did something weird, slitting almost like a cat's before returning to their usual round, red pupils. "I know."

That was both reassuring and completely *un*reassuring. If P.B. knew, if he was willing to admit to it that easily, then it was real. She had grounded in him, if not as much as she had in Sergei. Especially recently. He knew her, knew what her current felt like.

But if he wasn't panicking, then it couldn't be all that bad. Right?

She reached automatically again for her core, and stopped. There wasn't any comfort there. The thing that was wrong...it waited in there, lurking like an alligator just below the surface.

She couldn't worry about it. Whatever was going on, they could deal with it after all this was done. Or it wouldn't matter at all.

"I still need a few items," she said. "What's the weather forecast for tomorrow?"

It was as though her admission had never been made, his acknowledgement unspoken, and they moved on.

"Clear and cool, with a chance of scattered showers. Your basic spring in the city."

"Good. That's good." She held her coffee carefully in both hands, closed her eyes, and counted backward from ten. When she reached three, she was floating in the middle of that gray fog, comfortably supported while current-strikes raged in miniature below and above her. This was the center of her core, the essential of what she was. Not the way it had been, once; not clear and sharp and familiar, but good enough for now. The power waiting there was intense, slippery, loose, liquid. Blood-warm and salty.

Distantly she heard a familiar voice trying to tell her something, but the fog muffled it, and all she could feel was the current coursing through her veins like a sweet, sharp orgasm, filling and then fleeing and leaving her shaking in the aftermath.

A few more items. And she was ready.

The core whispered to her, reminding her. *Hard hands on her back, the hard floor under her. Hot anger and cold fear. Beast. Not-human. So dismissive, those voices. So puny, so vulnerable to her fury...and it felt* good.

She emerged from the depths, gasping, hoping that P.B. hadn't noticed.

He hadn't; it was all inside. Everything was inside.

Something was very wrong with her. Wrong, but strong. Wren shifted, uncomfortable with both sides of that awareness. Being strong wasn't always a good thing: the balance came in power and control. Too much control and you stifled the spark. Too much power, and the control failed, and you...

Her breathing steadied, and the gray fog cooled her fear. If that wrongness got her through the next few days, that was all right. She would do what needed to be done.

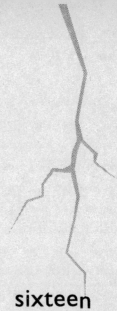

sixteen

The wind stirred the leaves overhead, and somewhere in the distance water was running. Background noise, pleasant but overrun by the murmur of voices and an occasional overexcited laugh.

"All right, people. Quiet down and count off."

Three or four voices chorused "One!" like the wiseasses they were, and Ron gave them an all-inclusive single-finger gesture. But it did the trick: the tension didn't go down any—that would take a miracle they didn't have—but some of the nervous babble softened, and the dozen or so figures gathered in the Ravine in Central Park stopped fussing quite so much.

This was their second meeting; the first one had been indoors, in civilized surroundings, to make sure that everyone got along reasonably well with each other, and that no flaming egos or not-so-hidden grudges surfaced under casual observation. Now, he was going to introduce stress and see what happened.

If he was very, very lucky, everyone would survive. Especially him.

"Right. This is just a dry run, so if things don't work perfectly— or at all—don't panic. Don't freak. Just sit back a bit and don't get in anyone else's way. All right?"

Fourteen Talent, chosen from the original list Wren had approved, for their skills, their smarts, and their willingness to draw blood first and ask questions later. Thirteen lonejacks and one Council member. Ron would have preferred a more even balance, but you took what you could get, and very few of the select Council members they had approached had heard them all the way through before walking out.

"So what's the boogie?" one of the men asked. He was heavy-set, with curly hair that was starting to gray, and looked like he should have been watching a baseball game in a crowded bar, not standing in a deserted area of Central Park.

"The boogie?" one of the younger men asked, mockingly, which earned him a slap on the shoulder from the first speaker. Ron sighed. Herding cats had nothing on organizing Talent. But he had told The Wren that he would get her what she needed. His specialization was procurement. So he would procure. One way or another.

"People." He got their attention back. "I need everyone to claim a number. Start with one: you—" and he picked a person at random, a middle-aged woman with black hair streaked gray like a badger's stripe "—and count off from there."

Given specific directions, they were able to accomplish it in short order, without too much joking.

"All right. Visualize your number."

"What?" A few of them looked at him as though he had lost his mind, while most of them seemed to understand the request.

"Visualize your number. Picture it in your brain, make it real. Like a spell, people! It's not that difficult for anyone more than five minutes out of mentorship, so stop groaning." He waited while they all looked inward. After a minute, he could sense them focusing, an intensity in the air that told someone sensitive to it that magic was in use.

"Good, good. Now reach out, gently, and feel for the number on either side of you." That took a little more effort, to both visually and magically feel the personal "signature" of their neighbor's current. Ron waited, checking his surroundings in the meantime out of instinct and nervous habit.

Off to the side, perched on the Glen Span Arch, a figure in jeans and a baseball cap was watching, accompanied by a towheaded woman dressed in black cobweb leggings and a red-striped sailor's T-shirt, Doc Martens on her feet. She looked cold, despite the black sweater tied around her waist. He didn't know her, but he could feel the current in her, and if she was with Danny, he wasn't going to worry about it. The ex-cop was the guy who had brought him into all this, him and Dr. Doherty. Danny was also The Wren's contact, the one who would, on the Day, relay the order to go. That was good enough for Ron.

There was a noise overhead, like the sound of a dozen squirrels scampering overhead. He didn't look up: there were many Fatae breeds living in the greenwoods of Central Park, and they would all be curious about a gathering of so many Talent, especially in days like this. He wouldn't be surprised if the waters of the Loch nearby didn't have an extra helping of water sprites who "just happened" to be around this afternoon. He fully intended to use them, once he introduced the stress factor.

That thought made him look toward the other end of the ravine.

What they were doing had the possibility to be dangerous, and while Central Park was the ideal place to practice—wide-open public spaces, with room to move—it was also a wide-open public space that anyone could use. Which meant that it was also a prime spot to be attacked.

Ron didn't think that the Silence would go after a group this large, but he wasn't the sort to not plan for the possibility.

Morgan couldn't be seen, down in the Ravine, but he was there with his own people, ready to prevent anyone—innocently or otherwise—from stumbling onto the session. The Null fighter had given his word, and he had proven he was to be trusted.

A motley crew he had here, Ron thought. A crew of would-be assassins, ranging from teens to geriatrics, protected by a kung-fu Null, led by a half-speed Talent, waiting on the word of a thief who was, if rumor was to be believed—and it usually was—about half a yard from wizzing, all to rescue brainwashed kidlings from the hands of Nulls who wanted to destroy everything that was wild and magic in the world, starting with them.

This had to work, he decided. It was too good a story not to be told, and if they didn't survive, there wouldn't be anyone to tell it.

"All right, let's get this started. Distracters, hit your marks!"

They scattered, forming a rough circle on the grass the way he had diagramed for them earlier. The sound of the Loch behind them was soothing without being an annoyance, and this deep into the Park, you couldn't hear any city noises at all. They could have been anywhere except one of the busiest, noisiest cities in the world.

"Remember, this is just a dry run," he repeated himself. "Don't overreach yourself. If you start to feel ill, or faint, then break off and—"

"Yes, Da," one of the teens called out. "We *know!*"

He laughed, reassured. "All right, you're all smarter than I am, I'll stop fussing. On the count of four. Four. Three. Two…"

Fugue state was how most Talent worked: it allowed them to blank out nonessential information and focus down into what they wanted to do. For those who had control issues, it created a safe place to trust, and for those who had rock-solid control, it brought them to another level of intensity.

Once they were out of mentorship, most Talent worked alone except in very special cases. Almost every lonejack preferred it that way. They were headstrong, stubborn, and each and every one of them was certain they knew the best way to do something. Even their sole Council member was more of a maverick than most Mages— he had to be to have agreed to join them despite the Mage Council's unspoken, unofficial-but-still-binding "don't get involved in the lone-jacks' battle or we will disown you" position.

The Wren asked them to combine their skills, to forge a new fugue state, a gestalt. And then to use that gestalt in order to pick off their enemies from a distance, one by one or group by group, however it worked best, while she went in on her Retrieval: an attack on two fronts. Theirs would be more deadly, but hers would do more damage.

Assuming it all worked, that was. Ron wasn't sure they could manage it, both the gestalt and the killing, but he hid his doubt outside his mind, and brought them in a controlled fall into the darkness with him, leading the way.

Here. Here I am. Touch me. Be with me. Trust me. Be me.

Signatures touched, current sizzled and retreated, then touched again, more delicately this time.

HeyHiDudeCool!SettledownFocusokFocuseveryone….

We did it!

We totally rock!

This is amazing.

Focus! A combined voice commanded them, stern and eager all at once, and the voices settled back into one. The strands of current combined, stretched, formed one thick braid and reached from the center of the circle, up into the sky....

Beautiful...

Now for the fun part. Ron reached out with a tendril that had been intentionally left free of the collective mind, and created a phantom wave charging directly at the bodies that stood like slow-breathing statues before him.

The enemy is in front of you—attack! Without breaking gestalt!

The cursing that followed was inventive enough to make him grin, before he was forced to get out of the way of the thwacking and stumbling that ensued.

Hold gestalt! he warned them, and then with another tendril of current, created a magical assault on the group-mind. *And defend!*

They were too busy to curse him, now.

Something was brewing, out there in the city. Something magical. Wren could feel it in the back of her head, something surprisingly light for all its intensity. She touched it, letting it sniff her the way one would a new dog, and then let it go. It didn't involve her, and she had other things to do today.

She was standing on the roof of an apartment building in the East Thirties, having taken the easy way of bribing the superintendent to let her out through the service exit. She had taken off her shoes and socks, and stood with her head tilted toward the sky, dressed only in a pair of blue jeans and a matching cotton pullover. Her leather jacket was stashed under the eaves with her shoes. The air was wet and cool, and she could feel the wind shifting around her, even though the flag outside the building itself was limp against its pole. Perfect conditions: moisture, instability, and lift. Spring, joyous spring, with the accompanying atmospheric disturbances. She could practically feel the particles touching her skin, sliding under the flesh and into her veins, meshing and matching with her current as it rose up.

There wasn't enough for a truly classic spring thunderstorm. There was barely enough for anything, if you didn't know exactly what to look for: the weatherman this morning had predicted a good day to eat lunch out in the park, if you could get away for an hour or so.

She was going to disappoint people in this neighborhood, if they'd seen that forecast.

Wren had always preferred wild current to man-made; she knew what to look for, what to pull, where to push, and how long to wait. More of a challenge, and more of a payoff.

Her core shimmered in anticipation. The current-fog was still there, shifting like a veil, but it was stilled for the moment, parting long enough for her to feel the shifting temperatures coming off over the ocean. Water wasn't the only thing in the air. It was weak, and distant, but it was there, like the scent of blood in the water. Sparks. Current. Whether it formed within electrons or was simply attracted to it no one had ever proven for sure, but lonejacks worried less about theory than application.

She crooked a mental finger at the swirling sparks and gathered her will. So easily. So terrifyingly easy to do that.

Wren was not quite a Pure, one of the Talent who had no obstructions to current in her system, but she was close enough to make others nervous, if they knew. She couldn't Transloc worth a damn without puking, and her remote viewing was laughable—God, what a tool that would have been, to be able to See where the object she needed to Retrieve was!—but almost all the smaller skills and not a few of the larger ones came naturally to her, once Neezer had shown her how.

But they all took effort. That was just how it worked.

Except now. Now, it was barely a question of thinking what she wanted current to do, and it did it.

Come to me.

Easy or hard, you weren't supposed to do this. Messing with the weather was a great way to recharge, and an incredible high if you did it right, but it also screwed with the entire global system, and it was damned dangerous no matter who you were.

No matter what had been done to you.

Give me your strength.

The stormlet resisted, wanting to slide down the coastline toward warmer water. Weather, like most lonejacks, was lazy. It went the easiest route, not the hardest.

"Sorry, kid. Not this time," she told it grimly.

Wren had faced the renegade FocAs before. She had gone skill-to-skill with them on the Bridge, and survived. Barely. And that had been when they were distracted, dealing with chaos and other Talent trying to kill them.

Now, she was going in alone. She wasn't trying to kill them. She was trying to save them.

Only one problem with that. From the things Sergei had said, the things that had been done to them, by the Silence? The ones she was going in to save weren't going to see it that way. They were going to resist being Retrieved. They were going to try to kill *her.*

She needed all the strength she could get. No matter where or how she got it.

Wren closed her eyes and slid easily down into fugue state, reaching into her core again and gauging how much she had, how much more she could take before she went into overrush, and burned out. Or worse.

Come to me, she called the storm. *Come to me.*

And like a reluctant hound called to heel, it came.

The rumble of thunder overhead was faint enough to be unheard by the million-plus workers inside the concrete and steel buildings, although people walking on the street paused and looked up at the mostly cloudless sky before moving on.

In an unmarked and unremarked office building on a small side street in Midtown, in a Spartan, guarded, and well-grounded room, Duncan rested his hand on the shoulder of one of his most trusted lieutenants, and squeezed gently. "Do it."

She nodded, and touched her control board with confidence, tapping out a code she was not supposed to know.

Across the city, lights went out, clumps at a time. If someone listened carefully, they could almost hear the howls of outraged consumers as lights flickered, computer screens died, phones went dead and air-conditioning systems sighed out their last. Down on the street, cars slammed on brakes and hit horns when traffic lights went dark, and a great sigh of relief rose up from various locations as the emergency systems for local hospitals and airports went online without hesitation.

New York City was used to blackouts. People had their emergency plans in place, their flashlights and their walking shoes, their alternate routes home. It was just another pain in the ass in the day of a major city. No big deal.

But the darkness kept spreading, from the small island of Manhattan outward into the outer boroughs and the suburbs of New Jersey and Philadelphia, up through Connecticut all the way up to Boston, and down the coast toward Delaware, fingers reaching into D.C. Pockets of power clicked on via emergency generators, and those who had lived through the great outages of decades before sighed and reached for candles and flashlights before the sun disappeared entirely from the sky and true darkness fell.

But some residents were inconvenienced more than others.

? ?

A mass query rose from the city, blended with curses as Talent felt their normal sources of easy current disappear. The overriding question was a familiar one: "Who did it this time?" Not every blackout or brownout was caused by a Talent overreaching or drawing down too much current at once, but it happened often enough to be a valid question.

As usual, nobody owned up.

Wren faded the query from her brain, refocusing her attention on what she was there to do. Tame current was all well and good, but the hunger in her was for something greater. Something wilder.

Valere! That call was a directed spike, impossible to ignore; she could not identify the voice, there were too many layers, too many echoes. No. She picked through the strands, recognized the taste of them, identified the whole from the parts; the Distraction, her ace in the hole. It had worked. But why then were they so panicked?

Valere! Ron, powered by the rest. *Everything's out! We can't touch anything, not anywhere! There's no power to draw on! We can't hold!*

An image came with the cry: a map of North America, the entire

East Coast flickering from illuminated to dark like reverse wildfire. But it didn't stop there; the darkness continued west, stretching fingers into Chicago and across the border into Montreal, down to Georgia and Florida, creeping across the country toward Los Angeles, San Francisco, and Seattle....

It hadn't happened, not yet. They were projecting their fears— the fear of every Talent. The Big Dark, an entire area gone dark in the space of five minutes. Every source of artificial current gone, and the rest of the country primed to follow, if the dominos continued to fall.

"Oh, *fuck*." She looked up into the sky as though to ask "Why me, God?"

Calm down! she sent back, more of a command than she had ever managed in a ping. *Hold!*

And the sky shaded blue into black as the storm, careless of mortal concerns, came sliding into town in response to Wren Valere's command.

seventeen

Hold!

Wren couldn't spare any more time to deal with panicked Talent freaking because their blankie had been pulled from them. The storm was small and localized, the way spring storms often were, but that didn't make it any less of a beast to handle.

To me, yes, here, to me, she told it. *Feel me. Recognize me, acknowledge my call.* It was all about control, especially here. And that control was rewarded when the storm cell centered itself directly above her, and opened itself to her.

Ten blocks away the sidewalks were dry, while on her rooftop the cold downpour drenched Wren through her clothing and to the skin as the clouds surged and thickened. Ten minutes the rain came while she waited, unmoving, a puddle forming around her bare toes. Ten minutes, counting off the seconds. The majority of her awareness was not in her body but much farther above, judging the readiness of the storm. It was delicate, delicate work, to not do it terribly wrong. Bad enough for her to be doing it at all: worse to screw it up.

Wren's fingers moved slightly, unconsciously, as though playing some unseen instrument. Her eyes flickered, her gaze moving restlessly over the street below; the majority of her attention might be elsewhere but some part of her was alert, nonetheless, to the needs and safety of the body.

Everything seemed to be calm, considering. Candles were appearing in apartment windows across the street, the newly lit flames casting shadows as people moved within the now-dark building. Farther down, car headlights moved slowly through the rain, picking their way cautiously through streetlightless streets. Cops were stationed at major intersections, but on the side streets, drivers—and pedestrians—were on their own.

Time passed, and her body, attuned to the resonances within the storm, determined that the mix of electrons in the upper atmosphere was coming to a satisfying blend. With an elevator-like drop, Wren felt out of the cloud-awareness, leaving the storm to the final stages of fermentation on its own, and landed back in her body with the slippery ease of an otter hitting water. She shuddered once, and then took a quick inventory of her physical condition.

Legs, sore. Arms, numb. Skin, soaking wet and shivering. She used a strand of current almost thoughtlessly, raising her internal temperature enough to still the cold. Her hair steamed slightly in the rain.

Save the power, part of her advised. *Blackout. No easy recharge available beyond what you take here.*

Her rational mind acknowledged the wisdom of that, even as her core scoffed—or would have, if it were able to do anything more than slither and hiss in anticipation of being so well-fed.

She stretched her arms over her head, feeling muscles from ankle to ears creak and release, ignoring the rain still coming down at a slower pace.

It was eerily silent up there on the roof: an occasional siren racing up- or downtown cut through, but otherwise all she could hear was the patter of the rain around her. Wren wasn't sure if the silence was real, though, or simply her perception: her ears felt as though they had been filled with felt, muffling all but the sharpest, loudest sounds. Storms were mostly silent things when they were growing and fading, which meant that coming out of one usually meant she was hypersensitive, not less.

The pings had stopped, too, leaving her brain blissfully unmolested. By now, most of the *Cosa* was probably dealing with the blackout the same way their neighbors were: eating the frozen goods before they melted, and bitching about ConEd's slow response time.

Without thinking about it, she scanned over the rooftops with visual and magical—currentical—awareness. Across the city there were molten pits of warmth, beacons in the dark. Emergency generators: some of them large, some small, all working to maximum capacity. She—any Talent—could sweep in and drain the current from them, if they needed to. It wasn't considered either smart or good manners to do it, though. Sometimes—often, especially if you were rushed or careless—harvesting like that could short out a few circuits, or cause a dip in output, and occasionally cause minor burns to the harvester and anyone who happened to be in the area.

You didn't touch the lights of Broadway for PR reasons. You didn't touch hospitals or emergency generators because if you did, people could die.

People will die anyway, if I don't have enough juice stored up to do this. That's different.

Is it? How? People are going to die anyway. Humans. Nulls, but human. You ordered their deaths, even if you didn't select them personally.

Wren shook her head to rid herself of the voices bitching at each other in her head. She didn't have time for moral discussions right now; no time, and no interest. Let other people worry about it, for a change.

She was tired of reacting. It was time to act. She needed to use this power building and breeding inside her, before it ate her alive.

On that thought, she reached out for the signature she had felt earlier, that braided rope of current. It was gone: She couldn't hear the grouped mind of the Distraction any longer. That wasn't entirely surprising; holding that mass connection for even a short time was draining. Doing it under stress, without access to easy renewal? Stupid. And they had been picked for brains as much as Talent. They would conserve their current for when it was needed. They would be ready for her when she called, less an army than a single weapon with multiple points.

And then people will die.

Yes, she acknowledged. *And then people will die.*

A shift in the air around her, a slight warming of the rain, made her look up again, letting the drops stream down her face and into her still-sodden hair. Almost time. The storm was almost ready for her.

She took a deep breath, then released it. *Focus.* No thoughts beyond what she was about to do, what needed to be done. The world doing its thing below her wasn't important. Or rather, it was, horribly so. That just made what she was doing even more important. The stakes had just been raised.

Up until now she had hoped to get in and out easily, cut the Silence off at the knees, and have the Distraction finish the job. Bloody, but simple.

Now, things were more complicated. At a minimum, the entire tri-state region was in blackout. That didn't happen. Not naturally. Not with such perfectly disastrous timing.

The Silence. She didn't know how she could be so certain, but she was. Which meant that they were readying their own attack—and soon.

The timetable just got jumped up.

So Wren called the storm again, coaxing and drawing a little more, pulling and holding it until it gave in to her shaping. And then she waited a few moments more.

She always knew, the instant before lightning formed; her core reacting to the anticipated jolt, maybe, or just a hyper animal awareness of danger. But she knew the moment opposing electrical charges slammed into each other, releasing and dissipating in a streak of lightning that blasted out of the clouds, straight toward her like a hawk on an unwary rabbit.

C'mere.

The bolt hit her dead center, and even though it wasn't a huge storm, that limited shock went through her like a tidal wave of energy. Such a small storm, to have so much power in it! She staggered under how smoothly it rode through her body, swelling to fill every available space. Her core reached up and sucked every erg of energy from it, like marrow slurped from the bone.

Mother of God! It *hurt.* It shouldn't have felt like that. Current could burn, could kill, but it never *hurt.* Something was wrong.

Something is wrong with me

I know.

Her current was normally bright and clean, electric blues, reds, and greens. It coiled in the pit of her core like snakes; cobras and pythons, dangerous and shy until coaxed. This...this was like being smothered by butterflies. Sharp-edged butterflies made of faceted black glass, edged with muddy red and gold. There were hundreds of them, thousands, and they fluttered and hovered and tore her to shreds.

And with every drop of blood she felt her core flare higher, hotter with power. Intoxicating her. Making her whirl and whiz up into a spiral of energy, of power.

Jesus wept, it was *incredible*.

Wren? A voice, sudden and shocked and concerned, in her head.

"Shhhhhh." A snake's hissing, whistling through her teeth. Butterfly wings, fanning a storm on some other continent. Black-winged butterflies, their eyes bright with power.

Wren!

Not human.

Creature.

Thing.

The feel of the cold stone under her body, their hatred hovering over her like a living thing, a weapon, the fires of hell rising to consume them all.

Current enticed, whispered, beckoned. Touch me. Take me. We can destroy them all. We can be free, forever....

Wren, ground! Ground, damn it! The voice was urgent, near-panicked, but the current's whisper was closer, more seductive.

Never again to be afraid. Never again to be weak. Never again alone...

You're not alone! That voice again, annoyingly inside her head, where she couldn't shut it out.

The power flared through her, impatient, before she could respond. *Use us,* the butterflies urged, and Wren fell into them, totally out of control, and felt herself shatter into a thousand red-tipped wings.

* * *

When the power went out, there were two customers in the gallery. Neither had been serious browsers, and they both left immediately. Sergei held out for as long as he could—another hour, watching the minutes tick by on his watch—hoping that the power would come back, but eventually he—like, apparently, most of Manhattan—decided it was useless.

"I'm calling it. Let's go."

An emergency light in the ceiling made their skin tones look like zombie flesh, and Sergei wondered, briefly, as though the thought might provoke the action, if there were zombies hidden somewhere in the *Cosa Nostradamus* like a crazy uncle in the attic, and if so, when they would crash the party. Because, really, that was all the past year had lacked.

Avert, he thought quickly. He was tired. He needed sleep. Or a drink. A drink, and then about ten hours of sleep. If the blackout held on, nothing would wake him up until he was done. Ideally, anyway.

"It's not closing time yet…." Lowell protested, still standing behind the counter where he had been arranging the brochures for next month's exhibit.

"Go home, Lowell," he ordered his assistant, wondering what the boy thought he could do, with all the power out. Carole had already gone home, happily, the moment he even raised the idea. She was young—still in college—and the idea of a blackout meant parties and mayhem to her, not annoyance and staying on the job.

"But…someone might…" Lowell was still handling the brochures, as though the right shuffle would make the power come back on.

Oh for the love of God and all his saints. The air-conditioning was off and his head was starting to hurt. "Go home. Nobody is going to rape and pillage the gallery just because the lights are out. Go home."

Lowell was clearly reluctant to abandon his post, as though one more customer might walk in off the deserted, darkening street just itching to drop a few thousand dollars on the hammered copper sculptures they were featuring this month. Or, worse yet, take one without paying.

"Lowell, I'm closing the gallery. You can either get locked in, or go home."

Sergei was already in his coat, waiting, by the time his assistant joined him at the door, and they walked out together into the oddly dark dusk.

Lowell didn't pout, but he was clearly unhappy. "Good night, Mr. Didier. I'll see you tomorrow."

"If the power's back on. If not, don't bother." Sergei doubted that the power would be restored by then, but he didn't want to depress the younger man further. He watched Lowell walk down the now-empty street, his shoulders hunched in as though oppressed by all the closed stores around him, and shook his head.

Yes, his earlier thoughts had been right: it was probably past time to bring Lowell into the management side. He had the eye, and the flair, and clearly loved to make money. And if he was stuck at the same level much longer, Sergei would lose him to another gallery, or an importer looking to expand, who would welcome his knowledge and passion.

The problem was how to manage it, without disrupting a successful routine or doubling up on responsibilities. Being truthful and objective, he wasn't ready to retire, or even take a less active role in running the gallery; thinking that he might would just lead to problems when he couldn't let go. Yet, he could do it for a short term, maybe use the time to work on his own connections outside of New York, and if Lowell took to the additional responsibility, they might be able to expand, maybe open another gallery in another city...

"I wonder where Wren would like to go," he thought out loud, purely out of habit, and then shook his head. No guarantee she'd want to go anywhere, with him. The thought of her leaving Manhattan...was almost as impossible as the thought of himself, leaving actually. He'd come here straight from college, and never looked back.

Sergei manually rolled down the grate over the gallery's store-front window, locking it with a heavy padlock. Normally he didn't bother—the alarm system was enough to secure the small window. But with the power out, even with the emergency system in place, he wasn't taking any chances. Despite his words to Lowell, Sergei was not as confident the city would remain well-behaved tonight, and there was more locked in the building than merely artwork. Wren had stashed things best not thought about in the basement storeroom.

"I should have listened to you and put in a current-based system, too," he told his absent partner. Except the reason he hadn't—because he would have needed a Talent around to arm it—still held. Maybe the next receptionist he hired should be a lonejack....

A crack of thunder rolled through the city, and Sergei hunched his shoulders and looked up reflexively. The sky had been clear when the blackout hit, but there was a definite storm front rolling in from the ocean, and the glitter that Wren had taught him to look for was...there. Yeah, there they were, hanging in the darker underbelly of the clouds. It could be coincidence. Or it could be a Talent messing with the weather to try to power up when every other source went down.

There were generators in the city, but they were off-limits. The *Cosa* didn't have many rules, but that was in the top five, from everything he had learned: thou shalt not fuck with emergency generators or medical/transit security measures.

"Wren?" He stared at the localized storm, wondering out loud if it was her.

No. She had been so wiped out, earlier this week; he knew that she had taken the time since then to top off her core. Which was totally an inappropriate metaphor—she wasn't a car to be refilled—but he was tired, and he was facing a hell of a long walk home if he couldn't find a cab, and...

And he really, really didn't want to go home. He wanted to *be* home, to fall face down onto his bed and not move for a week. But the effort involved in getting there was almost too much to contemplate.

"You're old, old man," he mocked himself. "Last blackout, you walked all the way home and up the stairs to boot."

Oh God. The stairs. Last blackout he had still been living over on Forty-Fourth Street. Damn. Living in his current, lovely, modern high-rise had many advantages, but not when the elevators would be running slowly, if at all.

A buzz startled him out of that depressing thought, and it took Sergei a second to realize that his cell phone was ringing, and another second to remember where he had stashed it. A fumble, and he got it open, the phone's glow an odd vision in the absence of any other artificial light.

"Didier."

"*Mein freund,* we have steaks that are melting. No, defrosting. Come, help us eat them!"

The voice was heavily accented, familiar, and delightful to hear, as was the invitation. Sergei felt his mood lift immediately.

"Horst, you are a man of impeccable timing and fabulous kindness. I'll be there as soon as I can. Pour me one of your evil brews. In fact, pour two. I'm thirsty."

He closed the phone and replaced it in his coat pocket, a sudden and unexpected grin lifting his face. Horst was one of his oldest friends in the city, a German restaurateur who had lived in the apartment across the hall when they were both struggling twenty-somethings, and it had been far too long since they had gotten together.

Plus, his fabulous, if yet-undiscovered, restaurant was only a mile or so away, and—more important—on the ground floor. No stairs required.

He thought about calling Wren to see if she wanted to join them, but decided against it. She had, incredibly, never met Horst, and now, with everything that was going on, it probably wasn't the best time to introduce them. Wren tended to get...focused, when she was preparing for a job, and this one was going to be a bitch and a half.

Besides...he felt almost disloyal thinking it, but while they had made huge strides, the bond between them had been damaged by both their actions and inactions. They were patching it, yes, repairing it, but it wasn't yet whole. They weren't yet whole.

She was still pushing him away.

Allowing them some time, especially considering the stress she was under...Yes. He would see her later.

Coward, his conscience taunted him.

Yes, he told it. *And tired, and hungry and given a valid reason to go else-*

where, especially to see someone who doesn't know Wren, or the Cosa, or anything other than what I am to the rest of the world. I need this break. So shut up.

It did.

eighteen

Extended use of current burned calories the same way a triathalon did: fast and steady. As a result, Ayexi looked even more like a rumpled hound than usual. His shirtsleeves were rolled to his elbows, and his tie had long ago been loosened and then tossed aside.

"The question is," he asked the people standing across the plans-strewn table in front of him, "can we keep going?"

The four Talent on his team looked at each other, then back at him. They were meeting in what they jokingly referred to as "the lab"—an abandoned warehouse on the waterfront that still smelled more than a little of fish. The warehouse was overwarm, even with all the windows open. Since there was no power running into the building any more, they had not been inconvenienced by the blackout; in fact there had been a moment of panic when they wondered if their rather intensive manipulation of current had *caused* the power failure, before they determined that the cause had been elsewhere, but it still raised the question of how—and if—they could continue the trials.

"We've been pouring a lot of our own current into the tests," Julia, the sole woman on the team, said. "If we continue, we may drain ourselves to the point where, even if we succeed, we won't be able to close the circuits to create the battery."

That was their charge: to create a battery that could hold the current offered by Talent outside their area; a repository for those gifts until they were needed. The *Cosa* didn't have scientists or technicians as a rule; past a certain level, sensitive electronics and current-manipulation fought for the same power, and current generally won. But that didn't mean they lacked people with the scientific and inventive turn-of-mind. Ayexi, between his own contacts and carefully placed rumors, had his pick of those available. Julia, Gordon, Sean, and Bernie had made the final cut. None of his people were under fifty; all of them had decades of experience manipulating both their own current and that of others, and they all blended their know-how with some serious wonder-why.

"Could we take some of the gifted current, rather than channeling it directly from the giver into the finished battery? It would require bringing in someone from outside before we were planning to, but..." The speaker looked around the small group, letting his voice trail out. Nobody outside that building, except The Wren and a few others, knew exactly what they were doing. Only a few more even knew of the offers that had come in from outside the region, offers that, while not strictly forbidden by either tradition or regulation, were certainly frowned upon, and for good reason.

Bringing another person into the project at this stage, someone not tied to the local community, was a risk. Sharing current was a lot like sex, and not only because of the intimacy. Unless it was taken in and then funneled out quickly, there was always a signature left in the current, and that could transmit more than just power—it could carry information along, too. Information you might not want to share with someone you didn't know. And there was a lot going on right now in their heads that Ayexi didn't think should get out, not even in rumor.

"It's risky. I say too risky." But George, who said it, looked regretful for all his caution.

"We're so close. Giving up now…"

Ayexi let them run the argument out. Talent were stubborn. More, they were egomaniacs. Even without any guarantee that what they did would ever be used, even knowing that nobody would ever know of their success if they managed it, took nothing away from the desire to make it happen.

"I think we can do it," Bernie said. "And it will have the added bonus of teaching us how to handle external current without siphoning any off, for the battery."

That got some self-conscious laughter. Most Talent got their first taste of current-training from their parents or mentor "feeding" them a little pretamed energy to manipulate, when they were still children, and the second thing taught, after control, was how to take it into themselves, by themselves. The idea of passing current along merely as a conduit, without "tasting," was one they were all a little amused by.

"Keep working," Ayexi decided finally, after listening to them go back and forth. "I'll find us a backup." Someone among those who had offered their current, who would not ask questions, but stand by to be used, without hesitation, on a moment's notice. Who wouldn't mind if four—five Talent took a bit of his or herself as they went. Right. Piece of cake.

First, though, he was going to have to update Genevieve. He didn't like to report bad news, but there was an upside: his "granddaughter" wasn't much on the creative side, but she knew how to wiggle out of tight spots; maybe her rather unique perspective would give her an idea that they could use.

The apartment building loomed in front of her—dark, the way everything was dark, up and down the street and across the avenues. Dark spaces, filled with darker shadows, pinpricked by occasional candles and flashlight beams. Wren staggered, one foot in front of another, not so much tired as overenergized. She could feel her skin humming, and every sound seemed sharper, every scent more pungent. Her skin itched, and she rubbed the back of her hands in a nervous action, hardly aware of it.

Her eyes glazed over, and she refocused them with an effort. There was light in front of her, stronger and more welcoming than a candle. She wondered for a moment if she was hallucinating, then she realized that it was coming from Bonnie's apartment on the third floor.

The light in Bonnie's window wasn't a candle. It was current. Wren could feel her core stretching out toward it, not to touch but to *take*. No matter she had just fed it; it wanted more.

She slapped it down the way you would a dog sniffing for table scraps, without any hope of actually disciplining it.

Focus. Control. Those were the bywords for dealing with current. You always had to maintain control, or risk being consumed.

Wren didn't feel like she was in control. She didn't feel like she was being controlled, either. It just…flowed, nice and easy and smooth. She could have lit up the entire building by herself, with one thought.

You need everything you've got, she reminded herself. *Don't get stupid just because you feel good.*

Her hair was still wet from the storm, and her jeans were uncomfortably damp and clammy, but she had dried her feet off before putting her socks and shoes back on, so her feet hadn't chafed walking home.

"I need a towel. And a soda." It struck her as funny, that she should be so wet, and so dry at the same time.

She opened the door and climbed the stairs, moving quietly. She didn't want to see anyone, especially Bonnie.

Why?

Good question. Wren didn't know. But it was important to avoid her. To avoid any member of the *Cosa*. She didn't know what they were doing. She didn't know what their plans were. They didn't know her plans. That was good. Why was it good?

Wren.

It wasn't a ping. It wasn't even a voice. More the memory of an echo. She brushed it aside, and unlocked the door to her own apartment.

She reached for the lights and then stopped, laughing at herself. It was dark now. Full dark, the way humanity had almost forgotten. No electricity. No source of easy power at the touch of a switch or reach of core.

Ayexi had reached her on the way home, a tight ping. There was so much pinging going around it was amazing the satellites weren't picking up the some sort of bizarre energy fluctuations over the city. He wasn't a good communicator, but he'd managed to get the highlights—or lowlights—across. She had agreed with his decision to continue, and given him her blessing. Not that he needed it. Everyone did what they did. What was needed to be done.

Ayexi's report had merely solidified her belief that this was no coincidence. The Silence had made sure there was no electricity for them to draw on. They had done it intentionally, damn the innocents injured, in order to cripple their enemy. To prevent a strike they knew was coming.

The Distraction had worked, before it was even put into play. The Silence was scared.

They damn well should be.

She grinned, a distinctly feral expression.

In the darkness, they would never see her coming.

Moving purely by memory, she went about the apartment, gathering all of her tools from drawers and closets. Her new slicks, still in the tissues they were delivered in. Rope, and Bonnie's hot-pink hot-stick. Her boots, the calf-high ones that moved like a pair of slippers, but supported her arch and ankles no matter what she asked of them. She had paid more than a month's rent to have them made, and had never regretted a penny of the expense. Her lockpick set. Metal claw-hooks that slid over the tips of her fingers, in case she had to do any climbing. A final addition to the pile: a small first-aid kit, with bandages and gels to stop bleeding, so she wouldn't leave any trace behind.

She licked her lips, and was reminded of her thirst. Going into the kitchen she pulled a can of diet Sprite out of the fridge and opened it, putting half the contents down her throat in one long swallow.

"Jesus, I needed that." Her voice sounded strange to her; too loud, too thin. Her face felt hot, and she rubbed the can across the skin of her forehead, trying to cool off.

"Prep," she reminded herself. "What else is on the list?"

She went to her office and pulled out a flat cloth wallet, filled with fifty dollars in unmarked fives and singles. It went on top of the pile of things she had already collected. She had been caught out once on a job without access to ready cash, and needed it. You never knew. She had Retrieved living things before, and anything could happen, even more than other Retrievals. She might have to put them in a cab, or...

She had no idea what she might have to do. Better to be prepared for everything you could think of, and not worry about the things you didn't until it actually becomes a problem. That was Sergei's training, bless him for an overcompulsive planner.

A tendril of current snaked out, as though looking for her partner, and she tucked it back without thought, although that sort of unsummoned behavior should have worried the hell out of her.

"Ready. Now to get set."

Wren took the pile and went into her bedroom, dumping the objects on the neatly made bed. She stripped off her wet clothing, dumping it in a corner on the floor. She went to the bathroom and toweled the last dampness from her body, then braided her wet hair into the tightest plait she could manage, pinning the loose strands against her scalp with plastic bobby pins. It wasn't pretty, but it did the job.

A scentless powder, head to toe, making sure it got between her fingers and toes, and behind her ears; all the places sweat—and scent—might accumulate unnoticed.

Satisfied, she went back into the bedroom and unwrapped the slicks. The material slid through her powdered fingers like a living animal made of heavy silk.

"Worth every penny," she told it, shaking the material out and sliding it up her legs. It was heavier than it looked, and would resist tears or snags better than the best wetsuit, without hampering her movement. And, best of all, it didn't cling in the wrong places: there was nothing more distracting in the middle of a job than having something creep in where it didn't belong. She pulled a pair of socks out of the drawer and put them on, considered the thickness and replaced them with another, heavier pair.

The rest of her kit went into a pack made of the same material as her suit. She looked at the pack, then hefted it, trying to decide if it was too heavy.

"If you need to drop something, you drop it," she finally decided. It wasn't as though the target wouldn't know damn well who had made the Retrieval. In fact, she was planning on leaving a very specific calling card. She *wanted* them to know, without the faintest, slightest doubt, who had kicked the stool out from under them, even if they could never prove it, or trace anything back to her.

She went to the top drawer of her dresser and opened it. In a static-guarded case, there were a number of small feathers. Some of them were plain, while others had a single bead on the shaft; a few silver, but most of them a clear glass. Each feather was a sort of calling card: pinfeathers from a cactus wren, given to her by a friend who lived out in the American Southwest years ago. Each bead was a precrafted spell—one of the few that could be prepared ahead of time without worrying about it fading or spoiling.

She hesitated, thinking, then took one of the glass ones. Silver was an antidote, in case she ingested or was exposed to a toxin. The glass bead contained a toxin-spell. She had so many because she had never taken one with her before. She'd never needed to. Never wanted to.

It was supposed to be fast-acting, and painless. She believed half of that claim.

She knew what the Silence was capable of. She would not leave herself in their hands, if the Retrieval failed.

She was about to leave when she hesitated again, and then reached past the box, taking out a dark green velvet bag about the size of her hand. Undoing the string, she pulled a knife out of the bag. The knife was the length of her index finger, and should have looked dainty, but didn't. The hilt was wrapped in cord, and the blade itself was a dark, ridged stone. It looked too dull to do any damage, but she handled it carefully nonetheless.

It was a voudon blade, blessed by a priest and sanctified in willing blood. Old magic. A gift from a dear and not quite sane friend, years ago.

Wren held it in her hand for a moment longer, and then she slid it back into the velvet bag, and then put the bag back into the drawer, and shut it.

Not this time. She had enough trouble already without calling on old magic, or gods she didn't quite believe in.

Wren looked around the bedroom, trying to decide if there was something else she needed, some last thing that would ensure success, or hold off failure.

No. You're procrastinating. Just go.

Yes. All right. Ready, set. Go.

She grabbed another soda from the fridge on her way out, popping the top as she went out the door, and had drunk all of it by the time she hit the street. She was so damned *dry* inside.

P.B. was tired, cranky, and he smelled of rat poison. He had been finishing up a courier job when the power snapped off, and his subway car was trapped underground. It had taken almost an hour for the cops and train crew to evacuate everyone, and that was only because it was an off-hour train. During rush hour...

Of course, during rush hour, there might have been fewer rats on the tracks. P.B. had been tempted to grab a few, just to freak Wren out, but he was honestly more of a pan-seared steak type than rat *au bleu.*

The thought made him hungry, and as he climbed up out of the subway exit with his fellow commuters/escapees, slouch hat in hand and overcoat draped on his sloped shoulders, he tried to remember if there was anything left worth eating in Wren's typically barren fridge, or if he should see if any wood-burning pizza places on the way home were still open, and pick up a pie or two.

He had just reached street level when it hit him, like waking up with a hangover. Without warning or cause, his mouth tasted nasty and dry, like he'd eaten bad fish; and his head hurt...except it didn't. His vision was a little too sharp, too bright, when normally he didn't see colors all that clearly, that vividly.

His day had been fine, up until then. All right, other than the whole being stuck in a train thing. Nothing strange eaten, or smelled, or heard. One person during the evacuation had looked like he wanted to start something with the short, furry freak in a trench coat, but P.B. had bared his teeth, and the guy had faded, not wanting to do a one-on-one in front of so many cops. So he was all right— no chance anyone had slipped him anything, or hit him with anything. Why, then, did he feel wrong?

He didn't feel wrong. That was the answer.

Wren.

He wasn't exactly expert at this, the mental tagging Talent calling pinging; it wasn't natural to him. P.B. didn't have to be expert, though, to find Wren in the ether. She was his lodestone, now, his due North, the reason he could ping at all. And the sense of wrongness was coming from her.

Wren!

There was no answer. She could hear him; he knew she could hear him. There was no way, now, that she could *not* hear him. They were linked, until such a time as she cut him off, and it would be forever her decision, not his.

And the link was still intact.

He didn't know how he knew that; he didn't know how he knew most of the things he knew about himself. His creator had not exactly been forthcoming with information before dying, damn the man into twice the hell he already occupied. But the demon knew this: that he had allowed Wren to ground in him, not once or twice, but multiple times. He had opened the locked door to himself and allowed her to find a foothold. She would forever have that access.

He had known that would happen, when he allowed her in. And still, he had done it.

In turn, in that openness, he had found a way into her.

That, he had not expected. His creator had never allowed that intimacy, that connectivity.

If she owned him, then he carried a bit of her inside him. Her core. Her *soul*.

Was it possible that she carried some of him with her? Was it possible that he—created servant that he was—had a soul?

None of it mattered. Let people who enjoyed thinking think on it. He only knew that he had promised. Promised Wren, that he would be there for her. Promised Sergei, that he would protect her.

He did not give his word. He never gave his word.

To these two humans, he had given his word.

"You're not alone," he whispered, stopping on the street as he felt an ache inside him that he recognized all too well. Loneliness. Not his own. Hers.

There's something wrong with me. Her voice, not so much afraid as resigned.

I know. He had wanted to say something different, to give comfort. But there was none to give.

A day later: different voices. Same meanings.

"*She's going to...burn out.*" Sergei, his face stone, his voice even, his eyes the only thing showing the fear and despair.

"*No, she won't.*"

"*The way she's—*"

"*She won't. I'm here. That's why my creator made me. Us. Demon.*"

He had made promises, not meaning to. Not realizing what they were.

Oaths. Binding. Damning. Everything had led to this moment.

Wren Valere was not his creator. She had never pushed, had never taken anything from him against his will. She treated him.... Like an equal. A friend. A *Cosa*-brother.

If she died, if something went wrong with her that he could have cured, could have prevented and didn't for the sake of vengeance, of retribution...

"Could you live with that?" His own question to Didier, only a few days before. He believed in what she was doing; supported her need to do it.

But no. If she died...if she died because he failed to do something, failed to be there for her.... He would not be able to live with that. He would not be able to survive that.

The demon reached out again. *Wren!*

There was nothing where that connection had been, just days before. No sense of her, no comforting touchback. Nothing but a high-pitched humming noise that made him want to cover his ears...

Except it wasn't coming from outside.

Wren? He did not dare hope. He dared not do anything except reach out...

The humming narrowed and then broadened out, as though it recognized the name and responded to it.

She was on the move. She was... He stopped, his small, rounded ears twitching involuntarily with rage. The stupid bitch was starting the Retrieval early. Without telling him, so that he could tell Danny to tell the Distraction to roll. *Without him.*

P.B. was moving down the street at double-time, slamming his hat on his head and dodging around pedestrians like a pro linebacker before he had even really thought about what he was doing.

Wren was in danger. Worse, she was in danger, and shutting him out.

He was so going to kick her ass.

nineteen

The city might be plunged into darkness, but that didn't mean everyone stopped working.

"Okay, pull the blood from the material...gently...I said gently!"

The formerly bloodstained cloth was now a gleaming ivory, as though it had been several rounds with bleach and hot water. The blood that had been soaked into it, on the other hand, now decorated the back wall in a half-sun splatter pattern.

"I tried," the erring Talent said, his voice reverting to a prepubescent alto. "But I'm shaky. I don't feel good."

The PUPI instructor was not unsympathetic: he could feel his core reaching out, hungry like a baby bird, too. But he let none of that show in his voice or expression.

"Let that be a lesson to you—we can't afford to coast along, thinking we can refill any damn time we like. What happens if you get sent out of the city on a case? Maybe someone offs someone else in the middle of a deserted campground, or a desert? Or in the middle of, oh, a city-wide blackout? Do you even know how to draw energy from anything that's not prepackaged?"

The point struck home, and stayed there.

"I'm sorry, Magister." The boy stared down at the cloth as though he could make the stains reappear by sheer force of will.

"Yeah. You're very sorry, brat." Now the instructor relented, tousling the boy's hair affectionately. "I know you are. And you won't ever let a day go by without checking your current, will you?" He looked down. "At least you had enough sense to splatter-guard your clothing." Not all of them did at first; you learned, after a few go-rounds, that lab-work could get...messy.

"So." He turned the boy's chair around so that they were facing the now-defaced wall. "Tell me about what we can tell from this splatter pattern."

That was a purely intellectual exercise, it wouldn't tax anyone's depleted core. Afterward, the boy could scrub the damn wall down. By hand, with water and cleanser, not magic.

And when daylight came 'round, maybe he'd take the boy for a drive out to the 'burbs, teach him how to find a ley line or two. Just in case.

"Stop! I said stop, damn it!" The cop swore under her breath and lengthened her stride, reaching for the gun by her side. The looter was younger, and faster, and probably knew—same as she did—that this particular alley ended in a locked gate that he'd be able to get over, and she couldn't.

On any other night she just would have reached out and snagged his ankle, used her abilities to make him trip and fall, and then cuffed the son of a bitch before he knew what happened. But tonight the only source of current was coming from St. Vincent's hospital around the corner, and be damned if she was going to touch that for some rinky-dink television set some rinky-dink fourteen-year-old thought he just *haaaaaaad* to have.

"Stupid pimply-faced son of a bitch," she said, and let her hand fall away from her gun. She wasn't going to shoot the idiot.

Her mentor had warned her about not keeping an eye on her internal current levels. She'd gotten cocky, living five blocks from a power generator. Now she—and the people of New York—were paying for that bit of stupidity.

"I promise, Judy," she told her long-departed teacher, watching the aforementioned pimply-faced shmuck throw himself over the fence, "the minute the power comes back on, I'll..."

Oh, who was she kidding? She was thirty years old and a set-in-her-ways bitch; one blackout wasn't going to teach her any new tricks.

Next time, maybe she would just shoot him.

Wren could feel the thoughts of the Talent around her as she traveled through the city. The panic levels were lower than they had been before, but the sense of self-disgust and resignation were palpable. It made her cherish the tiny glow of wild current fueling her; she didn't rely on others to provide her with power, no!

Although she had, more often than not. Honesty forced her to admit that. Honesty, and the memory of what it felt like to sip directly from the East River Generator. Jesus, what a rush that had been!

But none of it matched how she felt now, like her body should be glowing from the awesome amount of current rushing through her, buoying her every step.

Ease. Strength. Current. Power. The thoughts ran through her head, chasing and tumbling over each other, knocking against her skin until she felt the urge to explode with it. Something about them, about *her,* tugged at her brain, worrying her thoughts, then fled. She'd figure it out later. She felt too good to worry, anyway.

It was almost boring, how easy it was to go unnoticed, even as she walked right through a gang of teenagers gathered on their corner; if before she would have been able to dance naked in Grand Central without gathering a flicker more notice than she chose, now the Retriever wasn't sure she could get a firefighter to blink if she set herself on fire in front of him.

She would have giggled, if she were the giggling type.

Once the urge to laugh passed, the knowledge wasn't as good or comforting a thought as it should have been. What if she didn't want to be on fire?

You could control the fire, the current told her. *You could be the fire, if you wanted to.*

Did she want to? She hrmmmed, deep in her throat. Fire illuminated. Fire burned. Fire hurt. She remembered hurting, and she didn't like it. Better to stay here, surrounded and protected by her current, in the cool shadow of it around her, hiding her...

A voice broke into her thoughts. "Yo man, give it up! You ain't got the pow to powwow!"

Three teenagers, too young to be out this late, too old to be kept off the streets by anything other than a lock and key on the door. They were playing crackers—a version of that old schoolyard game where you rested your hands palm down in someone else's, and then tried to keep from getting slapped. It was a stupid game, testing reflexes and nerve, but when you added the "cracker"—the spark of current that went with the slap—it became a sly training tool.

If teens weren't even able to manage that, not even ten hours into a blackout, the collective *Cosa* needed a slap upside the head. That was bad. Bad, and lazy, and dangerous, and might get them all killed some day, if they weren't careful.

She ghosted past the three teens and, just for a laugh, sparked all three of them, hard.

The portraits of the founders lined the back wall of the control room, ten by twelve head shots rather than the more grandiose full-size ones normal to corporate America. The story was that the founders had refused to sit for paintings during their lifetimes, feeling it was too much arrogance on their part. These portraits had been commissioned long after their deaths, when the Silence moved into this building, and the current Board decided that they needed a more formal sense of history. As such, they were probably more flattering than actual depictions might have been.

Nonetheless, the first time he was allowed into this room, Duncan had studied the faces of the founders carefully, looking for clues that weren't in the official records. After that, he never bothered to notice them.

Today, the video monitors on the opposite wall were what held his attention.

"Sir." His aide was talking again. "Sir, we are taking flack for this. I don't know how the rumor started, but people are beginning to whisper. And where there are whispers…" He didn't finish the sentence. By "people" he meant a certain select few within the upper layers of the government, those who were privileged to know of the Silence, if not the specifics of what they were and what they accomplished. The history of their cause.

Duncan had no use for history, except as it proved his own beliefs and powered the future. The future he intended to bring, first to this city, then the country. He was not egotistical enough to think that he could affect the entire world, but he didn't have to. He simply had to start the fire burning.

"Sir, I know what you intended, but…the power will have to go back on by morning. We have no choice."

Duncan watched the screens, only half-listening to his aide as he observed the screen showing bodies milling about, checking weapons and adjusting gear in a room half a city away from where he stood.

"Midmorning, at the latest," his aide went on. "We can't afford to be known——or even suspected——as the ones who disrupted the work-flow. Another hit to the city, more bad news, and we might——"

"Relax, Marc," Duncan finally said. They were alone in the control room; even the half-shift had been released, to get home to their families, to reassure them that the blackout was just a temporary thing, one of those random occurrences that they could tell stories about for years to come. "We keep to our original plan, and we do not panic."

"Sir…"

"The ends will be worth the means. If we move swiftly enough, everything should be just as it was meant to be by the time the sun rises, and you will be able to be a hero to the people of the city, the man who gave them back their televisions and their microwaves."

Marc looked unimpressed with the promise. He was a good man, a more than competent man, and he would never see either side of a news camera, and nobody would ever know his name outside of these walls. So long as the job got done, he was fine with that. He just didn't want there to be any screwups.

"Are our people ready to move?"

"Of course." Marc seemed surprised that his boss even had to ask.

Duncan smiled, pleased by both the answer, and the instant emotional reaction. A good man, Marc was, and worthy of the trust the Silence placed in him.

"Of course. Send them on their way, then, with my wishes for a good hunt."

Marc nodded, and left the room, leaving Duncan alone with the display banks.

He breathed in deeply through his mouth, and then exhaled the same way, a long, drawn-out sound that was almost but not quite a sigh. Years of work, to come to this moment. Years of moving under the surface, of gathering friends and defanging foes, of letting lesser ills flourish in order to root out greater threats....

"Tonight. As the darkness holds us, we fear, and we hide. But the warriors move in the shadows, and with dawn, a new world will awaken..." He smiled, a satisfied, almost smug smile, and his expression was terrifying in the absolute absence of regrets.

"Camera, display seven." At his command, one of the screens switched to another view. Fourteen cots were lined up in a row, and fourteen bodies rested in them. Most were sleeping peacefully. A few were not, turning and tossing as though caught in some unpleasant dream.

"And you, children. Once the city is cleansed, the Board of Directors will have no choice but to accept that my means of attack are effective, and we will no longer have to rely on you and your sadly tainted gifts." A shadow passed over his face, briefly. "But you have served us well. I will make it as painless as possible. You have earned that much grace, in this mortal world."

The lights in the control room were dimmed, as usual. But when Duncan left the room, the hallways were just as dark. They might have a generator capable of lighting the entire building to full power, but there was no need to advertise that fact. And, since they had caused this hardship on the city, it seemed only right to share in it, as well.

Within reason, of course. Duncan had no desire to climb several flights of stairs, merely to prove a point.

The elevator chimed its arrival, and he got in and pressed the 'up' button.

Elsewhere in the city, one of the scenes Duncan had been watching went into action.

"Lock and load, people! Be ready, we're just waiting on the Man's word."

Adam was repellently cheerful, but the look on his face was hard and bitter. The orders had come down the night before, and they had been in lockdown within the building ever since then. Not, of course, that anyone was afraid they would not show up—no, every soul here was willingly sworn to the Silence, and the Silence was sworn to them. The lockdown was only to keep them safe, to prevent anyone from having difficulty coming back to work, any trouble getting into the city when the blackout hit. The blackout that was affecting their families, their friends. The blackout they had not been able to warn anyone about. It stung. But they swallowed it. They did what was needed, as they always did, to protect those who did not know the danger they were in.

"To protect..." It was a whispered refrain, up and down the room. Some of the voices were more convinced—and convincing—than others. It was part of their vows when they came to the Silence, more meaningful than any other oath they ever had or would take: to protect the innocent, to repel the darkness, to defend the light of knowledge, science, and civilization.

"I really don't like this." Jordana looked at the weapon in her hand, repelled by the lightweight feel. She was a fair shot with a gun, could handle a knife, preferred projectile weapons…but this *thing* made her deeply uneasy. She had seen what it did. The Actives called it a witchfinder. But it did more than find them. It *hurt* them.

She had grown up on fairy tales. There were bad witches…and there were good ones, too. Bad fairies…and ones that rocked babies to sleep, and churned milk, and…

"I really don't like this," she repeated, more to herself than any of her companions.

"What, scared?" Erik slid onto the bench next to her, lacing up his boots to make sure they were properly fitted.

"Bite me," she responded, but without any real spirit, putting the plastic tube securely in its holster. He was a Handler, too, about five years older than she was—they were both too old for this. But she wasn't sure she trusted some of the younger members; they had a look around their eyes, a looseness to the skin, that worried her. Like they didn't lose any sleep at all over their orders.

"Is this what you signed up for?" she asked. "Being sent out like a…like a team of hunting dogs?"

He shrugged. "That's exactly what I trained for. To rid the world of dangers. I'm the Silence's dog, and so are you."

"Maybe. Maybe." She rubbed at her face, as though to rid herself the confusion that deviled her brain. "But I just don't see how these people are such a danger. They haven't done anything to anyone."

He snorted. "That you know of."

"Exactly."

He didn't get it. She wasn't sure she even did. But all she could remember was the look on Didier's face, when he came into an Op-friendly bar that one night, looking for information. For allies.

They had accused him of caring more for his new friends than his old. They had called him a traitor, worse. Painful things had been said. Stupid, painful things.

"Don't your FocAs qualify for human status any more?" He had asked them that, and seen something in their eyes, in their lack of response, that had made him stand to leave. "Right. Excuse me then. I won't waste any more of your time."

And she had let him walk out. Had let him believe that she valued some human lives—innocent human lives—over others, simply because of what they were able to do. Like the color of their skin or the ability to sing, something they had no genetic control over...damning them to destruction.

Magic had to leave the world, for order to remain and civilization to thrive. There needed to be one set of rules for everyone. She believed that, as purely as she believed anything. This was a world of rational thought and accomplishment, and old fears and superstitions—and fairy tales—caused people to fear each other, to whisper of curses and hexes, to burn their neighbors and denounce their brothers and sisters, their parents and children. But tonight's orders...she became an Operative to help people. She became a Handler to make sure that Operatives were properly trained. This wholesale slaughter hadn't been part of any of her job description, either time.

But she didn't know what else to do. They were doing ill to do good, and none of it made any sense any more.

"Soldier up," someone called. "Word's been given. Let's roll."

She shuddered, and followed.

twenty

It was dark. Very, very dark. Dark the way city-dwellers weren't familiar with, the kind of dark that could freak you out if you weren't used to it——and sometime even if you were.

That said, Manhattan in early spring, during a blackout, was a lovely place. If you could ignore the dangers that might be stalking you. Sergei, full of tender steaks grilled over a peachwood fire, and Belgium ales, walked with the confidence of a man who knew that he did not present the image of an easy target. Let a mugger *try*.

If he tilted his head just so, he could see the spangle of the night sky overhead, spread out above the buildings. Lovely. As much as he loved the city, there were times he missed getting out past the suburbs, where you could actually see the entire sky, not just hints of it.

He wasn't the only person to note the stars: there were blackout parties going on everywhere in the city, some merely quiet gatherings, others more raucous as they too consumed beer and food before it could spoil, almost all of them spilling onto sidewalks or rising to rooftops.

If a person didn't know better, he or she might think that the entire island of Manhattan had become a giant nighttime tailgate and star-gazing party. The thought made him grin and shake his head. God, he loved this city.

Still, he wasn't totally lost to the reality. When there was a scuffle to the left of him, deep in an alley, he didn't speed up or slow down, but turned his head enough to judge if the scuffle was planning on coming out at him.

When it didn't, he was almost disappointed.

Things were happening elsewhere, *magic* things; he could feel it. Not the urgent sense of need that had gotten him out of bed and into the thick of battle back in January, but a less pressing awareness of danger. Whatever it was, however he knew about it, his presence wasn't required or requested.

And so he walked, slowly and deliberately, enjoying the cool night air, and found his steps taking him, not toward his own apartment, but Wren's.

Her street was, not surprisingly, hosting a block party of sorts. The far end had an impromptu blockade of traffic cones and dining room chairs set up across it to dissuade cars from entering—not that there was much traffic at nearly midnight—and there were at least three coolers filled with beer, open bottles of wine, and soda available for the grabbing.

Unlike some of the other parties he had passed, nobody had a battery-operated boom box blasting music. Instead a tall, long-haired man had brought out an old, battered guitar, and had been joined by another man with a harmonica, and someone else with some sort of percussion instrument, and they were having a relatively quiet jam session while other groups of people stood around and had conversations. There were no children; Sergei didn't know if this just happened to be a child-free street, or if they had all been kept to normal bedtime hours, despite the blackout.

Wren wasn't among the partiers. That didn't surprise him too much: she wasn't much for mingling, especially when she was preparing for a job. She knew all of her neighbors, and liked them, but with the exception of Bonnie, the other lonejack in the building, he didn't know if any of them had ever even been in her apartment, or if she had been in theirs.

It did surprise him that Bonnie wasn't out here; the young Talent never met a party she didn't like.

When he got to the building, he noted that all three windows of Wren's apartment were dark, then laughed at himself. Of course they would be. Even if she were burning candles, she normally kept the heavy shades drawn and the light wouldn't show through.

The apartment a few floors down had a full blaze of light going, however. Candles, and a glow that could have been a battery-operated lamp, or something a little more esoteric. Bonnie's place, he guessed. That was why she wasn't out on the street—she was hosting her own shindig.

One of those well-lit windows flew open, and a man stuck his head out, scanning the street. He disappeared, and the white-blond head of a woman replaced his, looking down to the street, directly at Sergei.

"Hey you!"

Whistle for the devil…

"Hey, you," he replied.

"C'mon up! We have ice cream that's melting!"

"You and most of the city," he replied under his breath, but opened the—unlocked, he noted with dismay—front door of the building and climbed the stairs to Bonnie's apartment.

There weren't as many people there as he had anticipated, and only one of them was Fatae. He suspected that the others were all Talent, simply because they seemed to recognize him.

Wren wasn't there.

"Where is she?"

Bonnie offered him a bowl of ice cream and, when he refused, shrugged and poured a hefty dollop of hot fudge over it, then dug her own spoon in.

"Don't know. Came home, she wasn't here. Didn't respond to a ping when the party started. It's been a little nuts around here… Talent tends to freak during blackouts. I figured a righteous ice-cream coma would do them good."

Sergei looked around, reconsidering. She was right—most of them did seem to be somewhat…wound up, despite the overdose of carbs they were ingesting.

"Wren never seemed to mind blackouts," he said, distracted.

Bonnie nodded. "Noted that about her. She likes to source wild. Smart girl. It's harder to do that, most of the time, but good to know how, at least. To be comfy with it, if needs be."

He already knew that Wren was smart. She was also AWOL. "So you haven't seen her?"

"Seen her, nope. Heard her, though."

"Oh?" His tone was a little harsher than he should have been, but Bonnie took it in stride. He made a mental note, again, not to underestimate the young Talent. Bonnie might look like a wisp of a Goth-girl, with her pale skin, paler hair, and mélange of depressing-funky clothing, but she was a PUPI, one of the hotshot investigators of the *Cosa Nostradamus*. More, Wren respected her, and her coworkers, to the point of being cautious around them. His partner didn't give higher praise.

"Yah, when the blackout hit." Bonnie bounced up and down on her toes; she clearly went into a sugar high, not a carb coma, off her ice cream. "Everyone was sort of panicking, yanno? Or not panicking so much as asking who shut out the lights. Because something this big? Either somebody seriously blew out the works, on a wizzing-out level, or a whole bunch of somebodies are going to get canned from cushy jobs in the electric-works."

"Wouldn't you know if someone wizzed out on that level?" he asked sharply. Wizzing was the ten-ton elephant in the room, for most Talent. As far as he had been able to put together, it was a combination of mental illness, nervous breakdown, and homicidal rage. It struck the most powerful, or Pure, of the *Cosa,* and it usually did so out of the blue, when they were reaching the prime of their lives. Wren's own mentor had wizzed, abandoning her three-quarter trained rather than risk staying near her when it happened.

She sucked absently on her spoon. "Maybe. Sometimes. It depends on what they were doing when it happened. Anyway, when it all went dark, I think Wren was mucking about with the weather."

"That rain shower?" He had wondered if it was her, but why?

"Yah. That rain shower that had way more mojo to it than an ittty-bitty shower should have." Bonnie shook her head, her hair—shorter now than the last time he had seen her—flying around her head like thistledown. "Like I said, she likes to source wild, and despite her best efforts I've got a pretty good feel for her signature by now—and don't let her know that, okay?" Bonnie's pale blue eyes looked up at him, guileless under the black eyeliner and shadow.

Right. If she was half as sharp as Wren thought, that was in no way shape or form an accidental slip. But he just nodded and pushed on. "The point, Bonnie?"

"Why was she sourcing? That storm, she had to be pulling it before the blackout hit, to nail it. So why did she wild-source, *before?*"

The question he was about to ask himself.

"Something's going down, isn't it? The blackout, Wren powering up..."

"As I remember being told, you didn't want any part of it," he said, taking out his cell phone and checking to make sure that he hadn't missed any messages. He hadn't. Also, his charge was running low. Damn.

It was a hard blow, and to give Bonnie credit, she took it squarely. "She's my friend."

And that was the right—the only right—answer, for him.

He had seven numbers in his speed dial. Two of them belonged to people who were dead now. He sent up a prayer to the gods that using a cell phone in an apartment of nervous Talents wasn't as stupid an idea as it probably was, then pressed number six and heard the call connect.

"Answer, damn it. Answer!"

P.B. didn't pick up.

It might mean nothing. The demon might—unlike Wren and Bonnie—be able to use electronic equipment without hesitation, but Sergei didn't know how often he actually did. Obviously he hadn't gotten around to getting an answering machine or service, yet.

"Have you seen P.B. recently? In the past twenty-four hours?" P.B. had promised he would be with Wren if he needed her. The demon had *promised* he would be there.

Bonnie shook her head, absently spooning more fudge-covered

ice cream into her mouth while she thought. "No. I was hanging with Danno yesterday, watching..." She looked up at Sergei over her spoon, as though trying to figure out how much he knew.

"Watching...?" he prompted her.

She flicked a gaze around the apartment, as though to make sure that nobody else was paying attention to their conversation.

"Team practice."

"Team...oh." The only thing he could think of, that she might refer to under those conditions, was the group of Talent she had declined to be part of—the ones who were supposed to be distracting the Silence when Wren made her move. He didn't know what they were actually planning—neither did Wren, from what little she had told him. Safer that way, since both of them were known—and therefore likely targets—of the Silence itself.

So far the Silence had only used their catspaw, the anti-Fatae vigilantes, but Andre's last message made it clear that "so far" was not the law of the land any longer. It was only a matter of time...

Time. Timing.

He snapped his phone closed, ending the call, and dodged around someone coming into the kitchen for more ice cream, heading for the door. Bonnie was on his heels, having picked up his sudden fear.

Wren's door was unlocked, and Sergei felt an unfamiliar sensation grab him by the throat and the balls. It only took a second to identify it: panic. He held it off, barely, stopping the girl when she would have gone racing into the apartment ahead of him.

"Bonnie. Has anyone been here? Did anyone tamper with the locks?"

She looked at him, and then reached her hand out, fingers pointing up, palm toward the door. Her eyes glazed over slightly, and her head cocked to the side. Accustomed to Wren's body language when she was working, Sergei had the sudden urge to take notes on the differences. Wren preferred to crouch, and almost always tilted her face up, not to the side. He wondered what it meant, if it meant anything.

"She leaves elementals here, usually?" Bonnie asked. Elementals were tiny creatures that lived in the current-stream, like particularly dumb watchdogs, Wren had told him once. "They're not curious about me—she's given them my taste. Yours, too. They're not upset about anything. They weren't set to guard...she left in a hurry but not under duress, and nobody's been here since then."

She blinked, and dropped her hand. "She just forgot to lock her door."

Sergei set his jaw and pushed the door open, already knowing what he would find: the apartment empty, her kit gone. She had started the Retrieval early. In a blackout, when she would be at a disadvantage.

"I'll take them when they're distracted." A flash of memory: she was sitting on the counter, in this apartment, her feet swinging, her hands moving as she talked. "When they have other things to worry about, when they're not expecting me."

Attacking from a position of weakness. Suddenly, violently, Sergei wished he had never taught an eager-eyed twenty-something anything at all about tactics, military or otherwise.

"Damn it," he swore, feeling the same weight of helpless anticipation that always settled on him whenever she was on a job. At least P.B. would be with her.

"It's on, isn't it?"

He turned to look at the other Talent, and nodded. She met his gaze evenly, then looked around the empty apartment.

"More ice cream," Bonnie said in a definite tone. "More ice

cream, and a lot more hot fudge, and then we're going to break out the hard stuff."

"Booze?"

She shook her head, looking very serious. "Butterscotch."

Despite his worry, Sergei started to laugh.

Just another job. Just another job. The details changed but the object was always the same: go in, Retrieve, get out. Nothing else interfered, nothing else mattered. Don't think about anything else. Don't acknowledge anything else exists.

Wren was cranky. She wasn't feeling the usual buzz she got when working. Maybe it was the silence around her: usually inside a building she could hear the humming of the wiring; depending on how juiced the system was, it was like hearing a friend talking in another room.

There was emergency power in the building, but it was faint, barely running the exit lights and backup systems.

Quiet, quiet. Too quiet. It was making her itch.

Wren had a sudden, ugly flashback to the House of Holding, the stone monastery where the Brothers guarded dangerous Artifacts, things that could not be allowed into the Null world. The House was a Dark Space, a location where no current existed.

This...wasn't that bad. Dark Spaces could drive a Talent mad. This was merely making her cranky.

Plus, there was some sort of grit in her socks. She wiggled her toes. Her feet had been clean when she put the socks on. The socks had been clean when she took them out of the drawer, and she'd taken a gypsy cab to the job site. So how had grit gotten in there?

Stop worrying about it. Job. Pay attention to the job. She could have used current to create enough static cling to hold her to the wall, could have slid down without using ropes or tools.

Could have, but didn't. Barely. She could feel the current surging in her, but held it in reserve. Never use strength when skill will do. An old cat burglar had taught her that, back when she first started. He'd been closing in on sixty, and could still rock the house because he used his brains more than his brawn.

Use your brain, Valere. Current is at a premium right now, no matter how good you feel. And when it goes, it's gone until power comes back up again. No storm going to roll into town to save your ass.

She rappelled her way carefully down the elevator shaft, praying to god that the power didn't come back on suddenly and squish her between car and wall.

God—or someone—was on her side, because she made it to the lowest level without too much difficulty. Letting her feet touch the floor, she slowly uncurled her fingers from the cables, flexing them to restore feeling in the tips. She removed the climbing claws and put them back in her bag, and pulled open the elevator doors.

Emergency lights were functioning here, unlike the upper floors, and the pale red sheen disoriented her for a moment. Her sight adjusted just in time to see a hand, seemingly unattached to an arm, coming down, aiming for her face. Wren ducked, blending into the darker red shadows of the hallway so that the body attached to the hand stumbled past her, overextending and falling facedown on the carpet.

Jesus wept....

He was wearing dark clothing, a black and gray mottled sweater, and pants. Not the thing you wore at night, unless you wanted to look like a shadow yourself. Thieves' clothing. Assassin's clothing.

Wren leaned over and touched the exposed nape of her assailant's neck, sending a focused charge down his spine. His legs kicked once, like a dying frog, and he went still.

She looked up, trying to get her bearings, her heart pounding way too fast for job-standards. "Jesus wept." Her voice cracked on the second word.

In front of her, two bodies blocking the way she needed to go were locked in the kind of hand-to-hand combat you didn't see in movies because it was too boring to look dangerous. Wren didn't make that mistake: the knife glittering in their joined grip was deadly, and she didn't know which one of them was going to end up in possession of it.

She didn't know shit, in fact, starting with who either of them were, what they were doing here, and why they were trying to kill each other. Or if either or both of them would turn on her next.

And the grit between her toes was really starting to piss her off.

Kill them! Kill them all!

The cry in her head was shrill and pained, like a cat whose tail had just been hammered. But before Wren would react, a soothing mental blanket was thrown over the first voice, trying to calm it.

It wouldn't be calmed. *Kill them! Kill them before they kill all of us!*

Wren winced under the anger and fear being broadcast in that command. But the two figures in front of her didn't seem to hear it, or if they did, they had more pressing things concerning them.

One of them was wearing the same camouflage gear as the guy she had taken out. The other wore street clothing: a blue sweater over black slacks. Dark, but not suspiciously so. Wren automatically rooted for that person, despite not having clue one what was going on.

The knife fight came to an abrupt end with a rough gesture by the left-hand figure in street clothes, the metal edge sliding into the chest of the camouflaged combatant with a meaty thunk, like the sound of a pig being slaughtered.

Wren had never heard a pig being slaughtered, specifically, but someone in the building had. She realized that in the same instant that she realized her senses were feeding his or her awareness, and that she was being fed the memory of pigs dying in return. Pigs, and the still-screaming voice, and the awareness of more, just out of range, reaching out to her: trying to get in.

Wren slammed her brain shut, flattening herself against the wall again as though the assault had been a physical one.

She was breathing heavy in a way none of her physical exertions had caused. This wasn't normal. This kind of sensitivity, this ease of current flowing through her…. What the *fuck* was going on?

You know.

No, I don't.

Yes, you do.

Yes, she did. *Something is wrong with me.* But she couldn't think of it, couldn't even say the word. Not now. She was committed; she had to follow through. Worry later.

The winner of the fight had fallen to his—her—knees. The woman looked up, her expression unutterably weary. She was not young, and there was blood staining the front of her shirt. Not all of it belonged to the other guy. Wren tensed, but didn't otherwise react. The woman hadn't proven herself an enemy…yet.

"Who…'re you?" the stranger asked, her voice as gray as her face.

"The Wren." There didn't seem to be any reason to evade the question, at this point. Not if the woman could see her, anyway. And showed no intent—much less ability—to lunge at her with the knife still held in her hand.

A lefty. Wren noted that fact, and felt her body adjust its stance, just in case. Morgan would be so proud. Assuming she lived long enough to tell him.

"Ah." It seemed to be answer enough. Sometimes infamy was useful. The woman's shoulders slumped. "Good. Get them?"

Wren frowned, confused.

"Get them…out of here." The woman let go of the knife, letting it fall with a soft thud onto the floor, and reached into the pocket of her pants. She rummaged for something, then, finding it, stretched her arm in Wren's direction, her fingers closed into a fist. "Do it. Use this."

Wren took the item from the woman's hand, trying not to let any of the blood touch her. It was a small button, flat black plastic, like a doll's eye, only larger.

"Doorway. Signals." The woman stared at Wren, as though trying to command her. "Safe for you to use. Get them out."

Wren slid the button into the thigh pocket of her slicks, where it barely made a bulge. "I will."

The woman nodded, then sank back onto her haunches, clearly out of strength. "Go. Hurry."

Wren went, stepping over the bloody body of the woman's opponent without looking down. Whoever the woman was, she was going to have to take care of herself.

The blueprints in her memory kept her on-track, and she made two turns without hesitation, and then came to a full stop. Three more bodies clogged the passage, blocking her way. They had fallen practically on top of each other, a macabre parody of a ménage à trois. She stepped closer, forcing herself to look. One in those dark cammos, the other two in civvies. All of them had been killed in hand-to-hand—there was no sign, as far as she could tell, of bullets or bullet holes in the bodies, and no smell of gunpowder in the air. Just jagged, gaping wounds, round burns the size of quarters, and puddles and splashes of thick, dark blood everywhere: bodies, floor, and walls.

Wren stepped over the pile, shuddering, and kept walking, a little bit faster, now. The stink of shit and blood was impossible to avoid, thicker and thicker as she went down. Bad things had happened here. Bad things. Recently. They might still be going on. *Be careful, Valere...*

Getting killed before she finished the job was not part of the plan.

She moved carefully, keeping her no-see-me steady, but didn't run into any other bodies, alive or dead. Lit only by those dim red lights, with no windows, with the weight of those bodies behind her, she felt as though she were moving through an underground passage directly into Hell.

The hallway widened, the office doors giving way to larger common areas, furnished with sofas and low tables, like a quality but not luxury hotel lobby. A Hell furnished by Ethan Allen. Nice.

The fact that her sense of humor hadn't run screaming entirely was reassuring.

According to the blueprints, there should be an entrance somewhere, in one of those common areas just about...there. Yes. She reached for her lockpick tools, feeling a faint anticipation at being able to do some violence herself, no matter how mild.

Except the door that was supposed to be secret, secure, locked-down, was open. The metal-sheathed-in-wood door was held that way by a body, propped upright as though it had staggered back and sat down hard, blocking the door from closing entirely.

A body that had no head—just a raw chunk of flesh that had once been a neck, severed veins still oozing blood—Jesus wept, she thought, so much blood—over its shoulders and onto the carpeted floor.

Wren stared at it. She knew somewhere a gag reflex was forming, but she also knew that it would never surface. Not while she was in this building. Not while she was on the job.

Humans had done this to each other. Had hacked and stabbed, burned and killed. Why?

If they could do this to each other…what had they done to the Talent in their possession?

She could feel herself shutting down, processing the stink and the sights through a filter that belonged to someone else. Someone far away. Another box, crammed full and locked down, slamming shut in her brain. She was nothing but boxes within boxes, and the gray mist over them all.

Leave it alone. If the fog lifts, you'll see. If you see…

She stepped over the body, and through the doorway into complete darkness. There were no emergency lights here, no security strips, nothing to lighten the oppressive weight. The air was stale and still; the air circulation systems were dead, too.

They weren't even trying to keep this portion of the building livable.

Current simmered into a boil, tingling just under her skin.

"Dark light come
shade night into dusk
let us see"

The blacklight spell kicked in, and the area around Wren was lit enough for her to see without blinding her or giving her position away. The moment she could see, she wished she couldn't.

The missing head stared at her from the small metal desk just inside the fake doorway. A good-looking face, once; healthy and still young. The expression was annoyed more than anything else, as though asking why she was wasting his time. Beyond the desk, the wall was smeared with a dark stain that Wren was pretty sure was only partially blood.

Are you here to kill us?

The voice was small and scared and vicious.

No Wren sent back. *No. I'm here to take you...* She hesitated, Doherty's words during one of their planning sessions coming back to her. 'Don't scare them. Don't challenge them. They're not used to having options.' *I'm here to take you the next step.*

It seemed to be vague enough not to be threatening. *Oh* the voice responded.

A figure unfolded from behind the desk. The dark stain was all over its hands, and the face was covered with a nasty bruise that was even worse in the black light.

They came to kill us.

"Who did, little brother?" She risked voice, but backed it up with a mental echo, in case the sound of her voice freaked him out. He started, but the echo seemed to reassure him.

Keeper's men. Keeper's women. Other Keeper's men and women fought them. We fought them. But it was hard. So hard. Not supposed to be that way. Keeper protects. Keeper doesn't hurt. Keeper keeps us safe and away from sin.

The visuals that accompanied the litany seared red into Wren's brain, and made the gray fog of her current seethe with hard, black sparks.

They had come to clean their mess, the Silence had. Had decided they no longer needed their FocAs, their twisted children.

Eleven Silence employees had been onsite when it happened. When the troops arrived, and ordered them to stand aside.

Four had. Seven had not.

Wren reached into the thigh pocket and felt the black button in her hand, practically felt it beating with the lifeblood spilled in this place. The woman had been one of those who resisted. Who defended her charges until someone came for them. It did not excuse what they had done before, what they had been part of, but...

"*I will bring them home,*" she promised those doomed, damned souls, feeling rage start to boil, deep down and low. "*I will keep them alive.*"

Others? she asked, projecting the feeling, as best she could, of fellows-in-danger, the closest thing she could approximate to friendship, a feeling that Doherty had warned her they might not understand.

Inside, he said. *I don't know how to get back in.*

An image of a door sliding open and shut came to her, along with a wave of frustration because the door would no longer open enough to get in. Despite the fact that he looked to be in his mid-twenties, he was reacting on the level of a five-year-old: knowing basic facts but unable to process them logically. She looked around, trying to match his visuals to the layout.

This was just a foyer, one final security check before getting to the heart of what was hidden here.

Let me, she said, and stepped around the desk. The plastic button vibrated in her hold, and the door hidden behind that desk slowly, reluctantly, slid open.

Onward into Hell, she thought, letting the black-tar current rise into her skin, welcoming the madness, and the strength it brought. *Damned souls only, please.*

She went through, the boy close on her heels.

twenty-one

Driving through New York City at any time was an exercise in quick reflexes and a total lack of fear. Tonight, without traffic lights to rein them in, cabbies and out-of-towners each thought they ruled the road, and the laws weren't even suggestions any more. Pedestrians stayed on the sidewalk, hoping the cars would keep to the streets.

And yet there were surprisingly few accidents. Rude and aggressive the drivers might be, but driving in any of the boroughs of New York City on a daily basis took a level of skill a mere blackout couldn't erase.

As the night passed, fewer and fewer cars were on the road, and the pedestrians found other places to be, either safely home in bed, or off at an impromptu celebration. A white van, paneled and totally ordinary, right down to the rude comments sprayed in paint and written in the dirt on the back end, moved down Atlantic Avenue in Brooklyn, cruising like an aged Great White shark before pulling onto a residential side street and pausing along the curb.

The engine cut, and the driver turned around to give his passengers last-minute reminders and instructions. "Do it quick, and hard. Don't leave anything behind."

"Anything" was left undefined. No random refuse. No evidence. No survivors.

There were ten operatives in the back of the van, half old-timers, half relative newbies. Most of the teams around the city were the same, varying only in size.

One of them opened the backdoor slightly and peeked out, making sure it was clear to exit. The van was double-parked next to a battered sedan. It was still too dark to see what make or model it was, even if anyone had cared.

The figures themselves wore dark pants, dark sweaters. Hands were cased in clear latex gloves, shoes durable leather with soft rubber soles. They all carried, not guns, but small tubes filled with plastic wiring and insulation, like some futuristic electricians come on a service call.

Someone cleared their throat, the sound unnervingly similar to the sound of retching. Someone else dropped something metallic on the floor, and swore softly.

"Get rid of that. No metal. Nothing conducive." The tone clearly said "you idiot."

"Try not to set off the alarm," one of the shadowy figures said as they exited.

"You really think anyone will notice, around here?" came the response, and another figure reached out, slapping the passenger-side door of the car next to them with the flat of his hand.

A whoop-whoop-whoop noise started screaming from inside the car, and the ten figures tensed, ready to jump back into the van if need be.

"See?" the Operative who had done the slapping said. "Nobody even notices."

The driver got out of the van and glared at them. "Stop screwing around. You have your target. *Move!*"

They moved.

Across the city, on the island and in the outlying boroughs, similar vans and sedans were pulling up to addresses, each one ticked off on a master list as they were approached, entered, and cleansed. Nobody saw them. Nobody heard them. Nobody stopped them.

Dora had been tasked with getting her brothers up in time for school. Never mind that there wasn't going to be any school today—not if the power didn't come back on soon—her dad told her to do it and she did it.

"Jimmmmmmy… Jim, get up."

"Doooorrra, s'stupid. No school." Jimmy's voice was muffled by the pillow over his head, and she was tempted, briefly, to hold it over his face more firmly. He must have sensed her intent, because he scooted out of reach, his sleep-puffy face emerging to glare accusingly at her. "Won't be any school."

"Dad said to get up."

She grinned at him at the change in his expression, mission accomplished, and went over to Michael's bed. He slept more soundly than his twin, and wouldn't wake up even if you yelled in his ear. She'd have to be considerably more direct.

"Spark him," Jimmy said, sitting up and watching from his own bed.

"Sadistic brat." Dora was fourteen to their eleven. She knew better. Even though it was tempting. They didn't get to use current, except when they were having lessons. Instead she reached down and pulled the covers off him, dumping them on the floor at her feet.

He slept on.

"Spark him. You know it works."

"I'm not going to get in trouble." The only light in the bedroom was the pale dawn light coming in through the windows.

"Why did Dad have us get up, anyway? I'm a growing boy, I need my sleep. All the medical boards say so."

"Dad said to get up. I don't ask why. You want to ask, he's downstairs in the kitchen, trying to figure out how to magic up some coffee."

Jimmy declined.

Someone drove up next door, parking on the street outside. There wasn't any overnight parking, and it was still too early. They were going to get a ticket, she thought absently. Car doors slammed: a sedan, or a minivan. Awful lot of people—maybe somebody's carpool coming in for early coffee?

"Huh. I still think——"

The shock threw him off the bed, knocking Dora flat on her ass.

"Dora!"

"Shhh..." She raised a hand, although there was no reason not to say anything. No reason not to speak. It was nice outside, but she was freezing cold. Whatever it was, it was happening elsewhere. And if they stayed very quiet, and didn't do anything, maybe it would stay elsewhere.

They heard a loud noise, then a softer one. Voices, muffled, and the sound of a front door opening and slamming shut again.

The birds had stopped singing.

Let them go next door. Across the street. Anywhere but here. Let that current-blast have come from somewhere else.

Jimmy scooted across the floor and shoved his way under her arm. She cuddled him the way he hadn't let her in years, not since he was a little kid, and they stayed there as the sun brightened in the window.

Michael slept through it all.

Her husband saw them first. "Get out of here!"

That was the first warning they had, that single shout. But it was all Sue needed. She had been preparing for over a year. Call her paranoid, but her family had escaped from Germany literally minutes ahead of the Nazis, generations before, and they still told the stories. She knew what hatred eventually came to.

This time, her family wasn't going to run.

Her mother had been a doctor. Her father a teacher. She would never debase the gift they had given her by using it to kill. But there were other ways to resist. Ways Nulls had created. When rumors of the Distraction filtered through the ranks, rumors of first strikes and payback, she knew what she would do.

By the time the men came upstairs, the forty-three-year-old woman was on the landing, waiting for them. Her and the double-barreled shotgun she had bought three months before.

She didn't have a permit to own it, but that didn't matter. She knew she wasn't going to be arrested. Not for possession, anyway.

And she was going to take them with her when she went.

When the man raised what looked like an empty plastic tube and aimed it at her, her first instinct had been to laugh. The shock that hit her when he triggered it was nothing compared to the shock of having her current drawn away and then returned into her system twice as hard. Her fingers convulsed around the trigger guard, and the bullets sprayed, uncontrolled, in an arc across the stairs.

She didn't take all of them with her. But she took enough.

* * *

Deep in the sublevels of the Silence's FocAs dormitories, Wren shook her head, a faint buzzing noise distracting her almost as much as the boy making like a second shadow behind her. She wasn't supposed to be distracted. She was supposed to have distracters working for her. By now, P.B. should have given them the word, started everything in motion.

She had told him, hadn't she? She couldn't remember actually talking to him. But she must have...

And what the hell are you waiting for? she asked the gestalt-mind, irritably, feeling the press of the damaged minds around her, the lone voice still shrieking in pain, somewhere deeper down in the building. Unthinking, she echoed it. *Kill them. Kill them all.*

Caught up in the pain, the anger, and the current running hot in her core, she did not realize how far, or how hard, she broadcast that last.

"You Lawrence Kohmer?"

"Huh? Yeah." The older man stood, pushing his chair back. They'd been halfway through the thirty-six-hour shift when the blackout hit, and while they were still ready for the worst, things had been calm enough to let them stand down a bit. He'd taken advantage of the quiet to sit down in the kitchen with a cup of now-cold but still potent coffee, and try to get through yesterday's *Times* when the interruption came.

The men who asked his name wore dark pants and heavy sweaters, like SWAT guys, but they wore them like expensive suits. He thought that if he looked down he'd see polished dress shoes sticking out under their cuffs. But he wasn't fool enough to look. You didn't need to be a genius to know these guys weren't with the City. Or any of the local news teams.

The third man in the triad took out a plastic tube, like an over-sized cigar case, and pointed it at the firefighter. "No, he's not."

"Excuse me?" Kohmer went for his wallet, arresting the movement when all three besweatered men reacted badly to his moving. "Hey, just going to show you some I.D., is all. If you're gonna serve me with papers or something, you wanna make sure it's the right guy, right?"

"It's not him." The third man sounded positive, and a little worried. "Or our records were wrong."

"Impossible." The first speaker had cold brown eyes, and he didn't seem to need to blink. Kohmer's shirt was wet down the back from sweat, despite the coolness of the evening air. They were the eyes of a hangman, the gaze of an executioner, staring right at him.

"Your records were right." The voice came from behind them, and as the three strangers turned to confront it, the plastic tube sparking as they moved, they were hit square in the chest by an impressive stream of water coming from a one-and-a-half-inch attack hose being held by the speaker.

The tube went flying, sparks arcing from it into the air, as though seeking a target.

The three intruders went down under the water like bowling pins in a strike. The man holding the hose wrestled it off, and the first firefighter, moving with a speed that mocked his age, had the non-speaking one in cuffs before they could recover. Burly men in FDNY windbreakers on over their jeans quickly tackled the other two, tying them up with similar speed, despite the water now covering the floor.

"Stupid fuckers," one of the firefighters snarled, being rougher with the cuffs that was strictly needed. "You come after one of us, you gotta deal with us all."

Having a Talent in the firehouse was a good luck charm. Having one like Larry, with strong Precog? Let the NYPD throw their magicals out—New York's Bravest knew when they had a good thing going.

"It's a good thing you told us something hinky was going down, Larry. Hey, what do you want us to do with—Larry!"

They turned to see their coworker on the floor just outside the kitchen, his normally ruddy complexion gone ashen-gray.

"He's having a heart attack!" one of them yelled. "Get the kit!"

"You idiot!" the man who had pretended to be Kohmer snapped, and dropped down to give manual assistance. The AED—automated external defibrillator—would probably make the situation worse for someone like Larry. They all knew that.

"Not…heart. Core," Larry managed to gasp. He lifted his arm, and they saw a round burnt-out circle on his chest, just under his name patch. "A fourth one, come in through the back. Got me…stupid…got away."

The faux-Kohmer tried to calm him. "You just stay still, man, you're going to be okay. You know the drill—save your strength…."

But the firefighter had already been running low, thanks to the blackout, and the witchfinder had taken the last from his core and turned it back on him, burning him out. There was no strength left to be saved.

He tried again, grabbing at his coworker's sleeve with shaky fingers. "Not…only attack. Everywhere. Go. Help."

"Man, we can't…"

"Help," he insisted, and then closed his eyes. In the gray haze, he Foresaw one last time: a woman, standing in the darkness. Falling into and swallowed by the darkness, an everlasting fall. *Kill them. Kill them all.*

Then a thousand tiny flickers of lighting descended upon her, lighting her from within in colors he had no words for. Her eyes blazed with actual fire, and her hair singed, and the world changed under her feet.

Larry didn't know who she was, or what happened. But with the last tendril of current he had left, he passed the image along to his sister, safely distant in Seattle. That final responsibility served, he left his body in the frantic hands of his coworkers, and let himself go.

Terry Kohmer woke suddenly, a hundred voices in her head. "Take me," they said. "Take me. Use me. Use me, hidden cousin. Use me. Save us. Save us all." And one strident voice insisting: *Kill them. Kill them all.*

Under it all, a salty wet stream of tears, a whisper of love, and she knew that her brother was dead.

She rolled over and looked at the clock: 3:00 a.m. It was just after dawn, on the East Coast. Had there been a fire, a deadly blaze? He had been sad, not frightened, not in pain. There was solace in that, but only some.

"Goodbye, baby brother," she whispered.

*"Use me."*Kill them.*

Terry frowned. The voices. Voices that came with the knowledge of her brother's death. The words meant something. What did they mean?

Use me, hidden cousin.

Cousin. The full impact of his sending came to her, staggering her mentally. A full hundred voices, a hundred different voices, all calling for their cousin.

Fatae. The knowledge came out of the voices, the strange accents and tastes to them. Only the Fatae would call a human cousin.

Hidden cousin.

Something important was coming. Something Larry had Foreseen before he died. Something important enough for him to send to her with his last scrap of strength.

She rolled over and poked her companion. "Who would be a hidden cousin?"

"Wha?"

"Who would be a hidden cousin?"

"Mmmphdonno. Someone's invisible?"

"You're no help at all."

"Mmmasleep."

"Who would the Fatae call a hidden cousin?"

"Zawren."

"What?"

Her companion yawned, then reached up to pull the pillow off her head so she could be heard better. "The Wren. That Retriever. If you'd listen to gossip every now and then instead of zoning out in boredom, you wouldn't have to wake me up to know these things."

"Thanks." She kissed her partner. "Go back to sleep."

She slipped out of bed and went into the other room to use the telephone. There would be time to mourn her brother later, after she had passed along his last message.

Kill them all.

She hesitated, then shook her head. That wasn't part of her brother's vision. It wasn't the voice of the Fatae. And yet, it lingered, the pain of it unforgettable.

Kill them all.

Ron was exhausted. He couldn't remember the last time he had slept. Yesterday? No, maybe the day before. At this point, he wasn't sure he could sleep even if they tucked him into silk sheets with a thousand-dollar whore.

The Distraction had tried, as best they could, despite the distinctly panicked "go!" message from P.B. coming far earlier than expected. The Wren had obviously decided to take advantage of the blackout and it made total sense, but it would have been nice to get more than ten minutes' warning.

Despite that short notice, his people had done everything he had asked, and then some. They had previously chosen a rooftop location in Manhattan to center on, radiating out across all across the five boroughs, and as soon as word came they were there, two Talent each at every location. The moment he triggered them, each slid into the gestalt as though they'd had a month of daily practices, instead of only the one.

Ron had stood with the map on that rooftop in midtown, and pinpointed each location, as per The Wren's notes. One by one, the Silence's holdings were targeted, their personnel identified, and homed in on.

And one by one, those Silence members fell, the cells in their bodies exploded as though by a direct lightning strike.

Death by electrocution would be the cause listed in their postmortems.

Ron lost count after thirty bodies. He stopped thinking, after fifty. By the time the gestalt faltered, there were over a hundred bodies downed by his command. Not even close to all, but damage done. Maybe enough to stop the beast in its tracks, certainly enough to draw attention away from the true target.

Then word came of the counterstrike, the Talent being eradicated in turn by dark-clothed Nulls with weapons similar to but far deadlier than the new hot-sticks some Talent carried. It was too soon and too large-scale to be retribution: the Silence had planned this, had likely set up the blackout to aid in it.

The sniper war had turned into a firefight.

Kill them. Kill them all.

He shook his head, trying to dislodge the faint, disturbing thought.

The call had come, and they had tried. But it was too much, even for his team, even fueled by the knowledge that every body they took out was one less to strike against them. They had faltered, fallen out of gestalt, and he had scattered them, sent them into hiding, into safety.

He had no guilt for what he had done. But the responsibility would never leave him.

Not for the ones he had killed; for the ones who had lived long enough to kill his own kind. For the Talent who died, when one more strike might have saved them.

In the aftermath, drained and aching, not knowing what to do, Ron had followed instinct, and ended up here, sucking down coffee and dealing with shell-shocked Talent as they came in. And they did come in, either following him or drawn by the same thing that had brought him in, some sense of safety in this space. Or maybe it was the cowboy coffee, which the owners were brewing over a probably illegal wood-burning stove in the back of the kitchen.

The blond from the park, Bonnie somethingorother, was slumped over her own coffee. Her eyes were bloodshot, and she had the twitches bad enough that Ron wondered if he should cut her off from the coffee. The Wren's tall, scary-eyed partner had brought her over sometime after midnight, before he disappeared with Danny on some mysterious, urgent errand.

"So many dead," she said now, speaking into the thick black liquid. "Can you hear them? Can you hear them?"

Yes. He could. Or rather, he couldn't. The absence of current where once there had been current was...loud.

"It's happening all over the city. It's a fucking massacre, is what it is." Megan was from the Council; her mother was a Council member, but she was friends with Kaylee who was mentoring Ron's little sister Gale, and the three of them had found their way to this coffee shop the same way everyone else did. following their instinct. There was only cold food and things that were about to spoil to go with the coffee, and the tables were lit by an assortment of candles that would have had the fire department down on their asses any other night, but nobody seemed to care. Nobody had the energy to care, literally.

And now, with reports coming in of attacks—of murders—all over the tri-state area...

It had become, de facto, the refugee gathering point, the source of what little information they had, the sending-out point of what little help they could offer.

And in all that, Ron had found himself by default the go-to guy. He wondered if this was the equivalent of a battlefield promotion, and did the best he could.

He looked at the Talent sitting in front of him, their exhausted faces proof of the strain they were under. "Tell everyone you can reach to get out of their houses, go somewhere they're not known. If they can't get out, stay low. Stay with Nulls they can trust."

"Who?" Livvy had the coffeepot in her hand, and a snippy tongue in her mouth.

"Damn it, I don't know, somebody must know a trustworthy Null!"

He looked around the space. So many Talent, gathered together. He should send them all away, make them find individual hiding places. But this wasn't a known address; it was as random as it could be...if they weren't safe here, in public, together, they weren't going to be safe anywhere.

And he didn't think they'd leave, anyway. Once again, he cursed the instinct that had made him sign up with Wren and her merry brand of troublemaking. He could have been all the way to Finland by now. He and Gale had relatives there. They said it was peaceful. Quiet. A little cold, sure, but global warming would take care of that...

Livvy was talking again, refilling everyone's mugs. "Talent'll survive. We know how to scatter and go low. I'm more worried about what's going on with Herself."

There had been no word from Wren, which was expected, and no word from—or sight of—P.B., which was not. Nobody had heard from the demon since that first, hurried message.

"Four different Foresees, all giving us the same information, in different ways. Fatae. Fatae offering themselves to the Retriever. Why?"

Kaylee shook his head. "Not themselves. Sparks, the girl from Seattle said. Small bits of light, like..."

"Like current." Ron said, sitting upright on the Naugahyde banquette seat like someone had goosed him.

"Yeah. But that's impossible. The Fatae don't have current. They're creatures of magic, but they don't use it. Can't. So how..."

"Stop asking how and start asking how!" came the terse response. Ron was already up and pacing, his brain set into forward gear again. The Foresee hadn't involved the Distraction, or any of the rest of the *Cosa*. Only the Retriever. That didn't mean anything specifically but it pointed to her as being pivotal. What she was doing was the point at which all hopes rested. The Wren... Or on what she was set to Retrieve.

He had an idea. It might work. It might not, but... It might. "Get the word out. Any Fatae who want to help, get them here. *Now,* or sooner than now! And get Ayexi in here, too! I want to know how far along they were with that battery!"

Suddenly he had a plan. It was a shit plan, but shit was better than none.

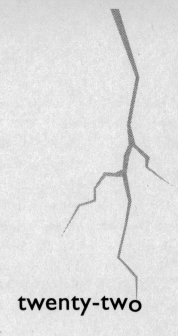

twenty-two

The car moved through the night, the headlights barely enough to cut through the dark. It looked like a junker outside, but the engine purred and the upholstery was not only intact but smelled good—a clean, fresh smell at odds with the age of the car.

"You take good care of it," Sergei observed; the first thing he had said since they got in.

"Spent too many hours in a squad car," Danny replied. "See no reason to spend any more of my life smelling stale smoke, vomit, and old burgers."

Sergei winced. "Nice."

"Yeah well. All the perks of the job. At least we never had anyone take a piss in the back seat. You'd be amazed how many guys decide the back seat of a cop car looks like a urinal."

Danny handled the lack of traffic lights with the disdain of his previous career, dodging the few cabs still on the road without even bothering to flip them off. If Sergei didn't know better, he would have thought the Fatae was bored. Only his tight grip on the steering wheel gave lie to that.

"You sure about this?" the ex-cop asked again.

Sergei gave a tight nod of his head. "Yeah."

He picked the gun up out of his lap and rechecked the chambers. The same result as the last three times he had checked: fully loaded.

Wren hated his gun. She hated guns, period, but she particularly hated this one. She had a small touch of psychokinetics, which meant that she could pick up the history of an object just by touching it. Most objects barely registered, but weapons? Weapons got her. And a weapon that had both blood and his touch on it? Bad. Very bad.

It had been a long time since he had carried a handgun on him, for that reason. But you never forgot the feel of it in your hand. The recoil of it in the instant after the shot. The smell of powder, blood, and shit in the air.

He had been a killer, once, in the name of Right. When he had stood against the darkness.

Tonight, he would become a killer again, standing in the shadows and shooting into the shadows. Not for Right. For revenge.

He tasted the thought in his mouth, and was satisfied. He could live with that.

"Coming up ahead, if you had the right address. Parking probably not going to be a problem tonight. You want close, or distance?"

The real question: Were they worried more about the getaway, or being identified?

"Close." He had the right address. If they walked out at all, nobody would be giving chase. If anyone did…they weren't going to need the car.

"You don't have to go in with me."

Danny spared time away from the road to give him a Look.

"Right. Forget I said anything." It wasn't just lonejacks who could be stubborn. Once Danny dug his hooves in, he didn't budge.

They parked at the far end of the street, sliding up to the curb smoothly enough to continue Sergei's mental vision of a metal shark in an empty sea.

He got out onto the sidewalk and looked into the sky. The buildings here were all short, and far enough away from the skyscrapers of midtown to see the sky. The stars were clear and sharp, and if he concentrated, he could see the Milky Way spread in a thick wave.

"Are you seeing this, Zhenchenka? Wherever you are, did you have the chance to see this?" He wished they could have gotten in a car like this, driven out of the city, sat on a hill somewhere, opened a bottle of wine, and pretended they could pick out constellations...

Maybe someday. Not tonight.

"You ready?"

Sergei slid the gun into the holster at his hip, and nodded. "Yeah."

Together, the two men walked down the dark street, the heels of Danny's cowboy boots making a faint clicking noise that echoed around them. The buildings on either side were simple three- and four-story buildings, lawyers and dentists mixed in with residential apartments. A comfortable neighborhood—one with middling crime reports that always shocked the residents.

The building they stopped in front of was single-use, five stories high, with one simple metal plaque on the front giving no information other than the building's street number.

Sergei walked up the front steps with the assurance of a man coming home after a long day. After a final look up and down the street, Danny followed.

The building was deserted. Sergei had expected that. The elevator was halted, the red emergency lights all that lit the building. Sergei knew that if he flicked a light switch, power would fill the room with illumination. Duncan would never leave himself without the basics, even if the rest of the damned country had to go without. Not because he was spoiled, or believed that he deserved them. Duncan's logic wasn't that simple, or straightforward, or that easily manipulated.

Sergei would not make the mistake Andre had, in thinking that he understood Duncan, that he could play the master of games.

He wasn't here to reason with the man, to find answers, or try to make him come to terms.

He was here to kill him.

"Third floor."

It was the last they spoke, climbing up the emergency stairwell together. Out of the corner of his eye Sergei saw that Danny had a handgun out as well. It was larger than Sergei's, and prettier. It wasn't any less deadly for having a burnished finish on the barrel or a filigreed frame, and Sergei wasn't about to mock him for having a cowboy gun, even if it did scream "overcompensation."

"Nobody's here."

"He's here." Sergei could taste him in the air. He knew exactly where their quarry was.

This wasn't the smartest thing he'd ever done, maybe. Wasn't the stupidest, either.

Third floor wasn't as luxurious as the lobby; the carpet on the floor was chosen for durability, not desirability, and the walls were painted plaster, not wood paneling.

"I expected something a little showier."

"They're not about the show. They like to tell."

Three doors down the hallway. Four. Five. At the very end, a set of double doors.

Silently Danny looked at Sergei. Sergei nodded without taking his gaze off those doors. This was it.

If either of them were Talent, they'd just blow the doors open. If either of them were Talent, they wouldn't be here.

"Open it," he said.

Danny reached forward and flung open the doors, stepping aside even as he did so. Sergei had already stepped to the other side of the door, so that neither one of them was in the direct line of anything that might come out through the door.

Nothing did.

His gun held up and ready, his finger resting just outside the trigger guard, Sergei sidled into the room. It was dark inside; not the pitch-black of no lights, but the hushed visibility of a movie theater or military command room.

There were seven screens set into the walls. Six of them were blank. One of them showed a narrow, red-lit hallway. The picture was clear, but there wasn't anyone in sight.

Sergei scanned the room, his gun ready, until he found what he was looking for.

"Did you bring me popcorn?"

The voice came from the chair in the center of the room. Sergei had his gun trained on the speaker by the time Danny could react.

"Really, Mr. Didier." Duncan pronounced it with the French inflection, perfectly. "So crass, to bring a weapon into my home. Please. I do not have a weapon aimed at you."

"No, you don't," Sergei agreed, circling around to face him. The Director of R&D and the puppet-master behind the anti-Fatae vigilantes: the architect behind the changes at the Silence. The man who had ordered the murder of at least one and probably more of his fellow Silence members, the murders of people who had worked for him, trusted him.

The man who had killed Andre Felhim, directly or otherwise, and made his body disappear.

Bile rose in Sergei's mouth, and he welcomed the bitter taste.

Duncan looked cool and relaxed, sitting in his chair. His linen shirt was open at the neck, the cuffs turned back.

"I would have thought your partner would want to be here for this. Although you can see that she is a bit busy." Duncan indicated the single monitor with a casual wave of one hand. He had been sitting there in the dark, watching her.

Sergei didn't look. Whatever Wren was up to, it was her job. Her responsibility. This was his. Division of labor, each to their strength.

He kept telling himself that. And he didn't look at the monitor.

Danny had retreated to the door, keeping an eye on the hallway, to make sure they weren't interrupted.

"This isn't about her," Sergei said. "It's not about them."

"Ah." Duncan sounded like understood. Sergei didn't think he did. It wasn't about Duncan, either. Or Sergei. Or even Wren.

"You can drop the leash, but a dog is still a dog." Except Wren had been right: Andre had never dropped the leash. Not really. Even from the grave he was still tugging it. That was all right. Sergei was a good old hound. He knew what to do.

"If you kill me, there will be no way to call off my Operatives," Duncan said, cool to the end. So sure that he had the better hand, he was willing to negotiate, to give away something out of generosity.

"They're not *your* Operatives," Sergei told him. "And there won't be anything left for you to call off, when this night's done." Duncan had played the game masterfully. None better.

Sergei didn't play games.

He raised his arm, sighted carefully, and gently pulled the trigger.

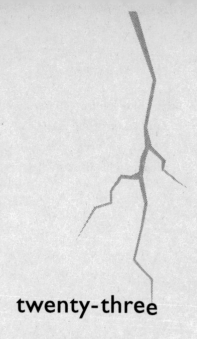

twenty-three

Wren was not having a good Retrieval. The stink of blood kept sliding into her nostrils, no matter how she tried to ignore it, and the boy skulking behind her was adding to the general feeling of creepiness. Her skin was on too tight under the slicks, and she kept touching the hot-stick in her pocket, despite there not being anyone to use it on.

"Ahhhgggghhhh!" The cry sounded out of nowhere, and Wren was knocked aside by a blast of current, her shoulder slamming into the wall.

"Son of a…" Her own current, already on edge and looking for an outlet, crackled red and black, aching to get out, to strike at the assailant.

"No!" It was a whisper, but it carried enough to stop a second attack long enough for Wren to drop to the ground and reinvoke her no-see-me, which she had dropped in her fury and desire to attack.

"Where! Where went? Kill!"

Feel much the same here, Wren thought.

"No, shhhhhh, she helped me!"

The boy who had come in with her. His voice was faint and scared, high-pitched and tight. But it was enough to stop whatever it was that had attacked her, and that fact gave her pause.

"They killed...they killed..." Her attacker had a stuttering voice, and stuttering current matching it. Oh, God. Current, surrounding her. Other Talent. The FocAs. They practically pulsed with current, all of them gathered behind the speaker. Four? No, six. Seven. Seven bodies, alive and Talented. Only seven?

She hauled herself to her feet, sensing more than seeing heads turn to follow her movement. They couldn't see her, but they knew she was there.

Earn their respect, Doherty had said. *It may be easier than getting their trust.*

"Who came?" she asked, the current easily holding her invisibility, even as they tried to find her. "Who did this?" She knew, but they had to say it.

"His men. The bossman. They came, they came and..."

"They said it was just another series of shots." A girl, from the back. Mid-twenties, if that. Bonnie's age, but her eyes were older. Decades older. "But we knew."

Yeah, Wren thought grimly. They would have. Not because of any Talent, though; if this Duncan bastard had sent in cleaners, they would have practically oozed intent.

They had come to clean up their mess. They had blacked out the entire seaboard, and tried to wipe out the evidence...

Something roiled, deep inside her, and this time she let it rise.

Oh, no, you don't. Rage took her, too easily, too sweetly. You don't get away that easy. You don't get away, period. *Kill them all....*

One of the Talent whimpered, the force of her current sweeping over them, crisping the air. Wren pulled it in, the black strands curling around the bones of her hands, streaking her skin as it rose to the surface. Sweet God, what had happened to her control?

She pulled back, concentrated. Unlike letting it loose, reining in current took control, more control than usual. Feeling steady again, she asked them: "Is anyone left?"

A few head shakes, and one of them mumbled, "No."

"None of us," a voice said, almost chanting. "None of them. None, and none, and none…"

"Jody."

"Jody?" Wren wasn't quite able to tell which one of them was speaking at any given time. Their voices all sounded the same, muted and flat, and her eyes weren't quite focusing in the black light.

"Nutritionist."

That was probably the funniest thing she had heard in days. Then again, she hadn't heard a hell of a lot that was amusing, lately.

"They hurt her. With the witchfinder. But she isn't a witch."

Seven Talent, borderline crazy, and a wounded, possibly dead nutritionist. Great.

Eight borderline crazy, a voice in her head amended. *We're all insane here except me and thee and I'm not so sure about me.* "Where is she?"

One of the females; a sturdy, solid woman with broad shoulders and thick brown hair that needed washing and combing, turned to look exactly where Wren stood. Her cloudy blue eyes weren't focusing all that well, but she knew where the Retriever was.

"Who are you?"

She also sounded almost sane. Almost.

"My name is Genevieve."

"Ayah. You're like us. But you're not. You're one of Them."

So much for sanity. The attack came so fast and hard, Wren couldn't get out of the way. Her current rose up in response, instinctively, automatically, without her having to engage her will at all. It wasn't responding; it was leading. She was a meat puppet under the flickering neon, the black sludge rising like strings to move her.

Jenny-Wren. Jenny-Wren. A familiar voice, almost lost under the snapping and crackling of current in her veins. All she had to do was twitch, just a flicker of a thought, and these annoying children would be gone, out of her way, annoying gnats...

Jenny-Wren. Sweetheart. No.

Only one person had ever called her Jenny-Wren. Only one person ever.

The black filaments tightened on her skin, and she soared up, past the fading echo of her name. Neezer had left her. He had abandoned her. Why should she listen to that last memory of his voice, the fading teachings that were all he had left her?

She refused the voice. Current filled her, stolen from the remnants in the walls, scoured from the flickering wires no longer carrying electricity, plucked from the very air around her. Electrons, too small for even the very best Talent to harvest, opened up to her and fed her.

God, it was glorious. She was a god!

Wren!

Weights on her feet, her ankles; turning her soaring flesh into stone.

No!

Ground! A demand, a command, a hard, white-furred fist grabbing her and pulling her back down into herself. Unlike the earlier voice, she could no more fight it than she could fight the blood in her veins.

The black filaments flared a dark green, and subsided, normal under-the-skin veins again.

She opened her eyes and was back in the facility. Six figures stared back at her, their eyes wide and scared. The seventh...

"Little sister. Little sister, I'm sorry." Wren went to her knees beside the fallen figure. "I didn't mean to hurt you."

Bright blue eyes stared up at her, the madness for an instant gone, shocked from her system.

"You came for us." A barest whisper, but clear, cognizant.

"Yes."

"You were late."

"I know. I'm sorry."

The girl sighed, and Wren felt ice swirl in her gut. "Little sister, stay with us. I'm a crap healer, but if you can hang in there, we can get out."

"There's...no escape. I saw you. On the Bridge. You tried to kill us, and now you've come for us. The Keeper's people kept us, and then tried to kill us." Those blue eyes were hidden behind heavy lids. "The world makes no sense."

"And it doesn't get any better, no matter what they told you." She reached out and touched the woman's hand. "But it's better than letting these bastards win."

She looked up at the others. "We have to hurry. When the ones you killed don't check in, they'll wonder what happened. We need to be gone by then."

No Retrieval ever went according to plan; she was used to improvising. This was just a little more juggling than she was used to.

"You, and you." Two males, who looked sturdy and undazed enough to be useful. "Carry her. Gently! Wait here."

She turned to the boy who had led her. "Keep guard." Possibly hopeless, but he had been the only one to get out. "If anyone comes, *anyone,* ping me. You know how to do that?"

He nodded.

"All right. Now, one of you. Take me to your nutritionist."

After a short, intensely whispered consultation, two of them— the youngest, other than her boy—were detailed to show her where they had left the injured Jody. The boys walked through the shadowy rooms, moving around furniture with the assurance of long-term familiarity. How long had they lived here? Wren couldn't even think of it.

There were cameras in every room—some of them still lit, indicating that they were recording. Wren wrapped herself deeper in no-see-me, resisting the urge to short the entire system. If nobody was here yet, that meant that nobody was watching. Shutting the system down might set off alarms, and bring unwanted attention too soon.

"Jody?"

The body was lying on a cot—one of several in the room.

"Jody?"

The woman was still alive; even in the low light Wren could sense the breath in her, the living energy.

"Hi."

The woman couldn't see her—between the dimmed emergency lights and her no-see-me, the voice might as well have belonged to the Invisible Man. But working with Talent, even a Null learned a few things, and the woman tried to focus her attention on where the voice was coming from.

"Who are you?"

Everyone seemed so determined to ask her that. Wren didn't think she owed anything to a member of the Silence who'd helped keep these kids locked up, though.

"Nobody you need to know about. Can you move?"

The woman shook her head. "Leg's broken. My knee. And I think a rib. I can breathe okay, but standing's not going to happen."

Wren had to make a decision. It didn't take long.

"Is there anything on the way out we need to know about?"

The woman shook her head. "I don't know. I wasn't...I was here to oversee the kitchen, make sure they ate healthy, not crap. When the others came in, I protested, and..."

Her head turned, and Wren could see the marks the kids had been talking about. Three large circles, burned into the flesh of the woman's neck and shoulder. Her own skin crawled, remembering the feel of that tube against her own face. "Witchfinder." If it left those marks on a Null...what would it have done to someone with Talent?

"I'll be fine," Jody was saying to her charges, lying through her teeth. "They'll take care of me. Go now. Go."

Unwilling, but equally unwilling to stay, the two former FocAs retreated back to the others, Wren keeping a nervous eye on the cameras as they went.

Time, always her enemy on a job, was running out. And she still had to get them out of the building, and into their new safe house.

The Distraction had damn well better be distracting. Otherwise reinforcements would be coming, and then it was all over but the screaming.

Her limbs felt heavy, the skin over her forehead too tight, like sunburn. Wren touched her core, carefully, trying not to rouse the sludge again. The snakes stirred, but they didn't have the manic energy of before. Damn. She had burned too hot. Simply *being* burned current: it was both a gift—there were no obese Talent, no matter how much they might eat—and a curse—even sitting still required you to refuel, eventually. The more you did, the hotter you burned. The laws of the universe worked on magic as much as anything else. The stories totally lied about that.

When they got back to the others, Wren took a quick inventory of her charges. One injured too badly to walk on her own. Four capable of walking, and probably running if need be. Two more, unknown but based on a quick once-over would probably give until their hearts burst. Whatever the Silence trained them to be, it wasn't quitters.

"Any of you high-skill?"

That got her a blank look, so she tried again. "Anything you're really, really good at, with limited effort?" If any of them could Translocate, they would have done it already, she suspected. Pity, that. Her attempts at Transloc usually ended with her tossing her guts on arrival, and she wasn't sure she was up to taking strangers with her. The one time she had brought Sergei along it had been a Transloc-or-die situation, and even then she'd barely made it.

"I can move things," one of the girls said.

"Right. Good. What's your name?"

"Rosalle."

Rosalle was at least partially Hispanic, her skin tone a little too ashen right now but her eyes were dark and alert, and in better conditions she was probably very pretty.

"Good. Anyone else?"

They looked at each other, and shrugged. There might be useful skills, but without someone to guide them, they seemed unable to identify anything.

Tick. Tick. Tick... Time, running out.

"Great. All right, Rosalle. I need you to do something for me. I need you to lift—what's your name?" she asked the prone woman.

"Allie."

"Allie. I need you to lift Allie. Not all by yourself, not all the way up. Just from her shoulders to her heels. Can you imagine that? Lift and lighten her, from her shoulders to her heels."

Roselle was shocky but smart; she figured out what Wren needed from her, and nodded. "She'll be easier to carry that way, if I take some of the weight."

"Exactly." Wren gave her a bright smile that she didn't really feel, and turned to the two men who were already supporting Allie. "Your job is to get her, and yourselves, out of here. Don't stop, no matter what. Don't help anyone else, no matter what. Don't do anything other than run, if that's what it comes to. Understood?"

They looked unhappy, but nodded.

"But where do we run to?"

Here Like an Internet link, the word connected to a visual in their brains. As she did so, she wondered if anyone had ever done that before. And then she wondered if she had just created the first mental mass mailing spam-link process.

"What is it?"

"A safe place." Mash's home. He was gone—one of the early victims of the Silence's campaign, but the legacy remained. Talent—young Talent, at-risk Talent—were safe there. If Mash had lived, would they have lost so many to the Silence? Never know, so better not to think about it. Doherty would be waiting, to help them. Doherty and his team would take over, then. All she had to do was get them there. Her mind circled around that fact, trying to take comfort from it.

Tick...tick...tick.

"Let's go. Stay close, walk low, and stay alert. Follow my lead, and if I tell you to go, you *go.* Got me?"

She looked at each one of them, memorizing as best she could their features, taking them inside her, holding them and weaving a net of neon threads around that memory.

"The *Cosa*'s children
the treasure of our blood
will be protected."

The words focused the intent, and the net tightened. To all intents and purposes, the eight figures disappeared.

Now, she told them. Fingering the button in her hand, she turned and opened the door, then closed it behind them again once everyone was through.

Two hallways, and...the main elevator shaft was out, with this crew. No way to get them out that way. The stairs? Too many; it would take too long. Could she risk starting the elevator itself? Wren tested her core, and rejected that idea. She might be able to do it, but she might not, and dropping the cage halfway up was not her idea of finishing the job.

Running through the blueprints in her memory, she tapped the nearest boy on the shoulder to indicate the change in direction. Like the tail of a lizard, the rest of them swung to follow.

Instead of going up, they went sideways. The hallway went from narrow and carpeted to wide and tiled, through a stainless steel kitchen. There was a huge metal bowl with fruit on it; Wren grabbed an apple as she went by, and was amused to see several of her charges follow suit.

The fruit wouldn't do much to restore current, but calories needed to be replaced, too. And these kids were too skinny: she wanted to sit them down to a double-pepperoni thick-crust pizza, stat.

God. Pizza. Yeah. And a side of pork dumplings. And about a gallon of diet Sprite and a six-pack of beer as a chaser.

Her food musings almost made her laugh, and the burble of laughter scared her. She really was losing her mind.

The thought snuck up, around every blockade she had put in its way, and finally plunked its ass in the driver's seat.

You're losing it.

There's something wrong with me.

I know.

Jenny-Wren. Be careful, Jenny-Wren.

She had been avoiding even thinking of it, ever since.... Ever since the tunnel underneath the theater. Ever since the black sludge had appeared. But she knew.

The fear every Talent lived with: wizzing. Taking in so much current that they burned out the normal protections. It made you more powerful…and irresponsible. Irritable. Dangerous. To yourself…and those around you.

Once you wizzed, you couldn't go back.

She had never forgiven her mentor for leaving her, when he felt himself start to wizz.

She looked back at the battered, scared Talent in her care.

She would not leave them. She would not hurt them. She. Would. Not. Wizz.

The back of the kitchen was where they were heading. Through the walk-in freezer, unsurprisingly *not* melting, and out the other side, to where large double doors were set into the wall.

"I always wondered how they got supplies in," one of the still nameless FocAs said. He sounded annoyed that he hadn't thought of it himself.

"It helps to have blueprints," she told him. "All right, here's where

it may get tricky." The fact that they hadn't been stopped, and no
alarms had gone off, merely heightened Wren's tension rather than
relieving it. Someone had to have noticed by now. It was too much
to hope that they could leave the building unnoticed. While they
were inside, they were mice in a maze, easy to track and control.
Outside? Outside chance favored them. And the Silence had to
know that.

Please God, let the Distraction have worked.

*Roselle. Can you open these doors? Don't try it yet, just feel it,
try to set yourself against it.*

Pinging wasn't meant for full conversations. The fact that she
found it so easy to do…

She shuddered, a full body ripple, when Roselle answered back,
riding that same band of current.

*I…yes. I think so. The doors are heavy, but they're wired, and
there's still some power in them. That will help.*

There was a pause, then Roselle continued. *The security
system's on. When I open it, the alarms will go off.*

Wren almost laughed. *Let me worry about that.*

Doubt came off Roselle in waves, but she didn't protest.

All right, guys. Wide-band pinging now, getting their attention
on her. Allie was the sole holdout—Wren couldn't take the time to
make sure that she had merely passed out. The guys carrying her
would have to deal with that. *Roselle's gonna open the door, and
I'm gonna deal with what comes after. All you have to do is get out,
and scatter. Do *not* stick together. Do not wait for anyone, do not
look back, and do not worry about anyone except yourself. Can you
do that?*

Normally a question like that, asked of a lonejack, would result
in dismissive laughter. A lonejack always thought of herself first. A

Council member would worry about their teammates—or so they claimed, but Wren's experience had been that they were as survival-oriented as lonejacks. The Silence's Talents were taken from both branches, but their training had been to place the organization above the individual—Wren knew that even without reading their training manual, having dealt with the fallout from Sergei over the years.

"I want out," one of them said, and the others nodded firmly. They'd be fine.

The taller of the two men holding Allie tugged slightly and took her weight entirely into his arms. "Easier to do it this way, once we're out."

She left them to get ready, and moved a few steps away.

Tick...tick...

Finally. They were coming. She could feel them, like cats circling the mouse hole. They were coming, and they were armed. Guns, and those things...

She felt a shudder come up, unannounced.

Witchfinders.

Witch*killers*.

No stoning, no drowning, this time around. Burning. They chose burning as the way the world would end.

She pushed the thought away, and thrust into her core, grabbing whatever current was there and pulling it, hard, into her system.

Her exhaustion didn't fade, but she was able to override it. The sugar from the fruit kept her body going, and the last flickering sweetness from the lightning surged. But the current was darker than it should have been, sharp and sluggish, like black-winged butter-flies in cold morning air.

It would have to do. She didn't dare reach deeper for any more.

Hello my darlings, she cooed at the alarm, slipping into the system without hesitation. Hours spent with wiring plans and a knowledge of how the Silence worked had made this as familiar to her as her own bed...in theory. In reality, there were edges and walls she hadn't quite anticipated, and it took her painful extra seconds to get integrated into the system. There, and there, and over here, yes....

A series of clicks, audible only to her inner ear, and she barely had to flash a signal at Roselle before the heavy mental doors were sliding open, soundlessly, and there were bodies flowing out...

And were met just outside by the crackle and spark of weapons, and screams of pain and surprise.

They had been anticipated. They had figured her out; they had hidden from her, and—

She saw one of the dark-clothed figures raise a tube to the slender boy she had rescued, and sparks arched...not from the tube to the boy, but from the boy to the tube, red and silvery blue. And then it returned, stripped of color, hitting the boy's skin and causing him to spasm in pain.

Current. Taking current, when they had already cut off all easy sources. Using their own current against them.

The black current rose on her skin again, mottling her usually pale tone into something bruised and angry-looking, purpled and sore.

They wanted burning? She'd give them *burning*.

Wren, no...

YES. P.B. She finally knew what it was he feared. Knew what her mind had been hiding from her, trying to tell her, ever since the tunnel. Knew, and didn't care.

She wasn't at risk of wizzing. She already had.

Nobody came back from wizzing.

If I burn out, if I burn into ash and madness, then let me choose the place, and the time, and the reason!

She reached down, and out, and as far around her as she could. Every strip, every scent of current, she took in. Even the scraps she would otherwise have ignored, the tainted energy, the faint flutters of every living thing. She took it, before the witchfinder could, and molded, and shaped it into her anger, her fear, and her frustration. The pain was nothing compared to the ecstasy, and she understood the seduction, at last, the intoxication of utter, heedless madness.

Wren...

She wavered, tied between the power streaming through her and the mental hand around her ankle, holding her to the ground.

Let me go, she commanded him.

Never.

Then help me! It was a scream of desperation, echoing down into the marrow of every Talent within a mile's length. She shouldn't have been able to do it: on a night where there was more chatter, more usage, she might not have been able to reach so far, even riding the edge of the wizzing the way she had been.

There was silence, shocked, and she could feel the scrambling of those Talents to send her what they could, to feed her.

But in that instant, a wave of coldness swept over the island, and the connection was broken.

Wren!

Chill darkness met the demon's call.

Wren, wreathed in black and purple current, burned out of control.

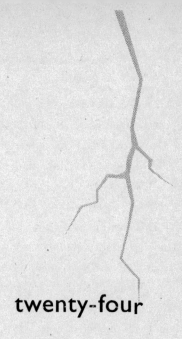

twenty-four

Kohmer's coworkers hadn't understood everything about him, but they knew he was a good guy, a stand-up guy, who had risked his life for them, and to help others. And that someone had killed him.

And that they had no way of bringing those killers to justice, even if the cops did manage to get something out of the ones they handed over. They couldn't leave the station, not when the entire city was in blackout, and they might be needed for God-knows-anything at a moment's notice.

So they did have one thing they could do.

They hit the airwaves.

"Yeah, that's right. Attacked one of our guys. Looked like some kind of stun gun, but sent him right into cardiac arrest. No. No, he didn't make it. I don't know who these bastards are, but there were four of them, and one got away, so ya gotta assume there's more, some kind of street gang shit, I don't know. Just keep your eyes open and your backs guarded. And pass the word."

Larry hadn't been the only one, even if he was the only one outed in their house. If word got passed, everyone would know. And be on guard. Plank Street Station had put out the word.

Which was why, three hours later, they met their first Fatae.

"You...this is where...to be?"

The creature was about a foot high, squat like a fireplug but somehow frail-looking. Its skin was brown and its eyes were black, and it had a shaggy mane of white hair that ran from a widow's peak on its forehead all the way down its naked back.

Mike—one of the firefighters who had taken down the intruders—was the one it approached, and he almost fell out of his chair when it spoke.

"What the hell are you?"

"You are place to be? For the gathering?"

"I...huh...what?"

The thing let out a heavy sigh, and turned to go, clearly disappointed.

"Wait!"

It waited.

"You're here...about Larry?" Mike was tired, not stupid.

The thing showed no sign of understanding, and he tried again. "About...the guy who got killed. The warning we sent out?"

The thing brightened. "The gathering. Yes. The vision he sent. Am here to give."

"Um..." The human had gone about as far as he could, with the knowledge he had, and was clearly floundering.

"It's all right."

A man stood in the doorway of the station house, wearing jeans, cowboy boots, a ragged leather jacket over a blue T-shirt, and an

NYPD baseball cap. "You made the mistake of being sympathetic. I'm afraid we're about to impose on that." He came farther into the station and offered his hand. "Daniel Henrikson. Used to be Patrolman Henrikson, but try not to hold that against me." The rivalry between fire and police departments was one of long and colorful history.

The thing tapped its foot impatiently, waiting for the two men to deal with the social necessities. "We help?"

The guy turned to speak to the thing, as though it was a totally familiar sight. "Yes, you'll get your chance. But you got here before anything was set up, and spooked your hosts. Why don't you take up meet-and-greet duty, while I arrange things?"

The thing nodded, and marched out the door.

"What?" Mike said again.

The guy—Daniel—grinned. It was full of understanding, and sympathy, and not a little apology. Even if the teeth were a little sharper than was comfortable to look at. "I know, it's a lot all at once. Let me explain. But I'll need everyone who's on shift. And anyone you think should be called in."

Pete was the first to speak, when Danny finished telling them about Talent, which they already knew, and the vigilantes, which they hadn't but made sense in light of what they did know and had seen, and the Fatae, which took more than a little getting used to.

"So, what you're saying, it's like a blood drive? These creatures donate their—what you call it, current? And then send out to the Talents being attacked?"

Danny made a sour face, as though annoyed he hadn't thought of that twenty minutes of talking ago. "Yes. Brilliant. Exactly. Except the surgery they need the blood for is going on *now*."

The firefighters looked around at each other, sitting on folding chairs and beat-up sofas, and Pete spoke for them all. "So what the hell are we waiting for?"

Less than half an hour later, the entire firehouse had been turned into an impromptu staging area. At the center of it, an older man barked orders, hovering over the object—a battery, the old guy called it—set in the middle of the garage, where the main truck had been.

The battery wasn't impressive: a large box made of some kind of frosted plastic. There was a device inside, but if you tried to look at it too long, your eyes began to burn from the strain, and you still couldn't describe what you saw, anyway. Kale, one of the firefighters, crossed himself and backed away. "It's alive," he said.

"So's that thing you left in the fridge from last week," Mike said derisively. "May save someone's life someday, if it turns to penicillin."

Rebuke taken, Kale went back to his job of directing the new arrivals to where they could be processed.

It was good that it was still dark, because he didn't really want to see what it was he was talking to. The good Lord made all creatures, and these things had come—at risk to themselves, if the stories were true—to help out people like Larry. So they were all on the same side and all that. But they still creeped him out. Especially the ones that looked like...

He didn't want to say it, but it was true. They looked like angels.

Elsewhere, firefighters mingled with Talent, drinking sodas in lieu of coffee, and monitoring communications both currentical—to use the phrase Valere had popularized—and short wave, keeping an ear on the city as best they could.

"I feel like I should be asking them questions about their sexual history," Mike muttered, checking notes off on a clipboard and directing a weird little guy in a red cap off toward the battery setup.

"Trust me," one of the Talent volunteers said in passing. "You probably don't want to know."

"Right," Mike said after a second's hesitation. "Point taken."

The mood was tense, bodies moving around in dimmed emergency lighting, but the firefighters were used to working under tense conditions, and here at least they knew that they were in control of the situation. Compared to what they'd dealt with in the past…hell, all they had to do here was house the contraption, let the human volunteers do their job with the fairy-folk, and if anyone came to try to shut them down…

Well, a firefighter never backed away from a good brawl.

"How're we doing?"

The voice was a deep growl, and it came from somewhere around Mike's knees.

"Jesus Christ Almighty!"

"Not even close." The thing—it looked like a huge kid's stuffed polar bear, the kind you'd see in FAO Shwartz around Christmastime, with a battered 1940s style hat on its head, except the dark red eyes moved and the teeth were white and sharp and real, and it was extending one huge black-clawed paw up toward Mike's face and…

"They call me P.B. Short for Polar Bear, showing a remarkable lack of imagination but decent observational skills. You look like a guy who's got a clue, so I ask again, how're we doing?"

"Um." He shook the offered paw. "Seventy-eight of the wee folk signed up and sent off, another—" he cast a practiced eye over the station house's common area "—hundred or so to go. We're moving them as fast as we can, but it would help if we had someone who could actually pronounce some of the names and…breeds, they're telling us."

"Right. I'll see what I can do."

The—P.B.—swaggered off, taking the hat off and slapping it against his side. "Danno! Talk to me! What's the status?"

It didn't make any more sense than before. In fact, it made even less sense. But for the first time since Larry was attacked, Mike was starting to think they might actually get through the night.

"Heads up!" someone yelled, and there was a sharp crackle, and a blast of rounded blue light exploded from the contraption, sending people and wee folk scrambling for cover.

"No more lemonjacques," someone called out. "They don't interface well."

"Right," Mike muttered, trying to figure out how you spelled that. "Don't work."

P.B. was standing next to the frosted plastic, peering at it. Mike handed his clipboard off to a rookie whose name he didn't remember, and stalked after him.

"How much charge does that thing hold?"

P.B. gave an eloquent shrug. "They don't know."

"How much is in it now?"

Another shrug. "They don't know."

Mike stared at the surface, not letting himself be drawn into contemplating what was inside.

"You know what happens to an overcharged battery? Especially if you charge it too fast?"

No shrug this time. "Yeah."

"Great." Now he understood why they had chosen a firehouse to pull this off in.

"It's not really a battery."

Mike was not reassured. "It's still going to explode if you screw it up."

"Yup."

Mike started to laugh. "Someone get the electrical kit out," he called over his shoulder. Carbon dioxide extinguishers probably wouldn't do much if this thing went, but a professional tried to be prepared. "And a water mister!"

"You're handling this pretty well, for a Null," P.B. said.

Mike looked at the battery, then around at the room full of creatures, then back down at P.B. "I've been a firefighter in this city for ten years," he said, and that was all that needed be said. Ten years, you saw a lot. Not much of it ever made sense.

"All right, folk, let's get this thing—"

He didn't get a chance to finish his order when the box flared, a hot red flash like a cross between fireworks and a wildfire. He ducked and turned instinctively, scanning the room to see who was nearest to the hoses.

But there was no flame to fight, just a light that hurt his eyes too badly to look directly into it.

"I think the battery works." One of the volunteers; his voice was dry, sardonic, and only a little bit shaky.

Mike nodded. Nothing left but to roll with the punches. "Good to know. What…"

P.B. staggered, almost falling against the battery before Mike caught him. The creature was heavier than expected, and his fur was softer plush than any toy of his daughter's.

"Wren, no!" the creature shouted, his raspy voice even hoarser, like he had been screaming for a long time. "No!"

Around them, all the human volunteers—all the Talent, like Larry—dropped like someone had taken a bat to the backs of their knees, and not a few of them tossed their cookies on the linoleum floor. A couple of his crew went down, too, their faces going pale and strained. The Fatae scattered, some of them making a distressed bleating noise that put Mike's teeth on edge.

Distantly, like someone shouting into a tunnel miles away, he heard P.B.'s voice again.

Wren! No!

YES! came back down the tunnel, fainter but even more anguished. A woman's voice, a woman in such distress that Mike's muscles tensed as though he were preparing to run back into a fire. Women sounded like that when their children, their babies, were caught in a burning building.

Wren! The yell was fading, even though P.B. stood right next to him.

Then help me!! The scream ripped through him, the anguish driving him down to his knees, even as he saw P.B. lunging for the battery, saw every Talent in the firehouse reaching out, their faces showing they heard the same thing he did: A woman, crying in rage and fury.

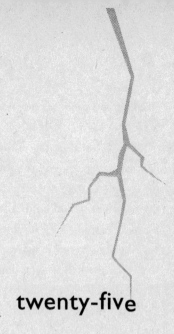

twenty-five

Inside the fire station, the Fatae were fleeing, out the backdoor, down into the sewers and up into the dark, cool air. They did not know what was happening, but they knew they no longer had any reason to be there. They had done all they could.

Everything now was up to the hidden cousin.

Inside, Talent picked themselves up off the floor, shaky but intact, some of them bleeding, some covered in their own vomit. Nulls, not sure what had happened but sure it wasn't good, righted chairs and tried to get some kind of answers as to where that sudden burst of light had come from, and if it boded well or ill for the blackout ending.

Then, against the walls of the fire station, shadows grew: long, slender figures dancing like dervishes, stretching and reaching. Slowly, those nearest noticed, even more slowly they turned, searching for the source of illumination, almost afraid to see.

Inside the battery an inferno grew, scarlet-red to indigo-violet, sparking and arcing silently within the frosted panels until those walls no longer seemed capable of containing it.

A hush fell over the entire station, the kind that they say only happens when someone famous dies, or something truly embarrassing is said, as everyone turned to stare, each silently praying that the containment would hold. Into that silence there was a solid, meaty thunk, the sound of a solid form hitting the battery: not to keep it together but to pry it apart, sharp black claws against the surface.

"What the hell are you doing?" Mike yelled, unwilling to get any closer, despite the instinct to pull the creature away from the battery.

"Trust me!" P.B. snarled over his shoulder, then turned back to the chore of tearing at the cube.

"Through me!" the demon demanded of the current stored inside, fighting against the well-constructed form in the instant before it broke free and destroyed them all. "Through *me!*"

It was insane. P.B. knew it was insane—and totally right. This was what he had been created for, what he had fought against, his entire existence. This was his purpose: not to run errands and carry messages. Not to defend physically, although his body was well-suited to that as well. But where the rest of the Fatae were made of magic, were the original source of the legends of a witch's familiar, he was not. He was made from flesh and fluid, bone and sorrow. He was created solely to be a channel for current, a repository. A living battery.

He had run for generations from that knowledge, that burden.

But like any good familiar, and good servant, he too had finally chosen whom he would serve. And he would serve unto death, if need be.

"Through me!" he demanded again of the stored current, and it obeyed, exploding out of the battery, out of the box, and into him.

Through him.

* * *

As though drawn by the activity there, black sedans pulled up in front of the firehouse, three, then five, then seven, and then two battered white vans, up and down the street, being forced to double-park to disgorge their passengers. Forty-plus figures, dressed in dark clothing and carrying nothing but small rounded tubes, they walked briskly toward the station, not caring who, in the early dawn light, might see them.

Their witchfinders had led them here. The witchfinders were so simple that they were never wrong. Such a gathering of current could only mean that this was the nest, the hive, the filthy refuge of the so-called Talent.

All over the city, war had been raging. This was where it would all end. Tonight. Now. Before another day came and went.

They walked in through the open bay doors, and were met by a wall of flesh: Talent and Null, side by side. Some were drenched in water, some covered in vomit, their faces pale and bruised from where they had fallen. Some of them carried makeshift weapons—fire axes, and sledges. Some were open-handed, as though waiting for weapons to be dropped into their grasp.

All of them were watching the approaching Silence Operatives, and none of them were welcoming.

"Kill them all," the black-clad leader ordered.

P.B. felt blood running from his nostrils and his tiny fur-covered ears, even as he sensed the others in the building leaving him, turning to face the new threat. It was too much for him to process. Wild magic. Old magic. The stuff of fairies and dragons, the oldest of the old blood and the youngest of the new breeds. The clap-your-hands and herb magics; the potions and the prayers; every incantation and exhortation ever uttered. All there, gifted by the Fatae, transformed through the battery into pure, strong, streaming current.

He couldn't handle it. But he did. The demon opened himself up to it all, processing the fire in his alchemical veins, his demon form, and sent out again through those veins, out to the waiting cores of a dozen, a hundred, a thousand Talent, here, and across the city entire.

P.B.'s lips pulled back in a rictus of a grin, the black flesh of his gums showing even as his eyes darkened and began to bleed as well, staining the white fur of his face a muddy brown. Strands of power went elsewhere as needed, but he saved the best, the most, for his master.

*Wren. Little sister. *Catch!**

A mile away and across the river in Queens, Wren dropped to her knees, her overstimulated core drained to emptiness. The children—her children—were surrounded, the damned Silence goons moving in, those damned witchfinders up and pointed and she couldn't do a damned thing. She was empty, so empty, and tired beyond pain. There was no more fear, no more anger; only sorrow hollowing out her core and leaving it barren and still.

She had nothing left to give, except that last bit of life-current they would take and use to kill her. They would die…they would all die. The Wren would leave her most important job unfinished, and that would be her damned legacy. Ashes, and dust.

A proper heroine would stand and laugh, be defiant, toss off a quip and take them down with her when she went. One of the heroines from the old movies Sergei loved so much would stand, and quip, and look good doing it.

Wren bowed her head to the cold floor, and waited for the end.

Wren. Little sister. Catch!

It was instinctive; even half-dead, Wren could no more ignore P.B.'s voice inside her head than she could her own heartbeat. She lifted herself up, physically and mentally, emotionally and psychically, and caught the strands of current he sent her.

Not strands. Cables.

They lashed onto her hands, visible in the dark kitchen as the strands wrapped around her skin, from fingers to elbows, sliding under her clothing, following the lines of her veins to her heart and down her spine, into her core and then out again. It burned, like acid in her eyes, and she would have screamed from the pain but her vocal chords, like the rest of her, was caught in the grip of the overrush of current and unable to do anything other than accept the input until it was done.

The sound of screams brought her out of it. In front of her, across the city, out into the suburbs. The hand of the Silence was reaching out with black-coated fingers, even as the night of darkness was coming to an end, the sun rising just over the watery horizon, and her people were dying.

There's something wrong with me.

No. Voices reassuring her, consoling her, lifting her. *You're perfectly, beautifully all right.*

You're all right.

The black threads skimmed over her skin, rising over her veins, but this time they were underlain by the more familiar gold, reds, greens, and blues of working current. They lifted her out of her body, her core overflowing with the gift of magic—powerful, tasty, unfamiliar in origin but all the more satisfying for it.

We are with you. An echo of voices.

I am with you. A single voice, familiar, blood-warm.

You are not alone.

"Down!" she thundered.

God, it was like…better than the best sex, better than the wildest thunderstorm. Like both at once, tied up in briars and pressed into her skin.

"Down!" she thundered again, and the flesh before her had no choice but to obey; where she had once been supine, now they lay with their faces to the floor, unable to look up, unable to run away.

She felt the storm fronts moving all over the continent, and yearned for them. A touch, a dispersal, and all the current holding this flesh would fall off and she would be free to clash and crash with the purest forms of current, to become them, with no muddy clay in the way.

Wren. Wren. Wren.

It was an itch in her brain she couldn't reach, a hand on her shoulder she couldn't shake off, and all that kept her focused. She was not alone. The hand that stayed her, the weight that grounded her, the heart that strengthened her…

Job to finish, Genevieve.

All at once, the power hit, and her core—and her brain— exploded.

Elsewhere, she saw humans battle, fists and blades against staffs and witchfinders, current dashing between them, taking out even numbers, one by one, on both sides.

Elsewhere, she saw Talented children huddled under beds as their parents were slaughtered.

Elsewhere, she saw Fatae, cowering in the sewers, in the trees, their own strength depleted to feed her, at the mercy of anyone who came by.

Elsewhere she saw her partner, a dark shadow over his heart, his hand holding a gun loosely, arm relaxed, head hanging low, and blood splattered on his slacks and his shoes.

Here, she saw the bodies of the former FocAs. Two would never move again. Three were in agony, their own current burning them where the Operatives—their former coworkers—had turned it on them. Two…they were crawling, trying to reach a weapon, any weapon.

Down, she told them, as gently as the wild current in her would allow. *Stay down.*

And then she reached out and grabbed a double handful of the darkest, nastiest current she could find.

Thou shalt not kill

Her sanity returned: a thin sliver of hesitation.

Thou shalt not kill.

Madness seemed to make more sense. *Thou shall protect your people.*

On the heels of that, a flash, not her own memory. Men, marching past. Bonfires burning high. Screams, and blood, and thick greasy smoke rising up to a God that didn't exist.

P.B., standing in a train compartment, pulling away from a Germany in flames: running away, again. Running this time to America, praying the madness would never follow him.

Thou shalt not allow a mass murderer to live.

You are not God.

Thou shalt not allow a blind faith follower to murder.

You can stop it. If you will.

The current thickened in her veins, waiting for her decision.

She would.

Once before she had ridden the edge of current into wizzing, although she had refused to acknowledge what it was at the time.

Once before, down in the tunnel, she had given way to it, out of fear, despair. Now she opened her arms and welcomed it, taking the damage, taking it and becoming it.

And the current took over, and she was tossed into the maelstorm.

Focus. Focus. Everything is in the focus.

She did not fight the madness. There was no fighting it. She fell into it, absorbed it, drew it into her...

And through her, into the demon who still held, connected, on the other side of the city, though running water divided them.

"Defend us against
the darkness in their hearts,
the hatred in their souls
the ignorance of their minds
the fallout of their *stupidity*."

She spat the last word, breaking the pattern of the spell and yet somehow increasing the impact. Blasts hit the humans, one after another. Unlike last time, she did not tear them apart but incinerated them on the spot. No remains. No residue. Remove them entirely from this earth, that was her intent.

There was silence. Silence from the Silence. She would have giggled, if she had the strength.

The black threads on her skin pulsed, urging her on.

All. All gone. All of them, not only on this spot, on this island, but everyone ever touched by the stench of the Silence. She would destroy them all.

The current was willing, but her flesh failed. If she were willing to let go entirely, to sever that last tie, to give over her will, the current would do it for her.

But she would be lost.

Wren. Little sister.

Wren? Another voice. A human voice. Null, impossible in the current-flow, and yet there.

The two-way tie became a three-way knot, soft voices calling her name.

The black threads pulsed again, pushing at her.

Wren hated being pushed. She looked down at her hands in disgust. They were black, tarry black. They were claws, not human. Not hers.

Kill them all.

The pain called for curing. Cleanse the city. Scour the world clean.

Genevieve. No.

The voice reached past her, tapping against the boxes inside. Searching, stretching. Lifting a lid here, there. There was so much pain inside each one. She was so tired. She was so tired she couldn't think.

Her fingers curled against her palm, and tears pricked hot and sharp against the inside of her eyelids.

Wrenlet. Wren. Genevieve.

Voices, calling. But the decision had to be her own.

The words came to her, stumbling but sure.

"My body.

My body, my soul.

My current, cleansed."

If she thought anything up until now had hurt, she had been mistaken. The agony that came as her own current seared the threads out of her veins, her mind, her core, was twice what even a Pure should be able to survive.

She couldn't hold it. Not knowing if she had gotten everything out, she let go, collapsing onto the ground, the little bit of apple she had eaten coughed up in a bitter green puddle. Her throat hurt, almost as much as her ribs, like she had been retching for hours.

Eve ate of the apple, and had been given bitter wisdom, and the pain of the ages. What had she learned? What had she become?

How many had she killed?

Not so far away, the sound of a car, and the psychic stink of intent coming with it. The Distraction had failed. Despite their best efforts, enough of the monsters survived. She was so tired, and they were coming to finish the job.

"Sergei…" One last call, her heart's need. Her heart, her soul. Her *partner*.

Two voices, as one. *We're coming.*

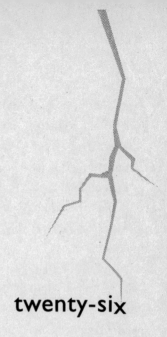

twenty-six

Sergei had never ridden in the back of a fire truck before. He couldn't say much for the comfort level, but there was no gainsaying the speed as they careened down nearly empty avenues, swerving around metro buses and random prowling cabs, into the Queens Midtown tunnel. In regular traffic, whatever that meant in New York, the trip from the station in downtown Manhattan to their destination could take anywhere from thirty minutes to two hours. He expected, at their current rate, to get there in twenty minutes.

It was half an hour too long. But even if there had been someone who was willing to Translocate blind to their destination, *and* take him with them, it was a moot point. Translocating took huge amounts of current, as he understood it, and it had taken P.B. some fast talking to get one of the Talent at the station to dig deep enough to grab Sergei without warning and Translocate him to the fire house in the first place.

If P.B. had known where the Retrieval site was, he might not have even bothered to take the time to do that. But he needed Sergei. Or

Sergei's brain, anyway. And his cell phone battery was dead. Deader than...don't go there, Didier, he told himself.

Sergei...

It might merely have been his imagination. Or not.

"I'm coming," he said to the faint voice, knowing she would not—could not—hear him. "I'm coming, *Zhenchenka*."

"Make it go faster," the demon muttered to nobody in particular. *"Faster."*

One of the firefighters—he had said he was a paramedic, claiming a seat on the strength of that—shook his head grimly. "You don't want it to go faster. These suckers are built for hauling capacity, not speed. Or tight turns."

They came out of the tunnel and hauled left unexpectedly, forcing everyone in the truck to grab on to handholds—what one of the firefighters referred to as the "Jesus bar"—to avoid being tossed to the floor.

"See what I mean?"

"Make it go faster," P.B. muttered again, ignoring the guy entirely. Sergei could relate. Every second was keeping them from Wren.

She had never asked for help before. Never. Never on a job. Never, period. She would accept help, when it came, but she did not ask for it.

He forced himself to stay calm. P.B. was hyperventilating like his namesake too long in a sauna, the brown stains on his fur a disturbing reminder of how wrong the evening had already gone.

"Drink your water," he told the demon.

"Yes, Da." P.B. was still breathing too fast, but he was smart enough to drink the water slowly, not chug it. The paramedic was watching him carefully, too, Sergei noted. Although what the man thought he might be able to do... Demon might be related to humans somewhere in their genetic stew, but that was no guarantee that any physical ailment or solution would work the same on both.

"Christ, are we there yet?" He couldn't crane his head to look outside; there were too many others in the way of the window. Almost eleven in the truck itself, and more riding outside. Most of them were firefighters. If they were stopped, they could honestly say they were responding to a call for help, if somewhat out of their area. More to the point, they were in better shape than the Talent back at the station, still recovering from a two-handed hit of psychic shock and physical assault.

"Bitch of a night," he said out loud, and got a low rumble of laughter from those close enough to hear.

"It's been a hell of a shift," one of them agreed. "Hell of a shift..."

"Ready your gear!" the call came back. Sergei checked his watch, and swore. The very expensive timepiece was now a very expensive ornament. The Translocation had fried it.

There was a reason he usually didn't wear it when he knew he was going to be around Talent. He had gotten careless, the past few months of isolation.

"New record," someone said, seeing him check. "Probably couldn't have gotten here faster by copter, even if they dumped you on the roof."

New York was a relatively compact city, even including all the boroughs. They had probably only traveled about fifteen miles, all told. It wasn't distance that killed you, it was the traffic.

The truck swerved again, and the driver swore. "We got company."

"Sedan or van?"

"A motor home," the driver responded in tones of amazement. Not the sort of thing you normally saw in the city, unless...

He saw P.B. have the same thought at the same time. "Gypsies." Some Talent settled in one location for their entire lives, to the point of homes being passed down through the generations. Others felt that staying in one place for more than a week was being too tied down.

A motor home out here, now, heading for the same location?

"Is it designed? Does it have anything on the sides?" P.B. asked.

"Yeah. Weird-ass looking eye on the back."

The demon saw Sergei looking at him, and nodded. "We got backup."

And then they turned onto another street, the tires screeching, and came to a stop, the engine and lights still running.

The firefighters knew their drill; they were off and out of the truck before it had finished shifting into Park.

"Holy mother of God" was all Sergei heard, and then gunshots. He was out of the truck, his own weapon drawn, scouting for cover and the gunmen at the same time.

"Down, everyone down!" he yelled, but the warning wasn't needed; every man off the truck had already gone flat, rolling or diving behind available cover.

Process of elimination; the three figures standing and shooting were his targets.

Part of his brain knew that he was shooting at former coworkers. Or not—it had been long enough; odds were his peers had not been part of the wet-work teams. But they might have.

They had chosen their path. He had chosen his.

Three figures. Seven shots, and all three were neutralized, if not dead. Good enough for fast work, in limited lighting.

"Go!" he ordered the others. "I'll keep them covered!" The M9 pistol had cost him a small fortune off one of his more dubious contacts, but right now he would have paid twice that amount for it, all over again. It wasn't fancy, or particularly elegant, but it packed a kick and a spare.

The firefighters and demon got up on their feet and moved in toward the active site; what looked like the loading bay off the side of the building, emptying into a wide alley.

Another round of shots fired off, followed by the yowl of someone being hit. And then the solid *thunk* of someone being hit with something decidedly low-tech.

"Got 'em," a voice called.

"Can't beat good old-fashioned human hands-on violence," P.B. said as he moved past the former Silence operative. Sergei shook his head. Only P.B. could say that with both irony and approval clear in his voice.

He let the others go past him; the desire to get to Wren's side was killing him, but he had an obligation to deal with here, first.

Two of the cammo-clad operatives were dead. The third was alive; bleeding badly but not mortally. "Stay or try to run, I don't give a damn," Sergei told him. "Just don't interfere. Your boss is dead. Nobody's going to save your ass this time."

The man nodded. His eyes were wide with pain but he was too smart to ask for help from this scowling stranger.

Sergei got up, feeling his knees creak with the effort, and followed the others around the corner. The sounds of fighting had already faded by then, other than the occasional grunts or cursing. No gunfire. That was good. His guys could handle themselves, so long as there wasn't any gunfire involved.

"My God…" Even in the predawn darkness he could see that there were bodies strewn everywhere, facedown or curled on their sides. The only thing missing from similar scenes of gore across the tri-state area tonight was that there wasn't the pooling of blood. These bodies had been taken down by something other than gun or knife.

And they weren't wearing black.

"The FocAs," he realized, already turning to look for the gypsies. A tall man and an even taller woman were off to the side; they could have been casual observers but something in their body language said that they weren't.

"You two! Over here!"

The two hesitated at being ordered around by a stranger, and Sergei lost his temper. "Did you come all this way to gawk? They need you, now!"

They could deal with it, or not. He, personally, didn't give a damn about them. About anyone except one small, slight form crumpled on the ground near the doorway into the building. Lodestone to magnet he went to her, sinking to his knees beside P.B., who had already gathered her up in his stumpy, fur-covered arms, holding her against his chest.

You forgot, sometimes, how much of the demon's bulk was muscle. All of it, pretty much.

Her eyes were open, but they weren't seeing much of anything. Her face was a disturbing shade of very pale green, and her eyes were bloodshot, although they hadn't bled the way P.B.'s had. A small mercy, there.

A quick glance at P.B. confirmed that she was still alive, but he reached over to feel for a pulse anyway.

She flinched away from his hand near her neck, so he moved— slowly—to take her wrist instead. Thready as hell, but there. Her skin was cold, though. Cold, and papery, like an old woman's skin.

"You look like hell, human," P.B. was saying. She moved her head slightly to follow his voice, but didn't otherwise respond. Something cold stroked Sergei's heart, and he shuddered.

"*Zhenchenka.*"

Her eyes closed, and her bruised-looking skin seemed to fade a little, as though becoming translucent.

"You did well, Zhenchenka," he told her.

"Failed."

The words were so faint, neither of them were quite sure they heard her.

Sergei looked up, looked around. The surviving Talent were being seen to by the gypsies, the paramedic hovering with his kit. Some were already being loaded into the motor home, presumably being taken to whatever location had—he assumed, knowing Wren's thoroughness—been previously arranged. The remaining Silence Operatives had been hauled off and tied up with what looked like quite convincing ropes, tied back to back with each other or to a nearby, unlit lamppost. The door into the building hung open, like a slack-jawed idiot, and the thought made him smile inappropriately.

He turned his attention back to the woman in front of him. "Job's done, Wren. Objects Retrieved and secured. I'd say you done good."

"Seconded," P.B. said, his voice still rough and scratchy, like he had a cold. "So let's go the hell home."

twenty-seven

"I can't believe you did it."

Wren on the sofa in Sergei's apartment, a blanket around her lap, a mug of green tea—disgusting stuff, but good for her, Sergei said—on the table in front of her, and a pile of magazines next to her. Three months' worth of *Popular Electronics* to catch up on, keeping up-to-date on things she might run into, and another pile of *Art World Monthly* for when the boredom became too overwhelming and she tired of daytime television.

She was already tired of it, but P.B. was fascinated. She was going to have to buy him his own television, because be damned if he was going to hang around all afternoon every day watching *Jerry Springer* and *Oprah*. She had almost sparked the very expensive screen into an early death, listening to the audience screaming for more blood.

"Why?" she asked him now, glad for something else to discuss. "Why is it so unexpected?"

"Valere. You're not quite the control freak some humans

are——" and he shot a pointed look into the kitchen "——but it's pretty damn close. And Bonnie? I mean, I like the girl, but Bonnie? Mistress of Perky Goth herself? You're letting *her* choose what color your apartment gets painted?"

"You're just jealous."

"Damn straight." He pointed his chopsticks at her, and scowled. "You're going to come home to black walls. And red floors. And sparkle powder on every metallic surface. And unicorns. Pictures of them, I mean. Getting the actual ones up the staircase would be a bit much."

"I don't think unicorns are part of the Goth culture," she said. "And Bonnie promised me no red."

"There's going to be sparkle," he muttered in tones of dire wrath, and went back to his kung pao chicken.

"Would sparkle keep you from mooching all the time? Because I'll call and tell her to add it, if it will."

She still felt…not weak, because she was alive, and the Silence was broken, and the *Cosa* was battered and damaged but still existed within the city she still loved, despite it all, and her apartment was even now being draped in drop cloths and readied with primer…so no, she didn't feel weak. But the energy to reach forward and pick up her mug nearly defeated her, so throwing something at the demon was out of the question, and he was taking advantage of it, damn him.

"So why now?" he asked, which was, she suspected, what he had really been wondering.

Wren finished the tea, making a face as she got to the bitter dregs. "Give me some more of the rice. And I don't know why. I guess…it was time for a change."

Time to finish making her stand. When Bonnie and her crew

were done, there was one thing left to do. She, and P.B., and Sergei were going to go back with a can of paint, and make one final enhancement: their handprints on the wall, the first thing you saw as you came in the door.

Her own statement of ownership. *This place is mine. I will defend it.*

Her apartment. Her city. Her people.

That thought brought them back around to the topic P.B. had been trying to distract her from originally, with his comment.

"You haven't given me the update yet." He had promised. She wasn't allowed off the damn sofa, much less to wade into the cleanup that followed the blackout, and Sergei had limited the number of people who were allowed to see her.

The Hidden Cousin; that damned nickname was about to become reality, the way Sergei was acting. Not that she really wanted an influx of visitors and gawkers. She looked like hell: that last push had eaten away ten pounds, at least, in twenty minutes, and her system was screwed seven ways from Sunday. And the fact that both of her guardians assured her that she looked better than she had when they found her…wasn't something she wanted to think about too long.

She hadn't told them everything that had happened to her. A lot of it was fading already. Some of it they already knew, some of it they guessed. Some of it she would take to her grave.

That thought made her spine twitch. It had almost come to that.

Seeing that she wasn't going to be distracted, P.B. put his carton on the placemat Sergei had set up to protect the coffee table. Demon were easier to housetrain than Talent, apparently. "Things are… tough."

That was probably an understatement of an understatement. In the weeks since the Before—and that was the only way she could think of it, the only way she could divide her life, Before what had happened, and after Before—the *Cosa Nostradamus* had spent most of its time licking its wounds and burying its dead. Only now did they have the time, and the current, to see what was left, and what needed to be repaired.

"We lost almost a thousand people."

The number didn't surprise her; she had felt so many of them, that night. When the current burned her up, and took her places she should never have seen, never have felt.

When she had wizzed, gone all the way into the madness, and somehow come back.

There was a gray haze over it all, still. P.B. told her not to try to chase it away; it was a bandage of sorts, keeping the pain to a manageable level. She didn't ask him what the hell he thought he knew about her pain; he was there, always. In the night when she cried herself into a stupor that passed for sleep. In the morning when Sergei created a surprisingly decent-tasting protein drink for her, to get her weight back up. In the afternoon, when Sergei stalked off for a walk, miles and miles of walking across town in the late spring sunshine, away from her, because she couldn't bear to have him near, because he couldn't bear to be near her, without one of them doing something that might be very, very dumb...

"A thousand people." She didn't want to know, but had to ask. "How many of them were children?"

"Wren."

"How many of them were children?"

"A hundred. Maybe."

A hundred. Better than she had feared. Worse than she could have prepared herself for. Easier to accept the death of people she had known, deaths in battle, fighting something, in some way, they had chosen to die for. Mourning children sucked the soul out of you, even if you never knew them.

A people that did not protect their children had no right to survive. Her mother had said that once, about why she was so careful about who she dated. A people that did not protect their children would *not* survive.

She had never mentored, because she had never known if she could muster the proper ferocity needed. Wren almost smiled. So much for that worry.

She should call her mother.

"And the Silence?"

P.B. shifted, even more uncomfortable with this question. "We never really had any idea how many there were. Sergei'd been away so long, and..." And the only ones they had any contact with within the organization were gone, either dead or gone into hiding with the destruction of the Silence.

"An estimate?" She had brought them to their death. Never mind they had chosen the path, she was still the one who had brought it to an end, by her command. Her current. She needed to know.

"Another thousand. Maybe as many as fifteen hundred, if we count the ones who just...disappeared."

A memory stirred, of bodies crumbling into dust at her command. She touched it, and let it go back into the shadows. Some day she'd retrieve those memories out of their boxes, integrate them with the other memories she was slowly, slowly reclaiming. Maybe. Or maybe not.

It was easier to think about new paint on her walls, and wonder what she would buy, to put up on those newly painted walls. And a new carpet for the hallway. And a rug for the main room.

Or maybe she'd just be happy with newly painted walls, for a while. No need to rush things.

Her head hurt again, and her skin itched. "God. Twenty-five hundred people. Gone. For what, demon? For what?"

"For survival."

His words brought back the memory of her mother's voice on the phone, in the first days after the Before. "All that matters is that you're okay, baby. That's all that matters to me."

Wren felt tears well up, but refuse to fall. She wasn't okay. She was never going to be okay. But she would survive.

"Hey."

Sergei had perfect timing. She leaned into his touch on her shoulder, luxuriating in the sheer *there-ness* of him. They had both been there for her, when she needed them, P.B. and Sergei. They had come when she called. Had somehow heard her, Null and demon. For obligation, and for love.

She could feel the demon within her, like another strand of current. The Fatae-loaned magic had faded in the aftermath, purging as quickly and as violently as it had entered her, and all the others. Old magic was potent, like whiskey, and gave you just as bad a hangover if you overindulged.

P.B. was more soothing, like the smell of peppermint and orange, the taste of excellent chocolate, the feel of a warm blanket on a cold day.

Sergei...was a Null. She could not feel him inside her any longer; the connection that had been forced into existence during those long hours no longer existed, had been burned out by the demand she put on it.

In duress, under extreme conditions, she knew it could be reforged: P.B. had been right, that night in his apartment: the connection between them was no flimsy thing. But for now, they were flesh to flesh only, and it was wonderful.

And that thought reminded her of how long it had actually been since they were flesh to flesh, and with that thought her entire body got into the act, waking up and starting to make demands.

Not yet, she told it regretfully. If they'd each had issues before, they had *subscriptions,* now. They still had things to work out, controls to be relearned, before they could trust themselves—and each other—again. She couldn't risk ending up right back where they had started, when it all went bad.

But they had time, now. They had time, and a real chance.

Not just to survive. But to *thrive.*

"Right." The TV flicked off, and the remote was tossed onto the coffee table. "I'm…going to take a walk." P.B. tried to sound offended, or affronted, but both humans could hear the snicker in his voice.

"You do that," Sergei said. "A nice, long walk."

The sound of the door closing behind him echoed for long seconds in the now-quiet apartment.

She rested against her partner's chest, felt his arms around her, and looked up to meet his lovely pale brown eyes staring down seriously, worriedly at her.

Things had happened to him, too. Things she didn't know about. She wasn't sure she wanted to know. She suspected: the Silence had been too strong a beast to fall simply because she took away its limbs…. The head had to have been taken as well; sliced and diced and the wound cauterized for good measure.

Her partner had always been a man with secrets, even now.

And the now was where they both were. Here. Now. Together, mostly.

The trick was to go forward from here.

She settled her expression into as serious a face as she could manage, her brown eyes as innocent as the things she had seen would allow. "So, when're you going to get us another job? My apartment makeover won't pay for itself, you know."

His startled laughter was the best sound she had heard in months.

* * * * *

Don't miss Blood from Stone,
the next step in Wren's adventure!